The nightwalker took one step forward and disappeared. Every muscle in my body instantly tightened as I fought back the swell of panic that erupted in my chest. Ancients could easily teleport from one spot to another in an instant. I couldn't do that. Not yet. However, I could feel the swell of power just a half second before he reappeared. There was a brush of energy against my back. Pivoting on my right foot, I twisted around and raised my sword in time to block the blow that aimed for my neck.

Praise for JOCELYNN DRAKE's DARK DAYS

"An intoxicating mix of jet-setting action and sparkling turns of phrase. . . . Filled both with action and satisfying characters. I wanted to slowly savor it, but I reached the end far too soon, left hungry and impatient for the next adventure."

Kim Harrison

"Darkly suspenseful and blessedly surprising . . . with prose as silky and enticing as her protagonist."

Vicki Pettersson

By Jocelynn Drake

The Dark Days Novels

NIGHTWALKER
DAYHUNTER
DAWNBREAKER
PRAY FOR DAWN
WAIT FOR DUSK

wait for dusk

THE FIFTH DARK DAYS NOVEL

JOCELYNN DRAKE

An Imprint of HarperCollinsPublishers

EOS

An Imprint of HarperCollins*Publishers*
10 East 53rd Street
New York, New York 10022–5299

Copyright © 2010 by Jocelynn Drake
Cover art by Don Sipley
ISBN 978–0–06–185181–0
www.eosbooks.com

First Eos paperback printing: August 2010

HarperCollins® and Eos® are registered trademarks of HarperCollins Publishers.

Printed in the U.S.A.

10 9 8 7 6 5 4 3 2 1

To the man who loves me and my cats

ACKNOWLEDGMENTS

I wish to thank my amazing agent, Jennifer Schober, as I know I would be lost without her guidance. I also wish to thank my wonderful and patient editor, Diana Gill, for demanding the absolute best from me. Thanks for always pushing me so hard!

wait for dusk

ONE

Pain exploded across my face, lighting up the black night. My body slammed against a hard surface before I slid limp to my knees, sending a fresh surge of pain up through my frame. The world around me was a blur of disorganized shapes and shadows, punctuated by splashes of red as something hit my jaw, snapping my head around. I landed on my back with a wooden thud.

I wanted to summon up my powers and set the bastard on fire, but the attacks were coming too quickly. My concentration was shattered. In the brief lull, I tried to assess the damage to see if I had any chance of striking back. My left knee had been shattered and my right leg was broken. My internal organs were swimming in my own blood, bruised, punctured, and damaged. My jaw felt fractured and my eyes were nearly swollen shut. I tried to shift to my side, revealing that at least three ribs were broken.

"You stupid bitch!" snarled a deep unfamiliar voice. For a moment I could almost convince myself that I had fallen into Rowe's hands. Only that naturi could possibly hate me so much as to beat me senseless.

"A nightwalker?" he demanded incredulously just before his foot landed in my stomach. My arms had been crossed over my middle, so my left wrist took the brunt of the blow, fracturing. I cried out as my mind struggled to hold onto the voice. I didn't recognize it. But then, I wasn't sure where I was or how I had even gotten there.

"A nightwalker? If I had known how things were going to work out, I would never have let you out of my sight in the first place!" His footsteps moved farther away as he paced the area.

"Who the hell are you?" I spat, sending a stream of blood over my split lower lip.

The creature sighed heavily, and I flinched as he walked back toward me. A large hand sank into my hair, twisting it around his fist before finally jerking it so I was facing upward. Squinting and blinking, my eyes slowly focused in the dim light on a face I was sure I would never see again: my father.

A scream became choked in my raw throat while I tried to lurch backward, sending slashing pain through my scalp as the creature refused to release my hair. His grin grew over his lean, old face becoming a mockery of the love and laughter I had seen on my real father's face.

Clenching my jaw, I closed my eyes and swallowed back a string of curses. I had to think clearly. This wasn't my father. It was obviously a shapeshifter, and one that could read my mind and my memories. The only creature that could possibly do such a horrible thing was a bori.

Gaizka! Oh God! We had failed to lock it up when we were on Factors Walk. The bori had gotten to me.

But even as the thought occurred to me, I knew it was wrong. LaVina grabbed me, using me to lock away the bori before it could steal Danaus away forever. LaVina had snatched me away from Factors Walk and taken me to this secluded location to beat me into oblivion. Or rather, it was this creature that had pretended to be the old witch LaVina so it could get closer to me and Danaus.

A growl rumbled in the back of my throat, warning him to back away, even though I had already proven to be a weak threat. LaVina had fooled us all. I should never have believed her to be a simple witch. I knew all the powerful witches from Charleston to New Orleans. This creature had snuck in, and we allowed it because we were desperate to cage the bori Gaizka. Now it was time for me to pay the price of not being more vigilant.

"You're not real," I groaned, clenching my fist against the swell of pain that swept over me as I tried to move.

The creature tightened his grip on my hair just before sending the back of his free hand across my cheekbone. A new pain blossomed across my face, causing my teeth to rattle in their sockets while a trickle of blood started to slip down my cheek.

"Did that feel real?" he mocked. He gave my head a sharp shake when I remained silent. "Look at me!"

My eyes snapped open and I stared into the dark eyes of the monster that held me. My body was broken and throbbing with pain. Without some help, I didn't have a chance to defeat this creature. I did not have the strength to summon up my powers to light this son of a bitch on fire, and too many bones were still mending from being broken for me to effectively move, let alone fight. If I was going to die, I would do it with my eyes wide-open and staring into the dead soulless eyes of my opponent.

"You're not my father. You're a shapeshifter. A bori." I could taste my own blood in my mouth as I spoke.

"Ahhh, my sweet child, you are not even close," he said, finally releasing his hold on my hair so that I unexpectedly thudded on the floor. "It's my own fault, though. I never should have waited so long to reveal myself to you." The creature paced away from me, waving his hands in the air.

As he spoke, I pulled my arms beneath my body and pushed myself up a little bit so I could look around. Shock tightened my muscles as I discovered that I was in the library at my own house. However, it looked as if a tornado had ripped through it. The shelves were all broken and the books had fallen into large piles around the room. My massive desk was overturned, while papers splattered with my blood were strewn about. Something inside of me shivered when I saw that my extensive collection of hourglasses destroyed. What little light came in through the window glittered and danced off the broken glass and piles of sand. Had my time finally run out?

"Let me start at the beginning." He spun on a heel to face me again, drawing my gaze back to the monster that still held the guise of my beloved father. "But you're going have to think for me."

Pain screamed through my body, causing my arms to tremble so badly that I finally gave up the fight and lay back down on the floor, trying to ignore the fragments of glass and wood beneath me. "Who are you?"

"I am your father," he said simply, spreading his arms out on either side of him, his hands held open as if welcoming me into his thin embrace.

"Impossible! My father is dead! He died centuries ago. He was human. You're just some pathetic mimic."

The creature was before me in a flash, grabbing my hair again so I couldn't look away. "Are you really so sure of that?" he demanded, laughing. Before my eyes, his features shifted so that his soft, wizened face grew younger and sharper in his appearance. His dark brown hair turned a bright shock of red that stuck out in all directions from his head. But it was his glowing lavender eyes that held me still. It was like looking at a male version of myself, and it was terrifying.

"This isn't real either," I whimpered. My mind was unable to comprehend exactly what I was staring at.

"Actually, you're right," he admitted with a slight shrug of one shoulder. "But then I doubt your little mind can fully comprehend the real version of me, so we're just going have to settle for the light version of the truth."

"I don't understand."

"Come now, Mira. Think just a little bit for me." Giving my head a little shake, he continued. "You know the old tales. Zeus comes down to earth from Mount Olympus in various forms and cheats on his darling wife, spawning an untold number of children, leaving the earth to be littered with all kinds of little demigods and nymphs."

A low, rough chuckle escaped me before I could stop it. "You're a god?"

With a growl, the monster slammed the back of my head into the shelf behind me, causing my vision to go black. I blinked a couple times, trying to regain my sight. The creature leaned close enough that I could feel its hot breath dance across my cheek. "Half dead and long forgotten from this world, but I am still here and here I will remain."

He pulled away, seeming to have control of his temper once again. "That old one wasn't the only one trying to maintain his immortality. We all had brief forays around this dark little mud hole, some having more success than others. Centuries ago, I appeared before your mother in the guise of the man that she was attached to."

When I managed to get my vision to clear again, I saw that I was once again staring into the face of the man whom I had always called my father. I gritted my teeth and tried to push away from the monster, but he held fast. My father had been a good, kind man, and his memory didn't deserve to be soiled in such a manner.

"So you're saying that you seduced my mother while pretending to be my father," I snapped, wishing I could put some distance between us. However, I lay as still as possible, hoping to give my body some time to heal. I would gather my strength, and as soon as I could, I would set this bastard on fire like a Roman candle.

The creature clucked his tongue at me and shook his head. "But, little one, he was never really your father. I am," he corrected. "But I am grateful for how he looked after you when you were younger and hadn't yet learned to defend yourself. Your mother proved to be utterly useless."

"My mother loved me!" I screamed, jerking forward.

The creature snorted at me as he released my hair. He changed back into the redheaded figure he had appeared as just moments earlier. "Your mother was terrified of you. Red hair, violet eyes, in a world that was filled with brown hair, brown-eyed children. Even worse, she was afraid of bringing another monster into the world. That's why she killed herself."

Putting my hands on the ground for a second, I pushed upward and lunged at the stranger, aiming to gouge out his eyeballs with my fingernails. Anger had overtaken my common sense. The creature just laughed as he easily captured both my wrists and slammed me back down onto the ground.

Running his tongue over his upper teeth, he smiled down at me, taking particular glee in revealing his next bit of information. "Yes, when you were but eight years old, she discovered she was with child again. Fearful of bringing another demon spawn into the earth, she walked into the sea, killing herself and the child."

"No!" I tried to lurch off the ground as fresh tears welled

up in my eyes. I knew I shouldn't believe him, but I did. My mother had simply disappeared early one morning when I was young and never returned. My father wept for her, but we continued on as best as we could. Something in me had always felt responsible for her disappearance, and I'd always known that she was dead. I just never understood why she had left us.

In response to my tears, the creature laughed as he released his hold on my wrists. I lifted my hands and wiped my eyes, sweeping away the blood and the dirt that had been smeared and crusted on my face.

"Who are you? What do you want with me?" I was tired of playing mind games with this monster. I needed to heal. I needed to find Danaus and know that he was safe. I needed to put my world back in order.

"Haven't you guessed by now?" he inquired, jumping to his feet with an eerie lightness. "I am your real father. The one responsible for your wonderful set of genes, your special gifts, and rather stunning looks."

"Whatever," I grumbled, causing his ebullient expression to deflate somewhat. "But who are you? Another bori? We shut Gaizka up. We can do it with you."

At this, he smiled. He slipped to his knees and crawled across the floor toward me, a smile widening on his sharp face. "In Africa, I've been called Ogo and Anansi. In Egypt, I was known as Keku. Among the Norse, I was known as Loki. The Native Americans referred to me as Coyote and Raven."

"Oh God," I whispered, trying to shrink away from the creature that was inches away from me. His frame seemed to grow so that his huge bulk hovered over me, blocking out the rest of the room.

A dark chuckle rose up from his chest and slithered over toward me, sending a fresh chill down my spine. "No need to be quite so formal," he mocked. "You, my dear sweet child, may just call me Nick."

"Wh-What do you want from me?" My brain failed to get past the sudden log jamb of thoughts that were nearly crippling me. I didn't want to believe it, but I was left with either the idea that he was actually telling the truth or that I had fallen in with another bori Danaus and I hadn't been looking for. Either way, I was in serious trouble.

At this, Nick frowned at me as he leapt back to his feet with an easy grace that bespoke of supernatural powers rather than any human finesse. Placing his hands on his hips, he paced away from me while shaking his head. "I knew I should have kept a closer watch on you, but after your initial display of powers, I thought you would be safe on your own for a while. Besides, I had other children to check on."

"There are others?"

"There were." He paused, giving a soft sigh. "Anything that failed to be as talented as you was quickly pruned like dead growth."

"Bastard." I grunted as I pushed into a sitting position. I was light-headed from the pain and my vision swam before my eyes focused on him again.

"What's a father to do? Can't have useless bits of my genes running aimlessly around," he replied as he slipped his hands in the pockets of his black slacks. "But I turn my back on you for a few short years, and when I look back you're a damned nightwalker! You soiled yourself, diluting all your wonderful powers and potential with that bori filth!"

I couldn't understand what he was talking about. "I'm stronger now than I ever was as a human."

"Stronger?" he snapped. "Unable to go out in daylight, dependent on the blood of humans. How is that stronger?"

"I'm faster and stronger than any human. I have the ability to read their minds and control their thoughts."

"And who's to say that you wouldn't have all of those abilities if you hadn't allowed yourself to be changed? You didn't give yourself enough time to develop. Now you're saddled with all these silly limitations."

"What the hell should it matter to you what I chose to do with my life?" I pulled my legs underneath me as I prepared to push to my feet. My legs were mostly healed and I felt that I would soon be able to stand. I didn't like the distinct disadvantage of being trapped on the floor while this creature paced the room like a chain-smoking speed addict looking to score his next fix out of my hide.

"Because I've got plans for you, my daughter," he admitted with an evil grin. "I've had to modify them a bit, but my plans for you still stand."

"I don't give a damn about your plans," I replied through clenched teeth. "I just want you to leave."

"Not yet. And trust me, you will care about my plans before I am through, for you sit at the center of it all."

I tried to pull to myself up by using a couple intact bookshelves behind me. "What plans?"

"Ahhh . . . no reason to give away my best secrets just yet." He laughed, wagging one finger at me. "Besides, there's something that you need to take care of first."

"I don't have to do shit for you!" Struggling to stand on my own as pain shot through the bones of my legs like a bolt of lightning looking for a grounding rod, I swallowed a scream.

"This is for the both of us." Extending one hand toward me, I felt a surge of energy fill my frame. In an instant I jerked to my feet, my arms snapping out to my sides, leaving me hanging in the air as if I were a marionette on a string. Jabari had exhibited the same ability to physically control me against my will. Danaus could force me to use my powers against my will. The bori could control me completely as well. And with no great surprise, so could Nick.

"I have had enough of this nonsense," he said with a harsh hiss. "No daughter of mine will be controlled by other creatures! Well, you will be controlled by no one but me."

"I can't help it!"

"Lies! You've never properly fought them!" With a wave of his hand, he slammed my back against a broken bookcase before pulling me toward him again. "There will be no more of this. You will not only fight them and keep them from controlling you, but you will learn to harness their own powers for your benefit."

An ugly bitter laugh escaped me as he stepped away and my head fell back. "That's nonsense if I ever heard it." I chuckled, letting my head fall forward again. My hair dropped down to crowd around my face, partially obscuring my vision of Nick. "Fight Jabari? He's centuries old. He could crush me with a thought if I so much as tried to defy him. He has some kind of power over me that I don't understand and can't fight."

The creature rushed toward me in a flash and wrapped his large hand around my throat. I felt his powers release me half a second before he flung me across the room and into the side of my toppled desk. A loud groan echoed through the room as both my body and the desk skid across the hardwood floor before finally hitting the opposite wall.

I slowly lifted myself into a kneeling position so I could glare up at him. "Don't you think I want to be free of Jabari?" I demanded. "I would love nothing more than to shove his damned powers down his throat and let him choke on them, but I can't. I can't fight him. Hell, I can't even sense his powers until it's too late."

"Then let me give you the gift you would have had already if you hadn't messed your life up with these bloody nightwalkers." He waved his hand at me and I found myself cringing, all the muscles tensing in my body as I waited for another wave of pain to come crashing through my frame. But it never happened. There was only Nick's laughter as he mocked my surprise and fear.

And then it came to me, as if a heavy veil were being lifted from the world. I could sense . . . energy. Different kinds of energy as it flowed in and around me. I could feel the earth and her steadily beating pulse. I could feel the hum of energy buzzing in my own body. I could sense the energy rolling off Nick in fat, swamping waves so it seemed to fill the air, suffocating me as I struggled to pull above its weight. It was unlike anything I had ever seen or felt before. Once, many months ago, I had sensed the powers of the earth, and being a nightwalker, I was always in touch with blood magic. However, the energy that tumbled away from Nick seemed to fit neither of these categories. He was a massive ball of power and something else . . .

"How about a test drive, father mine?" I mocked, pushing to my feet. Narrowing my eyes on his smug face, I tapped into all the energy swirling around me, not caring whether it came from blood, earth, or whatever Nick was, and let it fill me in a rush. I summoned up my powers and flung a round of fireballs at him with enough speed that I was sure he wouldn't be able to dodge them. And he didn't. The fire struck him in the center of his chest and washed over his body, covering him as if it were a second skin. His laughter bounced around the room as he took a step toward me, still covered in flames.

I stumbled a step backward, hitting the desk behind me, and steeled myself for the next round of blows as my mind frantically searched for another way of attacking. I had no weapons on me, only the power I had been born with. Running wasn't an option. Nick had already proven that he was faster than me. So I waited for my punishment for striking out.

But it never came. He laughed at me and extinguished the flames. "That's my girl," he said, and patted me on my bruised cheek. "Now you just need to use that energy you can sense against those who are trying to control you. Prove to me that you can harness their own powers for your means. Control Jabari. Control Danaus."

Something in my chest twisted at the sound of the hunter's name falling from Nick's thin lips. I wanted to keep Danaus as far from this creature as I possibly could, but I knew looking into his twinkling black eyes that it wasn't even a remote possibility.

"And if I refuse?" I lifted my chin as I clenched my teeth.

"Then you are useless to me as you are, and we'll have to start from scratch," he said with a grin. He pressed his hand into my stomach and leaned in close. "I can still undo what was done."

"What?" I demanded, my stomach twisting into a tight knot.

"Make you human again." My mind halted at the very thought. *Human. Again.* I couldn't ever be human again. I didn't *want* to be human ever again. I was a nightwalker. I had been a nightwalker for more than six hundred years. It was all I knew.

Nick sent a pulse of energy through my system and I felt a jerk in the middle of my chest as if something had tightened its fist around my soul. At the same time, my heart thudded in my chest and I took a ragged gasping breath, feeling like I had been holding it for the past six centuries. I could feel blood rushing through my veins and warmth pulsing through my body again. *Oh, no!* I was alive again.

"No!" I screamed, grabbing his hand with both of mine. "No! You can't do this! Don't take this away from me!"

"Then heed me, daughter of mine," he bit out. "Prove to me that you can wield the powers of the hunter and the Ancient, and I will leave you as you are. Otherwise, I will turn you human again and you will bear me a child to replace you."

"A child?" I stopped struggling as the horrible thought screamed through my brain. "But you said you were my father. It would be a monster."

"It wouldn't be the first monster I've graced this world with." Nick released me, and I slid down the side of the desk as my legs gave out. Sitting on the ground, I stared straight ahead, blind to the world around me.

"Listen to me, Mira," he said slowly, drawing my gaze back to his smiling face. With a wave of his hand, one of the silver-plated hourglasses that had been smashed to pieces reassembled itself in midair, leaving the black sand to collect perfectly in the upper glass chamber. Nick set the hourglass between my legs, tipping it so the sand ran into the empty chamber. "You've always felt like time was running out for you, and now you know why. I'm here and I'm waiting for you. Do as I ask and you shall be rewarded. Fail me and I shall make you human so that you can breed me a child to take your place. I will be watching, but remember, your time is running out."

Two

Valerio found me sitting in the middle of my destroyed library, my eyes locked on the hourglass as I tried to will the sand to stop falling. My thoughts were a shattered wreck and I was left bobbing in the middle of the black sea, clinging to the one thing that I had been sure was impossible: Nick could turn me human again.

After centuries of being a nightwalker, of endless nights of blood and violence, it was the one place where I felt I belonged. I was hated and feared by most of my kind, I had allies that would rather see me staked, but being a nightwalker was all I knew. It was home, and I couldn't go back now.

But my heart beat and blood rushed through my veins, if only for a moment. My lungs had burned until I took that first gasp of air, refilling them completely for the first time in far too many years. Worse still, my soul had been fully anchored within my frame as if it had settled back down in the hole that was now the home to the monster that craved the blood I fed on so frequently. For a flicker in time I'd been human again, and all I had felt was terror.

"Mira?" Valerio whispered, glass crunching under the hard soles of his dress shoes as he stepped into the room. He had magically appeared, streaking across the vast distance from Venice to Savannah. And for the first time in my existence, I had sensed the swell of power before he appeared and knew exactly who it was. Nick had truly awakened something within me.

Kneeling beside me, he slowly placed one hand on my shoulder, causing me to flinch. "Mira, are you all right?" I was wounded mentally and physically, and I needed time to heal and think, but I would get neither. Yet time was slipping away from me, and Valerio's unexpected presence in my domain indicated there was a new problem that needed my unique attention.

"Bring me Danaus," I commanded in a low voice.

"Is he the one that did this to you?" Valerio's hand tightened on me even though there was no change in tone in his voice.

"No. Bring him to me."

"Where is he?"

My eyes fell shut and I reached out with my senses, letting my powers wash over the entire city of Savannah and the surrounding suburbs in a great wave. To my surprise, I found Danaus exactly where I had left him—at Factors Walk. Had only a couple minutes passed when it felt like years?

Mira! came Danaus's instant reply when he sensed my touch.

Valerio is coming for you, I simply stated and then pulled quickly away, setting up mental barriers as I went. I didn't want the hunter in my head, didn't want him to know about the monster that seemed to be linked to my earliest beginnings, my weak pathetic human roots.

"He's at Factors Walk," I said, shoving a mental image of the location into Valerio's mind. The nightwalker jerked away at the unexpected invasion, releasing his hold on my shoulder, but I didn't care. "Bring Danaus to me now."

Wordlessly, my longtime friend and companion stood and disappeared from sight. I had enough time to reach out and pick up the silver hourglass that rested between my bent legs before Danaus and Valerio reappeared. With a grunt, I flung the timepiece across the room, where it to shattered into hundreds of pieces, sending out a spray of black sand like a plume of deadly smoke.

The hunter took one look at the room before grabbing a handful of Valerio's white shirt and slamming him against the nearest wall. "What the hell have you done?" he snarled. Danaus's powers bubbled up with his anger, filling the small, broken room with a warm haze of anger. This time, I felt as if I could reach out and touch those powers. And if I really wanted to, I could give them only the slightest shove and Danaus would boil Valerio's blood. This new power carried with it a haunting temptation, like low-hanging fruit just waiting to be plucked.

"He didn't do anything," I muttered, shaking my head as if to clear it from too many dark thoughts. Energies swirled around me like ghosts, each with its own demands and desires. "He found me like this."

Danaus released Valerio with a small shove and stepped over to me. Kneeling down, he placed one hand beneath my chin and forced me to lift my head. I knew what he saw. I was cut, battered, swollen, and bruised to the point of being barely recognizable. My clothes were shredded and I was covered in my own dried blood. From the moment that Nick had gotten me alone in my home, he had taken the time to beat me completely senseless so I didn't have a chance at fighting back. Didn't have a hope.

"Is Gaizka gone?" I asked, unable to stop the tremble that slipped into my voice at the mention of the bori that tried to steal Danaus away.

"It's gone." He cupped my face with both his hands and

looked me in the eye. "You saw it. The doorway opened and Gaizka was drawn back inside. Caged. Gone forever."

My eyes fell shut as a tear slipped down my cheek. "Forever," I repeated, bitterness eating away at the word before it could travel much farther than my lips. Forever seemed like such a pretty concept. Aurora and the naturi were supposed to be locked away from the world forever, but they escaped. Why couldn't the horde of bori that were waiting in their own little holding pen break free as well?

"What's Gaizka?" Valerio asked.

I turned my head toward the nightwalker, still resting my face in Danaus's hands. His warmth was wrapped around me in a comforting embrace, and I wasn't ready to leave it just yet and dive back into the cold brutal world that waited for me. "A bori who escaped. We locked it away again."

I opened my eyes to find Valerio standing with a somewhat blank expression. One hand was outstretched, with the tips of his fingers pressed to the doorjamb as if to steady himself as the room threatened to spin around him. I could easily guess that it was taking all of his strength and considerable willpower not to show the terror I knew was screaming away in his mind.

The bori, along with the naturi, were our greatest enemies. Yet where the naturi were content to simply destroy us, the bori were determined to once again control us. They were, after all, the creators of all nightwalkers. Centuries ago the nightwalkers and the lycans locked away the bori and the naturi, but recently our prisoners had been escaping their bonds.

"It's gone?" Valerio asked in a breathless voice. "You're sure it's gone?"

Pulling my face out of Danaus's grasp, I rested my head against the desk behind me and closed my eyes. "It's gone."

"It . . . Gaizka . . . did this?" Valerio inquired.

"Yes," I quickly said before Danaus could speak. It was a lie, but it was something I knew Valerio would easily believe. I still had no idea what I would tell Danaus when the time finally came, but for now neither man needed to know who had been in the library with me. I was trying to come to terms with it myself. I didn't need to think about the repercussions of other people knowing.

"But it's gone now," I said with a grunt as I tried to push to my feet. To my surprise, Danaus swept his arms beneath me and picked me up, cradling me against his large chest.

"You need to rest," he said firmly, starting to walk out of the room.

"She needs to feed," Valerio countered in a cold voice as he came to stand in front of the hunter, stopping him from taking me to whatever soft, comfortable location he had in mind. Bed sounded very nice. Feeding required more energy than I was willing to expend until the next evening.

"But I'm not going to get either, because I need to know why you've suddenly shown up in my domain," I said tartly, pinning Valerio with a dark gaze. "This isn't a pleasure visit, is it?"

"It's always a pleasure to see you, Mira." Valerio smiled, as some of the tension eased out of his strong shoulders. The destruction of the library, my appearance, and the mention of the bori had temporarily shaken up the nightwalker's usual unflappable calm. But he now seemed to be settling back into his usual self of untouchable poise and charm.

Laying my head against Danaus's chest, I listened to the steady rhythm of his heartbeat, letting the soothing sound push back the pain. Valerio and I had some kind of business to discuss, and I had a dark feeling I knew who it involved. "Danaus, either put me down or put me in the parlor. There's no rest for the wicked in this city."

A part of me half expected the hunter to simply drop me

on my ass exactly where he stood, but I must have looked pretty damn bad because he carried me into the main parlor and gently settled me on the sofa while he took a nearby chair to my left. Valerio followed us silently into the room, which was impressive considering the creaky, hardwood floors, but then Ancients had all kinds of special skills that we younger ones could only dream about.

Valerio walked over to the marble fireplace and turned around, his hands on his hips as he looked down at his feet, a frown toying with the corners of his lips. The nightwalker was weighing his words. If he was trying to be cautious, I knew it did not bode well for me.

"Out with it," I snapped. "You're not here for Knox." Yet even as I uttered the words, I felt a strange tightening in my chest at the thought of it. What if he was here to take back the nightwalker he had made centuries ago? Not only had I come to count on Knox to help me maintain the peace in my domain, but I also saw him as a good friend. I didn't want Valerio to snatch him away from me.

"No, this isn't about Knox," Valerio admitted with a shake of his head, sending a soft lock of hair down across his forehead. The nightwalker released a heavy sigh and stared at Danaus, who was frowning at him, looking distinctly uncomfortable. The last time he'd met Valerio, it had not been under the best circumstances. Both the naturi and the coven were trying to decide how to kill us, and Valerio was struggling to choose a side.

"I think it would be best if we discussed this in private," Valerio finally admitted, tearing his eyes away from the hunter to pin me with his dark gaze.

"If this is about the coven, he can stay," I grumbled as I slid into a sitting position. I gently placed my feet on the floor, feeling to see if my knee and leg were fully healed. Strength was returning to my battered frame and I felt that a lot of my aches and pains could be washed away with a hot shower. "Danaus has met the coven. He's been through hell with me. He can stay to hear this."

At this, Valerio finally frowned at me. "Are you saying that you've finally taken a pet?"

"No!" Danaus said, instantly lurching to his feet.

"No," I seconded in a softer, yet firm voice.

"Then what, Mira? Are you saying he's your equal? You, a member of the coven, are equal with a vampire hunter?" Valerio demanded, twisting the knife that he had plunged into my chest when he started this conversation.

I didn't know how best to explain it. Danaus had walked through the fires of Hell with me, survived attacks from both naturi and bori. If this creature was going to continue to watch my back, I couldn't keep secrets from him.

"It's complicated, Valerio. Let's leave it at that." Valerio gave me a skeptical look that implied far too much. *Leave it. It's not what you think,* I told him again, in thought, which only earned me a slight grin. The nightwalker positively reveled in being a complete pain in the neck.

Motioning for Danaus to return to his seat, I ran one hand roughly through my hair, pushing it out of my face. "Can we just get down to business?" I said to Valerio. "What does the coven want?" While Valerio had never mentioned it, I knew the coven was one of the few things that would drive the nightwalker out of the splendid comfort of the Old World into my domain.

"They want you," he stated, shoving his hands into his pockets as he leaned one shoulder against the mantel of the fireplace.

"For what?" Danaus inquired.

"They're convening, aren't they?" I asked, trying not to sound like I was whining, but I wasn't succeeding too well.

"Yes, and your presence has been 'requested,'" Valerio said with an amused little sneer.

Requested, my ass. The coven wanted to meet and have me officially inducted as a member. I had skipped some of the formalities when I joined the coven during the summer due to a desperate moment of need—if we were to have any chance at stopping the naturi. Jabari, one of the coven Elders, had been there to verify my petition, but I never received the official approval of the other two members of the coven. I had never given other nightwalkers a chance to challenge me. Hell, Our Liege could simply stop my ascent to the open seat by ripping my head off.

I swallowed a half-dozen snide comments as I rubbed my temples with one hand. I needed to rest and to talk to Danaus. Unfortunately, I wouldn't have the chance to do either until I got rid of Valerio. "Am I the only reason the coven is meeting?"

"I don't think so," the nightwalker said with a small sigh. "Keepers from domains all around Europe have been complaining about the recent naturi infestation. There's a chance that the coven might take some action at last, but it's unlikely it will happen unless you're there."

"I guess it's too much to ask that the keepers take care of their own domains like they're supposed to." I slouched on the sofa, dropping my head into my left hand while resting my elbow on the arm of the sofa. "It's not like it's the job of the coven to police the world for the naturi."

"It may be, now that they are running loose again," Valerio pointed out grimly.

"At least until Aurora has been taken care of," Danaus added.

That was doubtful. I had mortally wounded Aurora, but I wouldn't believe that the queen of the naturi was dead until I saw her cold corpse rotting before me. Besides, there was still Cynnia and Rowe. The naturi nation had too many would-be leaders waiting in the wings that could easily take up the cause once Aurora was killed. Unfortunately, with our penchant for infighting and betrayal, the nightwalkers were nowhere near as organized. Right now we needed a united coven to take on the naturi threat, and the ongoing war between Jabari and Macaire would keep us from ever being at our peak strength. To make matters worse, my presence on the coven would not help mend the gaping fissure that tore through the nightwalker ruling body.

"What were your orders?" I demanded, pushing my concerns regarding the naturi aside. I would have to deal with the coven first and survive that ordeal before I turned my attention to the naturi.

"Fetch you."

"Good dog." My wry grin succeeded in wiping any lingering smile from his face.

"Watch your step, Mira," Valerio warned. "My orders are to bring you to Venice immediately. I could grab you now and take you. In your current condition, I don't see how you would last too long."

Danaus shot to his feet and came to stand directly between Valerio and me. The hunter slid his hand up to the knife strapped to his side, while his own energy surged from his body to beat against me.

"It's okay, Danaus," I said, laying a hand on his arm. I gave it a gentle squeeze, trying to reassure him. It was touching that he was ready to kill my friend to protect me. "If Valerio planned to do that, he wouldn't have wasted time telling me."

Danaus stood in front of me, staring down Valerio for several more seconds before the hunter finally backed off, returning to his seat beside me.

"Tell them that I will board a plane just before sunrise today and be in Venice tomorrow night in time for a meeting of the coven," I said, lifting my head from my hand to look at the nightwalker directly.

"It's not what they want," he warned.

"But it's what I want, and as a member of the coven you have to obey my wishes. If Jabari wants me there tonight, he'll have to fetch me himself."

"I wouldn't put it past him." Danaus growled, shifting in his seat as if expecting to see the Elder suddenly appear before him.

"If you must, tell the coven members that I am tidying up some of my own naturi matters," I said to Valerio with an absent wave of my hand.

"Don't you mean bori?"

"No, I don't," I said sharply. "And after you relay the message, you may want to reconsider being present when I arrive. I'll be bringing Danaus."

"Really?" Valerio said, cocking his head to the side as he took a step closer to me.

"As my consort."

"Oh . . . really?" he asked with a deep chuckle. "That hasn't been done in . . ."

"Centuries, I know."

"And never with one of his kind."

"True."

A wide grin spread across Valerio's handsome face as he shook his head at me. "I wouldn't miss this meeting for anything in the world. I'll see you in Venice." With that, he disappeared in a small surge of energy, leaving me with Danaus and the mess that I was about to make.

Three

I was alone with Danaus. After days of running and fight-ing both the naturi and the bori, I had begun to wonder if we would ever have a quiet moment together. Things had changed between us, but I couldn't begin to describe how or why. I was afraid to put words to it for fear of destroy-ing what little positive ground had been made. My stom-ach twisted into knots and muscles tightened in my chest. There had been other men in my long existence, but none of those times felt half as delicate as what I currently faced. To make matters worse, there was a good chance that I was about to obliterate what progress had been made with my newest scheme, but in truth I was willing to take the chance if it meant that he was coming to Venice with me. I wasn't prepared to face the coven alone, and if Nick had his way, I would need to keep the hunter at my side for the time being.

"Do you plan to feed tonight?" Danaus asked, drawing my gaze back over to his face.

I shook my head. "I just need to rest a little before I make some phone calls."

To my surprise, the hunter stood and scooped me up in his arms again. He wordlessly carried me up the stairs to the bedroom with the yellow paint and a pretty striped comforter. The covers on the bed were twisted in disarray from someone who had slept in the bed the day before. A lump formed in my throat. Lily had slept in this room. Her sweet scent was so thick in the air that I could have closed my eyes and believed her to be standing right next to me.

But she wasn't. That sweet young girl was lying dead in Factors Walk, her body broken from when she had been thrown into the stone wall by the one nightwalker she seemed to trust above all others: Tristan. The bori had taken control of the nightwalker, forcing him to do things he would never think of doing.

"Danaus." I choked on his name as I grabbed his shoulder with my right hand. "Why? Oh God, why now?"

He sat down on the edge of the bed and gently gathered me even tighter into his arms. "You're going to see the coven. You have to deal with this now or it will sneak up on you in a moment when you can't afford to be weak," he said. His voice had grown rough and hoarse as he spoke.

"I liked her." My voice was muffled as I buried my face in his chest. "I truly liked her. She was smart and spunky and quick. She would have been safe at Themis."

"Yes, I liked her too," Danaus whispered into my hair. "She would have been safe at Themis. She would have been happy at Themis with James and the others."

I suddenly jerked my head up and pulled away from Danaus so I could look him in the eye. "It wasn't Tristan's fault," I declared in a rush, tears finally breaking back their barriers to stream down my face. "It wasn't his fault. He had no choice. It was Gaizka. Tristan would never have done anything to hurt her. You can't—"

"I know." Danaus smoothed back some of the hair from my face. He wiped away the tears from my cheeks, but they were only replaced by fresh ones. "It's not Tristan's fault. No one is blaming him."

"Is—Is he still alive?" Nick had stolen me from Factors Walk as soon as Gaizka was safely locked away. I hadn't a chance to check on either Danaus or Tristan.

"I honestly don't know. Valerio grabbed me before I could get to him."

A deeper sense of panic tightened in my chest and sent a trembling through my limbs. I couldn't stand to lose both Lily and Tristan all in one night. Both had been surrogate children for me, a vain attempt to replace the child stolen from me when I was human. I *needed* Tristan to be safe.

Closing my eyes, I reached out along the common mental path that Tristan and I had used on the rare occasion. I had once complained about his need to be in contact with my thoughts. Now I would give anything for that faint familiar touch.

Tristan.

Mira. The reply was weak and thready, but for the time being, the nightwalker was still alive. Unfortunately, the contact was thin and felt as if it would break at any second. Tristan was dying.

Tristan, where are you?

I didn't want to do it. I swear to you, Mira, I never wanted to hurt her. Overwhelming grief filled each and every word that crossed my brain. He, too, had lost a child during his human years, and now couldn't contemplate the fact that Lily had died at his hands.

It wasn't your fault. You know that. Danaus and I both know it. Lily knew that. She never blamed you. Please, Tristan, tell me where you are?

I never wanted to hurt her. I tried to fight it, but I wasn't strong enough.

I know. No one blames you. Please, tell me where you are? You need help. You're dying, Tristan. I can feel it.

I know. Those two words reached me in a pale whisper.

He wanted to die. He welcomed death rather than face an endless existence with the knowledge that he had killed a sweet thirteen-year-old girl.

Damn it, Tristan! You're not allowed to give up. I need you.

He didn't answer me, and panic took over. I was exhausted and in pain, but I wasn't willing to let him go without a fight. I had lost too many people over the years, and right now I just couldn't face the loss of yet another person I had grown to care for. Taking a tighter hold on the energy swirling about me, I scanned the city of Savannah until I located Tristan on Factors Walk. He hadn't moved from where we left him. Cloaking him from the view of any others that might wander down the alley, I turned my attention to locating someone who could help me.

Knox! I half shouted when my mind touched on the nightwalker's presence not far from the waterfront.

Mira? Don't shout like that! I'm driving. You could have startled me off the road, he teased in his usual lighthearted manner. I doubt I could have startled him if I wanted to. Right now I was just a massive force of energy.

Tristan's dying. You must help him.

Where?

Factors Walk. Get in and out quickly. Leave the girl's body for the cops, I directed, something dying inside of me to so carelessly leave Lily to people who didn't give a damn about her. I wanted her here in my arms where I could spend the next several hours weeping over her limp body. Instead I had to leave her to the humans. They were the only ones who could take care of her now.

What happened?

Later. Take him to my town house. Danaus and I will be there shortly to help. Save Tristan no matter what he says. Force-feed him if you have to. He must live through the day. I can't lose him, too.

I'll save him.

My body went limp at those three firm words. I knew Knox would do everything within his power to save Tristan's life simply because I wanted it to be so. I knew Tristan's wounds were deep and large, making his survival unlikely, but Knox would try for me. He would try for Tristan.

I slumped in Danaus's arms, the energy that I had pulled together to direct Knox and hide Tristan draining out of me. Knox would take care of everything for me. He would do whatever it took to save Tristan for me. Laying my head against Danaus's shoulder, I finally let the tears fall for Lily's death, the pain I had caused Danaus when I was forced to attack him, and for my own dark fate, which still hovered in the air.

Tristan will be safe, Danaus said, using our own personal path. I had no doubt that the hunter had been listening in to the conversation as he lingered in my brain. I didn't care. I needed that connection. To feel for just a brief moment as if I wasn't alone in the world.

I can't lose him, too.

You won't.

Every muscle in my body seemed to protest as Danaus helped me back to my feet. He remained close on my heels as we walked back down the stairs. My gaze skimmed over the shattered remains of my library, and I was unable to completely suppress the shiver that wracked my body as I turned my back on it and headed for the back door.

"We'll also need to discuss that at a later time," Danaus warned, causing my shoulders to hunch under that new weight. I still didn't have a clue as to what I was going to tell him, but right now the truth didn't seem like the best choice.

The hunter helped me ease into the passenger seat of my little silver BMW Z4 while I handed over the keys with only the slightest bit of hesitation. The car was a manual, and I was in no shape to be shifting gears. Besides, I still had a round of phone calls to make.

Danaus quickly whipped us from the quiet suburbs of Savannah to the historic district in record time, while I contacted my human assistant, Charlotte. She would make the arrangements needed to have my private jet fueled and ready for flight in a few hours, though she didn't seem pleased to be disturbed at such a late hour. It was only when I looked at the clock on the dashboard that I realized it was nearly midnight. I shrugged. I had more than seven hours to get Tristan settled before I needed to board the plane.

I closed my phone and released a heavy sigh of relief as we pulled up to my town house. I had reached my bodyguard Gabriel. Both he and Matsui were safe and completely unharmed. They were supposed to accompany Lily and Tristan to Themis in London, but when Tristan appeared at Factors Walk with Lily, I had feared the worst. Gaizka had shown on more than one occasion that it had no qualms about taking a life. But this time it seems the creature settled for a quick phone call, telling Gabriel that I had changed my mind about the London trip. Neither Gabriel nor Matsui were aware that Lily had been killed and that Tristan hovered at death's door. And for now, I didn't have the heart to tell them. I told Gabriel only that I would contact him again when I returned from Italy, but reassured him that the danger had passed. I don't think he believed me, but he allowed me to end the conversation without a fresh barrage of awkward and painful questions.

Tristan's pain assailed me as we stopped in front of the town house. His physical pain and emotional anguish filled the air as if they were a noxious odor that you couldn't escape. I pushed out of the car before Danaus could assist me and hobbled toward the front stairs, weaving between

the throng of humans who were shuffling zombielike up my
stairs and through my open front door.

"Mira?"

"They won't remember a thing," I reassured Danaus
quickly as I shoved my way into the house. Knox was
using all of his powers to summon anyone in the area
with a pulse to Tristan's side. To my surprise, I also found
Amanda kneeling beside Tristan, who sat on the parlor
floor, his blood seeping into the carpet beneath him in an
ever-growing pool. Amanda's hands were pressed against
his chest, trying to hold in the blood that was leaking from
the massive wounds. She had been keeping her distance
from everyone since she was briefly kidnapped by the
naturi a couple months ago. I had a dark suspicion that she
partially blamed Tristan for her capture, but apparently
she had come to her senses.

"He's fighting us," Amanda said when she caught sight
of Danaus and me. "He refuses to feed. He doesn't want to
live."

"I do." Kneeling between Tristan's bent legs, I took both
of his hands in mine as I thrust my presence into his mind. I
left him with nowhere to run. He hadn't the strength to fight
me, or the will. At my direction, he turned his head to the
first offered arm and bit down, drinking deep.

Knox and Amanda removed their presence from
Tristan's mind and turned their focus to the gathering of
humans. We would need a constant source of fresh blood
for a while as we waited for the wounds to heal enough to
hold in the blood. Behind me, I could feel Danaus's unease
about the feeding, and yet he remained by my side, one
hand resting on my shoulder.

Tristan was silent for nearly an hour as he fed on one
person after another. I controlled his mind, compelling him
toward one single act. It was not the same way that Jabari,

Danaus, or even Gaizka controlled me. I simply walked into his mind and amplified his basic instincts to feed. In his weakened state, he couldn't fight it properly. He didn't even question it.

Yet as his wounds closed and his strength grew, I could feel him beginning to stir. At first it was just a dark shadow of pain and horror, but it soon swelled into a great haze of anger. I gritted my teeth and prepared for him to finally shove me out of his mind, but it never came.

Why? The question drifted to me like a whispered secret, but held a wealth of anger. *Why did you save me?*

Because I'm selfish, I admitted truthfully. *I need you.*

You don't need me. You have Danaus. You have Knox and Gabriel. You have countless others.

And I need you just as badly as I need them. You are my family, my brother. I cannot stand to lose you.

I killed her, Mira.

Gaizka killed her! Not you!

He continued as if he hadn't heard me. *I can still smell her. I can still feel the softness of her skin and the sting of my hand each time it made me strike her. I can smell her fear and hear her voice echoing in my brain, pleading with me . . .*

I pulled free of Tristan's mind at that moment. His memories were too fresh and they were quickly becoming my own. I wanted to pull completely free of him and hide from Lily's violent death, but I forced myself to tighten my grip on his hands even as tears poured down both our cheeks. Lily would always haunt us.

Another hour passed before Tristan's bleeding had completely stopped and I deemed him strong enough to survive the day. Danaus helped the last of the humans out the door and down the stairs. They all held the memory of attending a Christmas party full of loud music and free-flowing alcohol.

They would all awaken the next day a little tired and head-achy, but glowing with a good memory.

Knox and Amanda got Tristan into Knox's car. He would take Tristan to my house, where he would spend the daylight hours recovering. Knox also planned to call Gabriel to add an extra layer of security, even though it was unnecessary. Gaizka was gone. There was no threat to Tristan's safety beyond his own fractured mind.

Danaus laid a hand on my shoulder and squeezed. I still knelt on the floor in front of the spot where Tristan had sat. Blood was everywhere. It was soaked into the carpet, smeared on the coffee table, and stained the sofa. Some part of my brain reminded me that it all needed to be cleaned, but I couldn't get myself to move.

"We need to go," Danaus said.

"I—I don't know."

"We need to go. The coven is waiting. Knox can handle things here."

"Tristan—"

"He will be fine. You saved his life tonight."

I shook my head as I took Danaus's hand and pulled myself to my feet. Tristan would live because of my actions tonight, but I didn't feel like I had saved him.

FOUR

We boarded my jet earlier than I had wanted. But the plane was completely fueled and the pilots were ready. My only reason for wanting to stall was that it was still three hours until sunrise and I would be trapped on a plane with Danaus. He was going to start demanding answers to a long list of questions I was hoping to evade for just a little while longer. But it simply wasn't to be.

After the door to the jet had been shut and properly secured, Danaus took my hand and led me back to the small bedroom at the back of the jet. He left me sitting on the edge of the bed while he walked into the tiny bathroom. Closing my eyes, I listened to the water running and the dull roar of the engines as they powered up. My thoughts drifted aimlessly along, first to the bori Gaizka and our narrow escape, and then on to Nick and his own dark demands. No matter where I went or where I turned, there was always someone dark waiting for me to mess up. At first it was Danaus, then Rowe, and Jabari, and Aurora, and Gaizka. Of course, there was always Macaire. He had wanted me dead even before I was reborn into a nightwalker. The problem was that I wasn't doing a very good job of cleaning off my list of people who wanted me dead.

If I was going to live much longer, I needed to do something about my enemies list.

My eyes popped open and I jerked upright when I felt the bed shift beside me. I hadn't heard Danaus's approach over the jet engines. He reached out with one hand to touch my cheek, but I lurched away from him. I was edgy and wary of the hunter when I knew he was going to come drilling for the truth.

Patiently, Danaus held up a wet washcloth in his left hand. "You're a mess."

"Oh." Taking a deep breath, I allowed him to turn my face toward him so he could begin to wipe away the caked on layers of dirt and dried blood. In my weariness, fresh tears welled up, but I held them back. How long had it been since someone had cared for me in such a gentle fashion? No easy answer came to mind. The years just stretched out in my mind like a black endless abyss.

"It's lucky it was dark when we arrived. The pilots might have called an ambulance rather than allow you on the plane," Danaus said as he tilted my head slightly to one side so he could clean along my right jaw.

One corner of my mouth quirked in a half smile. "I'm sure I've looked worse."

Danaus dropped his hand into his lap and heaved a heavy sigh that was barely heard over the engine of the jet as we taxied down the runway. "Not by much if at all. Between the bori, the naturi, and the coven, I don't think I know of anyone who has taken a beating like you and survived."

"You mean besides yourself?"

Danaus shook his head. "You have always taken the brunt of what they've all dished out. And through it all, you've survived."

"But . . ." I prompted when the word seemed to hang ominously in the air.

"But when you disappeared from Factors Walk, I thought you were dead. Never have I seen such terror in your eyes." Danaus slid his fingers into my hair and grasped the back of my head. He pulled me close so that his lips grazed my ear. "Tell me what happened. Tell me the truth so I can protect you. I never want to see that look again."

"Maybe you can't protect me," I said, pulling away from him.

Danaus gave a low growl as he stood and tossed the filthy washcloth into the entrance of the bathroom. He then turned and lifted me into the bed. He paused long enough to remove my leather boots before pulling the blanket up over me. While at the town house, I changed into some clean clothes and packed a small bag while Danaus grabbed his bag. We were at least prepared for a few days of travel.

"I will protect you," he proclaimed, sitting on the edge of the bed again. "But my job becomes much easier if I know what I am faced with."

I stared down at the blanket, propped up by a small mound of pillows. I was exhausted and hungry, but I knew we would get no rest until I spoke of what had occurred at my house. I briefly debated a string of lies that would be immensely easier to swallow than the truth that rested on the tip of my tongue.

But even as I settled on a lie, I found myself recalling a lonely church in Venice where Danaus divulged to me his darkest secret: his mother had sold his soul to a bori before he was born. He had risked horror and censure with that admission. He trusted me when he still had little reason to trust me. It was well past time that I did the same.

"My real father paid me a visit," I said, desperately searching for some logical place to start this ugly conversation.

"Jabari?"

I shook my head, refusing to lift my eyes from the blanket. Jabari might have been one of the nightwalkers that made me into a nightwalker, but he was not my father. "No. I'm talking about the creature that gave me this set of particular genes when I was born as a human." *Human.* Even that word seemed to be a stretch, but I didn't like my other choices.

"I don't understand. What happened to LaVina?"

"There was no witch named LaVina. That had always been my father in disguise watching over me. He apparently was waiting for his chance to get closer to me, to finally make his presence known. Gaizka gave him the opportunity."

Danaus reached up and gently brushed my hair away from my face, bringing my gaze up to meet his. "Mira, you're more than six hundred years old. This . . . thing . . . can't possibly be your father. I don't know of anything that could live that long and actually reproduce with a human. Unless, of course, your mother wasn't—"

"No, my mother was a normal human woman." I paused and shook my head. "You won't believe me. I hardly believe it myself. If he hadn't . . . I would never have believed it myself." A lump formed in my throat around the words that still needed to be spoken.

"Ryan's a warlock, and I doubt that he's more than three hundred years old. There couldn't possibly be an older warlock hanging out there," Danaus said, more to himself than me. "Not naturi or bori. Nightwalkers don't reproduce, right?"

"Danaus, you've never met a creature like this." I reached across the bed and took one of his hands in both of mine. I closed my eyes and pushed the words forward. "He calls himself Nick. But he said that in other cultures he went by names such as Raven, and Anansi, and Keku, and Loki."

Danaus lurched off the bed, pulling out of my reach when I finally reached names that he instantly recognized. The names were all different, but they all were names for the gods of chaos in the various different religions. The trickster gods of old. I was a child of chaos.

"Mira, this thing has got you fooled. That's impossible. A god? A dead god from another religion?"

"And what if I'm not? This creature beat me within an inch of my life and did it without breaking a sweat. It appeared before me looking like the man that raised me as a child. It threatened to make me human."

Danaus halted his pacing sharply and turned back to face me. "Make you human?"

"Don't get your hopes up," I snapped. "But yes. Nick said that if I didn't do as he demanded then he would make me human again so I could bear him a child to take my place in his master plans."

"Human?" Danaus slowly sat back down on the edge of the bed. "Such a thing isn't possible."

"With a touch, he caused my heart to beat and blood to flow through my veins. For just a second I could feel my soul settle back down into my chest. It only lasted a couple seconds but he did make me human again."

"Okay, just supposing that for a crazy minute your father is a god, what does he want?"

"He wants me to learn to control you the same way that you can control me. He wants me to learn to control Jabari as well," I admitted, cringing as I waited for him to explode at the suggestion.

"This Nick has to realize that Jabari is going to kill you the second he even gets the slightest indication that you can control him," Danaus calmly said. "Jabari wouldn't risk it."

"Let alone you."

A half smile tweaked his beautiful mouth. "What's the saying? Turnabout is fair play. I can't say that I won't fight you every step of the way, but it would only be fair considering how many times I've utilized your powers."

"Thanks. It's just until we find an edge over Nick, though I can't begin to guess as to how we're going to do that." Relief rippled through me as Danaus seemed to be taking all this information a lot better than I had initially expected. Of course, I knew that he didn't truly believe any of this. I had no doubt that he believed some other creature was playing a trick on me, trying to bend me to its will. For the time being it didn't matter what Danaus believed. I'd told him the truth, and I had a feeling he would come face-to-face with it soon enough.

"Why Nick?" Danaus inquired.

"What do you mean?"

"Why would he call himself such a common name as Nick?"

A knot twisted in my stomach. "Don't worry about it, Danaus. It's not important."

I knew the moment the name clicked in his brain. It was an old colloquialism that Nick was playing off of from Christian mythology, but Danaus was smart enough to know it. The hunter surged off the bed and crossed to the other side of the plane, putting as much space between us as possible.

"Old Nick! That's it, isn't it? He calls himself Old Nick!" Danaus barked at me.

"Yes, that's it," I said calmly.

"Your father is the devil. He's Satan. Old Nick."

"Another god of chaos, yes. This time he's just playing off Christian mythology. Look, it doesn't matter what he calls himself, the point is—"

"If he's the devil, that makes you the Antichrist!"

"Damn it, Danaus! Listen to me. I'm not some fucking Antichrist! You know me! I'm not evil, regardless of who claims to be my parents." I wanted to scream. I had just gotten around to convincing him that all nightwalkers weren't evil, and now it turned out that I was the love child of the god of chaos. It wasn't exactly a ringing endorsement for me and the rest of my kind. "Please, I need you. Don't abandon me now."

Danaus slowly walked back over to me and sat on the edge of the bed. He reached out and cupped the back of my head, pulling me forward so my forehead was pressed against his. "I trust you," he whispered in a shaking voice.

I understood what such a thing cost him. This was a man who had devoted his entire existence to fighting evil in an attempt to reclaim his soul. Now he was potentially siding with a creature that had been spawned by the greatest evil of all. He was siding with me based on the decisions I had made, the lives I had saved while we were together. I had earned his trust, and there was no greater honor in this world.

Placing a trembling hand against his cheek, I let my thumb run along his hard cheekbone. "Thank you." A spark of undiluted desire surged through me as my gaze settled on his parted lips. I wanted to lean in and taste him, drink him in for the first time after so many all-too-brief encounters. I could sense the same longing ignite in the hunter as the sound of his heartbeat increased in its pace. The tip of my tongue darted out of my mouth, wetting my lips. His scent swirled around me, dragging up memories of a distant sea bathed in sunlight. Danaus was so close. Another couple inches and I could feel him, taste him.

With a shuddering breath, Danaus pulled away from me first. He stood and paced the tiny room a couple times, shoving one hand through his thick mane of black hair while I settled back against the pillows. The hunter's willpower and self-control remained intact simply due to the fact that he feared the true nature of the creature that called itself my father. He returned to his spot on the edge of the bed when his breathing and heart rate evened out again, while I settled back against the pillows and closed my eyes, feeling more than a little frustrated.

"We still have a problem," Danaus announced. My eyes popped back open and my body stiffened. I thought we finally had everything worked out. "The coven. What are you planning with the coven?"

Curling up tighter in the covers, my gaze drifted away from him to dance around the small plane, anything so I didn't have to face his piercing gaze. "I don't know what you're talking about."

Danaus put his hand under my chin and forced me to tilt my head back so I had to look up at him. "Consort?"

Sliding my chin out from his touch, I released my hold on the blanket and pushed myself into a sitting position. I winced as pain stabbed through my body from too many bruised organs and fractured bones. I was almost completely healed from my encounter with Nick, but there hadn't been time to feed. My focus had been entirely on saving Tristan's life.

"When I took the vacant coven seat while we were on Crete, I kind of skipped some of the more important formalities. It's time to take care of those things." I ran my fingers over the blanket, smoothing it out, anything so I didn't have to look up at him.

"What formalities?"

"Any nightwalker has a right to challenge my claim to the open seat."

"Does that include members of the coven?"

"Yes."

"And your liege lord?"

"Yes," I murmured, my head dipping a little lower.

"Will Jabari help you?"

My hands stilled on the blanket and the world slipped away from me as I thought of the coven and its members. Jabari had been one of my three creators and my mentor. He could also control me that same way Danaus could. It expanded his power on the coven from a single seat to two, giving him an edge over his rival Macaire.

"If Macaire were stupid enough to challenge me directly, yes, I think he would. If Our Liege took issue with my presence, I don't think so. Jabari knows how to pick his fights, and I'm not worth getting killed over."

"And what about this consort business?" His voice hardened and I found myself inwardly cringing. I didn't expect him to honestly go along with this, but I had been backed into a corner. I didn't want to go into Venice alone. Sure, I was a member of the coven. I was also the illustrious Fire Starter. But I wanted someone at my back. I wanted someone among this horde that I knew I could trust. Valerio would only help me so long as it was in his best interest. Same with Jabari. I had no others that would be in Venice that I could call comrade.

"I need you with me," I said, trying to sound strong and confident. "I need you there with me, someone I can trust to watch my back. I won't lie and say there's no risk to you. If I'm killed by Our Liege, then you'll be next, and it won't be a quick death. But if I survive the challenges, then I want you there with me when the business of the naturi comes up."

"As your consort?" Danaus's voice had become surprisingly soft, like a gentle caress.

I let out a groan and buried my hands in my face. I wish he hadn't been there for that part. "It's not like it sounds," I muttered. "I need you there, in the Main Hall, at my side. But to do that, you need a title, a standing within my world, and there are only three grades when it comes to associating with the Elders. You're a pet—"

"Which is nothing more than a plaything."

"Yes. Or you're a companion, which is just a glorified servant."

"Or you're a consort," Danaus finished.

I paused, licking my lips as I dropped my hands back into my lap. "It's the closest I can come to putting you on equal footing with me. It means you are my . . . my . . ."

"Lover?" he supplied, and I cringed.

"Typically, but obviously not in this case," I admitted. "It means you're under my protection, you are held in very high regard to me, and anyone risks my wrath if you are harmed in any way. However, you have no power on the coven or within my world. It's just what little extra protection that I can offer you. No mortal has even held that position, and I honestly don't expect it to go over too well, but it's the best I can do."

"Do I get a say in this matter?" he asked.

I closed my eyes and shook my head, disgusted with myself. I was making all these plans, but I had not bothered with the most important thing: asked him if he was willing to go. The hunter had done his part. He had faced not only the naturi with me, but the bori as well. I needed him to stay close if I was to escape Nick's grasp for the time being, but he didn't need me any longer. He had sworn that he wasn't going to return to Themis. His life was his own now. He could go wherever and do whatever he wanted.

"Will you please go before the coven with me? It will be dangerous, and I will do everything within my power to protect you. I . . . I just want you there with me." I felt as if I was dangling out on a thin limb, waiting for it to break under the weight of all my hopes and fears. After everything that had happened, I wasn't ready to let him go.

Raising his hand, Danaus ran the back of curled fingers gently across my cheekbone in a caress so soft it nearly brought tears to my eyes again. "If I don't, I miss out on the latest news regarding the naturi. Maybe even a chance to hunt the bastards. Besides, going would mean that I get the chance to thumb my nose at Jabari and the rest of the coven by being at your side. I'm willing to take a risk for that kind of opportunity."

A surprised laugh escaped me before I turned my head and pressed a quick kiss to his knuckles before he could draw them away. "I think you're spending too much time around me. You're developing a seriously twisted sense of humor."

Danaus leaned forward and pressed a light, lingering kiss to my forehead, causing my eyelids to slip shut. "I'm willing to take that risk, too."

Five

Venice was a haven and a hell for all nightwalkers. It was the seat of the coven—the ruling body of the nightwalker nation. It had been the home of the Elders for centuries, and I expected it to remain that way for many centuries more. It was a piece of the Old World, slowly decaying but still grasping to her faded charms and dusty manners like a shield and sword against the hectic pace of the modern world.

The island of San Clemente rose up around us as we stepped off the boat and onto the stone dock. I stood with my hands resting on my hips, staring at the wall of trees before me. Nightwalkers crowded the island, watching me, anxiously awaiting my arrival. It had been more than a century since a new Elder took a seat on the coven. Elizabeth had risen to power from out of nowhere, destroying Adam to take his open seat. The coup had been a shock to many, and the other Elders declined to challenge her ascent to power. I hadn't been in the city at the time, but Jabari filled me in later with his own speculation.

Now, the Fire Starter was to take her place as an Elder on the coven. I would be the first in a very long time that wasn't a true Ancient. I had yet to reach that critical thousand-year mark and the various powers that came with that age. There would be some willing to challenge me to take the seat, but they had to question whether they were willing to take on Jabari as well. Even though we were at odds, it was no secret that I belonged in some strange way to the Ancient Egyptian nightwalker.

Frowning, I dropped my right hand onto the handle of the short sword I wore at my waist. A second, longer blade hung across my back, while an assortment of knives was strapped to my body at various points. I would not use my unique gift unless I was backed into a corner. For now, I was content to rely on the fighting skills I had honed over the many centuries. I needed to beat them with a sword in my hand. It was more than the rush of power that came from taking a creature's life with the edge of a knife. It was the assertion of my powers beyond my horrifying gift, which allowed me to burn any nightwalker to a crisp in a matter of seconds. They needed to fear me and all my skills.

"Are you ready?" Danaus asked as he came to stand beside me. The hunter wore a long, black leather duster that snapped in the growing bitter winter wind. He was also ready for battle. If things went poorly for me, he needed to at least have a fighting chance to get off the island.

I looked over at my companion, flashing him an evil grin. "Heavily armed and looking for love."

"In all the wrong places," Danaus added, with one of his rare grins.

We walked down the winding path through the wooded area to the massive building that housed the coven. It was a tall, dark stone building with a few slit windows. An imposing structure, with its wrought-iron banded doors and stark face. The exterior and surrounding grounds were not lit by any kind of lighting, helping to ward off any curious guests that might have wandered down the path from the nearby hotel. Danaus and I reached the home of the coven unmolested. All the nightwalkers were in the warmth of the hall, waiting for our arrival.

I paused with my hand on the door handle to the structure and let my powers flare out around us. After a while I simply stopped trying to count. More than one hundred nightwalkers waited inside for us. Danaus wouldn't have a chance if I was killed. I was beginning to have second thoughts about bringing him inside. I had felt that I needed someone there at my back. He was the only one capable of freeing me from Jabari's hold, should the nightwalker attempt to control me. He was the only one I could rely on to come to my side if I were injured. He was the only one I trusted.

"I'm not leaving," Danaus announced as he came to stand beside me.

"And miss out on this bloodbath?" I forced myself to smile at him despite my gnawing concerns. "I wouldn't dream of it."

Jerking the heavy metal handle, the door slid open. The cold wind rushed in ahead of us, causing the candles to dance on their slender perches. I raised my hands and the candlelight stilled and grew brighter, beating back the heavy shadows to reveal that we were alone in the vestibule. Danaus followed me in, pulling the door closed behind him.

After only a couple steps the set of doors barring our way to the throne room of the coven soundlessly swung open. Danaus drew his blade from his back, ready to take on any that approached us, but no one came. They were waiting for us, though. The hall was brightly lit, and yet the floor remained a dark pool of shining black marble. Jabari, Macaire, and Elizabeth sat in their respective chairs on the raised dais at the far end of the room, watching my approach. To my surprise, Our Liege's chair remained empty. I had been expecting him to make an appearance for this rather momentous occasion, unless he didn't actually expect me to formally ascend to the position of Elder. That dark thought slowed my steps a bit as I reached the doors.

My gaze danced around the room to find the three walls before the dais lined with hundreds of nightwalkers. So many faces I didn't recognize. None of them looked particularly friendly. I didn't see Valerio, but I knew he was there. Unfortunately, my eyes did light on Stefan and my frown deepened. The Ancient nightwalker looked at me with a fresh, burning hatred. He had been waiting to officially hit the millennium mark before he finally ascended to the open seat on the coven. I imagined that I beat him to it by a matter of weeks at the most.

Don't do it, I mentally said, pushing the words exclusively into Stefan's brain. The nightwalker had survived two attacks on Machu Picchu. He had fought the naturi beside me, and even helped me stop Danaus when the hunter was temporarily possessed by the bori.

It's my right to challenge you, Stefan snarled.

True, but I need you alive, and Jabari won't allow me to lose. I could feel his instant rage, but the nightwalker said nothing. He had planned on challenging me for the seat on the coven, and I suspected that he would actually have a good shot at defeating me if he acted quickly enough. However, we both knew that Jabari liked his edge on the coven, and he wasn't about to give it up if he could help it. For now, Stefan was willing to step aside, but I knew he would attack me the first chance he got away from the Main Hall.

Stepping farther into the room, I was hammered by a great swell of energy that pulsed out of the throng of nightwalkers that filled the hall. The air was glazed in red, and I felt as if I was moving through a thick wall of heavy mist. The feeling was both energizing and irritating. Their energy was at odds with my own, as if just slightly off center. I couldn't grab it, couldn't use it. It would have been like trying to cram a square peg in a round hole. The only bits that felt in harmony with my own powers flowed from Danaus beside me and Jabari before me. Unfortunately, I wasn't willing to try to use their powers at this exact moment. If I were about to be attacked, it didn't seem a safe time to go out on a limb and try something new.

In the center of the room, I stopped and gave a sweeping bow to the members of the coven, but I couldn't keep the smirk off my lips. Jabari was outwardly grinning, practically beaming at the prospects of putting a puppet on the open seat. At the same time, Macaire appeared to be positively livid, his wizened face twisted in anger. He knew that it would be only a matter of time before Jabari used me to make a play for his head and heart. Only Elizabeth seemed unmoved by the proceedings. She'd been no fan of mine after I slaughtered her companion Gwen last summer. However, such things were a fairly common occurrence when one dealt with the coven and its court. It was wise not to get too attached to anyone.

"I am Mira, daughter of . . . many," I announced, twisting the words in my mouth before releasing them into the air. Unlike all the other nightwalkers, I actually had three makers: Sadira, Jabari, and Tabor. Oddly enough, only Jabari remained. "I am the Fire Starter and I have come to claim the open seat on the coven. Are there any who would challenge me?"

A heavy silence filled the air as I stood waiting for anyone to step forward. I knew what they were thinking. Would I stick to my oath that I would not use fire while on the island of San Clemente? It was an old promise I had been forced to make shortly after being reborn, because I was burning through too many Ancients. During my last visit, I had broken that promise in an attempt to save my life and

Danaus's. I had done it when I lost my temper at the presence of a naturi in the Main Hall.

"I challenge you," announced a deep voice in a heavy Russian accent. I flinched before I could stop myself. I didn't need to turn around to see the speaker. I knew the voice, knew the accent. The Ancient nightwalker claimed all of Russia as his domain. I hadn't expected to see Yuri there. He'd distanced himself from the coven during the long centuries and had never before expressed any interest in becoming involved in the politics of our people.

Turning slowly so I could see the nightwalker over my left shoulder, I arched one eyebrow at him. "Do you think I am not concerned about what is best for our people? Do you think I will not endeavor to protect our kind from the naturi?"

"It is hard to believe that you are concerned about the best interests of our people when you've got a known hunter at your side as a pet," Yuri snapped.

"Consort," I corrected, which sent up a gasp and a murmur of conversation around us. I looked around to find that even Jabari had stopped smiling. Consort meant that I had not bent Danaus to my will as he may have hoped. The hunter was the only one capable of blocking Jabari's control over me. I was trapped between them, a toy both children were fighting over.

"Consort? A human and a nightwalker hunter as a consort?" Yuri demanded, as if his mind failed to fully comprehend what I was saying.

"Yes, he is my consort and I will protect him from any who would take a step against him," I replied calmly. "Do you oppose me because I would not be the best for our people, or because of the people that I associate with?"

"Both. You would drive us into war with the naturi. You would leave your 'consort' to run free hunting us."

"War with the naturi is inevitable." I turned around to completely face him, my hands resting on my hips. "Aurora is free. Rowe is free. The great horde of the naturi race is free. If we hope to survive, we face war with them. They are not interested in coexistence. Not so long as Aurora leads them."

"And the hunter?"

I shrugged. "He protects mankind and our secret. Is that not in our best interest?"

"He has no place among our people, not after killing so many of us!"

"And how many of us have you killed?" That question stopped him, his raised fist dropping back to his side while his face contorted with a fresh surge of anger. Yuri was like any Ancient. He had made a name for himself by killing countless nightwalkers. It was no different than Jabari, Macaire, or even me.

"You will not become an Elder," he firmly said, taking a step forward so he was separated from the rest of the crowd.

"Then you must come stop me," I said, opening both of my arms, welcoming him out onto the floor. My smile never wavered as I glanced briefly over at Danaus. His face was expressionless, but I could feel his powers above all the others, beating against me. He was continuously scanning the area, using it as a warning system against any who might try to sneak up on us. *Go stand beside my seat and watch your back,* I directed him.

You watch your back, too. The hunter casually strolled over to the open seat on the dais and mounted the three small stairs. It was all I could do to suppress a wide grin when I saw him place one arm on the back of the seat and cross his left foot in front of his right in a relaxed stance. He appeared utterly confident that it would be only a matter of minutes before I was sitting in that seat.

Drawing the short sword from my side, I waved one hand at Yuri, inviting him out onto the floor. The Ancient stepped forward, shedding his heavy, floor-length fur coat to reveal a pale bare chest. The creature was thin and bony, like an animated skeleton wrapped in medical gauze. His brown hair was wild, sticking out in every direction from his head as if he spent his nights running among the wolves he controlled. From his waist he pulled out a long wicked knife. Twisting his wrist, the blade caught the flickering candlelight, winking at me.

The nightwalker took one step forward and disappeared. Every muscle in my body tightened as I fought back the swell of panic that erupted in my chest. Ancients could easily teleport from one spot to another in an instant. I couldn't do that. Not yet. However, I could feel the swell of power just a half second before he reappeared. There was a brush of energy against my back. Pivoting on my right foot, I twisted around and raised my sword in time to block the blow that aimed for my neck. Metal clanged against metal, sending up a brief clash of sparks. Yuri looked genuinely surprised when I pushed him away from me. He had been expecting to take me completely by surprise and end the fight with a single blow.

"You're going to have to try a little harder than that," I sneered. In a flash of steel, I sent a flurry of blows in his direction, keeping him backpedaling. Not one had been aimed to be a killing blow. I was simply proving to him that I was better than he anticipated. I would kill him in a moment, and I would do it without using my powers. The gathered horde of nightwalkers needed to know that I was just as dangerous when I wasn't using them.

Yet no matter how fast I moved or swung my sword, Yuri was always faster. As an Ancient, he always would be. Backed to nearly the dais, the nightwalker caught a blow aimed at his chest, easily halting the blade before it could pierce flesh. He smiled before pushing me off of him. I slid more than a yard across the slick black marble, the soles of my shoes squeaking as I struggled to stop myself.

"You've improved since I last saw you," Yuri admitted as he closed the distance between us.

"I've had six centuries to practice." Yuri had appeared before the coven many years ago, when word hit that a fledgling nightwalker that could control fire was making her first appearance. I had been a freak show for all to see as they tested both my strength and endurance. I lasted longer than most, but in the end I broke like all of those before me.

Yuri lunged at me with incredible speed, swinging the blade to remove my head. I barely raised my own sword in time to stop it. The vibrations down the blade nearly shook my hands loose, leaving them stinging from the impact. Muscles burned as I struggled against his greater strength. I was beginning to question my earlier vow. The Ancient was both stronger and faster than me. He had more powers than me. My chances of winning on skill alone were growing dim.

Again the nightwalker vanished before my eyes. Immediately, I sent my powers out from my body, tapping into the energy that surrounded me. I sensed Yuri just before he reappeared behind me. Spinning around, I ducked lower into a squat and slammed the flat of my blade into the back of his legs. The impact was enough to send him sprawling onto his back. Kneeling beside him, I drove my sword down into his chest before he could roll away, narrowly missing his heart. At the same time, he lifted his blade, shoving it through my shoulder.

Our matching cries of pain reverberated through the air as the scent of blood filled the hall. Jerking my sword from his chest, I pressed the tip into his throat.

"Will you yield and swear to follow me?" I demanded through clenched teeth.

"You have not won yet," he bit out, twisting the blade that was still in my shoulder. A low moan escaped me, but I held my own sword steady in my hand.

"It's over," I said firmly. "This is your last chance to walk away."

To my surprise, Yuri disappeared. I slammed into the floor, my free hand sliding in his blood as I tried to stop myself. A wall of flames shot up around me as I pushed to my knees again. Pain pulsed down my arm and across my chest. The flames had been a reflex reaction to save myself from being stabbed in the back.

Yuri reappeared beside me. He grabbed a handful of my hair, but before he could tighten his grip, I pushed on the floor, using his blood to slide out of his reach and through the dancing flames. Regaining my feet, I threw a knife at him before I stepped back into the circle of fire. The blade embedded itself deep in the creature's stomach, bending him over in pain. With no remorse, no hesitation, I raised my sword and chopped off his head.

The headless body collapsed at my feet, while the head rolled several feet away. With a snap of my fingers, the wall of flames vanished as Yuri's body became engulfed in flames. Walking over, I kicked his head toward the dais so it lay before my chair like a trophy.

"Who's next?" I shouted, extinguishing the flames so that only my voice echoed through the heavy silence. No one moved. No one spoke. Even wounded, I was still a threat they were unwilling to take on. I was not an Ancient, but I would take my seat on the coven as an Elder regardless of whether I truly wanted it.

This arrangement will not last, Stefan whispered in my head.

I smiled as I turned to face the three seated Elders before me. *You're right. This won't last. Just give me time and I will hand you an open seat,* I promised. I didn't always agree with Stefan and his outlook toward the other races. However, he was strong and he would help me stand against the naturi. I needed him alive and seated on the coven beside me if my people were to survive the long nights that were approaching.

"It seems there are no others willing to cross you, Mira," Jabari said, beaming at me like a proud father. "Once again I recognize your claim to the open seat on the coven."

My gaze turned to Elizabeth and Macaire, waiting. All the members of the coven had to recognize my claim on the open seat or they had to challenge me. After my fight with Yuri, I was weaker than I had been when I first walked into the Main Hall, making me potentially easy prey for Macaire and maybe even Elizabeth. Both held grudges against me for their own particular reasons. My muscles tightened, increasing the pain in my shoulder even as it struggled to finally heal. My hand tightened around my sword, sending a stabbing pain through my arm, but I was ready.

"I recognize your claim to the open seat on the coven," Elizabeth declared in a clear, ringing voice that filled the enormous chamber. She lifted her chin a little and even graced me with a small smile, as if daring me to question her motives.

My gaze then turned to Macaire, whose face had grown red during the past few minutes as his rage mounted. I was willing to bet that the nightwalker had goaded Yuri into challenging me, confident that the powerful Ancient would make quick work of me. But yet again Macaire had underestimated me and my determination to live.

"I recognize your claim to the open seat on the coven,"

he announced in a dark growl, his hands tightening on the arms of his chair.

I bowed my head slightly to him, my grin growing wider. It was official now. I was an Elder on the coven that ruled the entire nightwalker nation, and I had at my side a hunter that was part bori. My people might never forgive me if they found out the truth, but I was doing what I believed was for the best.

"As my first act as Elder, there is some old business that I would like to clear up," I announced. Gazing around the room, my eyes finally lit on a slender blond nightwalker with icy blue eyes. My smile dimmed as I walked over to him. Lucas took a step backward, bumping into a nightwalker standing directly behind him.

"Mira, I—" he started, but I didn't allow him to get any further. Grabbing the front of his shirt, I tossed him into the middle of the open floor before the coven. The young nightwalker scrambled to his feet and tried to edge closer to his master Macaire. However, I darted across the room, intercepting his movements.

"What grievances do you have against my companion?" Macaire demanded as he shoved to his feet.

"Many," I said in a low voice. "Don't I, Lucas?"

"Please, Mira," he pleaded, trying to take a step away from me, but I had already begun to circle him, keeping him trapped in the center of the floor.

I waited for him to say that he was simply following the orders of his master, but the nightwalker stopped himself before he could incriminate Macaire. The Elder would only go so far to protect him, and neither of us believed that he would cross me directly.

"Last summer you were in Savannah trying to incite a rebellion with Bishop among my people. You lingered in my domain without presenting yourself to me. You attacked me and you attacked my guest." I stopped pacing. "Do you have any excuse that you can offer up?"

"Please, Mira, I had no choice," Lucas pleaded as a tear streaked down his pale cheek.

"Really? Why is that?"

"I—I can't . . ." he said, his words seeming to drift away. If he offered up an excuse that saved him from me, he would not escape Macaire's wrath.

"That's what I thought." Balling my right hand into a fist, I punched through his chest so I could grab his heart. I wrapped my fingers around the cold lifeless organ before ripping it out. The nightwalker gave one little jerk before falling over before me. He never cried out. He never fought me. But then, he never had a chance.

I waved my empty hand over Lucas's body, lighting it on fire. I tossed the heart on the burning body and turned back to face the coven with a wide grin on my face. All the aches and pains I felt earlier had left me as I was filled with a rush of adrenaline that came from killing both Yuri and Lucas. My fangs poked against my lower lip and a part of me yearned for another battle, but now was not the time. Macaire had returned to his seat, his eyes unmoving from the flickering flames behind me.

"My debts are settled," I said, and then walked over to my seat on the coven. Blood dripped from my fingers to the floor as I paused before the three short steps that led to the open seat. Danaus had straightened from his relaxed stance and stood like a soldier behind my chair at parade rest, ever ready to protect me. I stared at the gold chair, every muscle and thought screaming for me to not take this place on the coven. It was a road I had never planned to go down. I wasn't supposed to get involved in the politics of my people. I had sworn that I would live out the rest of my existence in peaceful anonymity in my beloved Savannah. But my people were running out of time, and I had no choice but to step forward if we were going to defeat the naturi.

Raising my chin, I walked up the last three steps and sat down in the stiff gold chair, looking out on the massive gathering of nightwalkers before me. No one looked particularly pleased with my arrival as the newest Elder. In fact, most looked horrified or angered by my presence. But it didn't matter. I would do whatever it took to defeat Aurora and the naturi that threatened our way of life.

Unfortunately, first I would have to take care of Macaire. Killing his companion Lucas had essentially been an open declaration of war, which only pleased Jabari. He had been looking for a way to finally get rid of his chief rival on the coven. The Egyptian Ancient was wise enough to fear Our Liege, but had no qualms about being the driving force on the coven. However, to achieve that, Jabari had to finally be rid of Macaire—the one nightwalker that had opposed him for more centuries than I cared to count.

It was fitting that I would continue to be the wedge dividing them, since that seemed to be the only role fit for me since I had first been reborn. Macaire could not control me, and Jabari had never been willing to share me with the Ancient.

Macaire's time was winding down. He had been given his warning with the death of Lucas. He couldn't step down. It was a sign of weakness, and other nightwalkers would seek to take advantage of that weakness at the first chance. No, if Macaire wished to survive, he would need to kill me before Jabari and I got around to killing him.

Six

The naturi were attacking.

The cry went up from every domain keeper that stepped before the coven that evening. Dozens came forward, frightened and angry that their territory was now the hunting ground for countless naturi during both the daylight and evening hours.

I could see the bitter accusation in their eyes. Our world was overrun with naturi because I had failed to stop them at Machu Picchu. It didn't matter that Macaire tried to forge an alliance with the naturi or that we had been outnumbered on that Peruvian mountain. It didn't matter that the coven had acted too slowly to counter the threat Rowe posed. It didn't matter that Jabari had wasted time trying to kill me when he should have been helping me. All they knew was that I had been sent to stop the naturi and now they were running free.

I sat in silence, enduring their dirty looks and sneers as they whined about daylight raids on nests and hunting parties by moonlight. The shapeshifters had turned against us, controlled by the animal clan within the naturi. I didn't expect the witches and the warlocks to stay friendly much longer, considering that Ryan and Danaus were no longer on speaking terms, because of me. The head of Themis was not only a powerful warlock in his own right, but also wielded a great deal of clout within the magic users' community. Our world was falling apart and we needed to start taking some steps to preserve and protect what we could.

"What have you done to protect those within your domain?" I snapped after listening to what had to be the tenth supplicant. My limited patience had finally reached its end.

"We're being slaughtered during the daylight hours," the nightwalker complained, flashing me an ugly glare. It was all I could do to not set him on fire that second, but I tapped down the urge.

"Any nightwalker that doesn't know how to protect his lair and keep it secret deserves to be staked and dragged out into the sun," I snarled, lurching forward so I was perched on the edge of my seat. "We've grown too sloppy and complacent over the long years. We've been the dominant species for centuries. The naturi should not have an edge over us!"

The nightwalker took a brave step forward as he balled his fists at his sides. "What about the lycans? They're hunting us as well."

"Have you spoken with the pack alpha?"

"No, not yet," he replied, his voice losing some of its earlier strength.

"Talk to the alpha. Set up limitations as to where the lycans can roam during the night hours."

"They won't agree—"

"They will if they want to continue to live and be free of the naturi," I argued, cutting him off. "And start hunting down the naturi, damn it!"

"What about the humans?"

I slid back from the edge of my seat and rested my head in my hand as I put my elbow on the arm of the chair. "What about the humans?" I repeated. My head was beginning to throb. This was growing tiresome, and I was confident that we weren't making any real progress. During the early years of my existence, when I was living with Jabari, I spent many hours hovering on the fringe of the coven because it meant that I was close to my mentor. I don't recall that time being as particularly tedious as it was right at this moment.

"They're being slaughtered at an alarming rate. The police aren't going to buy this serial killer garbage we've been feeding them for much longer. It's only a matter of time before the truth gets out. We won't be able to protect the secret for much longer if the naturi continue their rampage unchecked."

"Then check them!" Jabari growled. "The coven cannot be everywhere at once fighting the naturi. These are your domains. Police them as you are supposed to or step down and let someone else take care of what you can't."

"But the coven can be in a few select places, looking into the matter and making an example of the naturi that are there," Macaire smoothly interjected, jerking my head in his direction.

Taking a slow breath, I forced a brilliant smile on my lips as I looked at him, trying not to flash my fangs at him. "That is true," I agreed sweetly. "Do you have someplace particular in mind?"

"Actually, I do. Budapest."

"Budapest? Have we heard from her keeper this evening? I don't recall that one," I said, maintaining my polite demeanor while fighting the urge to grind my teeth. The Elder had something up his sleeve and was simply waiting for me to step into his trap.

"I have been contacted separately by nightwalkers that live within the city limits of Budapest," Macaire replied, smiling back at me. "I have also been seeing a growing number of reports out of that city regarding human deaths under mysterious circumstances. Someone must act quickly to quell the chatter that is starting to hit the human media."

I slouched in my chair, staring blindly out at the crowd of nightwalkers fanned out in front of me, watching my every move. I hadn't visited Budapest in years. I wasn't even sure who her keeper was now. However, it didn't take a rocket scientist to guess that the keeper was most likely loyal to Macaire.

"Budapest is a vital stronghold for our people to the east," Elizabeth chimed in.

"It's long been a haven for our kind, but our numbers there have dwindled," Macaire stated sadly. "We need to protect what is ours."

"Shall you be going then to check it out?" I leaned forward in my chair so I could clearly see him around Jabari.

Macaire looked over at me, a wicked grin growing across his old, soft face. "I thought you would be best suited for this endeavor. You have proven to be quite adept at ridding an area of the naturi. I thought that you might be able to assist the nightwalkers of Budapest. You could clean out the region and make it safe again for our kind while settling the humans as well."

Should I be concerned? I asked Jabari secretly.

You should always be concerned when Macaire is involved.

I should have just killed him instead of Lucas.

Yes, that may have been the wiser choice, Jabari agreed with a rumble of laughter rolling through my brain.

Of course, then you would no longer need me.

True, he admitted.

It was enough to make a person scream. Even the one ally I had on the coven wanted me dead in the end. Only the hunter at my back seemed to worry about whether I lived or died. At least he wanted me to live another night for reasons other than how I could be used to his benefit.

"Who is the keeper of Budapest?" I asked, sitting back in my chair again. I was stalling. I didn't want to go and fight the naturi again. Most importantly, I didn't want to go into a domain that was ruled by a nightwalker loyal to Macaire. However, if I could steal that bit of backing from the Elder, it would weaken him. He would have fewer allies to rely on. It would bring him one step closer to being removed from the coven.

"That is unknown," Macaire admitted. "Since the death of Geoffrey more than two centuries ago, no one has formally stepped forward to claim the territory."

I didn't buy it. There were exceedingly heavy concentrations of nightwalkers in Paris, Budapest, Vienna, Prague, and Berlin. I knew the keepers of all those domains save Budapest and Vienna. Of course, it was well known that Valerio made his home in Vienna and anyone causing problems in that city had to answer to him. He may not have held the title of keeper, but the city belonged to him. I could only guess that Budapest was managed much the same way by a nightwalker I wasn't currently familiar with.

Going to Budapest was dangerous, to say the least, but I would only be faced with the naturi and a nightwalker that didn't like me much. It didn't seem to be that bad a situation. If I was lucky, Rowe would be hanging out in Budapest, giving me a chance to remove his one remaining eye. Traveling to Budapest would also give me the opportunity to steal something from Macaire. The potential rewards outweighed the risks, as far as I could see.

"I shall travel to Budapest and look over the situation. I'll remove the naturi from the region," I said with a nod of my head. "However, it seems such a waste to just send out one Elder when there are four of us. Wouldn't it be a more effective example if we all struck out in separate domains and cleaned them of naturi?" I waved my right hand out toward the horde of nightwalkers closely watching me. "Our people have come forward for our help. Would not a strike from all four of us be the best use of our resources?"

"We all have domains that we watch over—" Elizabeth started, but I was quick to cut her off.

"Yes, and I've been careful to leave my domain in the capable hands of one I trust to watch over things while I am away. Surely, you've done the same. I imagine that you can spend a few nights away from your domain and the coven in support of your people."

I sat back in my chair, fighting back a smile. There weren't too many nightwalkers that would welcome a visit from an Elder, let alone have one temporarily set up shop within their domain, even if it meant getting rid of the naturi. Not many would thank me for this suggestion. However, I was unwilling to be the only one on the coven that got her hands dirty. I had been sent to Crete and Peru to stop Rowe. I was now being sent to Budapest to fight the naturi for some unknown keeper. I would not be the errand girl of the coven. They had to fight as well if we were to succeed against the naturi.

You will pay for this suggestion, Jabari growled at me. "I think this is an excellent idea. With the death of Yuri, I will travel to Russia and check over the situation in Moscow and St. Petersburg," he announced.

I was impressed and worried. Jabari was from Egypt. He lingered there in his free time even after countless centuries. He hated the cold, but he was willing to travel to Russia in the dead of winter. He had something else up his sleeve beyond the need to destroy naturi in Yuri's domain. I quickly pushed the concern aside. I had no plans to travel to Russia, no intention of traveling that far from my own beloved Savannah. Let the Elder claim the region, extending his reach to more than what Alexander the Great could even call his own.

"Following that train of thought," Macaire began, straightening in his chair as he spoke, "I shall go to Spain. After the death of your maker Sadira, a power vacuum has been left behind. There is no one there to keep order. I shall restore calm to the region."

Should I warn him about the wind clan near Barcelona? Danaus inquired.

A smile tweaked the corners of my mouth, forcing me to bite the inside of my cheek to keep from letting the smile fully form. *No, let him figure it out on his own.*

Pushing to the edge of my seat, I looked down the row to where Elizabeth sat. Her tiny figure seemed to be engulfed in the chair. She sat with her back ramrod straight, her dainty hands folded in her lap. I struggled to imagine her in a fight with the naturi, but then Sadira could have passed for someone's grandmother, not a vicious killer. When it came to nightwalkers, looks were frequently deceiving.

"If I might make a suggestion," I politely said, lifting my hand. "You may want to consider traveling to London and the surrounding region."

"London?" she repeated, arching one eyebrow at me. "Why there? There is no keeper of London, none in all of the United Kingdom."

"True, but it has a high population density of humans and there are still a number of nightwalkers there, despite the fact that the city has no keeper. Wouldn't it be prudent of us to stake a claim in the city before it is lost to the naturi?" I countered. "We could at last establish a power foothold in the region, and it's not too far from your own beloved Paris, correct?"

What are you doing?

The question nearly echoed through my brain as both Jabari and Danaus made the demand at almost the exact same second.

I'm trying to see where her loyalties lie, I told Jabari. *I don't think she's with Macaire and I know she doesn't stand with you. Handing her a new domain could give me insight into where she stands.*

I then switched to my secret path with Danaus. *I'm dangling a bit of fresh meat in front of Ryan. I want to see if he will try to access the coven through Elizabeth if he thinks he's lost his entrance through me.*

My reasons for sending Elizabeth were multifaceted, but neither man needed to know all of them. If Elizabeth didn't side with Jabari or Macaire, she might soften toward me at last if I handed her a way to easily extend her own domain. London and the surrounding region wouldn't be an easy place to control, but it was another high-profile city like Paris.

"I will go to London," she announced, nodding toward me. She eyed me suspiciously for only a moment before turning to look straight ahead again, dismissing me.

"It is decided, then!" Jabari announced, pushing to his feet. He raised his hands over his head, causing his robes to sway about him. "This meeting of the coven is at an end. We will meet again when all four members have gathered here in Venice after the completion of their tasks."

The nightwalkers filed out of the front door of the Main Hall, while Elizabeth and Macaire slipped out a side door that led to the underground chambers. The air was heavy and silent, but I could feel the telepathic chatter as they discussed this unprecedented move by the Elders to rid the region of the naturi. The Elders rarely did anything beyond their silly amusements here in Venice. To take action, to actually take up arms against an enemy, hadn't been done in centuries. But then, we hadn't had an enemy to strike against in many centuries.

To my surprise, Jabari lingered behind, along with Valerio and Stefan. The Elder returned to his seat while the two others stepped forward. Valerio gave a sweeping bow to me, grinning ear to ear, while Stefan stiffly bowed his head.

"Budapest, eh?" Valerio said, inspecting his fingernails. "It sounds like fun. I'll join you if you'll have me."

"You standing against the naturi? I struggle to see what's in it for you," I said, unable to keep the shock out of my voice. Valerio preferred the background, watching as others took risks. He knew when to step forward and take the benefit for himself when the opportunity arose. If anything, Valerio was a lover, never a fighter.

"Budapest is but a short jaunt from Vienna. I would prefer it if this naturi . . . infection did not spread to my own sweet city," he replied, and I was happy to drop the issue. That was an explanation that I could understand. He was finally stepping forward to protect what he considered his. Of course, I was willing to bet there was more to it, but he would never tip his hand if he could help it.

"I wish to assist you as well," Stefan stated brusquely. "I have had my own issues with the city of Budapest. There is a personal matter that I wish to look into if you would allow me to join you."

"That's fine with me." I wasn't going to press Stefan for more information because I knew I wasn't going to get it. I didn't trust the nightwalker, but I was willing to bet he was going to give me a little room since I had promised him a seat on the coven. He was going to give me a little time to deliver on my promise before he attempted to take my own seat. "Unless you want to arrive separately from me, my plane will leave shortly after sunset for Budapest."

Both nightwalkers gave me a brief bow before disappearing from the Main Hall. I turned in my seat to find Jabari watching me with a thoughtful look on his face.

"It's killing you to see me sitting here when you were so close to killing me just a few months ago," I teased, grinning over at him.

"It is an unexpected turn of events, but not one I find unpleasant."

"For now, you mean."

"True," he conceded. Jabari was pleased I was on the coven so long as it benefited him. The moment I no longer gave him an edge was the day he would kill me. He had already started looking for ways to replace me. Luckily, I had an ace up my sleeve that he didn't know about. Unfortunately, I had to find a way to escape his control without him being aware of it. Sure, Nick was demanding that I learn to use the powers of my keepers, but it wasn't something I was confident I could do in secret. If Jabari discovered that I'd found a way to escape his control, he would kill me in an instant. I was too dangerous without someone holding my leash.

"Is there anything I should know about Budapest before I set foot on her soil?" I asked, directing our conversation back to the more important matter at hand.

"Don't trust Macaire."

"I gathered that much. Who's the keeper?"

"I do not know. Macaire has been known to frequent that region, so I turned my back on it. You will benefit from having Valerio on hand."

I sighed and shoved one hand through my hair. "Unfortunately, Stefan is a mixed bag."

"He wants your chair," Danaus said, speaking for the first time since stepping foot in the Main Hall. His deep voice seemed to echo through the silence and vibrate through my chest.

"He wants a chair on the coven. I'd be happy to hand him someone else's," I muttered, not needing to comment out loud exactly whose chair I would be willing to hand over.

"I can offer you no help with Budapest," Jabari continued, ignoring my comment. "Be on your guard. It has always been a place for powerful creatures. Both lycans and warlocks call it home, as well as nightwalkers."

"I'll be careful."

"Do not trust Stefan. He has been known to side with Macaire on occasion," Jabari admonished one last time before disappearing from sight.

Danaus came around to stand beside my chair. I looked up at the hunter and smiled at him, some of the tension finally oozing from my shoulders. I still had a long road ahead of me, but for now, the worst had been pushed aside. I survived my first meeting on the coven and been forced to kill only two creatures. I had a dark feeling that it would mark a slow night for me. My reign on the coven would be short, but it would also be washed in the blood of my people and that of the naturi.

"How do you think it went?"

Danaus shook his head at me, fighting back a smile. "I wasn't expecting you to declare war on your first night. It was a bold move."

"Macaire has to know where I stand. I'm not going to take any shit from him, and he's not going to be able to win me away from Jabari like he hoped last summer."

"And Budapest?"

"He knows the keeper of Budapest. I have no doubt that he's issuing instructions as we speak. There may be naturi there wreaking havoc in the city, but it's also going to be a trap. I—I can't ask you—"

"I'm going," he declared before I could stammer out my wishes.

I smiled up at him, barely suppressing the urge to kiss him. Danaus had been there when I was in attacked by naturi in London, Crete, and Ollantaytambo. He was there went we mounted the attack on Machu Picchu. He was there when I struggled to piece together the crumbling order of my own beloved Savannah. He had been there through it all with me. At this point I couldn't imagine fighting the naturi without him. Of course, there was also the chance he could take out a few nightwalkers as well, which would make him more than happy.

A part of me wished I could tell him that he didn't have to go, or that it was too dangerous for him to accompany me. I wished I could tell him that I didn't need him, considering that I had Valerio and Stefan at my side, but I couldn't utter the words.

"Thank you," I murmured, hating the blush I could feel stealing up to my cheeks.

Placing his hands on the arms of the chair, Danaus leaned down and pressed a light kiss against my forehead. "I am your consort. You go nowhere without me," he whispered, his lips brushing against my temple. I smiled, resting my head against his jaw. Apparently when I named him my consort, I wasn't the only one staking a claim. And for once, I didn't mind.

SEVEN

Budapest glowed about us, shining like a golden crown surrounding a shimmering river of glass. The news revealed that a fresh blanket of snow had fallen over the city during the day, leaving it glistening under the stars. The last time I visited Budapest, the three sectors of Buda, Óbuda, and Pest had not yet been joined into a single city. She had been in the process of rebuilding from yet another battle that left many of her amazing buildings scarred and gutted. But still, this jewel of Central Europe shined and thrived.

After leaving our hotel at the foot of Gellért Hill, we caught a taxi that was now taking us across Erzsébet Bridge toward lower Pest. The bridge rose up around us, white and slender like a woman's arm reaching across the Danube. Farther up the river I could see the Széchenyi Chain Bridge standing solid in all its stone and golden glow glory. There was beauty around every turn in this city, with its exquisite architecture and stunning statues and monuments. A part of me wished we weren't here on business but actually had some time to wander down the lovely streets and possibly visit the Parliament Building or any of the castles that dotted the landscape. Unfortunately, the exquisite Saint Stephen's Basilica was out of the question—the magic held by holy places of worship like churches, temples, and synagogues kept nightwalkers out.

"You seem quieter than usual." Danaus finally drew my gaze back into the car. The hunter sat next to me, his long black coat wrapped around him against the bitter cold outside. The temperature had dipped close to zero that night, and the wind gusted off and on, swirling the snow about us.

"It's been a long time since I was last here." And even then, the memories were not so great. I had been running with Valerio at the time, and causing more than my fair share of mischief. I wasn't always the good little girl that I was now, and Valerio was no help on that front. The nightwalker had a wicked sense of humor and a dangerous definition of fun.

"I doubt that's what's preoccupying your mind."

A smile tweaked the corners of my mouth as I looked up at my companion. "You know me too well sometimes," I said, then shook my head. "I cannot begin to guess at what Macaire has in store for us. He would not have sent us to Budapest unless he had something special planned that would finally get me off of the coven and permanently out of his hair. And if he can get rid of you in the process, all the better for him."

"It can't be too complicated." Danaus shrugged, his shoulders brushing against mine. "Either the keeper in Budapest is extremely old and strong, making it unlikely that you'll be able to defeat him. Or there are a high number of naturi here, making it impossible for us to win against those odds."

My frown deepened. It was the same two scenarios that I had come up with as well, and it didn't make me feel any better. "A single Ancient keeper doesn't stand a chance against both of us. And neither do the naturi. We've wiped them out before. We can do it again."

We can't. We can't combine our powers as we had before, Danaus countered, switching to our private path in the event that our driver could actually speak English. We had lost our greatest weapon. Through the combination of our powers, we could destroy our enemies with a thought. However, the downfall of that ability was the fact that it sent the soul energy directly to the keeper of Danaus's soul, a bori by the name of Gaizka. We had just finished locking him away once again at a great cost. I was in no hurry to have yet another run-in with the bori.

"Macaire doesn't know that," I replied. "I'm sure he still thinks that we can wipe out the naturi with a thought. I can't imagine what edge he thinks he finally has over us."

"We'll figure it out." I wished I felt that same confidence Danaus exuded, but then I'd had more experience dealing with the Elders than he did. They were careful plotters and evil manipulators. They acted with purpose and caution so they could be sure they knew that the outcome would fall in their favor. It was rare that you could surprise an Elder, and even rarer that you could escape their schemes.

"When was the last time you were in Budapest?" I asked, happy to change the subject.

"The Turks called this place home at the time," he replied, putting his last visit sometime during the late fifteenth century to the early sixteenth century.

I slid my fingers through his open hand beside me. "A lot has changed since then."

"And yet some things have not." He stared down at our entwined hands. His fingers remained loose, not truly holding my hand, but at the same time he didn't pull his hand free of my touch. "Mira, I—I'm not sure I can do this."

"Do what?"

Danaus raised our hands. "This? We're so different.

We've got pasts that we can't escape. Pasts that are going to eventually get in the way. I don't see how we're going to make this work."

"I'm not worried about making something work. It's about enjoying each other's company while we have it," I said, fighting to hold onto the fragile smile that was perched on my lips. My muscles in my chest tightened nervously; I could feel him already pulling away from me before we had taken any real steps forward, and despite what I said, I did want to make this work.

"What if there is nothing between us but lust?" He lowered his voice as if this was some dark topic not fit for human ears.

I lowered my voice as well and slid closer to Danaus, so my shoulder touched his. "Is that such a bad thing? At least it is the start of something; something that we could possibly build upon." I reached up with my free hand and slid my fingers along his jaw, loving the fact that he no longer drew away when I touched him. I could feel the energy balled up inside of him. He was stiff and anxious, but he didn't move away. The urge to kiss him welled up inside of me once again, the need to taste him. Instead, I dropped my hand back into my lap and lay my head against his shoulder.

"The road ahead of us is dark," he warned, but at the same time his fingers tightened around mine.

"But we're no longer alone."

Giving Danaus's hand one final squeeze, I sat up and pushed to the edge of my seat so I could lean across the front seat to speak to the driver. While my Hungarian was more than a little rusty, I still managed to direct him to drop us off near an empty corner in City Park. I could feel Valerio and Stefan lurking in the region. We were close to our meeting place, and I preferred to walk the rest of the distance without the watchful eyes of any humans nearby. I handed over six thousand Hungarian forints as he pulled the car to a stop. It more than covered the fee for the taxi ride and was a nice enough tip that he didn't ask any questions about us being dropped off in a lonely part of a park near midnight.

Danaus slid out of the car, releasing my hand, and I followed behind him, shoving my hands into the pockets of my long coat in an effort to fend off the bitter cold. With a jerk of my head, we started walking in the direction in which I sensed Valerio. Stefan's presence was a bit shadowy, as if he were quickly flitting from one place to the next so I couldn't keep a clear sense of where he was, and yet he wasn't cloaking himself completely from me.

After a few dozen yards along a winding path, Valerio stepped out of the shadows, blocking the light from a nearby streetlamp. He wore a heavy coat that stretched to his ankles, while a thick scarf was wrapped around his neck. The cold was little more than a nuisance to most nightwalkers, but he dressed so that he easily blended in with the humans. Plus, he liked to keep up with the latest fashions.

"Have you found someone worth talking to?" I asked as we joined him.

"She's up ahead. From what I've been able to discern during the past few hours, she tends to hold court here most nights."

"Keeper?" Danaus inquired.

"Doubtful. She's old, from what I understand, and long used to getting her way, but no one has used any term with her that has even a vague resemblance to the term 'keeper.' It sounds like she's just an old nightwalker," Valerio said with a shrug.

I frowned, not liking what I was hearing. Old nightwalkers were extremely territorial and hated to play nice with other old nightwalkers. Unfortunately, as much as I hated to admit it, I too was an old nightwalker, and I was long used to getting my way. It frequently made for ugly clashes, as one was forced to finally give way to the other, usually through bloodshed and possibly an unexpected death. "What's her name?"

"Odelia," Stefan said, gliding out of the shadows to my right. I was relieved to see that Danaus didn't flinch. I had not sensed Stefan until a second before he officially appeared, and I doubted that Danaus had sensed him at all. Stefan was just trying to prove to me that he was my superior when it came to powers and experience. I, on the other hand, wasn't in the mood to play. We had bigger concerns, and the sooner Danaus and I got out of Budapest, the better it would be for all those involved. We needed to get back to Savannah.

I stared down at the snow-covered ground as I wracked my brain for a memory of someone by that name. I had known too many nightwalkers over my long life, and too few of my memories were good.

"Do you know her?" Danaus asked.

"I may have encountered her a time or two," I admitted with a shake of my head as I looked up at Valerio and Stefan. "But I don't truly recall her. The name sounds vaguely familiar. Do you know her?" I asked Stefan.

"She's about your age. Long, dark hair, dark eyes," he said, as if reciting a grocery list. "She's arrogant, stubborn, and short-tempered."

I snorted and started walking again. "You've just described most nightwalkers."

Danaus fell into step beside me, while Valerio and Stefan followed close on my heels. Only Danaus's footsteps crunched in the snow. We nightwalkers had lived too many years of moving like a summer breeze across an endless field to make noise now. There was no question where we were headed. There was a large concentration of nightwalkers up ahead, and it didn't take much to sense their energy floating in the air.

"What is this place?" Danaus asked as we turned a corner and started to walk up the circular drive of a large neo-Baroque building. Outside, a large statue threw down a massive shadow as if it were guarding the place. Several large domes rose up in the night, while the gray stone front was marked by tall columns and enormous windows that reflected back the light that shone off the snow.

"It's the Széchenyi Baths," I replied.

"A Turkish bath?" Danaus said, obviously surprised. I understood why. Most of the time when we were meeting up with a powerful nightwalker, they preferred to hold court in a dark, human-crowded nightclub where food and sex were easy to find.

"Not a true Turkish bath, though there are still some in the city" Valerio said. "This one wasn't discovered and re-built until the early twentieth century."

"And when was the last time you were here?" I asked, arching one brow as I looked at him over my shoulder.

"More than three centuries ago, as you may recall," he said, sliding me a sly smile that brought a blush to my cheeks. But then most of our memories would stain my cheeks red. "As to how I knew about Széchenyi, I had some time to read while I was waiting for your arrival." To my shock, the nightwalker pulled a small travel guide out of his pocket and flashed it to me before returning it to his pocket.

"Always prepared for any eventuality," I mocked, then turned my attention to the small grouping of nightwalkers that stood by the front doors. The welcoming committee didn't look as if they were ready to let us pass into their private club, fellow nightwalkers or not.

As we drew close to the front doors, the three nightwalk-ers fanned out, blocking our entrance. Their hushed conversation stopped and they adopted a variety of bored and uninviting looks. It was all I could do to not giggle. The oldest of them wasn't more than three centuries old. Hell, their combined ages couldn't equal Stefan's age, or probably even Valerio's, not that the nightwalker would admit to it. They didn't stand a chance in being able to stop us on their best night. I completed a quick scan of the entire exterior of the bathhouse and the entryway as well. They were the only ones guarding the place.

Are there no old nightwalkers within the city beyond Odelia? I inquired of Stefan. These three could barely stop a determined human if they wanted to. Why put something so young on guard duty unless there was no one you were truly guarding it against except humans?

Not many, from what I had been able to gather, he replied. I could sense his distaste for the private communication, but he at least understood that this was not the type of conversation one had with the help.

Seems odd for a city so old. From my experience, old cities attracted old nightwalkers. They had old hiding places, old traditions, and old languages they were able to cling to.

Odelia may have cleaned house in order to solidify her power within the city.

It was a distinct possibility and was not totally unheard of. Removing any nightwalker that was relatively close to your age removed any potential competition in the region for your dominance. But in truth, it was odd for such an old city to be in the hands of one so relatively young. Budapest should have been in the hands of an Ancient at the very least. I was beginning to wonder if I was potentially cleaning house so Macaire could move in. To my knowledge, the Elder preferred to linger in Rome, never traveling too far from the coven seat in Venice.

"What business do you have here?" asked the eldest of

the nightwalkers in Hungarian as we finally stopped before them.

"We're here to enjoy a midnight swim," I replied easily in Italian. My Hungarian was still too rough, and traditionally, Italian announced to any nightwalker that you were from the coven. Unfortunately, this pronouncement didn't go over as I expected. The three nightwalkers looked at each other in confusion, clearly unable to understand what I had just said to them. In fact, I was stunned speechless when Valerio finally had to repeat what I had said in Hungarian.

This is wrong, I said, directing my thoughts to both Valerio and Stefan. *They are all more than a century old. Should they have not all appeared before the coven already? At the very least, the oldest should have been brought before the Elders. Has the tradition stopped here in Europe?*

No, Valerio replied, his tone betraying some concern. All nightwalkers eventually appeared before the coven. All nightwalkers first learned Italian by pleading for their lives in that elegant language.

"He cannot enter," the oldest of the three declared, pinning Danaus with a dark gaze. "Only magic users are permitted inside."

"What must he do to prove that he's a magic user?" Valerio inquired before I could argue. I was already growing weary of this trio, but then I was just another spoiled nightwalker long used to getting her way.

"He must cast a powerful spell of some sort on one of us," one of the nightwalkers said with a disbelieving smirk.

"Fine," I snapped in Hungarian. "Danaus, kill that one." I pointed to the one who had spoken. He simply smiled at Danaus and me. For a moment I almost pitied him because he couldn't sense the energy that circled around the hunter, but my pity for him dissipated before it could fully form.

I can't do it, Mira, Danaus whispered in my mind, stunning me. I looked over at him, struggling to keep my mouth from falling open. This nonsense from a creature that seemed to chomp at the bit every time I tried to restrain him from killing a nightwalker?

What are you talking about? Boil his blood. Gaizka won't benefit from that bit of magic, I argued.

It's not that. I've never killed a nightwalker that didn't attack me first.

You must. If you don't, we'll have to leave you behind, and then all three of them are going to attack you. When the hunter continued to frown at me, I finally relented. *All right, boil his blood until he begs for mercy. You don't have to kill him.*

Satisfied with that arrangement, which shocked me more than I cared to think about, Danaus raised his hand toward the nightwalker I had indicated. Around me, I could feel his power swelling in the air, warming me like the summer sun breaking through the clouds. The smile slid off the lips of the young nightwalker and he looked down at his bare hands. The skin undulated as if something were crawling beneath the surface. With a whimper, he threw off his long coat as he ran out into the snow. His long fingernails tore at the bare flesh on his arms, revealing blood that popped and hissed as it boiled just beneath his skin. He released a bloodcurdling scream as he dropped to his knees and plunged both arms into the calf-deep snow, trying to cool the heat that was steadily building within his body, but it wasn't enough.

Closing my eyes, I reached out for the stream of energy flowing between Danaus and the nightwalker. I gathered up my own powers and merged them with the stream, giving the spell a little boost without directly controlling Danaus. The nightwalker shrieked, his body twisting and contorting at odd angles before he finally flopped back into the snow, silent and dead. We had completely melted his organs, destroying his heart.

I didn't mean to do it, Danaus whispered to me. *I lost control.* I could feel the horror rolling off him. He only killed nightwalkers in self-defense in his mind. This had been murder.

It wasn't your fault, I murmured back to him, but then quickly dropped the connection. Now was not the time to explain that I was attempting to manipulate Danaus's powers in accordance with Nick's orders.

"What did he do?" demanded the youngest of the two, taking a step back away from the hunter.

"Boiled his blood," I murmured, still starting at the dead body as I thought about the ease with which I'd been able to amplify Danaus's ability. It had been far too easy, now that Nick had adjusted my own sensitivity to the energies around me.

Turning my attention to the two remaining nightwalkers, who were still staring at their dead companion, I waved my hand and the young one was instantly engulfed in flames. He managed to run a few feet away, hurrying toward the snow to put himself out, but the fire ate through his body faster than he could stumble. He collapsed at the edge of the drive, his body little more than a hot ember.

The remaining nightwalker pressed his back against the wall next to the doors, his eyes wide with fright. "You may live to tell your mistress that the Fire Starter, two Ancients, and a hunter are knocking at her door and we will come in," I snarled in rough Hungarian. My translation was close enough because he grabbed the door handle and jerked the old, heavy door open before darting inside in a blur of movement.

"You're a coven Elder," Valerio reminded me needlessly

as he reached for the door and held it open for me. "You really should introduce yourself as such."

Stepping inside, I threw him a dirty look. "Normally, yes, but these pathetic creatures haven't been before the coven. They don't know what it means to be an Elder. Fire Starter is self-explanatory."

Valerio flashed me a wry grin. "True."

My trio of companions fanned out behind me as we stalked through the interior of the Széchenyi Baths. The walls were painted a pale yellow accented with white columns and ornate molding. The sound of laughter and splashing water echoed through the cavernous halls, forcing me to check several times as to how many people we were facing. Up ahead, the concentration of power was impressive. There had to be more than a dozen nightwalkers, along with a scattering of both lycanthropes and other human magic users.

As we crossed through a final archway, we came to a large room that held an enormous pool. Steam rose up from the water, filling the air with a heavy mist, which helped to diffuse the dim lamplight that glowed from above and in remote corners around the room. Nightwalkers, lycanthropes, witches, and warlocks, lounged in the water and along benches. We were the only ones still wearing clothing. At the far end of the room, the nightwalker I had spared was kneeling next to a female nightwalker lounging on a heavily padded divan. Her damp pale skin glistened in the thin lamplight.

"I'm guessing that's Odelia," I muttered, shoving my hands into my pockets.

"Astute observation," Stefan commented from behind me, making me wish I could just singe him a little bit. Unfortunately, I was willing to bet that I still needed his assistance before I could finally escape this city.

Frowning, I led the way across the room, weaving my way between the naked bodies. A few looked up at us, halting their conversations, but most seemed content to ignore our presence within their nighttime refuge. When we were standing before Odelia, the nightwalker languidly rolled onto her back and propped her head up on her hand while resting her elbow on the back of the raised side of the divan. The nightwalker from the front door backpedaled, quietly edging away from our group. Fear still filled his eyes, making him more than a little wary of us. I preferred it that way.

"You must be the Fire Starter," Odelia announced in heavily accented English.

"And you're Odelia," I replied, balling up my fists in the pockets of my heavy coat. I was fighting the urge to strip it off. The heat in the bath was stifling, but I kept telling myself that we wouldn't be there too long. I could suffer through it.

"You've heard of me?" she inquired, arching one eyebrow at me.

"Not until five minutes ago," I admitted, crushing her little hopes to dust. "Heard of me?"

"Who hasn't?" she said with a delicate snort. "The nightwalker that can start fires with a thought also has a human that can apparently boil the blood of any creature he sees. It makes for a nightmarish combination."

"Oh, and it gets worse," I said, a grin finally blossoming across my face. "I'm now an Elder of the coven."

"Oh," she whispered, sitting up just a little straighter. At least she was old enough to know what it meant to be a member of the coven. It was a position that didn't just demand respect, it screamed for it even as it killed you. "I didn't realize that Tabor's seat had been claimed."

"The news is still spreading throughout the various domains, though I am surprised that it has yet to reach Budapest. You're not that far from Venice."

"I apologize for your less than gracious welcome," she said, rising to her feet. "I had no idea that a member of the coven would be gracing us with her presence. Can I offer you a seat? Or maybe some refreshments? I like to keep a warm meal on hand for anyone who gets thirsty while at the baths."

"I'm afraid this isn't a social call. I am looking for the keeper of this domain," I announced.

Odelia's face crumpled as she returned to the edge of her divan. She folded her long fingers together and placed her hands on her knees. A lock of her long brown hair fell over her shoulder, partially covering her left breast. "Budapest doesn't have a keeper."

"How can a region this large, filled with nightwalkers, not have a keeper?" I snapped, growing more irritated the longer I remained in this bloody city. "There are more powerful creatures in this city than in most other large cities throughout Europe. By my guess, you're more than six centuries yourself, and I know I've sensed others around the city that are older than you. Someone has to have laid claim to the region."

"The last keeper of Budapest was a nightwalker by the name of Harold, but he left the region unexpectedly more than a century ago. No one has heard from him and no one has stepped forward to take over the city," she explained with a slight shrug of her shoulders. Odelia pushed backward so that she was once again lounging on the divan. "In truth, we haven't had a need for a keeper. The city remains quiet, and as you can see, the various races get along just fine."

"And the naturi?"

Odelia's eyes dropped down to the ground and she chewed on her full lower lip. "They moved into the city just about a month ago and we haven't been successful in getting rid of them. We've learned to hunt in packs now, and the lycans stay away from certain parts of town where they have been known to gather."

"Who is taking care of the naturi?" Valerio inquired, slipping graciously into Hungarian. Odelia turned her gaze on the oh so sauve nightwalker and smiled coyly up at him. I thought I was going to be sick.

"His name is Veyron," she purred. "He is the oldest of the nightwalkers within Budapest, and he's taken on a sort of brotherly role in the city, watching over the younger nightwalkers."

"I've heard of him," Stefan interjected. "He's not yet an Ancient."

To my surprise, Odelia actually glared at Stefan for just a blink of an eye before smoothing out her expression once again to smile up at Valerio. "He is the oldest of us all."

"Which makes for a very young group of nightwalkers," I observed. "How is it that such an old city has not attracted more powerful nightwalkers?"

"I can't really say," she said, once again shrugging her shoulders as she dragged her gaze up to me. "We've managed quite well without them underfoot."

"Is Veyron the one in contact with the coven?" I asked. "Macaire informed us that Budapest was having problems with the naturi."

"Veyron would be the one that you want to talk to. He has a place in Buda in the Castle District where he sees visitors. I'm sure that he would be more than happy to see you. In fact, I can go right now and tell him to expect you." Odelia swung her feet around to place them on the ground again, but a wave of my hand kept her seated on the dark red divan.

"Don't bother," I said, struggling to keep from frowning. "We'll find him. We want to wander around the city and look into the naturi matter firsthand before we meet with Veyron. Thanks for your assistance." I turned away from Odelia and took a step toward the door when my eyes fell on the enormous bath once again. Laughter rose up from the water and people splashed, kissed, and engaged in other forms of entertainment. Something caught my eye and had me turning back toward our host.

"Who is the alpha for the Budapest pack?" I inquired.

"His name is Ferko," she replied slowly, watching me with a cautious eye. She knew better than to lie and say that there was no alpha for the local pack. A pack of lycanthropes didn't exist without an alpha. It was impossible. "He's not here. He typically doesn't visit the baths until a week after the full moon, and it's usually only for an hour or two."

"Not the social type, is he?"

"Not really," she agreed, ignoring my sarcasm.

"Thanks for the information," I said, waving at her as I turned.

"Are you going to get rid of them? The naturi?"

"It's what I do." Killing naturi seemed to be the only thing that I was good at.

Eight

I paused as I started to walk out of the large bathing chamber. Valerio was staring at the enormous pool where nightwalkers and lycanthropes splashed and laughed together completely oblivious to our presence. A wide wicked grin spread across my companion's face, and I fought the shiver that crept up my spine. He was thinking of something evil, and a part of me grew excited by the prospect. Valerio always knew the best amusements.

"Only a fool would inquire as to what is passing through that devilish brain of yours," I said as I came to stand beside him, with Danaus just behind my shoulder.

"So many wonderful traditions have been lost here," Valerio said. He shoved his hands deep into the pockets of his coat and rocked back on his heels.

"You're a coven Elder," Stefan added as he stood on the other side of Valerio. "They should be cowering before you. They should be trembling before the power of the coven."

"They don't even know what the coven is." I placed my hands in the pockets of my coat and looked over the gathered masses. I was a member of the coven. What's more, I was the Fire Starter. I was the one that had taken all the risks when it came to saving our people from the naturi. They should have feared me.

"It should not be allowed to continue," Stefan declared

"Then I suggest a little fun as a way of celebrating Mira's ascension to the coven. Some entertainment," Valerio announced, clapping his hands together.

A slow smile slid across my lips. "Did you have something in mind?"

"If your consort would be kind enough to keep an eye on the door against any runners, we could play a few games with the nightwalkers," Valerio replied.

"Runners?" Danaus inquired.

"Vampires who try to leave before the party is over," Valerio explained.

"Feel free to kill them should any of them cross your path," Stefan growled. "It is your specialty, correct?"

"I can handle it," Danaus bit out, glaring at him.

I placed a hand on his arm, drawing his gaze back to my face. "Allow the lycanthropes and the other magic users to leave here unharmed. Our . . . games don't include them unless they strike first."

"And if they strike at me as they leave?"

"Oh, feel free to boil their brains from their skull," I said with a chuckle. I gave his arm a final squeeze, widening my smile to try to reassure him that everything was going to be fine, but I was growing a little shaky myself. It had been a long time since I'd taken part in nightwalker games, and never as a member of the coven. My role had always been that of either prey or predator. What's more, Valerio was involved, which meant that this was going to be extremely bloody. For a creature that didn't like to get his hands dirty, the nightwalker had a twisted sense of humor that stretched more than a mile wide.

I watched Danaus walk from the bathing room, his

shoulders straight and stiff. His head never turned toward the nightwalkers that eyed him as he left the room. He was above all of them. He was above this type of violence as well. When he killed, it was in the name of justice and protection. Too often when nightwalkers killed, it was in the name of amusement. Not for the first time, I wondered if our way of life would be our downfall, not the naturi. We said we were weeding out the weak and culling the herd, but in truth we were just thinning out an army that we desperately needed against what was coming. But it was too late for doubts now.

"The Elder has changed her mind," Valerio announced in a loud voice that echoed through the enormous hall as he turned back toward Odelia. He shed his heavy coat and unwound his scarf from his neck. "We have not had a chance to properly celebrate Mira's ascension to the coven, and she has declared that some games are in order."

"Of course," Odelia said, sliding gracefully from her divan. A stiff smile lifted the corners of her mouth. "We are happy to find some way to amuse the great Elder."

"You may clear the chamber of all those who are not our kind," Stefan directed coldly, with an absent wave of his hand before shedding his coat.

"But we've always included the lycans and the magic weavers in our activities," Odelia argued.

Stefan halted and frowned down at the naked nightwalker. "How long has it been since you were last before the coven?"

"Several centuries. I was quite young," she admitted, clutching her hands together before her flat stomach.

"Obviously," Stefan said with a heavy sigh. He stared down his long Roman nose at her and fixed his iciest stare on her. It was enough to make me nearly giggle out loud. "The shifters and such have complained in the past that we play too rough, so Mira is generously allowing them the chance to leave. I suggest they take advantage of it."

Odelia was smart enough not to ask any additional questions as she stepped up to the pool and politely announced that tonight's gathering had become a private affair due to the presence of a coven Elder who wished to be entertained. I didn't exactly come away sounding like a welcome guest, but more of a tolerated nuisance. I smiled to myself. Odelia had no idea what was ahead of her.

To my delight, Valerio shoved the divan with a loud screeching sound across the tiles so that it was now facing the largest open area outside of the pool like a throne. He spread his coat over the divan and Stefan did the same directly after him. I smiled as I lay my coat on the divan just before stretching out on it. Now I could be sure I wasn't touching any of the area Odelia had lain on, as if she were a creature beneath me. And in truth, she was, now that I was a coven Elder. They all were.

Once I was settled on the divan, Valerio and Stefan came to stand on either side of me, rolling up their sleeves above their elbows. Energy pumped and vibrated from them in their excitement about what lay ahead. I could easily understand their enthusiasm. The naturi were knocking on our door, demanding dominance in our world. Valerio was aware of a bori making a brief visit. It seemed all our nightmares were coming to life. They needed a little time to blow off some steam.

"Counting Odelia, there are fourteen nightwalkers in the hall along with three shifters that have decided to stay behind," Stefan said.

"Pick a number, Mira," Valerio said, his tone growing more giddy as the time approached.

I arched one brow at him as I gazed into his glowing eyes. "What game are we playing?"

"I thought we would give them a lesson in Italian," he replied. It was an old and popular game in the coven among the fledglings. The new nightwalkers were brought before the coven and beaten to a bloody pulp until they either learned to beg in Italian or died first.

"Nine."

Stefan nodded, looking over the assembled masses climbing out of the pool and watching us warily. "Nine seems like a fair number."

Kill the lycans immediately, along with any nightwalker that may be tied to them. Leave Odelia alive if it is possible. She may be useful later, I said softly in their brains so that no one else would know of my plans.

"Shall we begin?" Valerio asked, seeming to chomp at the bit to be set free on the nightwalker horde.

I waved my hand toward the gathering and smiled. "At your pleasure."

The violence was fast and intense. There was no running or escaping it. Stefan and Valerio seemed to be everywhere at once. Though I couldn't hear it, I had no doubt they were whispering to each other telepathically, directing each other when one or two would attempt to make a break for the door.

With a smile, I finally sent up a wall of flames in each of the doorways that circled the enormous pool. Before the rules were even set up, Valerio and Stefan singled out the lycanthropes and brutally slaughtered them in a wash of blood and broken limbs. They had been given their warning that this was a nightwalker-only party. Odelia gasped and took a couple steps backward, her trembling hands covering her mouth. Normally, I would have immediately directed Valerio or Stefan to eliminate her as a potential shifter sympathizer that could cause me problems later, but I let it pass. I had a feeling she might prove useful later, considering that she was one of the oldest nightwalkers in Budapest.

After the lycanthropes had been taken care of, Stefan and Valerio turned their attention to the young nightwalkers. The trick was to get them to try to speak in Italian. This wasn't going to be the easiest of tasks since most spoke only Hungarian or German, while it appeared that a small smattering knew some English. The first three lost their tongues and were left curled up on the floor, gurgling blood as the wound attempted to close. When Stefan questioned them a second time, the trio naturally couldn't speak, so he and Valerio tore them apart in a spray of blood that now coated the pale yellow walls.

A small group made a run for the pool, potentially hoping that neither Valerio nor Stefan would be willing to get completely soaked in their hunt of the nightwalkers. To protect my companions and keep everyone together, I placed a second wall of fire around the thermal bath, blocking that potential escape route. One unfortunate fellow didn't stop in time and was enveloped in flames. He flailed around the room, waving his arms and rolling on the ground. I could have put him out, but there was something about the way his screams bounced off the high walls and domed ceiling. I closed my eyes and let my thoughts drift back to the nights I lived with Jabari. I thought of the many entertainments I had taken part in at the coven Main Hall. So many had died there, and their screams had sounded so similarly. For just a brief moment it was like coming home.

Mira? Valerio inquired silently.

Sorry, lost in a happy thought.

As long as you're enjoying yourself.

You, too.

He paused with his knee dug into the back of a nightwalker's neck while the poor victim's left arm was being stretched behind his back. *It was always more fun when you were at my side.*

I chuckled and shook my head as he resumed torturing his prey until the nightwalker's skull finally cracked on the hard floor. Valerio was walking temptation. He was dripping blood and grinning at me like a madman with a meat cleaver, but there was something right and warmly familiar about that grin. I knew that violence was a part of his soul because it was a part of mine as well. At the same time, I knew the soft touch of his fingertips as they skimmed over my naked flesh. I just needed to remember that those nights were over and Danaus was now at my side.

I'm content with a spectator's role tonight. There will be plenty of time for me to strike while we are in Budapest, I replied. Yet at the same time, I forced myself to grip the sides of the divan cushions to hold myself in place. A part of me was longing to be washed in blood with them, but I was an Elder now and wasn't supposed to get as dirty as I used to. Of course, I had a dark suspicion that I wasn't going to change that aspect of my personality just to please the coven. I was a hands-on kind of girl.

While it was only a matter of minutes, it probably seemed like a lifetime to the nightwalkers that were herded into a small corner of the bathing room. Odelia was among them, parts of her pale body smeared with the blood of her comrades as they jostled and bumped against each other to escape Valerio and Stefan. Six had been killed already, besides the lycanthropes. I could see Valerio and Stefan mentally sizing up the remaining three. When I had given them the number "nine," I'd chosen how many would die that night.

My gaze danced over the huddled masses. A couple had managed to squeak out *"clemenza"* after some prompting from both Valerio and Odelia, winning them exactly that—a moment of mercy. Another surprised us all when he said *"perdona la mia ignoranza."* Stefan had been more than a little perturbed by the development because I think the An-

cient had singled him out for slaughter, but he'd spoken more
Italian than the rest of the group so he was permitted to actually leave the bathhouse with his life intact. I was even
kind enough to signal ahead to Danaus that this one was to
leave the Széchenyi Baths alive.

It was only after I had been staring at the crowd for a
moment that a smug face finally stood out to me. He was
leaning up against the wall with a large towel wrapped
around his body like a toga. His red hair was damp and
standing on end about his oval head, while piercing lavender
eyes watched me. It was Nick; I knew it without a single
doubt. I didn't need to scan the air for his signature surge of
power. I knew, looking at him with his red hair and lavender eyes, that this was the creature who was supposedly my
father. I could only guess that he had sensed me using my
powers and decided to make an appearance to make sure I
was abiding by his wishes.

Shoving off the divan, I stalked across the bathing room,
my heels clicking ominously in the growing silence. Valerio and Stefan had stopped in the middle of tearing apart a
nightwalker and stepped back as I approached the crowd. I
heedlessly stepped among them and grabbed Nick by the
arms. Slamming him against the wall, I grinned as his head
hit the tile drywall with enough force to crack and dent it.

"You have no business here. I will handle it," I growled
in a low voice.

"That's not enough and you know it," he taunted, referring to my little jolt of power with Danaus's. The muscles
in my chest constricted and a knot formed in my stomach.

"I doubt it ever will be."

"You're going to have to try harder than that my—"

I cut off his words by pitching him through the thick wall
of flames that encircled the pool. There was a loud splash
and an ominous thud that was muffled by the water as he

hit the bottom of the pool. I clenched my teeth and started to walk back toward the divan when I heard a slap of flesh against concrete. I turned to find Nick climbing back out of the pool, stepping through the flames as if they weren't even there.

I stood there like the rest of them, frozen in shock. Everyone naturally assumed that he was a nightwalker and had just succeeded in crossing through the flames twice without even getting singed. Nick took advantage of my shock. He rushed me, closing the distance between us in a flash. He slammed me into the wall with enough force that I nearly went through the first layer of the wall to the brick exterior. I grunted and my vision blurred.

Still dazed, I looked up at him with a smile. At the same time, I slammed my fist into his chest and pulled his heart free. He took a couple stumbling steps backward and shook his head at me. I knew it wouldn't kill him. If he truly was a god, I didn't think there was a way to kill him. However, he was kind enough to oblige me this small thing so that too many questions weren't asked about his odd presence.

"I'll be watching," he promised just before he was engulfed in flames not of my making. His whole body and the heart in my hand crumpled to ash in a matter of seconds, wiping away his existence, but not his frightening memory. He was watching me, waiting for me to perform my tasks like a good little puppet.

"We're out of here," I snapped, turning back toward the divan. I grabbed my coat from the divan and jerked it on, while Valerio and Stefan joined me. A touch on my cheek from Valerio caused me to still, my nerves easing back to some semblance of peace and control. Nick had rattled me, but Valerio had succeeded in giving me back a little bit of my peace again.

"Did you enjoy tonight's amusements?" he asked.

"Yes, you and Stefan were stunning. As always."

Valerio bowed his head to me and then leaned in and pressed a kiss to the vein on my jugular, leaving behind a smear of blood. Stefan followed tradition, but went for a less intimate location. He gently took my right hand and pressed a kiss to my vulnerable wrist where my pulse would have been. The bloody marks were signs of approval on my part of their performance in tonight's games. If I had not approved of their work, I would not have allowed them to touch me.

As we walked past the remaining nightwalkers, I spared Odelia a quick glance. "See to it that this mess is properly cleaned up before the dawn." We then continued back out into the cold Budapest night where Danaus was patiently waiting for us.

"Sounds like you had a good time," he said as he wiped the blood off one of his long knives. Two lycanthrope bodies lay at his feet, massive cuts stretching from deep in their stomachs to their throats. In a couple quick moves the hunter had gutted both of his attackers.

"Looks like you had a little fun yourself," Valerio said appreciatively as he nudged one of the dead with the toe of his shoe.

"They tried to get back inside after they left. No invitation. No entrance." Danaus shrugged his shoulders and I could see a smile toying with the corner of his mouth.

"So are you going to tell us who the mystery man was?" Valerio inquired, pinning me with a direct gaze. My companions had been kind enough to wait until we left the main bath. Otherwise, it might have raised too many questions in front of Odelia and the others. I shoved a trembling hand through my hair, pushing it out of my face as I struggled to come up with a viable excuse. I didn't know anyone in Budapest, hadn't been to the city in ages. I shouldn't have been able to make such a comment, but Nick was hanging about, causing problems in my life.

"He's no one important," I grumbled, keeping my gaze straight ahead.

"I thought you didn't know anyone in Budapest," Stefan countered, stepping directly in front of me so I was forced to look at him.

"I don't. At least, no one of consequence," I snapped, quickly sweeping past him.

"What was he referring to?" Valerio prodded.

"Not your concern. It has nothing to do with this matter that has brought us to Budapest. It's something personal."

"Is it going to interfere with our investigation?" Stefan demanded.

"No."

I felt confident that I could conclude this investigation into Budapest without worrying about Nick, but I was also confident that he was going to interfere with the rest of my life. I had gotten my first taste of true power when I tapped into Danaus's abilities. Nick and I were both sure that I wouldn't be able to resist using him yet again, particularly if my life was on the line. For now, I was at his mercy, but I would find a way to escape these bonds even as I found a way to escape Jabari and Danaus.

Nine

Valerio and Stefan stood under the lamplight in front of me, their hands buried in their pockets as a brisk wind swept through the park. Danaus remained a silent shadow just behind my shoulder, gazing down on me and the lies that I was carefully weaving for all those who would listen. I needed to find a way to escape my Nick conundrum before it got someone killed. Unfortunately, it wasn't my most pressing problem at the moment.

"If we're here to eliminate the naturi, I don't understand why we don't just hunt them down and destroy them," Valerio said, pulling the two sides of his open coat more tightly around his body. His brown hair fluttered a bit in the wind while his eyes teared up in the cold.

"We have more to do here than deal with the naturi," Stefan declared, standing stiff and tall, as if unaffected by the growing cold, which I truly doubted. Valerio was starting to look cold, and I knew that the nightwalker was older than Stefan. Old age didn't allow you to be completely immune to the elements, no matter how he wished to appear impervious.

"So I gathered," I murmured. "Macaire would not have sent me here unless he had other thoughts in mind. The naturi are a concern, but it doesn't sound like they are the reason why there are no Ancients within the city. That is what concerns me. Where have all the nightwalkers gone?"

"Maybe you should ask your consort," Stefan suggested, turning his narrowed gaze on Danaus.

"I've not visited here in several centuries," Danaus replied sharply, taking one step closer to Stefan. "I've hunted no nightwalkers within the city limits." The Ancient nightwalker also took a step closer, trapping me between them. I pressed one hand against Stefan's chest, while shoving my shoulder into Danaus's chest, keeping the two separated before I got squished between them.

"Enough!" I said, raising my voice. "Themis and Danaus are not responsible for the slaughter of Ancients and you know it, Stefan. Killing off Ancients isn't that easy. I suspect either Macaire's been cleaning out the territory for his own private use, or somehow this Veyron has found an effective way to kill them so he can take over the domain."

"Why do we care?" Valerio interjected, drawing my gaze back to him, as both Danaus and Stefan took steps away from each other. I dropped my hand back to my side and straightened my stance. "Nightwalkers die all the time, many killed by our own kind, not to mention the naturi. Why should the Ancients of Budapest be any different?"

I shoved my hand back into my pocket and shook my head as I looked at the ground. The snow had been packed down beneath our shuffling feet so it was nearly a sheet of white ice. It also bothered me that none of the nightwalkers seemed to know or care anything about the coven. But then, that seemed to be a smaller concern at the moment. "Because when this war grows with the naturi, we're going to need every Ancient we've got on hand to help stop them. We can't afford to lose them in silly territorial squabbles. Besides, if Veyron has found a way to kill off Ancients, wouldn't you like to know what it is? After all, Vienna is just a hop, skip, and a jump away from Budapest."

"So what do you want to do?" Stefan demanded.

I looked up at him, a frown pulling at the corner of my lips. I had yet to understand why he had decided to tag along on this little mission, and I had a sneaking suspicion that I wouldn't like it when I did finally learn the reason. For now he seemed willing to play along, but I needed to be cautious about which direction I sent him in. If Veyron was killing Ancients, I didn't want him getting too close and risk losing him when I still had a need for his skills. Also, if Veyron was killing Ancients, I didn't want Stefan getting too close and learning the secret of how to do it before I did.

"See what you can dig up regarding this Ferko. I want to know about the Budapest pack. I want to know their size, their average age, and a gauge of their strength. I also want to know how long they've had this easy alliance with the nightwalkers in the area." There was a good chance that if I was going to go up against Veyron, I would also be taking on Ferko and his people as well.

"And where do you want me?" Valerio asked.

"Quietly, see what you can dig up on Veyron. Find out where he holds court and if he actually has a family. Just watch without drawing too much attention to yourself." It was a great risk sending Valerio digging after Veyron, but of the four of us, he had the best chance at quietly gathering information. Valerio had managed for centuries to hide his true age from all the nightwalkers around him, and I was one of the few that knew he was actually an Ancient. Furthermore, he had a knack for sneaking in and out of a place unnoticed by other nightwalkers around him.

"And what will you be doing?" Stefan groused.

"I thought Danaus and I would go back inside and enjoy the mineral bath." I jerked my thumb back toward the enormous building that loomed behind us. "We're going hunting for naturi, you ass!"

"Naturi? Mira, you can't—"

I held up my hand to halt Valerio's words in mid-sentence. "It's like you said, we're here to take care of the naturi problem. Danaus and I are going to do some scouting tonight. We'll try to find where they are hiding out and how many are in the region. Our goal won't be to wipe them all out in one quick swoop."

"Why not?" Danaus inquired from behind me.

"Because if we do, then we'll have no reason to stick around and spy on Veyron and his little clan of fledglings," I said with a smile. Besides, I didn't think it would be that easy to dispatch the naturi, given that Danaus and I no longer had our greatest weapon at our disposal. We'd have to cut through the naturi the old-fashioned way, one by bloody one.

Needing no further guidance from me, Stefan immediately disappeared from sight. I closed my eyes and scanned the region. I couldn't sense him anywhere nearby, but that didn't mean the nightwalker wasn't cloaked.

"You don't trust him," Valerio announced.

I cracked one eye open and looked at my companion, a frown pulling at one corner of my mouth. "Not a bit. I can't begin to guess as to why he elected to join us. You, I sort of understand, though I don't trust you either."

"That's because you're a smart girl," Valerio said. He leaned forward and pressed a quick kiss to my temple. "You kids be careful and have fun. We'll meet up again at your quaint little hotel room tomorrow night."

"Looking forward to it," I grumbled just before Valerio disappeared as well.

"I don't like him," Danaus declared when we were finally alone.

I threaded my arm through his and directed him back

down the sidewalk, winding out way through the park. "I never really expected you to. He's not the type to take things too seriously. He likes to play with his food when he gets the chance."

"I'm surprised I haven't staked him already."

"Me, too," I agreed softly. Valerio liked to live dangerously, playing with both humans and lycanthropes whenever the opportunity arose. Only the coven could make him toe the line, and that was simply because he didn't want them controlling his life.

We walked more than a block in the cold, the snow and ice crunching beneath our feet. The distant whirr of cars racing down the nearby busy streets could be heard, but even that sound was fading as most people retreated to their homes and away from the cold for the night. Pausing at a street corner, I huddled close to the hunter, trying to use his body to protect me from the wind.

"What did this little show of power accomplish tonight at the baths?" Danaus demanded. "Besides unnecessary violence and senselessly risking your life."

"I taught them to fear the coven. I taught them that the true power lies with the coven and not with this little love fest that Odelia and Veyron have created here."

"It taught them to fear you, and fear doesn't win you allies in this war."

"But fear will keep the dagger out of my back. Fear may keep them from willingly being my allies, but it will keep them from trying to kill me. It's the ones like Stefan that don't fear me that I worry about."

"How could Stefan not fear the power of the Fire Starter?"

"Because he knows I'm weak now, as weak as I was when I was human."

"How can you say that? You're stronger now than ever before. You're an Elder on the coven."

"I have a consort now and that makes me vulnerable. You are my weakness, and those in power know it now." ·

"Mira—"

"You're worth the risk a thousand times over. Never doubt you are worth the risk."

I pulled away from Danaus and cleared my throat. We needed to talk of other things besides his impact on my life. We had bigger concerns. "Can you scan for the naturi? Get a sense of how many are in the city?" I asked, looking up at him.

"I'll see what I can find for you." Closing his eyes, I could feel him send his powers out from his body. They washed out over the city, sliding across the river, up through the hills of Buda and down across the flat plains that composed Pest. At the same time, I slipped into the hunter's mind, viewing the world through his eyes. I could feel little balls of energy that were different from the energy I sensed in nightwalkers. It was similar to the earthy tones I could sense from the lycanthropes, only stronger. I had thought these bits of power were only more lycanthropes, but I'd been wrong. I had actually been sensing the naturi, thanks to my new gift from Nick.

Pockets of them were scattered throughout the city and in the outlying woods beyond the city limits. A thicker concentration wasn't too far from us. Their power was dense in the air, clouding everything around them.

"Is there an island in the Danube near here?" Danaus asked, his voice barely above a whisper.

Shutting down my own powers and pulling out of his mind, I concentrated on what I could remember of the city. "Yes, there's actually three islands in the Danube near Budapest. Is that where they are located?" I was impressed with Danaus's skill. I could pick out a vague sense of direction, but I had no real feel for distance.

"Most of them are."

"How did you know they're on an island?"

"There's a large blank spot around them where there are no signs of human life. The only spots in the area that would match such a thing would be the river that cuts through the middle of the city." The hunter rubbed his eyes and the bridge of his nose with his thumb and forefinger before looking down at me. "What did you see?"

A sheepish grin graced my mouth as I stared up at him. I had made no attempt to cloak my presence in his mind. In truth, I hadn't thought about it. My main concern was trying to see if I could sense the naturi as well. I could, to my surprise, but with nowhere near the skill that Danaus could.

"Little balls of earth energy. I sensed them earlier but I thought they were just more lycanthropes," I admitted, and then immediately regretted my words. I was no longer accustomed to hiding things from Danaus. I was used to him knowing everything I knew.

"How is it that you sensed them?"

I dropped my head and clenched my teeth, cursing my stupidity and carelessness. "Things have changed since that night in Savannah." I forced each word out as if it was stuck in my throat. "Nick gave me the ability to sense all types of energy, but I'm still trying to sort it out. I'm nowhere near as skilled as you when it comes to sensing the naturi."

To my utter shock, Danaus ran his cold hand across my cheek so that he was now cupping the back of my neck. He pulled me forward and pressed a kiss to the top of my head. "He was inside of the bathhouse, wasn't he?"

"How did you know?"

"I sensed your rage and fear."

"I'm afraid he's going to kill you," I whispered.

"You'd never allow it."

Blinking back tears, I turned my head and pressed my lips to the palm of his hand. "Thank you for your confidence in me." It was all I could say. He was giving me his trust, and as I had already proved once tonight, I didn't deserve it.

Ten

After some discussion, Danaus and I decided we would pursue a small group of naturi hanging on the edge of the city at what turned out to be Szobor Park. I suspected that if anyone knew I was in the city, they would expect me to go straight for the gathering on one of the islands in the Danube River, but I wasn't willing to step into that trap just yet. It was bad enough that I had willingly walked into whatever trap Macaire had set for me. For now, I was avoiding the bulk of the naturi on the island. I wasn't sure how we would reach the island just yet, and I feared a trip out on a ferry would put me in the clutches of the water clan once again. My last encounter with the water clan in Savannah nearly cost Danaus his life.

Unfortunately, neither Danaus nor I were familiar with Budapest. The hunter knew a vague location of the group of naturi, but neither of us could give directions or a landmark to taxi driver. As a result, I was forced to dip into Danaus's mind while he scanned the region for the naturi. At the same time, I was in the mind of the taxi driver, directing him as best as I could toward our ultimate destination. My powers were strained as I struggled to separate the two minds, while leaving enough of the driver conscious so he could effectively operate the car without plowing us into the first semi we passed. I was shaking by the time we reached Szobor Park, the strain making it one of the longest thirty-minute drives of my life.

I had done this trick before with other nightwalkers, touching multiple minds at once with little problem. But then, everything was easier when I was dealing with night-walkers. The mind of a human was too easy to completely consume. Meanwhile, I had to maintain my own guard against Danaus so he could not see some of my own dark secrets as we were intimately linked together. I didn't expect the hunter to go wandering around in my mind while we searched for the naturi, but I wasn't about to leave the door hanging wide open either.

At Szorbor Park, my hands were trembling and my head was throbbing from the strain. I released both Danaus's and the taxi driver's minds at the same time, glad to finally be free of them. Slumping back against the seat as Danaus paid the fare, I closed my eyes and drew in a slow cleansing breath. The pain started to ebb and I became aware of the energy steadily flowing from Danaus. It pulsed and brushed against me, a reassuring heat that seeped into my chilled frame. The hunter was continuously scanning the area for the naturi to make sure we weren't going to be attacked before we even stepped from the car.

"Are they coming?" I pushed into a sitting position as he opened his door.

"Not yet. Feels like they actually moved deeper into the park," he replied as he slid out.

I followed behind him, unbuttoning my coat as I moved. My weapons were hidden beneath the heavy folds of my leather coat, and I needed to be able to easily access them. "Where are we?" I may have been giving directions to the taxi driver as I pulled them out of Danaus's brain, but that didn't mean I had even the slightest clue as to where we finally ended up. I frowned as I looked around the empty expanse. We were on a lonely strip of road, well outside the city proper. We weren't going to easily find another taxi back to the hotel, assuming that we had little trouble dispatching the naturi. Grabbing my phone, I typed in the phone number for the taxi company written across the side of the car door. If we couldn't get another taxi, I'd be forced to hotwire a car. Unfortunately, I was trying not to stir up too much trouble in the city just yet. I wanted to meet this Veyron first, and then I would be happy to cause as much trouble as I wanted.

A red brick wall rose up before us with three tall openings. There were two large windows within the wall that housed a pair of enormous stone statues. I walked over to one, squinting in the darkness until I finally made out the cubist vision of Karl Marx's face. Cocking my head to the side, I took a step back and smiled.

"It's Statue Park," I said, talking mostly to myself.

Danaus stood next to me as he looked up at the statue of Karl Marx and Friedrich Engels. "I don't know it."

"It's also called Memento Park by some." I shoved my hands in my pockets and walked over to the other statue. I didn't recognize the face, but it matched some of the Communist themes I had seen in pictures. "I read about this place. About a decade ago the city leaders gathered up all the Communist statues from around the city and placed them together in a single park. Preserving history, but keeping it carefully corralled in a single location so it can't bleed into the present."

"So, I'm guessing that we should be careful and try not to damage the statues," Danaus said.

I smirked at the hunter over my shoulder. "It would be preferable. I don't expect that the city will be able to easily replace anything that we break tonight, and I'd hate to be responsible for destroying this interesting bit of history."

Taking a couple steps backward, I crouched on the balls of my feet for a second before taking a running leap into the air. It was with a sigh of relief that I easily landed on the top of the red brick wall despite the coating of snow and ice. Squatting down, I stared out at the broad swath of level ground that sparkled in the snow before me. Apparently the park was closed during the winter, because no one had bothered to shovel the snow from the walkways. However, I could still make out the outline of six large circles in the earth around a larger central circle. There were no trees in the park to hide behind, but I could easily make out more than three dozen statues. And somewhere in there, five naturi were hiding. I could feel the pulse of their energy, but it almost seemed blurry, as if their powers were obscured by the energy coming from the earth.

I, on the other hand, stood out on the wall, my hunched body outlined by the moonlight. Let the naturi know I was coming for them. With any luck, my appearance and active hunting of the naturi would finally draw out Aurora, or maybe even Rowe. I was ready to remove the head from either one.

"Let's go," I said as I took a step off the wall. I landed easily, my knees flexing under the impact. My left heel slipped slightly as I hit the snow but I kept my balance. Meanwhile, Danaus took the time to pick the lock at the front gate. A loud squeal resounded through the frozen wasteland as he pushed it open. I flinched at the sound, glaring at him over my shoulder. I wasn't exactly trying to be sneaky, but at the same time, I wasn't trying to wake the dead either.

"Where are they?" I asked when the hunter was finally standing beside me.

"Toward the back of the park, holding very still."

"Blending in with the statues, I'm sure." Reaching inside my coat, I pulled a short blade from where it was strapped to my waist. A second blade was removed from where it hung at my hip. "You take the right and I'll take the left. We'll meet at the back of the park."

"Shall we make this interesting?" Danaus inquired as he also pulled a blade.

I arched one brow at him and lowered my weapons. "Fighting the naturi isn't already interesting?"

"Most kills wins."

"First to use his or her powers automatically loses," I added with a grin. Danaus nodded, one corner of his mouth lifting. "And my prize?" This caused Danaus to pause, his newborn smile slipping from his face.

"What do you want?"

My smile only grew, but I knew better than to ask for anything really interesting. He'd never agree to it and our fun would be lost. However, I still had to go for something that might make him sweat just a little bit so it would be a real competition. "A favor."

"You want a favor?" he repeated.

"Yes, I want the right to hold a favor in reserve with you."

Danaus stared at me in silence, weighing the danger of owing me a favor. At the time, I knew he was considering the odds of whether I would actually beat him in a race to hunt down the five naturi. He would need only three to beat me. This was going to be a close thing no matter what was at stake.

"I'd like the same prize should I win," he finally said, surprising me.

"All right," I agreed slowly. I hadn't considered the chance of him actually requesting the same thing. Of course, what was the danger? The bastard could control me if he truly wanted to, and it wasn't like he could ask me not to feed. It was both too dangerous for those around me and just generally impossible if I really needed to feed.

With the contest settled, Danaus headed off to the right, quickly becoming little more than a hulking shadow in the darkness. His crunching footsteps echoed through the silent night, announcing his approach. Meanwhile, I moved soundlessly through the darkness, weapons drawn. Large shadows rose up around me, cast by the moonlight glazing the various statues and random bits of brick wall that worked to section off the park.

I paused as I passed the first circle to my left, and fanned out my senses so I could try to pick out the naturi. Their energy danced in the air, but it was all hazy and unfocused. Confident that I hadn't left a naturi at my back and they were all still in front of me, I edged around a small brick wall and entered the second connecting circle.

"Why have you come here, bloodsucker?" called a voice out of the darkness. It sounded like it had come from the far edge of the park. It was an easy target for me to home in on, but I knew that the other four naturi stood between me and the speaker. They weren't about to make it that easy for me.

"Looking for you." The cold, silent air carried my words across the distance. "And hoping to find Rowe."

"The traitor is not here."

"If you go find him for me and bring him here, I might consider letting you live," I taunted as I edged away from the wall. Tightening my grip on the blades, I moved across the second circle, allowing me to put some distance between the statues and myself. The approach left me exposed and vulnerable, but then I wasn't the type to hide and wait for my prey to come to me.

"We want nothing to do with that traitor." The voice laughed, the sound bouncing around the park. "Besides, we outnumber you. You're the one that should be pleading for our mercy."

"Never again," I muttered under my breath. I had begged for mercy at Machu Picchu when I was tortured as a fledgling. I had pleaded for them to kill me and release me from the overwhelming pain. I would never beg for anything from the naturi again.

My only warning was the soft ping of a taut bowstring being released. I spun around, dropping to my left knee, but I reacted too slowly. The poison-tipped naturi dart embedded itself in my left shoulder blade. Pain screamed down by arm, causing my hand to open. My knife fell to the snow with a muffled thud. I swallowed a cry, gritting my teeth to hold it in. My left arm was useless as I waited for the poison to finally run its course through my body.

Raising my right arm, I blocked the blow aimed to remove my head. A brief flash of sparks from the impact with my short sword lit up the night. My opponent looked to be a teenager with his fresh face covered in a sprinkling of freckles and his unkempt, windblown brown hair standing on end. But looks could be deceiving. This creature was likely older than I was, with ample battle experience.

As he lifted his sword over his head for another blow, I aimed my own sword for his stomach, hoping to disembowel him. He was fast. He shifted his stance, easily blocking my thrust. I needed to finish him quickly. I was trapped on my knees and there were four more of them running around the park.

The naturi looked over my shoulder for a split second as he moved to slash at me again.

"Shit," I hissed. Dropping my left shoulder, I rolled away from my opponent and the naturi that had come up behind me. As I moved, I scooped up the knife I had dropped with my left hand. While I'd regained the ability to use that hand, it was still weak. I wouldn't be able to block with it and my aim would be miserable if I attempted to throw anything.

Unfortunately, rolling to my feet caused the dart in my shoulder to dig deeper, sending a fresh wave of pain through my body. I swayed once on my feet before the pain finally ebbed a bit. Blinking once, my gaze focused on the three naturi arrayed before me. At the same time, a pair of gunshots shattered the night, bringing a frown to my lips.

That's one, Danaus said, touching my mind. The hunter had taken the lead by making the first kill. However, with three naturi before me and a fourth lurking somewhere in the darkness, my main concern was not about winning our little contest, but surviving it. Of course, I wasn't about to admit to the hunter that I was in trouble.

The naturi that had attacked me earlier moved in again, while one of his companions also swung his blade. In a flash of silver glinting off the moonlight, I blocked both slashing blows, causing the two naturi to take a step backward. Clenching my teeth, a soft grunt escaped me as I threw the knife as hard as I could at the naturi that had yet to attack me. However, my left hand still lacked both speed and accuracy. The naturi easily deflected the knife, sending it spinning off into the night.

A pair of shots rang out as Danaus pursued the other naturi that had yet to appear at my back as I'd expected. That left three standing before me.

That's two, Danaus kindly informed me.

I swallowed a snide reply, cursing myself for not taking the time to pack my Browning. I still didn't like guns and avoided carrying them whenever possible.

"Two of your companions have been killed. This is your last chance to escape before you lose your lives as well," I said.

"A chance to kill the Fire Starter is worth any risk," one of the naturi said, bringing a frown to my lips. I had yet to use my gift and still they recognized me. I wasn't ready to be considered enemy number one among the naturi.

"Besides, we have you outnumbered. You haven't a chance," said another naturi.

"Not for long," I growled. Grabbing another knife off my leg with my left hand, I swung around at the opponent on my left. He blocked the sword aimed at his chest but wasn't fast enough to stop the knife I buried in his lower abdomen. Unfortunately, my back was left open. Pain screamed through my body as another naturi stabbed me in the back. I moaned as I jerked the knife loose from the naturi's stomach. Stretching around, I stabbed the other naturi in the thigh, but the move drove the sword deeper into my back.

The naturi pulled the sword from my back, bringing a gush of blood from my body. Wildly swinging my short sword, the naturi took a cautious step backward, giving me more space before they once again moved in for the kill. Danaus was coming toward me, but I had a feeling he wasn't going to make it in time. Blood was pouring out of me and I was growing weaker by the second.

Desperate and trapped, I needed to take them out as quickly as possible, but we had agreed not to use our powers. Unfortunately, I needed to start using Danaus's power if I was going to escape Nick's wrath.

Stepping backward, I drew in a deep breath and held it as I pushed down the pain threatening to overwhelm me. I reached out into the air with my mind, pulling the energy that was radiating from Danaus toward me. He wasn't going to like this at all.

With the energy balled up in my hands, I threw it at the three naturi standing before me. I had to wait only a second before they stumbled back, screaming and clawing at their skin. At the same time, Danaus cried out, his grunt of unexpected pain echoing across the open park.

Mira! he called, but I ignored it. I focused the energy on my enemies, cooking them from the inside out. The energy didn't fill me the same way as when Danaus was controlling me. I could feel it flowing out of the hunter and directly into the naturi before me. Danaus groaned, but it wasn't a sound of pain, but of release. Over the blossoming anger and frustration coming from him, I could sense an underlying feeling of joy and pleasure. It was as if the use of this power provided him with a growing sense of relief. Regardless of what he felt, I knew that Danaus was going to strangle me when I finally released my control over him.

The trio of naturi dropped their weapons and fell to the ground, writhing in pain. Their skin blacked and finally cracked, allowing the boiling blood to ooze out. The screams were finally reduced to choked, gurgling cries of pain before they were silenced permanently.

With a wave of my hand, I released my hold on Danaus, cutting off the power that flowed to the bodies of the naturi. The hunter's heavy breathing was the only sound that carried across the park besides the sound of the wind. Slowly, I turned to face Danaus when the sound of clapping drew my attention back toward the three naturi. A tall figure walked out of the darkness, a pair of black wings extending from his back as if he were part bat. *Rowe.*

The one-eyed naturi had haunted me for months, his memory chasing after me no matter where I went or what I did. He had aided Nerian in torturing me when I was first captured by the naturi more than five centuries ago. He tried to kidnap me when I was in London with Danaus only a few months ago. He fought me on Crete yet again when he broke the seal that bound the naturi in their world. Onetime consort of the queen of the naturi, he focused all of his energy on freeing his people. Now he was banished, an outcast, because he was twisting earth magic with blood magic—an act forbidden by the naturi.

"Rowe," I snarled, tightening my grip on my sword as I stepped over the bodies of the dead naturi to close the distance between us. "I expected you sooner."

"Healed from our last meeting?" he asked, pulling a sword from his waist as he folded his wings against his body. I swallowed back a growl that rose up in my chest. The last time I encountered the naturi, he had shoved a knife deep into my back while I stabbed his wife-queen in the chest at Machu Picchu. I barely survived, but at least Aurora had barely survived the meeting as well.

"What do you want with Budapest?" I demanded when I finally had control of my temper. "Has Aurora come to roost here, and you're clinging to the hem of her dress, hoping for a reprieve?"

"I want nothing from Budapest. My few followers contacted me the second they discovered that you were lurking in the region. I'm more than happy to grab you and hand you over to Aurora. I have no doubt that she would be pleased to have you again after the damage you wrought in Peru," he said with an ugly sneer.

"Buying your way back into her good graces?" My laugh sounded forced and uneven as I struggled to focus over the pain in my back. "She's not going to take you back. You've dealt in blood magic, scarred your body, lost your golden glow. You're not one of them now. Never will be!"

"She may never take me back, but I promise that you won't survive my attempts to return to my people." He lunged at me, sword pointed at my chest.

I stumbled a step backward, knocking his sword away with my short sword. Pain twisted in my back as I moved, threatening to swamp me. My body was healing, but too slowly for my liking, particularly while I was facing Rowe. Unfortunately, I doubted that Danaus was willing to back me up after everything that I had just put him through. Yet at the same time, I couldn't summon up the guilt I felt that I should. The hunter had controlled me in the past to save both of our necks. How was what I had done any different?

As my footing grew firmer, I matched Rowe blow for blow with the sword, looking for an opportunity to finally relieve him of his head or his heart. The naturi was too dangerous to be left alive. He wanted to kidnap me yet again, and I would not fall back into the hands of the naturi.

Rowe smiled at me despite the fact that I was pushing him backward a step for every step that I took forward. The evil grin was enough to stop me in my tracks. I couldn't take the time to try to scan the region for more naturi, as the distraction would leave me vulnerable to attack from him. I stopped walking forward, darting my eyes from left to right, but saw no one besides my opponent.

"Where is Cynnia?" he demanded, surprising me. I hadn't seen the naturi princess since we left Peru, and in truth, I didn't expect to ever see her again. I tended to kill first and ask questions later when it came to the naturi, regardless of their allegiance to Cynnia or Aurora.

"I haven't seen her."

"Don't try to protect her. She needs to be killed for her betrayal of the crown," Rowe said, his smile slipping from his face.

"Even if the crown tried to kill her. She doesn't have the right to protect herself from her own sister?"

"Not if her sister is the queen. Aurora passed judgment on her. She needs to face her fate, and you need to stop protecting her."

I didn't like this. Did the naturi actually think I was protecting the rogue princess because I had stood by her earlier at Machu Picchu? The little rugrat had used me for protection. After the battle at Machu Picchu, she took those that were willing to follow her and disappeared into the coming dawn. I hadn't heard from her, and I prayed I never would.

"I don't know where she is. I wouldn't protect her. She's on her own now. Besides, Nyx seemed fully capable of protecting her little sister. Maybe you should go looking for them instead of harassing me. Hand them over to your ex-wife."

"I will find them," Rowe stated, the tip of his sword wavering in his growing anger.

"Fine. Just keep me out of it. I don't want to be a part of your war," I responded, my own grip tightening on my sword.

"You are a part of our war now. Aurora wants you and her sisters dead. I will deliver that to her."

The sound of footsteps crunching across the snow caused me to draw my last remaining knife from my side and clench it in my fist. However, a part of me relaxed almost as quickly as I recognized the cadence of the footsteps. Danaus was drawing near. The hunter might not be happy with me, but he wouldn't knife me in the back while I faced off against Rowe. He would at least wait until he was standing in front of me.

"Get out of here, naturi!" Danaus growled. "You're outnumbered and we could kill you with a thought. Get out of Budapest. We'll hunt you down another night."

Rowe cocked his head to the side, his eyes flitting between Danaus and me before his mocking smile returned. In the same second, he threw out his wings and caught the wind that was sweeping over the land. He took to the air, disappearing in the thick black of night. I stared up at the sky for several seconds, waiting to see if the sky grew heavy with clouds, signaling that the naturi was calling up a thunderstorm. But it remained clear, sparkling with starlight.

As I lowered my head, Danaus roughly grabbed my arm and slammed me into a nearby brick wall. Pain exploded in my back as my wound hit the wall a second before the back of my head smacked into the red brick.

"What the hell—" I started, but swallowed the words when I looked at his face, twisted with rage. I stiffened and raised my chin as I prepared for this fight. The hunter had been content to let Rowe go because he was determined to take a pound of flesh out of me.

"What the fuck do you think you were doing?" Danaus demanded, stunning me. Such foul language was definitely out of character for the hunter, but then I had left him more than a little pissed by controlling him earlier.

I shoved the knife I was holding back in its sheath at my side, but kept the short sword in my hand. I didn't think I would need it but didn't quite feel comfortable being unarmed around Danaus. "Killing naturi," I said tartly. "The deal was that we couldn't use our own powers. Nothing was said about using each other's powers."

"You used me!" he shouted, making me press closer against the wall.

A hollow ache radiated from my back, but it was nothing compared to the ache that suddenly began to fill the empty void in my chest. Guilt and horror had finally begun to set in. I had hated Jabari and Danaus every time they controlled me, taking away my right to choose. I hated being little more than a marionette for their enjoyment. And then I'd done the same thing to Danaus. I could make whatever excuses I wanted to make, but it didn't get around the fact that I'd done the one thing I hated more than anything else in this world. I had used him to save my own skin. And sadly, I knew I would do it again in order to escape Nick's reach.

"Now you know what it's like to be treated like a puppet on a string," I said in a low voice. "Now you know what it's like to have all your choices taken away."

"Is that what this is about? Getting even?" Danaus said, some of the anger draining from his tone.

"No, I—" I started, but stopped abruptly, swallowing the words that fluttered through my mind. I wanted to apologize, but had never received words of apology from either Danaus or Jabari. Neither ever had a doubt about what they were doing to me. They had their reasons, and at the time, they always seemed like good reasons.

"You had no choice," Danaus said, deepening the frown on my lips. I had a choice. I could have used my own powers to destroy the naturi. I could have cried for help, allowing Danaus to make the choice to use his powers to save me. I could have said no to Nick and faced my fate. I could have let the naturi kill me. I had choices. I just made the selfish one.

"I was trapped. I couldn't beat them. I should have asked you for help. I made the wrong choice and I'm sorry," I said, letting my eyes fall shut. I took a deep breath and shook my head as if to clear it. "But I have to learn to control your powers. If I don't, Nick will grab me. He's going to make me human again."

Danaus reached up and brushed a loose hair from where it had blown across my cheek. "Being human again wouldn't be so bad."

I jerked away from his touch and scowled at him. "I won't go back to being human. Not to please you or Nick. I'm a nightwalker and that's how I plan to stay, so don't get your hopes up."

"I don't want you to change," Danaus said.

"I'd be fool if I didn't know you'd prefer me to be human."

"Anything other than nightwalker might be easier to accept," he admitted. But in the next second he completely stunned me when he leaned in and pressed his lips to mine.

It was a short kiss, a gentle brushing of the lips that warmed me down to my toes. When he pulled back, I was still speechless.

"Of course, I'm learning there are some advantages to seeing a nightwalker," he continued.

"Such as?"

"You're more durable that other women I've known. You've certainly lasted the longest."

A snort escaped me as I failed to stop the amused smile that formed. "I had no idea you had such a gift for flattery."

Pushing off the wall, I walked away from the hunter with my head bowed as I headed for the entrance to the park.

"You owe me a favor," I muttered under my breath.

"What?"

"The bet. I won, I killed three naturi with your powers, not mine. I won. You owe me a favor," I said, not bothering to look up at him.

"If you think I'm going to deliver on that bet, you're insane. You used me!" he snapped.

"I'm sorry about that."

Danaus dropped into silence as he walked beside me back to the main gates that barred the entrance into the park during the nighttime hours. I glanced over my right shoulder to find him watching me with the corners of his mouth pulled down in a frown. His shoulders were slumped and his hands dangled empty at his sides. We both seemed more than a little beaten despite what proved to be a relatively easy fight. It should never have gotten so out of control, but it was for the best. If I didn't find a way to adequately control Danaus's powers, Nick was going to make me human again. It was a risk I wasn't willing to take.

Danaus's voice was a dark rumble that swept around me. "Promise me that you're never going to do that again."

Pulling my cell phone out of my pocket, I looked up at him as we exited through the large wrought-iron gates. "I'll make that promise the day you can do the same for me."

A frown marred the hunter's lips and pulled his eyebrows together over the bridge of his straight Roman nose. His beautiful blues eyes sparkled in the moonlight as anger once again filled his frame. He knew he would not get a promise out of me because he couldn't make the same promise in return. With the naturi surrounding us and the coven trying to kill us at every turn, he couldn't relinquish control of his most powerful weapon. He was trapped in my world now, and he wouldn't give up his control over me until one of us was finally dead.

Eleven

Sunset came too early the next night. After returning to the hotel from Szorbor Park, Danaus headed out into the city while I returned to the hotel room we were sharing on Gellért Hill. I could have used a bite, but I wasn't in the mood for hunting. I was in the domain of an unknown keeper and Rowe was lurking about. In the meantime, I had with me two nightwalkers of questionable dependability. Valerio looked out for himself first and foremost, while Stefan would rather see me dead so he could have my seat on the coven. The situation was far from ideal from my perspective. I needed to get home before this situation got even more out of control. Unfortunately, returning to Savannah wouldn't solve my dilemma with Nick. I couldn't even begin to guess at how I would deal with such a creature.

With a sigh, I jumped in the shower and then pulled on a clean change of clothes. I had packed enough to get me through a week, but I was hoping that this trip abroad wouldn't last me quite so long. My own domain was wounded and sore, needing my strict attention before the rift between the shifters and the nightwalkers grew any wider.

Stepping out of the bedroom into the main living room of the hotel suite, I found myself faced with Valerio instead of Danaus. A frown tugged at my lips as I looked around the room, as if the hunter were lurking in some remote corner, but he was nowhere to be found.

"He's not here," Valerio confirmed.

"Where is he?" I demanded, hating the petulance in my tone.

"Don't know. He left the hotel room as soon as I arrived and didn't say where he was going." Valerio sat in one of the comfortable chairs that ringed a dark wood coffee table. My bare feet sank into the thick carpet as I crossed the room and dropped into one of the chairs opposite him. "Trouble in paradise? Lovers' quarrel?"

I flashed the nightwalker a dark look and then turned my attention back down to the coffee table before me. There were a pair of picture books on the surface that showed tourists all the wonderful sights within Budapest. A secret part of me wished this would prove to be an easier task than Jabari had led us to believe, and that Danaus and I could take some time wandering these old streets together. However, between Nick and Rowe, such a hope was promptly crushed.

"Mira—"

"Let it go, Valerio. It's none of your business."

"Unfortunately, it is my business," he countered, drawing my gaze up to his face. "If you're distracted with romantic thoughts, it could mean my life. It is my job to protect the Elder of the coven, after all."

I tilted my head to the side as I stared at him in surprise. "Would you protect me?"

He smiled. "Of course. You are one of the few nightwalkers still in existence that I would dare to refer to as a friend."

"Valerio, I'm quite confident that I am the only nightwalker in existence that you would call friend, but that still doesn't mean you would risk your neck for me."

His smile grew wider and an evil twinkle filled his eyes. "I never said anything about risking my neck. I only said that it's my job to protect you. We must be reasonable about these things. You certainly wouldn't want me to die for you."

A soft chuckle escaped me as I shook my head at my old friend. Valerio would never change. He looked out for himself above all, and always looked for the situation that best served to give him the advantage. It surprised me that he had taken my side months ago when I was on the outs with the coven, but then the move proved to be to his advantage when I finally claimed the open seat. I was beginning to believe that he was both smarter and more dangerous than I ever gave him credit for.

"So, you've become involved with the human and now it's not working out how you might have hoped," Valerio observed. I opened my mouth to argue with him, but he held up one hand, halting the words on the tip of my tongue. "Please, don't waste our time by denying it. You made him your consort. You've been working closely together for months now. If you didn't kill each other, it was inevitable."

Flopping back against the back of the chair, I crossed my arms over my chest and crossed my left leg over my right knee. "Nothing is inevitable."

Valerio shook his head at me. "But things aren't working out, are they?"

"No," I said softly. We technically kissed and made up at the park, but I could still feel the anger boiling inside of him.

"I'd be surprised if they did."

"We're not that different."

"Yes, Mira, you are." Valerio presented me with a patient yet condescending smile. "You're a powerful nightwalker and he's a human. You're an Elder on the coven, and he's a nightwalker hunter. There is a vast canyon separating you and Danaus, and I don't think you will ever find a way to bridge that gap."

"We'll find a way," I said stubbornly, but I could no longer meet his eye. My gaze dropped down to the shiny tabletop, trying to ignore the truth that was ringing far too clearly in his voice.

"Let it just be a fun interlude. Do not involve your heart in this matter."

"As if I would be so stupid and foolish," I scoffed, but it was a lie and Valerio knew it.

"It took you decades to recover from Sean, and I heard about Michael," he murmured, leaning forward in his seat. He reached across the table and placed his hand on my knee. "The men in your life don't last a long time, and you are the one left standing with a broken heart. Love is a beautiful thing, but you're an Elder now. You can't afford such weakness."

He was right. I had loved Sean with everything that I was, but his death had finally driven me out of Europe and to the New World. And the loss of my sweet Michael because of the naturi had made me sullen and reckless. The men in my life lived short lives and died painful deaths. But something in my mind screamed that Danaus was different. He was older and wiser than his predecessors. He had his own gifts and could survive and thrive where the others had not. At least, that was the lie I was currently telling myself.

"Love is not a weakness," I countered, pulling my knee out of his reach.

"It leaves you vulnerable. They could use your attachment to Danaus against you," Valerio warned.

"And risk the hunter's wrath? I doubt it. A few may try it at first, but they will not survive his anger at being used like that."

Valerio sat back in his chair and stared at me with new-found interest. "You sound very confident."

"Danaus will not tolerate being used." I knew it firsthand. I was lucky the hunter was still in the city. He could have caught the first plane out of Budapest the second the sun rose and never looked back. I was praying that some thread of compassion he felt for me was holding him to Budapest. "He hasn't lived as long as he has in our world without having a few skills of his own. He will outlast the others."

"It will be interesting to see," Valerio stated, scratching his chin.

A knock at the door drew my attention away from the nightwalker. Pushing out of my chair, I walked to the door while scanning the hallway with my powers. An unknown human stood on the other side of the door. She was alone in the hall. However, there were two nightwalkers downstairs in what felt like the lobby of the hotel. Meanwhile, I could feel Danaus coming down the hall toward the suite. A part of me relaxed as a soft sigh of relief slipped past my parted lips. He was returning to the room.

Opening the door, I was greeted by the sight of a tiny young woman with flowing blond hair and bright blue eyes. She was thin and pale, wearing a wispy thin top and soft flowing skirt that brushed against her ankles. A thick pearl choker was wrapped around her slender neck, with a silver ring in the front. A fragile smile lifted the corners of her rosebud mouth, but there was worry in her gaze. She was afraid.

"Are you Mira?" she asked in a musical voice.

"I am," I admitted, only when Danaus was standing directly behind her. His hand rested near a knife that he always kept at his side. The hunter stared down at the top of the woman's head, a frown marring his handsome face.

"I am Sofia and I have been sent by Veyron to invite you

to his home this evening," she said. Her soft, breathless voice danced around us like a summer breeze. It seemed to hold no threat or cause for concern. I frowned. I didn't trust her. She seemed too helpless and fragile, but appearance could far too easily be deceiving. And yet I could sense nothing out of the ordinary about her.

"Come in," I said, waving for her to enter the hotel room as I stepped out of the way.

The young woman kept her head down as she entered the dimly lit suite. She came to an abrupt halt when she saw Valerio standing before the seat he had been in just moments ago. Her hands remained twisted before her thin body as if she couldn't relax enough to allow them to hang limp at her sides.

"This is Valerio," I introduced, motioning toward the nightwalker. "And the dashing gentleman behind you is my consort Danaus."

Sofia scooted farther in the room, turning so she was facing the three of us. "It is a pleasure to meet you," she said, her gaze darting about the room. I knew she was looking for Stefan. Odelia would have informed Veyron of my presence along with the presence of my companions. As if he knew that he was needed, Stefan appeared in the room, standing just behind Sofia. It was all I could do to smother the smile that was trying to rise on my lips. Danaus gave Stefan's presence away when his eyes shifted from Sofia to the nightwalker standing behind her.

"Oh God!" she cried in her soft voice as she turned to find him there. She jumped away from him and covered her mouth with both of her hands.

"And this would be Stefan," I said, finishing the introductions with a little more glee than I should have felt at scaring a human. Danaus glared at me, but I shrugged it off. It was just a bit of harmless fun, and any report she brought back to Veyron would make the nightwalker pause in his dealings with us. Regardless of what Danaus thought, there was a method to our madness.

"I am assuming that Odelia told Veyron of our presence in Budapest," I began, drawing Sofia's attention back to me.

The young woman dropped her hands back to her waist, where she continued to twist her fingers together, and turned to face me. "Yes, Odelia stopped by last night and told Veyron that you had come to look into our naturi problem."

"You know about the naturi?" Danaus interjected when she would have continued.

"Yes, of course," she said softly, flashing the hunter a weak smile before turning her attention back to me. "Veyron would like to welcome you into his house and to Budapest properly. Would you please appear at his home tonight?"

"We would be happy to meet with Veyron tonight," I said, resisting the urge to frown at Danaus. "We have several matters we would like to discuss with him." The hunter apparently hadn't realized that Sofia was Veyron's pet, and this didn't bode well for the rest of the evening. I was beginning to wonder about the wisdom of bringing him along, but if I told him that he couldn't go, I knew it would cause even greater problems. I had taken him into the heart of the coven, for god sakes. A late night meeting with a powerful nightwalker shouldn't be a problem for us, but I knew it would be.

"Excellent! Veyron will be quite pleased that you're coming," she said, seeming to relax a bit for the first time. Reaching inside the left sleeve of her shirt, she pulled out a folded piece of paper and moved to hand it to me. I took a step back, while Stefan stepped forward and intercepted it. It was all done smoothly, like a dance we had practiced over the long years of our association, but in truth we had never done such a thing before. However, it was the practice of the

Elders not to receive anything directly from an underling if other nightwalkers were about to act as our assistants. Stefan knew the drill, and I was proud of the fact that I hadn't actually reached for the paper. The tradition was a mix of protection and elitism. By touching the paper she tried to hand me, I was putting myself at risk of any spell that might have been attached to it. In addition, an Elder never lowered him- or herself to accepting something from any lowly creature if could be helped.

"It—It's the address and directions to Veyron's home," she stammered, her eyes darting from Stefan to me.

Mira, Danaus said in a warning growl.

She's in no danger, I replied in my most placating tone. His weakness for humans was going to be our undoing in the end; I knew it.

"Odelia said that you are an Elder on the nightwalker coven," Sofia said in a low voice, but it came out sounding like more of a question.

"Yes, I'm an Elder."

"And the Fire Starter?"

"Yes," I hissed, smiling wide enough to expose my fangs. Whatever safety she felt by living under the protection of Veyron's name slipped away as she came to realize she was in a room surrounded by powerful nightwalkers and a human that I called my consort. If I had come to town with the explicit desire to anger and destroy Veyron, then my first stop would be through Sofia, and the two nightwalkers that were making their way up to the suite would never be able to save her. If Veyron treasured her so much, he never should have sent her. But then, she was in no real danger. I didn't mind raising the heart rate of a human every now and then, but if I was angry with a specific nightwalker, I usually took my temper out on that nightwalker, not his underlings.

"If there is nothing else, you may return to Veyron and

tell him that we will be appearing at his home later this evening." I extended my hand toward Stefan, who laid the piece of paper in my palm.

"Yes, of course," Sofia said quickly with a bob of her head before she scurried back to the door. Everyone remained silent as Danaus opened the door and closed it again then secured the lock.

I glanced down at the piece of paper, noting the clean, elegant handwriting. It was obvious that a woman had written down the address and some brief directions to the place that lay somewhere in the Castle District. With a frown, I handed it over to Valerio, who also examined the address.

"Is this truly his place or is it a trap?" I asked, shoving my hands into the pockets of my black dress slacks. I hadn't been in the mood for my typical leather pants and confining top, but settled for a pair of cotton slacks and a mint green turtleneck. It was far from intimidating, but as Sofia proved, I could be intimidating even without my leather and knives.

"It is the address for his home, but I think it is also a trap," Valerio said. Folding up the piece of paper, he handed back to me and I shoved it in my pocket.

"Find anything of interest last night?" Stefan inquired.

"He's not the keeper," Valerio stated with a heavy sigh. "No one uses that term. However, he is one of the oldest nightwalkers in the region, if not the oldest. His name is frequently connected with Odelia's when it comes to who is making the edicts in the city."

"Is there any indication that Veyron and Odelia may be fighting for control?" I asked.

"None. There has been no indication that they are anything but in total harmony at all times."

I shook my head and walked a couple feet away from where Valerio sat in his chair and then paced back. The only thing I could come up with is that Veyron and Odelia were actually lovers and were sharing the domain, but that situation was doomed to fail at some point. Nightwalkers typically didn't play well with other nightwalkers, particularly when emotions and shared power were involved. Hurt feelings and wounded egos did not mend so easily. "Lovers?"

"Possibly," Valerio said with a shrug of his broad shoulders. "Just so long as they are both permitted to have other affairs as well. Sharing the domain, you think?"

"They have to be," Stefan interjected before I could speak.

"It's rare, but it has been done before."

"If we're here to take out both of them," Danaus said in a low, dark voice, drawing all eyes to where he leaned against the doorway leading into the suite, "it will ultimately leave a power vacuum since there are no old nightwalkers in the area. That's dangerous."

"Valerio is just a quick jaunt away in Vienna," I said, waving my left hand at the seated nightwalker. "He can easily hop over and keep the peace if necessary."

Valerio pushed to his feet and took a step around the coffee table toward me. "Now, Mira, there's no need to volunteer me for more territory than I need. I'm not even technically the keeper of Vienna. I can't go extending my territory to include Budapest as well. Besides, as an Elder on the coven, shouldn't you have a domain in Europe like the other members?"

"I keep my eye on Savannah. That's enough," I snapped.

"And having a domain on two continents may ruffle more than a few feathers on the coven, I am sure," Stefan said, earning a glare from me, over my shoulder. But despite my dark looks, the nightwalker was correct. Jabari had a good chunk of Africa, Macaire claimed Rome, and Elizabeth hung close to France. While I was always the first to deny it,

I was overseer for all of the New World. I had always taken the approach that I was nothing more than an ambassador for the coven since my domain was exclusively Savannah, but I knew that nightwalkers across the region bowed to my will because I was the Fire Starter. Claiming Budapest as well as the New World would only upset the various member of the coven.

"Well, everyone can relax. I'm not claiming Budapest," I said, trying to keep my voice from dropping to a frustrated growl. "I've got Savannah and that's more than enough for me. We should get going. Danaus and I will take a taxi to Veyron's place and then I'll contact you when we arrive so you can pop over."

"It may be better if we follow you by the air," Valerio suggested. "You never know. He may decide to launch an attack when you're en route to his place if we're separated."

"We'll be fine," I said, then looked over at Stefan. "Find anything interesting with Ferko?"

"Just where they will be hunting tomorrow night," Stefan replied with a cold grin.

"Tomorrow night?"

"Full moon," Danaus said, leaving me cursing my absentmindedness. I had completely forgotten about the full moon. The local pack would meet tomorrow night, since they would all be forced to shift. The urge to hunt would be overwhelming, and they would need the strength of the alpha to keep the group under control.

"I'm guessing that I'll find out tonight at Veyron's what has dragged you to this city," I said, arching one eyebrow at Stefan. The nightwalker had not come because he had any real desire to protect me. He didn't care about whatever Macaire had planned for me. His main concern was a seat on the coven. However, I was willing to bet that something important had happened in his life surrounding the creatures of Budapest and he had tagged along to take care of a personal matter. I knew that he would have to tell me soon, or it was going to interfere with my own investigation. I was already on edge with Rowe in the city, and it didn't help that I was faced with a tag-team ruling party. I needed to know that Stefan wasn't going to run off and take care of his own agenda.

Stefan gave a little snort as one corner of his mouth quirked in a grudging smile. He had underestimated me. "I imagine you will."

"Fine. We're out of here. Be on guard while you're in the city. Rowe is in town and he's not happy," I announced as I grabbed my heavy coat from where I had laid it across an open chair.

"The one-eyed naturi from Machu Picchu?" Stefan inquired. "The one that wants your head? When is he ever happy?"

I pressed my lips into a firm line as I turned back toward the bedroom so I could pull on a pair of socks and boots before we left. Rowe was only happy when I was hurt and bleeding. Rowe would only be happy when I was dead.

I paused near the center of the room, every muscle in my body freezing as I extended my powers beyond the confines of the hotel room. Something powerful was coming.

"Danaus! Blade!" I ordered. I was completely unarmed, but the hunter tossed me a knife from across the room. I caught it with my right hand and turned it toward the growing source of energy. Valerio and Stefan didn't question me as I could feel their own powers begin to fill the air.

To our combined surprise, Macaire appeared in the room, standing so the point of my knife was just centimeters from his heart. He took one look at the blade and raised an eyebrow at me. "I take it things are not going well."

I hesitated in withdrawing the blade, but finally forced

myself to lower it to my side. "I've never been one to welcome unexpected visitors."

"I came to offer my assistance since I am the one that directed you to Budapest."

"While unnecessary, your presence is most appreciated," I lied through my clenched teeth. "I take it that everything went well in Spain."

"All is quiet in Sadira's former domain. Some of her children still reside in her old castle. Otherwise, the naturi threat has been removed from the area."

He made the comment about Sadira's former domain and her poor children as if I was supposed to feel some kind of twisted remorse about her death at Machu Picchu. The only regret I felt was that I had not been the one to actually kill my maker. The old bloodsucking witch got what she deserved, and now it was time for her precious children to learn to stand on their own two feet.

In the meantime, I truly doubted that Macaire had accomplished much on the naturi front. Danaus had been there weeks earlier and cleared out the region. I couldn't imagine that there was much for Macaire to do. Besides, the Elder was far more interested in seeing me get killed off one way or another.

"We had our first encounter with the naturi last night," I said. "Rowe is in town and appears eager to have his hands on me again to hand over to Aurora." I suppressed a barrage of nasty thoughts about Macaire. The nightwalker liked to tread through the minds of others, and I had no desire to have him listening in on my thoughts of him. "I'm confident that we'll succeed in eliminating him at long last when we remove the naturi threat from the region."

"Really? I'm surprised, considering that he's been giving your problems for so long. Why do you think you have an edge this time?" Macaire inquired with a wicked grin.

"He doesn't have the same kind of support of his people as he has had in the past. He's an outcast; a traitor. They are going to be unwilling to help him, making the naturi an easier target to hit."

"Will you be hunting him down tonight?"

I shook my head. "Not tonight."

"We've been invited to a private gathering," Valerio volunteered.

I turned Danaus's knife over in my hand, watching the silver blade reflect the light. "It seems that Budapest is far more interesting that we initially thought. We all came to town assuming that we were dealing with naturi, but I'm afraid there has been a serious breakdown in the ruling system that we have set up."

"What's going on?" Macaire demanded.

"That's exactly what we're trying to figure out. The Ancients are dead. None of the younger nightwalkers are going before the coven. And this Odelia that I met last night claims there is no keeper of Budapest. It's chaos, and it cannot be allowed to continue."

"Really? I had no idea the situation was so dire."

"I'm surprised. I thought you knew. I assumed it was the reason you chose me to come to Budapest—to clean up this mess."

"My concern was the naturi, that is all."

"You said that you were familiar with Budapest, correct?" Danaus interjected, where Stefan and Valerio were not bold enough to tread. "You should accompany us tonight to Veyron's. Perhaps the two of you could shed some light on what has happened to this poor city."

Macaire stiffened at being addressed directly by Danaus, but was forced to nod at the invitation. "I have heard of this Veyron and I would be happy to accompany you."

I chuckled as I turned my back on Macaire and walked

over to Danaus to return his blade. "Two Elders gracing a single nightwalker's doorstep. What a rare honor!"

I'm sure that's exactly how Veyron will see it, Valerio said sarcastically in my mind. He was still cautious enough not to directly cross Macaire. I had recently killed the Elder's companion, making him a walking powder keg. The littlest thing could set him off, and no one was particularly happy to discover that he was now in town.

"You can get the location from Stefan or Valerio," I called over my shoulder as I walked toward the bedroom with Danaus following behind me. "We'll meet you there in approximately thirty minutes." My final words were punctuated by Danaus slamming the door shut behind us. Let them figure it out on their own. I didn't want Macaire traveling with Danaus and me. He wasn't supposed to be there in the first place, and I didn't like it. I was beginning to feel even more trapped, surrounded by Nick, Rowe, and now Macaire. I was quickly running out of options and people to help me.

Nick had been right. Time was running out for me.

Twelve

There was no mistaking that Danaus was still angry with me from the previous night. The hunter refused to look at me as we climbed into the taxi. He stared out his window at the night-drenched city while I told the taxi driver where we were going. So much for trying to make this fragile relationship work. We were two damaged people, warped by too many years on this earth and too many violent encounters with the various races. We couldn't trust others and we couldn't ask for help. Valerio would have said we were doomed from the start, but I refused to believe it. I had managed complicated relationships with nightwalkers, lycanthropes, and humans over my long existence. Why couldn't I make it work with a half-bori vampire hunter?

I gazed across the taxicab at Danaus, taking in the way the light slid across his strong features as we rode down the busy street. His dark hair brushed his shoulders, nearly obscuring my view of his blue eyes. I swallowed a sigh and turned my gaze back to my window. I knew what he wanted. A promise that I would never control his powers again. I just couldn't do that with Nick making my life a living hell each night.

"Was it necessary to frighten the woman?" he finally growled at me after we were in the car for several minutes.

"This time, yes, it actually was." It was a struggle to keep the sarcasm out of my voice. "She will carry back to Veyron stories of me and my companions. Veyron needs to know that the Fire Starter is here and she will burn through his domain if necessary."

"You mean your already dark reputation wasn't enough to convince Veyron? You needed to scare some poor, helpless human as well?"

I held back my next comment and stared out the window. I truly doubted there was any real reason to pity the poor girl. She looked like she was well taken care of, by the quality of her clothes and the expensive choker that ringed her neck. The woman was obviously Veyron's pet, which meant that she was accustomed to dealing with nightwalkers. And she carried some value to Veyron since he went to the trouble of arranging a pair of bodyguards for her.

"You needn't get so worked up about the girl. I have little doubt that she can take care of herself."

Danaus opened his mouth to comment but I didn't hear it. A large bundle of magic energy gathered in the air just above out taxicab as we waited at a red light. There wasn't time to search out who it was or what the reason for the ball of magic was for. It didn't feel right, and I had survived countless centuries by listening to my instincts. Grabbing a handful of Danaus's leather coat, I jerked him forward while I crouched down as much as I could in the backseat of the tiny taxicab.

"Get down!" I shouted just before a large explosion reverberated through the air, causing my eardrums to rattle in my head. Something large slammed into the side of the taxi, flipping the world upside down. I was thrown into the side of the taxi with Danaus landing on top of me. His elbow crashed into my jaw while the back of my head hit a combination of the glass and the street as we turned over. The whole world changed from darkness to a flash of white light as the taxicab rolled onto its top and I was crushed under Danaus's weight. The noise of the metal scraping along the street was horrendous, clogging up all my other senses besides the horrible sense of pain.

Danaus finally shifted on top of me. Around us I could hear the shuffle of feet and the cries of terrified voices from the people that crowded this busy section of downtown Budapest. My body ached and my thoughts felt fuzzy, as if they were covered in cotton. There was a warm wet spot on my temple where my scalp had been cut and I had a sneaking suspicion that I had cracked my skull when we turned over. A part of me just wanted to lie there, but I couldn't. A creature was lurking somewhere outside the car, desperate for my undivided attention. I wasn't about to disappoint him.

Are you okay? I asked Danaus, using our private path. I had begun to cloak myself from the human onlookers so I could sneak out of the car.

Been better. Driver's dead.

Yeah, well, it could have been us just as easily. Stay here and play dead. I'm going to go look around.

I can help.

Keep an eye on the crowd if you can. I'm not sure what hit us or if it's gone.

Sliding out beneath Danaus on a bed of broken glass, I crawled out through the back window, which had been smashed. It wasn't easy to weave through the people that were gathered around the overturned car, trying to get a look in at Danaus. I was cloaked, but I wasn't sure how long I would be able to keep it up. My head was throbbing and the world swayed around me, keeping me off balance.

Outside of the crowd, I scanned the thoughts of the people, reviewing their memories. They were filled with confusion and fear, as no one could recall what had pummeled the side of the car. Only that something hit it with enough force to flip it over and send it skidding across the street. In the most anxious of those gathered, I inserted the memory of a car slamming into the side of the taxi before it drove off. It wasn't a pretty image, but it was more settling that the gaping void that filled their minds now.

I scanned the area for our attacker but no one stood out initially. There was a heavy feeling of magic and power in the night, but I couldn't tell if it was residue from the spell that had been cast or if the attacker was still in the region. The only thing I was confident of was that our attacker had been a warlock or a witch. The magic in the air didn't feel like a nightwalker, and lycanthropes didn't use magic. Even a naturi would have had a different feel to it.

A knot twisted in my stomach as I switched my focus to scan specifically for Nick. I had to wonder if he had struck out at me simply because I was not making progress fast enough, but I couldn't sense him. Of course, that didn't mean the bastard wasn't lurking somewhere close by, watching the show.

Energy thickening in the air was my only warning before I was slammed into the side of a building with a crushing force. My hold on my cloaking spell wavered once, but I managed to keep a grip on it so no one saw me flying through the air. Three ribs broke, puncturing once vital organs that now only seemed to be source of pain for me. Smashed against the wall, I gazed around the area to see a figure outlined by the moonlight as the person stood at the edge of a building.

With a smile, I summoned up my powers as a fourth rib threatened to break under the pressure pinning me against the wall. Fire flared around the figure that was casting the spells, but just as quickly the fire was extinguished with a hand wave. That was why I didn't go picking fights with warlocks. You find one with just enough skill, and my ability to manipulate fire no longer gave me an edge. However, the distraction was enough to free me of his magical grasp.

Sliding down the side of the building, I was relieved to see Danaus crawling free of the car. I considered reaching for his powers but squelched the thought just as quickly. The hunter was already angry with me. No reason to make the matter any worse, though I knew I would have to eventually.

Danaus, the rooftop across the street, I directed as I tried to push to my feet.

Got it. I felt the warm brush of his powers as he gathered the energy around him just before sending it across the street to our attacker. The figure jerked sharply and then ran from the edge of the building, moving out of our line of sight. Danaus dropped his hand and muttered a soft curse. He couldn't boil the attacker's blood if he could no longer see him. The magic user had escaped, but at least we were both still alive.

Too often nightwalkers were seen as the most dangerous of the supernatural creatures because of our need for blood to survive. However, warlocks and witches were frequently the most brutal of the others simply because there were too few of us strong enough to stand up to them. The only thing we had in our favor was that warlocks and witches didn't frequently feel the need to strike out at the other races. Like nightwalkers, they were content to fight among themselves.

With a few solid mental pushes and a little misdirection, I finally managed to extract Danaus from the crowd gathered around him and the car. He stumbled over to where I was leaning against the wall, a frown creating lines in his brow.

"Warlock?" he asked.

"Or witch. Apparently we have an admirer in town besides Rowe," I grumbled in a low voice, still trying to avoid the attention of the crowd that was now being dispersed by the newly arrived police and ambulance. I squinted my eyes against the flashlights on their cars, which bathed the area in bright shades of red and blue.

"Earth warlock or witch?"

I shook my head and instantly regretted it as it felt like my brain had sloshed around in my skull. "No," I replied with a soft groan. "The magic felt like blood magic. Crisp, clean, familiar. This was a blood magic user who was looking specifically for us."

"Maybe you," Danaus quickly countered. "I don't have any enemies in this part of the world."

A little snort escaped me as I looked up at my companion. "My enemies are your enemies now, my friend."

Danaus's frown eased as he put his hand under my chin and tilted my head up so he could get a better look at my face and the blood that was now smeared across my cheekbone and jaw. "You should have just left me in Savannah," he said.

"And leave you out of the fun? You'd never forgive me," I teased, finally succeeding in erasing the last of his frown. "How bad does it look?"

"You're a mess," he said, dropping his hand back down to his side.

"You're not," I griped. "Of course, you're the one that landed on me." Looking around the area, my eyes finally settled on an elegant hotel just down the block. It was a safe place to clean up before we continued on to Veyron's. I knew I couldn't show up on his doorstep looking like I had just survived a car crash. With a gentle jerk of my head, I motioned for Danaus to follow me down the street.

"Any clue as to who our new friend is?" he asked after we were several feet away from the crowd of people. His pace was slower than usual, but then I think he was more worried about me and the limp I had developed. The broken ribs I had sustained from the second attack mixed with the aches and pains from the car crash were slowing me down. My body was healing, but it was also starting to demand that I stop and feed. Unfortunately, that wasn't an option with Danaus hanging on my coattails. Of course, if Veyron was half the host I expected him to be, I wouldn't be surprised if he offered appetizers.

"No idea," I muttered. "The only person I know that could have pulled such a spell is Ryan, and that wasn't Ryan."

"No, that wasn't Ryan," Danaus agreed. He had only gotten a brief glimpse of the person on the rooftop, but it was enough to know that it wasn't the lanky, white-haired man that ran Themis. We had had a falling out with the powerful warlock, but I was relieved to see that he hadn't made an appearance in Budapest with the sole purpose of making our lives more difficult. He was undoubtedly saving that for a more special occasion.

Wincing against the bright light that filled the hotel lobby, I paused in the middle of the room, staring up at Danaus, who was watching me as if I looked like I was about to fall over. "Not a word of this is mentioned at Veyron's," I declared. "He can't know that we're having trouble in his city. I want Valerio or Stefan to look into the warlocks and witches first."

"If he's as powerful as everyone seems to think he is, wouldn't he know who the most powerful warlocks are?"

"If he's smart, he will. I just don't want him to know that he's not the only one trying to kill me."

"Veyron's trying to kill you?"

"Of course. Why else would Macaire have sent us here? Macaire needs me dead, and for some reason he's sure that Veyron has an edge. If Veyron knows a warlock or a witch is gunning for me too, he may try to strike while I'm in the middle of a fight with the other bastard."

"Doesn't a meeting with Veyron and Macaire together seem unwise if they both want you dead?"

"Possibly, but you're watching my back. It will be fine."

"Go clean up in the bathroom and I'll meet you right here," Danaus said, pointing me toward the restroom near the back of the lobby. There was no use in continuing the conversation. I was determined to discover exactly what Veyron and Macaire were doing in Budapest.

With a sigh, I shuffled toward the bathroom, peeling off my coat as I walked. It was splattered with my blood, but as far as I could tell, none of my blood had gotten on my sweater. I would need to burn the coat before I appeared at Veyron's, but otherwise he wouldn't be able to tell that Danaus and I had been in a bit of a scuffle.

I couldn't begin to guess why the magic user had attacked us. The only one that might be even a little angry with me was Ryan, and I didn't think it would be his style to send someone else after me when it would be more to his advantage to manipulate me back to his side. I was far more valuable to him alive than dead, particularly if he was looking to get a toehold of control on the coven.

This magic user was also striking me at a bad time. It wasn't enough that I had to worry about what Rowe was up to, but I had to try to guess why Macaire had sent me to Budapest in the first place. Sure, it was to die, but why here? What edge could Veyron actually have over me and Danaus?

Of course, there was potentially an even darker reason as to why Macaire sent me to Budapest, but it was too horrible of a thought to contemplate. And besides, there was absolutely nothing I could do to stop him.

Thirteen

Veyron's house was naturally an enormous affair with old beveled glass windows and a gray stone front. The courtyard was brightly lit with an array of old lampposts and a pair of electric wrought-iron sconces next to the front door on the face of the house. Tall trees with gnarled branches like the bony fingers of the dead reached out across the yard, casting great shadows over the area. The bare branches clacked together in the wind, while snow swirled around our feet. As we stepped out of our second taxicab, both Valerio, Stefan, and Macaire appeared just behind us, wrapped in their coats, while I stood in only my sweater and dress pants.

"What took you so long?" Stefan inquired with a frown.

"And what happened to your coat?" Valerio added.

"We ran into some unexpected problems. I'll tell you later," I growled under my breath as I walked up to the front door. I didn't want Macaire to know about our little run-in with the warlock if I could help it.

Before anyone could ring the bell, the door was pulled open by a stiff-looking human in all-black attire. He didn't ask who we were, but wordlessly waved for us to enter the house. It was all I could do to keep my face perfectly blank as we were led through one opulently deco-

rated room after another toward the back of the house.
I kept a nice, comfortable home in Savannah, but this
house dripped money and classic Old World charm. There
was furniture throughout the place that was more than a
couple centuries old and all in pristine condition. Silver
and gold candelabras glowed with candlelight throughout
the rooms, while fires flickered and danced in every fireplace we passed.

Yet despite the opulence, we saw no one but the servant
that was leading us. There were no sounds in the home but
the echo of our footsteps across the marble and hardwood
floors and the crackle of fire eating at logs in the fireplaces.
I scanned the house to find that there were a small collection of nightwalkers in the direction we were headed, while
nearly two dozen humans were hidden around the house. I
was willing to bet that the humans represented a collection
of servants and pets for Veyron. I inwardly cringed, dread-
ing how Danaus was going to react should he be faced with
the humans.

As we entered what appeared to be a garden room with
large windows that reflected back the lamplight, a nightwalker with copper-colored hair pushed to his feet. He
placed one hand on his waist and bent low toward me and
Macaire as he smiled broadly at us.

"The great Fire Starter, Mira," he announced in a thick
Hungarian accent. I noticed that he spoke in neither Hungarian nor Italian, but English. It was a neutral stance for him.
He bowed to me, but he wasn't using Italian and he simply
referred to me as the Fire Starter.

"Thank you, Veyron, for welcoming me and my companions into your home," I said. Turning sideways, I waved
toward Danaus and the others. "This is my consort, Danaus,
and these are Valerio and Stefan. And I'm sure you're already acquainted with coven Elder Macaire."

"Welcome, sire," Veyron said, bowing a second time. "We have not formally met since my appearances before the coven have always been very brief."

"Truly?" I said. "I assumed that you knew each other since Macaire said he had been contacted directly about the naturi problem in Budapest."

"I have heard from various emissaries of the city, through my pets, that there was trouble in Budapest," Macaire said. "This is the first chance I have had to officially meet Veyron," he added, making me want to choke. I had no doubt that those two knew each other and knew each other well. This was a bunch of lies in an effort to get me to lower my guard.

"No matter," I said with a flippant shrug of my shoulders as I forced a smile onto my lips. "The important thing is that we are here now to fix this poor city."

"And it is an honor to have two Elders and their companions in my humble home. Please, everyone come in and rest yourselves. Let me summon some refreshments for us," Veyron said as he returned to his seat. I personally could have gagged at all the pleasantries and silly formalities, but I knew it was expected. Of course, the great irony was that I was seated with the vampire most likely hired to kill me along with the man that had hired him, and we were expected to play nice just because it was expected of us. I would not be accused of not playing by the rules.

As Veyron sat down, I noticed that Sofia had stepped out of the shadows and taken a seat on a little cushioned stool next to his chair. I claimed the seat across from Veyron, my eyes drifting over to the woman. Meanwhile, Macaire, Valerio, and Stefan sat near me, while Danaus remained standing just behind my shoulder, his arms folded over his chest as he glared at Veyron. I counted myself lucky that he was playing this nicely with the powerful nightwalker.

Veyron ran his hand over Sofia's head as if petting an obedient dog. "And this is my little pearl, Sofia."

"Yes, we've met." I forced a smile on my lips as I dragged my gaze back up to Veyron. "She's quite lovely."

"Thank you," Veyron said, positively beaming at me as if he were a proud owner.

We had only a moment before eight humans walked single-file into the garden room and came to stand next to me and Veyron. There were four men and four women, all appearing to be under the age of thirty. There were blondes, brunettes, and even a redhead, with varying body types, appearances, and, from what I could tell, different blood types—all for the discerning palette.

"Please," Veyron said, motioning toward the eight appetizers arrayed before me.

I let my eyes sweep over them as if I were weighing the selection. Yet in truth I was stalling. I was trying to figure some way out of this, but I knew there wasn't as Macaire rose and chose a healthy-looking young man with blond hair.

I'm going to feed. It's good etiquette, I warned Danaus, trying to keep the conversation between the two of us.

I guessed as much, he replied. Anger rolled off of him in waves, brushing against my side as I pushed languidly to my feet.

No one is going to get hurt, I continued, trying to make sure he wasn't going to do something that would get us in deeper trouble than we were already in.

Are they here of their own free will?

I don't know, but I know that they won't remember anything of what happens here tonight.

With that, Danaus became completely silent, blocking me as much as he possibly could from his thoughts. I stepped over to a tall man with dark brown hair and brown eyes.

I ran my left hand over his chest and smiled as his heart picked up its steady pace at my touch. I dipped into his mind to find that his name was Frank and that he was a college student studying physics. And while it shouldn't have been necessary to check, I found him to be wholly human. It took only a slight push on my behalf to put him in a trancelike state. He was no longer aware of the room or its occupants. For a brief moment in time there was only me and the pleasure that I promised to give him. A lopsided smile lifted his lips as he looked down at me.

Just before I lifted my mouth to Frank's neck, I looked over my shoulder at Danaus to find the hunter glaring at us. His whole body was stiff and his hands were balled into fists. I smiled at him then turned my face into Frank's neck, burying my fangs deep into the vein there. His body jerked once before he let out a soft sigh of pleasure.

My mind was deep in his, sending through him waves of exquisite pleasure, losing him in a mind-numbing bliss. At the same time I nearly became lost in that same wave. It had been too long since my last meal, too many long, cold nights of fighting and nearly dying. I had needed this more than I was willing to admit. The blood and the young man's embrace washed away the cold and the fear. It wrapped me up in a safe world that didn't include the naturi and the bori. The only thing that could have made this better was a different set of strong arms.

Feeling better, if not a little evil, I reached out to Danaus's mind, sending to him the same warmth and pleasure I was basking in. It was a weak, filtered version of what he had encountered at the First Communion just a week ago, but it was enough to earn me a low growl that undoubtedly caught the attention of my other companions.

Stop it, Mira, Danaus snapped silently.

Leave off. You're enjoying it and you know it.

I don't want to. The surprising admission was enough for me to close the connection between us. I finished my meal alone after a couple more minutes. As I closed the young man's wound, I thought about grabbing another, but I didn't need to gorge myself. I would have the chance to feed again later.

After guiding Frank to a chair near the doorway into the garden room, I resumed my seat, barely resisting the urge to run my tongue over my teeth. "Thank you. That was a welcome snack," I said with a nod of my head to my host.

"Are you sure you won't take more? If they are not to your liking, I can summon others for you. Older perhaps? Or younger?" Veyron offered like any attentive host. I waved off his comments and turned my attention to Valerio and Stefan.

Both nightwalkers silently chose from the remaining humans that filled the room, using the same care I had shown, to my great relief. Valerio wavered at times between putting his meal in a trance and leaving them conscious so he could enjoy the fear that pumped through their veins. Leaving them conscious would only anger Danaus, and everyone knew it. I was simply grateful that neither Valerio nor Stefan took the opportunity to start a fight with the hunter.

Unfortunately, Macaire was taking advantage of the situation to try and provoke the hunter. He not only fed on three separate humans, but made sure they were fully conscious during the entire affair so their terror could be felt and heard in the room. When the first male failed to elicit a response from Danaus, Macaire switched to a pair of thin, weak females who were far more vocal in their fear. The Elder drained them within an inch of death, and they crumpled to the floor with an ugly thud. They had to be carried out by some of Veyron's other servants.

Throughout it all, Danaus didn't even flinch. I knew the hunter had seen far worse in his days of battle and through his exceedingly long existence, but Macaire was only succeeding in proving to Danaus that he had been right all along. Vampires were simply bloodsucking monsters without a care for the human race beyond a source of food. Macaire proved that we were soulless creatures that weren't worth saving. In that flicker of a moment, I didn't blame Danaus for all the nightwalker deaths he had caused. If any of them were like Macaire, they deserved what they got.

When the trio of nightwalkers returned to their seats and the humans filed back out of the room, Veyron's eyes drifted to Danaus and a grin slowly crossed his features.

"I am loath to ask such a favor," he began, his gaze still locked on the hunter. "But I am wondering if you would permit me to try him. I have never heard of the famed Fire Starter keeping a pet. I am interested to know what makes him so unique."

"No!" I snapped, lurching to my feet. "No one touches him. Danaus is not a pet. As I said earlier, he is *my consort*." Around us, candlelight flickered and flared brighter and higher on their wicks as I unconsciously tapped into powers that had been a part of me since birth. Something important to me was being threatened, and I was going to defend it with everything that I was. Veyron would not touch Danaus.

Stefan and Valerio also rose to their feet as if to protect me, while Danaus remained standing as still as a statue beside me. Macaire lounged in his chair, watching the proceedings with a smirk on his thin lips.

Veyron was wise and remained seated, offering both of his open hands to me as he immediately backed away from his request. "I meant no harm in my request," he backpedaled. "I never meant to offend you or your consort."

I nodded stiffly, returning to my chair, followed by Valerio and Stefan. "Danaus is not to be touched by another creature." I left the unspoken threat hanging heavy in the air. If I were to never feed from the hunter, then I would never allow another nightwalker to touch him. I didn't want him to be tainted in such a fashion. He was not like any other human I had met, and it wasn't just that he was part bori. He was different, and I wanted to preserve and protect that difference from the rest of my kind.

"Forgive me. I understand his importance to you. In truth, I don't think I could ever allow anyone to touch my dearest Sofia here," Veyron said as he once again stroked the back of her head. I half expected her to start panting or purring as she turned her wide blue eyes up at him and a delicate smile lifted the corners of her bow-shaped mouth.

"Perhaps he would like for me to get him something to eat or drink," Sofia suggested in a soft, almost hypnotic voice.

"Yes, of course. How thoughtless of me! I am not accustomed to entertaining humans," Veyron said with a laugh.

Sofia rose to her feet as if supported by air and started to glide out of the room when Danaus shocked everyone by finally speaking. "I can accompany her," he volunteered.

"There is no need to trouble yourself." Sofia smiled sweetly up at him, while I fought the urge to chew on my bottom lip in troubled thought. I had not expected this from Danaus. I had thought he would want to remain close while we were in talks with Veyron, but now he seemed anxious to slip away with Sofia. I wasn't sure what he was up to, but a part of me knew that I wouldn't like it.

"I don't mind," Danaus said. "It would give me a chance to see more of this exquisite house."

"Yes, take him with you, Sofia," Veyron said with a wave of his hand. "Get him something to eat and show him my home while I speak with the Elders." I bit my tongue and forced a smile on my lips as I relaxed in the chair across from my all too gracious host. He thought he was doing Danaus some great favor, but I knew that the hunter had some devious scheme up his sleeve.

Stay out of mischief and be wary of the other nightwalkers in the house, I warned as he left the room with Sofia.

As soon as the door closed, I turned my full attention back to Veyron. I was more than ready to get down to business and complete this little dance we had started. "I'm surprised that Odelia is not here to join us."

"I didn't know that you were expecting her to be present," Veyron replied.

"She seems to hold some power within the city. And so do you." I was curious if there was any lingering animosity between the two that I could irritate. It could prove useful later. "I will admit that I'm a bit confused when it comes to understanding who the keeper of Budapest is. It is unknown to myself and the other Elders of the coven who truly rules this city."

Veyron settled his right ankle on his left knee as he sat back in his chair with a smile. "There is no single keeper of Budapest. There's no need."

"Who keeps the peace?" Valerio inquired.

"There's no need for anyone to enforce the peace in the city," Veyron replied. "There are no struggles for power, no fights over territory here. All the nightwalkers here are somewhat younger in age and are content to go their own way."

"It's not all peace and love in this city," Stefan declared in an ominous voice that dragged everyone's eyes over to him. The nightwalker sat stiffly in his chair with his hands gripping the arms. It was one of the rare moments when I'd seen him express any kind of emotion, and it was obvious to everyone that he was more than a little angry.

"What has happened?" Veyron's smile lost some of its earlier wattage, confronted now with open hostility from a nightwalker that was older than him. Should this encounter rise to blows, there was no promise that either Elder would step forward to stop Stefan.

Lifting his chin, Stefan unclenched his jaw enough so he could speak. "A month ago I sent my assistant here to pick up a package for me. She arrived by private jet. She came to the city and checked into a hotel, but that was the last that was heard of her. The package was never picked up and nothing has been seen of my assistant."

"If you need help acquiring your package, I'm sure I can assist you. I am familiar with many of the shopkeepers throughout the city," Veyron said with a nonchalant wave of his hand.

The arm of the chair that Stefan was sitting in creaked as the nightwalker's grip tightened. "I am not concerned with the package," Stefan bit back in a deadly soft voice. "I want to know where my assistant is. She is to be returned to me."

Veyron gave a sad shake of his head that left even me wanting to rip it off. "I'm afraid this is the first I have heard of the matter. I'll do what I can to help you find her."

"I believe it will be in your best interest to help me because I plan to dismantle this city until I do find her," Stefan snapped.

"What's her name?" Macaire inquired politely.

"Michelle," Stefan replied, his voice losing some of its edge. "She is just over five feet tall, with brown hair that hangs down to her waist. Her eyes are brown and there is a sparse sprinkling of freckles across her nose."

"How old was she?" Valerio asked.

"She *is* 221 years old," Stefan said, surprising me. I had not expected his assistant to be a nightwalker. But then, by the detailed description he gave and his refusal to face the fact that she was most likely dead, I was willing to bet that Michelle was more than just an assistant to him. I hadn't expected Stefan to actually have any kind of emotions for anyone beside himself. Of course, it made sense. Nothing would force Stefan to volunteer to come on a mission with me unless it was very important to him. And by his tone of voice, Michelle was very important to him. For a brief second I wondered if it was Michelle that had truly brought Stefan to Budapest and not some elaborate plot cooked up between him and Macaire.

I frowned, biting back a comment. It was very likely that Michelle wasn't still alive if she had disappeared more than a month ago. Nightwalkers didn't just disappear. There was always the chance that she had run from Stefan and was hiding somewhere in the East, where things were a little wilder and less closely monitored by the coven and its keepers. In the East, it was easier to slip in and become lost among the other nightwalkers, creating a new identity for yourself.

However, I was reluctant to accept this theory. Stefan seemed to truly care for Michelle, and I assumed he'd know if there was a possibly that she would run. Of course, love can make us all blind at times.

"If she was in town a month ago, you may consider contacting Ferko," Veyron suggested, scratching his chin with his right hand. "He's the alpha for the local pack. Sometimes the lycans can get a little rough when it's close to the full moon. I hate to think it, but there is a small chance that she may have fallen in with a rough crowd while she was in town."

"Is that a problem in Budapest?" I asked, raising one eyebrow at him. "Locals harassed and potentially killed by the lycans?"

"Not really." The nightwalker shrugged, looking for all the world as if none of this conversation truly mattered to him, and in truth it shouldn't if he didn't consider himself the keeper of Budapest. "Of course, the time of the full moon for the shifters is always a dangerous time of the month. Sometimes people go missing. I'm sure it happens everywhere."

"Actually, it doesn't." My voice grew colder, losing its congenial softness and warm invitation. "The alpha for the pack in my own domain keeps a tight control over his people. Humans and nightwalkers do not go missing in my domain." Sitting back, I tapped my finger on my lips in thought. "Macaire, please correct me if I'm wrong, being as I am new to the Elder position," I began, pausing to smile over at him.

"Of course," he replied with a stiff smile of his own. "What is on your mind?"

"I don't think the coven is comfortable with this current arrangement."

"How do you mean?" Macaire said, sitting up a little straighter in his chair as he slid closer to the edge of his seat.

"As a member of the coven, I have to admit that I'm not comfortable with the regular disappearance of humans and nightwalkers within the city," I said, dropping my hand back into my lap. "And if I'm not comfortable, the rest of the coven couldn't possibly be comfortable."

"Macaire has never expressed any concern about the arrangement for the city," Veyron admitted thoughtlessly as he started to squirm in his own chair.

"Correct me if I am wrong, fellow Elder, but I don't think you are fully aware of the situation, considering that you spend the majority of your time in Italy," I said. "Speaking of which," I added, turning my attention back to Veyron, "why are the fledglings of Budapest not making an appearance before the coven, as is tradition?"

"It was my impression that we were no longer following that old tradition."

I gave a little snort and shook my head as I looked over at Macaire. "Could you ever see us giving up such a time-tested tradition as breaking in the fledglings in Venice? It's positively absurd!"

"It is the only way to teach them where the true power of our people lie," Macaire said through clenched teeth.

"Respect," Valerio said. "The young nightwalkers here have no respect for the coven, the Elders, or even when they see a true Ancient," he added as he picked a piece of lint off his dark slacks. He couldn't resist putting another nail in Veyron's coffin. I had no doubt that he knew where I was going with this and was now simply egging me on.

I heaved a heavy sigh and looked down at my hands folded in my lap. "This can't continue."

"It can't be!" Veyron said, nearly coming out of his chair.

"But it is. Shifters are killing nightwalkers and humans, endangering the secret. Nightwalkers are not appearing before the coven, which is the only place they can properly learn what it means to be a nightwalker and understand their place in the world. This is unacceptable, and I know I speak for the rest of the coven when I say this cannot continue."

"What are you planning to do?" Macaire demanded in a slow, deceptively even voice.

"The only thing I can do," I said, before sucking in a deep, weary breath. "I will take over as the keeper of Budapest."

"But you can't!" Veyron cried, jumping out of his chair.

"Why not?" I asked, one corner of my mouth lifting in a smile as I settled back in my own chair.

Veyron squirmed in silence for several seconds before he finally found his voice and a viable excuse for his objection.

"You're already the keeper of a city in the New World. How would you manage to be in two places at once?"

"I would spend an extended period of time here, remaining until I felt that the city was on the right track before I returned to Savannah," I stated. "And in truth, now that I am an Elder on the coven, it is probably best that I remain in Europe so I can be close at hand to Venice. I may actually hand over Savannah to my assistant. He would do an adequate job at managing the city."

Veyron slumped back in his chair, his hands balled into loose fists on his knees. He was trapped, and it was all I could do to swallow laughter. If he didn't want me to claim the keeper position for the city, he would have to step forward and claim it himself. Of course, considering the poor job he was currently doing, there was a good chance I would steal it from him anyway.

"Do you have an objection?" I asked oh so sweetly, flashing my fangs at him as I smiled. I looked down at Macaire, who could only nod stiffly at me as he settled back in his chair.

"No, of course not," he said, a bit too quickly to be considered believable. "Your presence would be a welcome addition to the city."

"Yes, this will help keep you close at hand for when you are needed at the coven," Macaire said. "We were recently discussing that it may be time for you to take a domain within Europe," he added, making it sound like it all had his stamp of approval, when I had little doubt that he wanted me nowhere near Budapest.

"Excellent. Then I claim the position of keeper of Budapest. See to it the word is spread throughout the nightwalkers of my new domain," I declared.

"Is there anything else you wish?" Veyron said through clenched teeth as he bowed his head to me.

I glanced over at my companions, and Valerio shook his head, looking completely amused by the entire proceeding. Stefan, on the other hand, continued to glare at Veyron, as he held the nightwalker responsible for the disappearance of his assistant. "Yes, spread the word that we are looking for a nightwalker named Michelle. I demand that she be found, or at least it must be discovered what happened to her. We will speak with Ferko and his pack tomorrow night."

"Tomorrow night is the full moon," Veyron reminded me.

I smiled at him again and leaned forward a bit. "I can't think of a better time. I like to make an impact on those I meet."

Veyron pushed back, his hands gripping the arms of his comfortable chair, almost mirroring the same posture as Stefan. Neither he nor Stefan was particularly happy, but at least only one of them wanted my head at the moment. Stefan was content to wait until a more opportune time, when it would most benefit him.

"Since you are now the keeper of Budapest, I am assuming that you are going to take care of our current naturi infestation," Veyron said in a low voice.

"I have already started. Danaus and I hunted down five naturi last night at Szobor Park," I informed him, taking exquisite pleasure in watching his frown grow deeper. Unfortunately, my joy was short-lived as I continued to speak. "However, we discovered that one extremely dangerous naturi is in the region. His name is Rowe and he's something of a zealot among the naturi race. Now that he knows I'm here, he could increase his slaughter of both nightwalkers and humans as he hunts me down."

A twisted smile flashed across Veyron's face. "So your presence here has actually made it more dangerous for nightwalkers?"

"Par for the course when it comes to Mira," Valerio said, earning a dark look from me. "The naturi tend to flock to her instead of running away. That happens when you're enemy number one among their entire race."

I forced a smile on my lips as I turned my gaze back to Veyron and shrugged. "That happens when you're known for slaughtering countless of their ranks over the long centuries. Their survival is dependent on my death."

"Will you be able to get rid of them?"

"It would be nice, considering that this particular naturi gave you such problems at both Crete and Peru," Macaire added, making me wish I could throw something at his head.

"I will take care of Rowe. The one-eyed naturi will not leave Budapest alive."

"One-eyed?" Veyron asked.

"He wears an eye patch. Scarred face. Black hair, swarthy skin. He really doesn't look like much of a naturi any longer, but he still thinks like one."

"So, while you're in town, you're going to rein in the lycans, hunt down the naturi, and teach the nightwalkers how to act like proper nightwalkers?" Veyron said with a sneer.

"Well, I thought I would start there. Those aren't the only things on my to-do list," I said, my smile never wavering. "But if I'm going to get anything done, I can't remain here. I need to get out on the street." Pushing out of my chair, I mentally reached out to Danaus and told him that we were leaving.

Veyron accompanied my group to the front door, where Danaus and Sofia were now waiting for us. Turning to Veyron, I nodded my head to him and smiled. "Thank you for all your assistance. I think you will be pleased with how Budapest improves while I am here."

"Yes," he said with a slight hiss as he held open the door for us. I led the way out of the house, with Danaus following on my heels. Macaire, Valerio, and Stefan were directly behind us. There was no mistaking the soft chuckle from Valerio when Veyron slammed the door shut.

"Only you would have the nerve to step into a domain and steal it right out from under a man," Valerio said as he slipped his arm around my back and rested his hand on my hip.

"He had ample opportunity to say something, and he didn't," I replied with an evil grin as we walked away from the house, toward the dimly lit street. "If I was out of line, I am fully confident that Macaire would have called me on the matter," I said, motioning toward the Elder with one hand.

"You are correct. Budapest is not how I remember her, and I am sure that you can get her back to her glorious former self," Macaire said with a slight bow of his head. "Now if you will excuse me." Without another word, the Elder completely disappeared from sight without giving another word of reason.

Stefan started to talk, but I held up my hand and scanned the region. I wanted to be sure Macaire was completely gone before anyone said anything that we might regret. We now had an extra pair of ears that we needed to worry about. When I was sure he was nowhere in the area, I dropped my hand and nodded for him to continue.

"But two domains on two continents? Didn't you just get through saying you weren't going to claim Budapest as your newest domain?" Stefan asked, needling me simply because he could.

I shoved one hand through my hair, pushing it away from my face as the wind picked up. "This is only a temporary arrangement. I will give up one of my domains once everything is settled again and the coven is happy."

"Give up Savannah?" Valerio asked.

Hearing the words spoken made my stomach drop. In that second I knew that I couldn't give up my beloved Savannah. It was the only place since becoming a nightwalker that I felt I could call home. I didn't care about Budapest—claiming the seat of keeper here was simply a way of taking control of the situation and finally forcing Veyron to act.

Unfortunately, I found myself faced with enemies on four fronts. The naturi were constantly at my back, while the nightwalkers, warlocks, and lycans were arrayed in front of me. I just prayed that the companions I had brought with me stayed by my side through the upcoming massacre, particularly now that Macaire had decided to haunt the city. And I knew it would be a massacre.

"Shall we go?" Valerio asked as his hand tightened on my waist.

"No, wait! Danaus and I can catch a taxi." I tried to pull his hand off of my side but he wouldn't budge.

"No, it will take too long," Valerio said. "Time to get you somewhere safe before Veyron decides that he's not going to wait around for you to improve the city."

I opened my mouth to argue but the words never escaped my throat. Valerio summoned up his powers and we disappeared from Veyron's front yard and instantly reappeared back in my hotel room. I twisted out of his grasp the second I felt my feet on firm ground again, and I drew in a lungful of air to shout for Danaus when the hunter and Stefan appeared next to me a second later. The air escaped me in a useless rush. I hadn't trusted Stefan to bring Danaus there. I didn't trust Stefan as far as I could throw him, but I was now grudgingly willing to give him the benefit of the doubt, considering the loss of his assistant.

"Leave us," Danaus said in a low voice. "Mira and I have something to discuss."

Valerio and Stefan didn't hesitate. Valerio disappeared instantly, and Stefan was directly behind him with a soft snicker.

I looked up at the hunter and frowned. This wasn't going to be pleasant. Whatever he had learned during his time with Sofia was about to come back to bite me in the ass. I knew I never should have left him alone with Veyron's pretty little pet.

Fourteen

Danaus shrugged off his coat and tossed it over the back of one of the chairs as he paced the room. I settled in the open seat and crossed my left leg over my right knee, trying to steel myself against whatever the hunter was about to drop into my lap. My stomach and jaw clenched as I watched him shove one hand through his dark hair, pushing it away from his face.

"I want us to free Sofia," he announced. This was definitely going to get ugly.

"Why?"

Danaus stopped pacing and pinned me with a dark glare. "Why?" he repeated as his right hand balled into a fist. "She's a prisoner. That vampire is holding her against her will."

"I'm not sure if I believe that." I shrugged as I relaxed in my chair. "And even if she is, I am willing to bet that she got herself into that mess in the first place. It's not our job to get her out of her current predicament."

"So, you're saying no?"

I drew in a deep breath and released it slowly, as I reminded myself that Danaus wasn't accustomed to my world. There were limitations as to what I could do without causing

a storm of trouble that I wasn't willing to deal with at this
time. I already had enough on my plate.

"She's a pet, Danaus."

"I figured out that much myself," he snapped, but I ignored him and continued.

"She's a pet, and most of the time that's a position a
human attains willingly because she or he is enamored
of the nightwalker. She's treated well, I'm sure. I've seen
poorly treated pets, and she's not been abused. In fact, judging by the clothing and jewelry she was wearing, it looks as
if he's treated quite well."

"You don't know that!"

I finally frowned as I uncrossed my legs and slid to the
edge of my chair. Danaus put his hands on the back of the
sofa that separated us and leaned forward so he could look
me directly in the eye. "She's a prisoner," he growled. "He
restricts her movement. He feeds off her. He shares her with
his friends. She's just an object to him."

"Sounds like a pet to me. Nothing too surprising in any of
that treatment." I paused, searching for some way in which
he could accept Sofia's arrangement. "Look, Danaus. She
got herself into this situation. She's just going to have to deal
with it. If she's lucky, he'll get bored with her. Hell, it's likely
that we're going to have to kill Veyron eventually, so she
will be free after all. We can't just waltz in and tell him to
free her."

"Why can't we free her now?"

I shook my head and glanced down at my hands clasped
in my lap. "It just isn't done."

"What the hell does that mean?"

"She's Veyron's pet." I pushed to my feet, which also
caused Danaus to straighten to his full height. "You don't
steal another creature's pet unless you want to start a war. I
don't want her. I don't want to spend the rest of her existence

protecting her. It's bad enough that I just claimed Budapest as my second domain. I don't need to steal away another nightwalker's pet when he's got her under his protection. My reputation can't afford to get any blacker."

"You certainly had no problem stealing Tristan from Sadira when we were in Venice," Danaus accused.

"The court of the coven was going to kill him, and Sadira wasn't going to do anything to stop it! I didn't have a choice. I couldn't stand by and let it happen. I promised him that I would help him get free of her," I argued, finally raising my voice.

"And Nicolai? What was your excuse there? You can't tell me that you weren't taking a major risk by confronting Jabari and the entire coven by taking the werewolf off their hands. You knew that you were going to spend the rest of his existence protecting him from Jabari."

"Damn it, Danaus! You were there. They were going to hand Nicolai over to the naturi. There was a chance that he could have been the next sacrifice that would break the seal. We couldn't take that risk. Nicolai had to be removed from the coven. There was no choice."

"Convenient," the hunter sneered. "You've got an excuse for both of them."

"Is Sofia in danger? No!"

"You don't know that."

"Veyron likes his little pet. She's not in any danger so long as she obeys him. He will protect her and she knows it. Sofia isn't in any danger from the coven or the naturi. Hell, she's probably the most well-protected creature in all of Budapest."

"But she's not free."

"That's not our concern."

"She's human and she wants her freedom. That makes it my concern," Danaus said. He glared at me for several seconds as if waiting for me to agree with him, but I didn't say a word. "I'm going to help her." He turned and started to walk out of the hotel room.

With a growl, I put one foot on the sofa cushion and leapt over the back. In a couple quick steps I was in front of him before he could reach the door. I placed my hand on his chest, stopping him.

"You're not going anywhere," I ordered. "You try to free her and you're going to start a war. We still need to get rid of the naturi and discover why it was so important to Macaire that we come here. Freeing Sofia is not part of that deal."

Standing so close to Danaus, something caught my attention. I drew in a breath to release an aggravated sigh when I noticed a new scent in the air. It was everywhere around us, filling the tiny hallway that led to the rest of the hotel room as if there were another person standing directly between us. I released the breath and drew a second, checking to make sure that I hadn't lost my mind.

I could smell Sofia. Or rather I could smell her perfume. It was everywhere. I slowly lifted my hand from Danaus's chest and sniffed my hand before jerking it away again. The smell was even stronger. It was coming from Danaus.

"What have you been doing?" I asked. Horror filled my voice as I pressed my back against the door.

"What are you talking about? You're changing the subject—"

"What have you been doing? I can smell her. She's everywhere." I suddenly pushed off the door and leaned into Danaus so my nose was just inches away from his chest. The scent of Sofia's perfume smacked me across the face, sending me reeling away from the hunter once again. "She's all over you!"

"Mira, you're being ridiculous."

"Am I? You come to me reeking of this other woman, demanding that I help you set her free. What am I to think? For a moment I thought your interests lay with me, but apparently some pathetic human has caught your attention. What is it, Danaus? Is it because she's a helpless damsel in distress or just because she's human?"

"There's nothing going on. When I told her that I would help her escape Veyron, she threw herself on me. She gave me a hug and a kiss on the cheek. Nothing more."

A low growl escaped me as I grabbed the front of his shirt and slammed him into one of the walls. "You allowed her to touch you! You're mine! Don't you understand that? I made you my consort before the coven and the entire nightwalker nation, and you're choosing a human over me already."

"I don't belong to you! I'm not your pet!" Danaus roared, trying to push me away from him, but I wasn't budging.

"No, not pet. I gave you a greater position. You are my equal before the coven. My beloved and protected consort." I released him then, giving him a little shove as I walked back over to the door and leaned against it. "And you come to me smelling of her."

"She's a helpless human trapped in a bad situation. We need to help her," Danaus replied, avoiding the issue that it appeared as if he had already found my replacement. My stomach tightened and I clenched my teeth. I didn't need this now. I was more concerned about taking care of the naturi threat in Budapest, killing Rowe, and avoiding being killed in the process.

Shoving both hands into my hair, I turned my back on him and stared at the door that led to the hallway of the hotel. I needed more time to look into this matter with the naturi and try to find out why a magic user was trying to kill me. Also, I was sure that Stefan would prefer if we did something about his missing assistant before I went stirring up more trouble.

"We need to wait, Danaus," I said, forcing the words out in a calm, even tone as I turned back to face him. I was trying to be reasonable. I was trying to give him the benefit of the doubt and help him after all the times he had helped me. Yet Sofia's scent felt almost like a physical barrier between Danaus and me.

"And what if she doesn't have time for us to wait?" he demanded.

I dropped my hands back to my sides with a heavy flop. "Has Veyron done anything to make her think that he plans to kill her sometime soon? I mean, that would be why we'd try to save her—because Veyron plans to kill her, and not because she's grown bored or something?"

"She wants her freedom," Danaus said firmly.

"Yeah, well, don't we all," I muttered, though I'm sure that he heard me. I felt trapped. I didn't care about Sofia and her problems. I had enough of my own, and I wasn't willing to risk my neck for every poor soul that crossed my path. I'd be dead in a matter of nights if I took it on myself to try to protect the world. But then again, that was what I was trying to do every time I took on the naturi.

Drawing in a deep breath, I closed my eyes and tried to find a center of calm in all the anger and frustration buzzing around inside of me. "Give me a few nights. Let me try to take care of Veyron, Rowe, and a few of the other problems in the city before I try to figure out what to do with Sofia. Maybe we'll just get rid of Veyron and that will take care of it."

"Will that actually work or will she just be swallowed up by another nightwalker once he's gone?" Danaus demanded.

"What? Just say it finally! What do you want from me?" I demanded, losing my hold on my temper yet again.

"I want her to come to Savannah with us!" he shouted back.

"No! Absolutely not!" I knew if I saw Sofia right then, I'd pulled her hair out and pluck her eyes from her skull. I'd turned my back on Danaus for only a short time and the little tramp decided to poach something that I had just begun to consider was mine. "She's not coming to Savannah!"

"You're jealous," Danaus accused.

"You're damn right I'm jealous. There's no way in hell she's coming into my domain with you," I snarled. "If you're so desperate to free her, fine. Before we leave Budapest, we'll get rid of Veyron, and she'll be free. But from there, she'll be on her own. I'm not going to be her personal protector. If I'm going to take up that role, then she will be my pet and I'll keep her on a leash so tight she'll long for her nights with Veyron."

"I can't do this any longer. It's not working," Danaus said, throwing his hands up in the air as he walked away from me.

It felt as if a vise were suddenly gripping my heart, threatening to crush it. I was losing Danaus before I'd even had a chance to truly enjoy his companionship. But then, I had no doubt that everyone would have said our would-be relationship didn't have a prayer of working. I had wanted to try, though.

"You didn't give us a chance," I whispered. "I may be jealous of Sofia, but you make it sound like I have every reason to be. You can't get over the fact that you just might be attracted to a nightwalker—the evil ones. So when a pretty human crosses your path and winks, you jump on her like a dog on a bone."

"Don't make this about us. It's about freeing a helpless human from a powerful nightwalker. It's about protecting humans from your kind. That's what I do," Danaus said, turning to glare at me. "I'm going to free her."

"Then you have to choose between me and Sofia," I replied, putting my hands on my hips. "The only time you will be able to successfully free her is during the day, when Veyron and all the other nightwalkers are asleep. That will leave me unprotected, and there is a very good chance that Veyron is going to send someone to kill me in the morning now that I have taken Budapest right out from under him. You save her, you'll be killing me."

"I can't leave her."

"She's in no danger."

"You don't know that," Danaus grumbled.

"No, I don't, but I do know that I'm in greater danger than she is at this moment. Are you really going to choose her over me?"

"My job is to protect humans, not vampires," Danaus replied. He grabbed his coat from where it lay on the chair and jerked it on. I barely had a chance to step out of the way before he pulled open the door and stalked out into the hall, slamming it shut behind him. It was still several hours before sunrise, plenty of time for him to plan an attack on Veyron's home and steal Sofia away. He was going to start a war that I wasn't willing to fight. Of course, that was assuming I would survive that long.

My stomach twisted into a tight knot and I descended slowly to my knees in front of the door leading out of the hotel room. He had left me. Danaus, the one creature I'd been able to depend on to protect me during the past several months, had left me to protect someone else. Tears welled up in my eyes, but I clenched my teeth and sucked in a sharp breath as I held the tears back, refusing to let them fall. I would not cry over Danaus.

We hadn't had a real chance at making this work. He was a hunter and I was his prey. Did I really think that he could ever come to care for me? It was impossible. Danaus longed to be a real, normal human. It was understandable that he would be attracted to the thing he wanted more than his next breath. I represented everything he didn't want to be, everything he didn't want to be a part of. His enemy.

If Danaus wasn't going to help me, then I had to find a way to help myself. I wasn't about to curl up and die just because I could no longer rely on the hunter to protect my back when I was at my most vulnerable. Closing my eyes, I reached out with my mind, seeking the one person left in the area that I felt would prefer to see me rise the next night. Valerio instantly reacted to my mental touch. I could sense his immediate concern and unease. No words had been necessary. He knew that something terrible was wrong. But then, above everyone else, Valerio knew me best. Maybe even better than Jabari.

I didn't even have a chance to regain my feet before he appeared in the hotel suite, still wrapped in his thick coat and scarf. He looked down at me for only a second before scanning the rest of the suite with his eyes and his powers to determine that we were truly alone.

"Did I disturb you in the middle of someone?" I asked as I pushed off the floor with one hand. I was too tired to even use my powers to rise to my feet. Valerio reached out and caught my free hand, helping me.

"No one is more important to me than you," he said smoothly, causing one corner of my mouth to quirk at the pretty lie. "Where is the vampire hunter?"

I looked down at his chest, avoiding his question with one of my own. "Can I stay with you? I am assuming that you're flitting back and forth from Vienna each night."

"Of course you can spend your day with me." Valerio reached up and smoothed some hair away from the side of my face. He laid his hand under my chin and forced me to look up at him. "What has happened? Where is Danaus?"

I stepped away from Valerio and forced my shoulders to straighten as I took a couple steps over to one of the chairs in the living area. "He left." Those two words sounded indifferent, but something inside of me fractured, leaving shards digging into my soul.

"Why?"

"He wants to free Sofia."

Valerio's footsteps were muffled on the thick carpet as he approached me. He laid a hand against my lower back as he came to stand beside me. "And you told him no." I remained silent, staring blindly at the wall opposite me. "You did the right thing. Sofia is just a pet, and you can't go interfering where it won't benefit you."

"He's convinced that she wants her freedom and he is determined to help her."

He slid his fingers up my spine in a reassuring caress. "She made her choice. If she wanted her freedom so badly, she should never have agreed to give her life over to Veyron."

"Danaus doesn't see it that way. She's human and wants out. He has to protect her from us."

Valerio reached around and gently grabbed both of my shoulders so he could turn me to face him. "Mira, dearest." I tried to pull out of his grasp, but he refused to release me. "He's a hunter. He's human. Not one of us. He doesn't understand our world, he can't. A blind man could have seen what was happening between you two, and I hate to tell you that it just won't work."

I knew I wanted the impossible, and I didn't need to hear how wrong I had been from Valerio. It was like twisting the knife in my heart a little more so that I would finally learn my lesson not to care for anyone. Others in my life had died because of their association with me. Danaus, on the other hand, had chosen to walk away from me. For a moment I couldn't decide what was worse.

"He left. I think he went to free Sofia during the day," I whispered, resting my forehead against Valerio's shoulder.

"Then you stay with me. We'll deal with the repercussions tomorrow evening," he said. I didn't need to tell him that Danaus had chosen to protect the human over me, or that Veyron would undoubtedly send men to kill me during the day. I didn't need to actually say the words. Valerio knew and he was willing to take me in.

"Don't tell Stefan," I said, wrapping one arm around his waist.

"I won't." He brushed a gentle kiss across my temple. "But you have to remember that we've all had troubles with a human every once in a while during our long lifetimes. I'm sure Stefan has had his fair share of problems."

"Yes, but if the others find out that there has been a . . . a falling out between Danaus and me, they may take that as a sign to start hunting him."

Valerio pulled back so he could look me in the face. "You're still protecting him?"

Leaning back into Valerio, I nodded. I had pulled Danaus into these dark waters, and I wasn't about to leave him to the sharks. We might not see eye-to-eye on some matters, but that did not mean I was willing to turn my back on him. I just couldn't. I still needed him.

Fifteen

When we disappeared from my hotel room, I naturally
assumed that I would be seeing the richly decorated
rooms of Valerio's Vienna home when we reappeared.
Instead I found myself wrapped in Valerio's arms outside
the Nyugati train station in Pest. Pushing against him, I
moved out of his embrace as I scanned the region. I could
feel Valerio's powers blanketing us, so no one saw us
suddenly pop into existence in this part of town beyond
the handful of nightwalkers I could sense in the immediate area.

I shoved a heavy lock of hair out of my face and paced
away from my companion. "What are we doing here? I
thought we were going back to your place."

"The night is still so young, Mira." Valerio reached for
me again, but I dodged his grasp as I walked away from
the noise of the train station. Despite the late hour, a heavy
crowd of people lingered in the area nearby, along with a
mix of nightwalkers. My heels crunched in the dirty grit
of the street and I found myself tightening my arms on my
chest as the wind picked up.

"What do you have in mind?"

"You just became the keeper of Budapest," he said,

throwing his arms out wide. "Don't you think you should celebrate? Maybe spend a little time with your people?"

"Knock some heads around and instill some fear," suggested Stefan as he stepped out of the shadows nearby, joining us.

I frowned and shook my head as an uneasy feeling sank into the pit of my stomach. I had lost Danaus, and now Valerio and Stefan were drawing me deeper into their own plans. I didn't like this at all. "So how long have you two been planning this little party for me?" I asked, forcing a smile onto my lips.

"Since you announced that you were the new keeper," Stefan said, matching my smile.

"It is tradition, Mira," Valerio interjected quickly. "Anytime there is a change in leadership, it's customary for the new leader to go out and be seen among her people."

What Valerio and Stefan were truly saying was that it was customary for the new keeper of a domain to go out and sacrifice a few nightwalkers as a way of officially kicking off their reign—washing it in blood. They weren't lying, no matter how much I wished at the moment that they were. I had started my own reign of Savannah in a tide of blood. While our numbers had been small at the time, more than half of the nightwalkers in Savannah and the surrounding regions died when I declared that I was the new keeper of the area.

Unfortunately, after last night's bloodbath and my fight with Danaus, I found myself no longer wishing to wash the world in the blood of those around me. I wanted to slip into a dark quiet corner and let the world forget about me. I wanted to escape the notice of the naturi, and Nick, and the coven. But standing there in the cold with Valerio and Stefan, I knew I wasn't going to get that. I was a powerful nightwalker, a coven Elder who had just claimed one of the oldest cities in Central Europe as her domain. It was expected of me to make an appearance and shed some blood.

I swallowed a heavy sigh as I straightened my shoulders and turned my attention to Valerio, who had been watching me far too closely. After my falling out with Danaus, he knew that I was feeling more than a little weak and vulnerable. He was trying to cheer me up the only way he knew how—with violence and chaos.

"So what place have you chosen for me to make my appearance? I would prefer for it to have a large impact on the nightwalker population, since we shall be dealing with the shifters tomorrow night," I announced, trying to keep my voice sounding bland and even a little bored.

Valerio's smile widened. He could see right through me, but at least he knew that I was willing to go along with his little game. "You're going to love this place. From what I had been able to tell, it's popular with both the tourists and the locals. It's open late and draws a huge bloodsucker crowd. It's the perfect place for us. It's called Bahnhof and it's just behind the train station."

I shrugged my shoulders, shoved my hands into the pockets of my slacks and followed both Stefan and Valerio through the street. We carefully wove our way through the crowd and used a little bit of mind manipulation to get through the front door ahead of the line of people waiting to enter the bar. I paused at the entrance, some of the tension easing from my shoulders at the pounding music. From floor to ceiling the place was decorated in old railroad memorabilia, which only seemed fitting since the place was right next to Nuygati train station.

We slowly pressed through the crowd of humans, making a sweep of the two separate dance floors as well as the different secret niches modeled after railway cars. I could feel the eyes of every nightwalker on us as we walked through the place. They remained silent observers for now. As far as they knew, we were trespassing in their private domain. Of course, they could have also heard about last night's slaughter as the Széchenyi Baths. Either way, they were giving us some space for now, but it was only a matter of time. I was waiting to see who blinked first. Considering that Stefan's lone assistant hadn't escaped the city, I was willing to bet that the nightwalkers of Bahnhof were going to press us first. I just needed to give them a proper reason.

It didn't take me long to find it. Toward the back of the train-themed dance club was a private car filled with nightwalkers and the human pets that clung to them like bits of fleshy jewelry. This was the exclusive club car. The so-called best seat in the house. And naturally, being the new keeper of Budapest, this had to be my seat.

I stood in the doorway and smiled down at them in silence, my arms hanging loose at my sides. They all looked at me with varying degrees of dislike and disinterest. One female seated farthest from the entrance into the secluded area frowned at me as she unwrapped her arm from around the shoulders of a thin, sickly white human with wind-blown hair.

"This is a private party. It would be best if you left," she warned, leaning forward on the table. Considering that nearly twenty people were crammed into the tiny area, the table was littered with surprisingly few drinks. There were more nightwalkers than humans in that tight region, and no one was bothering to keep up appearances that they were just average customers of the club. This behavior simply wouldn't do.

"Yes," I said in a low hiss as my smile widened. "This is a private party and we have come for this set of seats."

A low round of laughter rumbled through the car as they

shifted restlessly in their chairs. I smiled, chuckling as well.
I was older than all of them. This wasn't going to be a contest. This was going to be a slaughter.

*Keep anyone from escaping out onto the main floor. I
don't want to cause a panic among the humans,* I directed
Valerio and Stefan.

*You're determined to drain all the fun out of this, aren't
you?* Valerio whined.

*I'll leave the humans to you and Stefan. I just want the
nightwalkers.*

"And where do you get this notion that we're going to
move for you?" the female demanded. "You don't belong
here. You should leave this city and go back to your own
home." This time I felt a not so subtle mental shove as she
tried to mentally direct me to do her bidding. It lacked finesse, strength, and even cunning. It was both crass and in-
sulting that she even attempted it on someone of my years
and experience.

I didn't even give her a chance to move. In a flash I
reached across the table, grabbed her by the throat, and
dragged her across the tabletop. Drinks were sent flying in
every direction, but the sound of breaking glass could barely
be heard over the roar of music coming from the other end of
the club. Pinning her to the table with one hand, I raised the
other above my head and bathed it in flickering blue flames
so that I now had everyone's full attention.

"Listen to me, you worthless piece of chum, I am Mira. I
am the Fire Starter, a coven Elder, and the keeper of Budapest. Do you know what that makes you?" I growled, leaning close so that all she could see were my glowing lavender
eyes and long white fangs. The female shook her head as she
held the hand wrapped around her neck with two trembling
hands. "My personal plaything for the rest of the evening.
If you're lucky, you'll prove to me exactly why your maker

didn't kill you the second you were reborn, because right now you're seeming extremely useless to me."

Two humans stupidly attempted to rush me at the same time in hopes of freeing their precious companion. Throwing the female nightwalker back to where she had been seated earlier, I didn't hesitate as I snapped both their necks in the blink of an eye and set another nightwalker on fire for edging too close to me.

Chaos erupted in the small booth at the sight of the fire. I stopped thinking and only reacted to the hands reaching for me and the knives that suddenly appeared, glinting in the firelight. After nights of running and fighting naturi, bori, and nightwalkers, I just stopped thinking and let my emotions run free. Limbs were ripped and broken. Screams were quickly muffled, lost in the roar of music that rumbled through the club. Valerio and Stefan appeared beside me, splashed with blood and smiling like devils at the carnage spread before them. In a matter of only seconds twenty people lay dead, both nightwalkers and humans. Hadn't even thought about it.

Stepping onto the table, I walked over the mess and claimed the seat at the back of the niche, pushing bodies out of my way. With a wave of my hand, a couple orbs of fire appeared in the air and hovered above the table, casting the blood-soaked booth in a frightening light. I looked around at the mess I had made and I wanted to be sick. I hadn't lost control in years. I hadn't killed a human in centuries. Not since my days with Valerio and Jabari, when I was young and reckless, had I caused such death and destruction. And yet despite my superior strength and vicious skill, they kept coming at me. They hadn't tried to run in fear or plead for their lives. They just attacked me, and I killed them because . . . because killing was the only thing I was good at. Killing them meant taking my own life back one person at a time. I was tired of being hounded by Rowe, Nick, Macaire, and too many others to count. If I killed them, then there were a few less people in the world that wanted to kill me.

After staring blindly at the severed head of one of the nightwalkers that had been in the booth, I blinked a couple times and looked up to find Stefan and Valerio sitting on either side of me, while other nightwalkers crowded the opening to the private little niche. Horror stretched their handsome features and widened their luminous eyes. I could hear "Fire Starter" whispered among them in both Hungarian and rough English.

None of them cared that I was a member of the coven. They didn't care that being an Elder made me a creature that demanded instant respect within the world of the nightwalker. They only cared that I was the Fire Starter, and with me came the instant threat of a painful and brutal death. Of the twenty, only one person within the booth had died by fire. They rest had been ripped apart by my bare hands. I was washed in their blood so that it was soaked into my clothes and dripped from my chin.

No matter what I did or where I went, I would always be the Fire Starter first and above all else.

Lifting my chin a little, I smiled at the nightwalkers that were cautiously watching me. "I am Mira and I am the new keeper of Budapest. I'll be in town for a few nights along with my companions. I hope you will make us feel welcome."

The response from the group was overwhelming silence, but I could feel a buzz in the air as many of them spoke with each other telepathically. I continued to smile at them, soaking in their fear and terror like a drug.

"And if you're wondering, I have already visited with Odelia and Veyron. They are both aware of my new position within the city," I added, just twisting the knife a little more.

A few of the older nightwalkers that had been around

long enough to potentially see a regime change within a region lingered long enough to welcome me to the lovely city of Budapest and offer their services. However, most silently filtered back into the crowd of humans. In fact, most of the nightwalkers had left Bahnhof within twenty minutes of discovering the slaughter. I was simply too dangerous to remain close to. There was no telling whether I would decide to strike out at more nightwalkers. By now the killing at Széchenyi Baths was well-known among the Budapest nightwalkers, and now there was the bloodbath at Bahnhof. Death followed me wherever I tread, and no one was willing to stand in my path.

I looked across the table so find both Valerio and Stefan relaxing against the bloodstained cushions, appearing at ease with the world. They had nothing to worry about. They were both my protectors and instruments of my destruction. They were immune to my fits of rage, need for chaos, and desire for fear among those that surrounded me. I knew that this type of behavior was expected as I took my place within the city and as a member of the coven. The only problem was that it was starting to make me ill, even as I got better at the destruction as time slipped past. I was beginning to believe that I was the daughter of chaos.

Sixteen

The next night, the hotel room looked like a bomb had gone off. The walls were pockmarked with bullet holes and the furniture had been trashed. Glass from broken picture frames littered the floor so that the carpet now sparkled in the light coming through the window. Releasing Valerio, I took a couple of cautious steps into the room, my mouth hanging open as I dragged my eyes over the chaos. Danaus sat on the floor with his back pressed against the door that led into my bedroom. His clothes were torn and bloody. A knife was held loosely in one hand while a gun rested on the floor next to his other hand. He looked up at me, confusion filling his face.

"How the hell did you get here?" he demanded, pushing slowly to his feet.

"I stayed with Valerio during the day. He just brought me back."

He pointed at the bedroom door with the knife. "You mean you were never in there?"

"No." I shook my head, my eyebrows snapping together over my nose at his tone. "Didn't you ever look in on me? You never checked?"

"No!"

"You left me!" I shouted back, refusing to feel guilty that he had defended what amounted to an empty room. "I told you that Veyron's men would attack me during the day. Did you think I was going to stay here unguarded and vulnerable during the daylight hours while you went after Sofia?"

"I didn't go after her," he admitted, lowering his voice to a normal level again.

"But you left."

Danaus narrowed his eyes on my face as his frown grew darker. "And you thought I would choose her life over yours."

"Yes." There was nothing else I could say. He left. He left the hotel room and I assumed that he was going after Sofia. Where else would he have gone after our argument? "Your leaving the room signaled to me that you were going after her. I would have been alone during the day, left vulnerable to . . . to this," I said, extending my hands to encompass the destroyed room.

"I went down to the hotel bar for a drink," Danaus snapped. "How could you think that I would honestly leave you alone? I stayed at your side in England when the naturi attacked. I was with you in Venice and Peru. Why would I leave you now?"

Because I thought you cared about Sofia more than you cared about me.

I was spared from having to answer out loud by the sudden appearance of Stefan in the center of the room. His eyebrows were raised and his lips twitched as if he was unsuccessfully suppressing a smile. "Had a bit of trouble during the day?" I wanted to smack him. Now was not the best time for jokes. Not when both my temper and Danaus's were already burning away on a short fuse.

"Who came here?" Valerio asked in the growing silence as Danaus and I glared at each other. I wouldn't feel guilty about leaving. He had left me with no indication that he planned to return to the room before sunrise, and I wasn't going to roll over and die to suit him.

"Lycans," Danaus replied slowly, finally lifting his gaze from me to Valerio, who stood just behind my right shoulder. Stefan's face was wiped clean of the smirk that had been twisting his lips. The lycans were currently harboring the blame for Stefan's missing assistant, and they had already been on the top of my list of things to take care of. If they had attacked Danaus with the intent of killing me, then the local pack didn't stand much chance of surviving the night.

"Are you sure?" Valerio inquired.

"He knows a lycan when he sees one," I replied as I walked through the room, toward the windows that looked out on the city. Lifting my eyes up to the black sky, I frowned at the full moon that shone down on me with her shimmering silvery light. The shifters would be at their peak strength tonight. It was fitting.

"Faster than normal humans," Danaus said. "Stronger. They carried with them a thick sense of power that couldn't be missed. The air smelled like a forest after the rain. There was no doubt that they were all lycans. There were three of them. However, one held back at the door during the fight. He may have been a warlock."

"Warlock?" I spun around to look at Danaus again, blocking some of the light that tripped into the room from the window. My black shadow was swallowed up in the dark room, adding to the bleak atmosphere.

"Warlock," he repeated. "He didn't cast any spells, but there was something about the way he stood and carried himself. As if he was above it all."

"Sounds like a nightwalker to me." I crossed my arms over my stomach as I leaned my shoulder against the window frame.

Danaus looked up and flashed me a grim smile. "I know a vampire when I see one."

"Yeah, I guess you would. Warlock, then," I grumbled.

"That's . . . unexpected," Valerio added.

Stefan shook his head, frowning. "Werewolves don't form hunting parties with anyone else. They hunt in tight formation with only their own kind."

I stared at the floor that sparkled with glass strewn over the thick carpet. The appearance of the warlock made me think that maybe he had been sent to make sure the job was done properly. I was beginning to believe that maybe Ferko had not been the one to send them. I had always believed that Veyron would send someone to kill me, but I'd been anticipating humans—not lycanthropes or warlocks. I found this development even more unsettling.

"I'm assuming that no one was killed, considering that there are no bodies," I resumed, pushing my thoughts to the back of my mind for perusal later. Our main concern at the moment was the shifters. I could worry about their alliances later when I had a chance to beat the information out of Ferko.

"No one was killed," Danaus stated, "though I have doubts as to whether one of them would survive the next few hours, considering I stabbed him near the heart. He was bleeding pretty heavily."

"Did the warlock attack you?"

"No." He finally shoved his knife in the sheath on his waist and then returned the gun to the holster at his lower back. "He never moved from the closed door."

"His job was to get them in and out of the hotel unnoticed," Valerio commented. "Silence any noise that rose from the room while they took care of their little task. When word gets out that they failed to kill you, they are likely to try again. You can't stay here."

"I'm not leaving the city again until this matter is taken care of," I told him. "This is my domain, after all."

"That's ridiculous!" Stefan snapped.

"After we take care of the lycans and Ferko tonight, anyone else will be reluctant to approach me, regardless of who is giving the orders." I pushed off the wall and walked back across the room toward Valerio and the door. A frown pulled at the corners of my mouth as my eyes strayed over the stuffing that protruded from the sofa cushions and the blood that had soaked into the carpet. It had been a pretty little room, and it was a shame that it was destroyed by the shifters. Of course, I was even more surprised to discover that Danaus had come back to the room, that he'd protected me without ever looking in on my helpless form.

"Shall we go?" Stefan asked, motioning toward the door. Danaus reached for his coat on the floor, while Stefan stepped around me.

"Danaus, you can remain here," I said. "Get some rest. You've already had a long day." I preferred to keep him with me, but if he had been trapped in a fight with three lycanthropes earlier in the day and unable to sleep, he wasn't going to be at his peak fighting ability. We were going after an entire pack of lycans during a full moon. This was one of more dangerous things I had done. I wouldn't be able to watch his back.

"I'm going," he growled, shoving one arm into the sleeve of his coat before fully pulling it on. "I can identify the ones that tried to kill you." He wasn't going to bother to change clothes. I, on the other hand, had acquired new clothes and a coat while in Vienna, thanks to Valerio.

"They're all going to be in wolf form," I reminded him. "By now they would have all met in the woods and shifted. We're going to have to hunt them down one by one in the woods."

"Yes, but they change back when they're dead or unconscious," Danaus countered.

The smirk returned to Stefan's lips. "We'll get the ones
that tried to attack Mira. We'll get them all." It was the ugly
truth I was hoping that I wouldn't have to reveal to the hunter.
Lycanthropes had attempted to attack not only the keeper of
a domain, but also a member of the coven. We had to wipe
out as many of them as possible to make an example of them
to anyone else in the region who thought to rebel against my
rule.

"How many of them are there?" Danaus asked, seemingly unmoved by our intent.

"Unknown."

Valerio shifted from one foot to the other, his expression
grim. "Judging by other packs in large European cities, there
should be at least a dozen of them, but it's unlikely that there
are two dozen." My expression matched his as I looked at my
old friend. Valerio wasn't the type to get his hands dirty. The
few fights I'd seen him in, he had been positively vicious.
But then, the fights had been one-on-one with another nightwalker. I didn't know if he had any experience fighting a pack
of shifters. Unfortunately, I did. It wasn't going to be pretty.

"Then you're going to need my help." Danaus said,
heading toward the door. As Valerio and Stefan started to
leave the room, I grabbed Danaus's sleeve, stopping him.

Thank you for protecting me, I said silently, so the others
could not invade this private moment.

I protected nothing, he replied, anger still filling each of
those words.

You protected me. Few have done so, I pressed, holding
him still when he tried to take a step away from me.

Valerio—

*Valerio gave me a place to sleep. He did nothing more.
You fought for me.*

I promised to protect you. His words softened in my brain to something that resembled a lover's caress as his anger dissipated. *I will protect you above all others. I promised.*

"Save the longing looks for another time," Stefan called from the doorway, snapping us out of our brief moment.

Danaus and I still had a long way to go, but at least I knew that he hadn't abandoned me for a human. The giant black chasm that still separated us needed to be closed, and I had my doubts as to whether that was even possible. But I was willing to try. He had not left me for a human. It was a start.

For now, I had to put thoughts of my rocky and fragile relationship with the hunter aside. I had to hunt down some lycanthropes, and I was sure that Danaus was going to see a side of me I preferred to keep hidden from him. I didn't want him to discover that I was struggling to hide the smile of excitement pulling at the corners of my mouth. I didn't want him to know I was eager to be in the woods, chasing them down, hearing their screams of pain. They had attacked Danaus, tried to kill me. I was ready to make them pay.

Seventeen

The woods were thick. An oppressive silence weighed on us as we trudged through the blanket of snow. The crunch of our footsteps echoed through the cold, crystalline night. Ducking under low branches, I was grateful Valerio had acquired a pair of black leather pants, sturdy boots, and a black turtleneck for me. My new, long black coat flaired behind me as I walked.

There was no doubt that the lycans were gathered up ahead, and there was no sneaking up on them as we crunched through the snow. By my count, we were faced with sixteen lycanthropes of varying ages and strength. There was one in particular that was rather strong, which I could only guess was Ferko—alpha of the Budapest pack. I smiled, causing my fangs to brush against my lower lip. Ferko and I needed to have a nice little chat about who was truly the ruling power in Budapest.

After walking more than a mile in the bitter cold, we came to a clearing in the middle of the woods. Some of the shifters had already changed into wolf form. Their thick coats protected them from the wind that was starting to kick up, pulling the snowflakes from the trees above us and swirling them through the air. A low growl rumbled through

the circle, but there was no other noise to be heard. Opposite me stood a man with long, shaggy brown hair and
eyes that seemed to be their own void of darkness. He stood
bare-chested in snow, his shirt and coat dropped carelessly
behind him.

"Ferko, I presume."

"Fire Starter." His voice rumbled within his chest like a
roll of thunder.

"I believe we have something to discuss."

"And what would that be? Your new position as nightwalker keeper of Budapest?" he said in a mocking tone that
left me clenching my teeth, but my smile never wavered.

"I'm more concerned about the lycans that you sent to
kill me during the day," I replied casually, as if we weren't
discussing the assassination attempt on my life.

He shrugged his massive shoulders, holding his hands
open and empty out toward me. "I don't know what you're
talking about."

"I didn't think you would, but if you're kind enough to
give me the name of the warlock that accompanied your
men, I might let some of your people limp away from the
forest tonight." An eerie lavender light glowed from my
eyes, matching the rising glow coming from both Valerio
and Stefan. We stood on the edge of battle, and there was
no way of avoiding it. I was simply giving Ferko the chance
to save the lives of some of his people. A good leader would
have considered my offer. Ferko didn't.

"Again, I don't know what you're talking about." If he
wasn't still smiling at me, I would have considered that he
might have been telling the truth. Unfortunately, it didn't
matter. His people had to die for the attack that was launched
on Danaus.

"Danaus?" I asked, turning my head toward the hunter.

"The blond over there." Danaus directed my gaze to the

shifter that stood near the edge of the ring with a gray wolf on either side of him. One of the wolves flattened its ears against its head and growled at me, returning my smile to my lips. We might have spotted two of the culprits behind the day's battle. "I don't see the other two. They may have already shifted."

"Kill the blond and anyone who has already shifted into wolf form," I announced, locking eyes with Ferko. Only he had the power to stop the slaughter of his people. Of course, he thought his people actually had an edge in this battle because they outnumbered us. Not a chance. I had two Ancients with me. They were older, faster, and stronger than all the lycans combined. I was the Fire Starter. And Danaus, well, he was a monster from nightmares that left a scream lodged in your throat when you woke with a start.

"I don't think you want to do this," Ferko said with a smug smile.

"No, you don't get it. I've been looking forward to this." I lowered my voice slightly, directing my attention back to my companions. "Leave Ferko alive. There's information that I need. Kill all the others."

"You're an angel," Valerio purred as he shed his heavy coat. Folding it neatly, he laid it over a nearby tree branch so it wouldn't get dirty. I looked to my left to find Stefan doing the same thing. I suppressed a wild laugh at their delicate sensibilities and priorities before a bloodbath.

Stefan and Valerio took a step forward toward the shifters, and they immediately scattered into the darkness. Both the men and women that were in human form were throwing off clothes as they ran through the forest, so it would be easier for them to shift into wolf form. Ferko winked at me once before he also darted into the black wall of darkness that enveloped the woods surrounding us.

"Have fun!" I laughed just before Stefan and Vale-rio darted after them. It was only a few seconds later that I heard my first wounded whimper rise up in the night. A young nightwalker was fairly matched with an experienced werewolf, but an older, experienced nightwalker held the edge in a fight against a shifter. We were stronger, faster, and generally more brutal. However, a lycanthrope was not without its own edge, since they tended to hunt in packs. It was rare for three powerful nightwalkers to come into the woods and hunt shifters. Of course, if any lycans escaped us tonight, there was still a chance they could hunt us down during the daylight hours and eliminate us as retribution. It was how this game was played.

I glanced over my shoulder at Danaus, who held a knife in his right hand. He was waiting for me to move. "Are you going to be all right on your own?"

"I survived many centuries without your watchful eye. I think I can manage this minor scuffle."

My laugh echoed through the night as I ran across the clearing and instantly became washed in the darkness of the forest. I dodged low tree limbs and moved almost silently across the snow-covered ground. My powers bounced back to me like sonar, revealing the locations of the werewolves. Four were ahead of me at different spots, waiting for me to blindly pass by so that they could all jump on me.

Palming the knife that was sheathed on my right leg, I darted to my left and leapt on the back of a wolf that wasn't expecting me to attack from that angle. He jerked his head around, clamping his teeth down on my left forearm as I buried my blade into his rib cage. The wolf yelped in pain, releasing me. Blood poured from my arm, but I ignored it as I wrapped it around his throat and pulled him over on me as I fell to my back in the snow. Yanking the knife from his ribs, I plunged it into the creature's stomach and twisted it, causing another cry to go ringing out into the night. A bubble of laughter rose up in my chest and some of the tension from earlier in the evening eased from my shoulders. I was back in my natural element and it was great.

My only warning was a low growl from a second wolf just before it attacked me. A set of sharp fangs bit into my throat, causing a gush of blood to spray across the white snow. I released the half-dead wolf I had been holding, pushing its limp body off me as I yanked my knife free. With a grunt of pain, I swung the blade at the wolf, but I missed when it leapt away from me before I could carve into its hide. A third wolf launched its heavy frame at me, aiming to land on my chest. I caught it with my foot in its tender underbelly, kicking it away from me.

Rolling back to my feet, I pocketed the knife as I stalked over to the wolf that had bit me in the throat. Blood dripped down from his jaws as it growled at me, its hackles standing on end as I approached. With a bark, it leapt, mouth open in hopes of taking a fresh chunk out of me. I grabbed the top and bottom of its jaws and pulled them sharply apart, breaking its lower jaw and neck at the same time. It didn't even have time to let out a whimper of pain before it died.

I dropped the carcass to the ground and smiled as I turned back to the wolf that had tried to jump on me. With long bloodstained fangs showing, the wolf growled at me as it backed up several steps. Its large yellow eyes reflected the moonlight. The creature crouched for a second as if it planned to leap at me, and then darted off into the woods like a brown blur in the darkness. I chuckled and gave chase, happy to spend the evening running through the thick forest after my prey. Dodging low branches and leaping over fallen trees, I found that my body hummed with energy and pent-up excitement. This was the thrill of the hunt, and it was the closest I would ever come to once again feeling alive.

The wolf dove, jumped, and barreled through the woods, weaving among the trees as if it were made of the wind. I followed close on its heels, not quite catching it as I played it cautious on the slippery snow-covered ground. I didn't need to catch it. It would grow weary before I would.

Something heavy landed on my back as I passed beneath a small rise. I hadn't been scanning the area for other lycanthropes and my prey had managed to lure me into a simple trap. With a swing of my arm, I knocked the creature off my back before it could do any kind of significant damage. Laying on my stomach, I threw out my hand toward the wolf that was about to jump on me again. Flames instantly engulfed my prey, burning brightly in the night. The creature lurched away from me, rolling in the snow as it tried to put the flames out. Its cries suddenly became a woman's shrieks as she changed back to human form, the pain making it impossible for her to remain a wolf. And then she lay dead before me.

I scanned the area, only to find that the wolf I'd been chasing had run off, most likely frightened beyond rational thought at the sight of the flames. This might be little more than a deadly game between nightwalkers and lycanthropes, but I played to win.

Three were dead, leaving thirteen to my other three companions as I headed back to the main clearing where we had initially met. With any luck, we'd have most of this cleaned up in a matter of minutes before we could finally turn our attention back to Ferko. Unfortunately, I wasn't as alone as I initially thought I was.

"Bravo, Fire Starter! Show those animals who's dominant!" shouted a mocking voice down from the trees, accompanied by clapping.

I clenched my teeth and took a couple steps backward, palming the knife in my right hands once again. I knew that voice. I would always know that voice. Rowe had found me once again, and he sounded like he was ready to play.

"Rowe!" I replied in the same mocking tone as I looked at the trees before me. "It's been so long since we last met. Come down and play."

"Gladly," he growled. The wind gusted through the trees so that their limbs swayed and crashed into one another. I looked up in time to see him gliding down toward me out of a nearby tree, his black leathery wings thrown wide behind him. I dove out of the way of his flashing silver blade, sliding several feet in the snow before I regained my feet.

The naturi grinned at me, twisting his short blade so it winked at me in the moonlight. I kept my distance from the one-eyed creature, as I had only a knife with me. I hadn't been planning to go up against the naturi this evening, just the local werewolf pack. And that was more hands-on than fighting the naturi.

Rowe lunged at me first, bringing his short sword down in a slashing motion, hoping to open a vein or two. I dodged it while trying to keep my feet beneath me as I moved through the snow-slick forest.

Mira! The naturi are here. Danaus's cry along our private link screamed through my brain as Rowe swung at me again. I narrowly missed having my head removed as I slid to my ass in the snow. I hadn't been cloaking the hunter's presence, and I had a feeling that Rowe was just following him around with the expectation that I would be in Danaus's shadow.

I noticed, I growled in response. I blocked Rowe's blade with my own, and quickly pushed it off as it slid down toward the handle, threatening to remove my hand at the wrist. *Get over here before more of the shifters find me!*

Leaning back in the snow, I grabbed a handful of snow and flung it at the naturi, hoping to temporarily blind him.

Rowe took a step backward to avoid the white spray, giving me the chance to push to my feet again. I backpedaled, wishing I could divide my attention enough to scan the area for lycanthropes. That was the last thing I needed—to be attacked from behind by an angry shifter. Unfortunately, I was too closely matched with Rowe and couldn't afford to split my attention.

"And I thought you wanted me alive so I could be brought before your precious wife-queen." I darted behind a particularly thick tree as he swung his blade at me. A heavy thunk echoed through the forest as the metal buried into the bark at the last second. I lunged forward as he tried to pry his blade loose. Rowe slid out of my reach and pulled a knife from his belt as he abandoned his sword.

"Oh, I do," he said breathlessly. "But that doesn't mean I can't wear you down a little bit, shed a little blood before I hand you over to Aurora. I'm sure she won't mind if you arrive less than perfect."

"I'm sure she won't mind at all," I replied, swinging my blade at him so he was backed against a tree. "She never could handle me when I was at my peak."

"You have never seen Aurora at her peak strength! She will crush you!"

"Yeah, yeah. Heard that one before and here I still stand."

In response, a low howl filled the air, only to be answered by two more that were ominously close to my current location. The werewolves were closing in on me and my combatant. I wasn't sure if they would bother to attack Rowe as well, but I couldn't get my hopes up. Besides, Danaus was supposed to be drawing close. He would even the odds.

Afraid that I would soon find a lycanthrope at my back, I waved my free hand out to the side. A low wall of flames sprang up from the frozen earth and surrounded us in a flash. Danaus would be trapped on the outside, but I hoped that the shifters would be trapped on the outside as well as I took care of Rowe.

"Don't worry," Rowe purred. "I'm not going anywhere."

"I'm not worried about you. I'm just making sure this stays a private party."

Rowe lunged at me again with his knife, hoping to get inside my reach so he could bury it deep in my stomach. I caught his hand while I tried to stab him. Unfortunately, the naturi captured my wrist as well, locking us in a deadly stalemate. My arms trembled under the exertion and I gritted my teeth. We were fairly matched in strength, but the ground beneath our feet was wet and frozen, making our footing unsteady. A wrong step and someone could far too easily slip.

"Give it up, Mira," Rowe snarled between clenched teeth. "Come back to Aurora with me. I promise to do what I can to get you a quick death."

"The only way I am willing to die is with Aurora's heart in my hand."

I tightened my grip on his wrist, hoping to shatter the bone, but it wouldn't give under my grasp.

"I will kill her. Someday, I will finally kill her."

"Never!"

A sudden crash of thunder echoed through the forest and the wind picked up. Fat flakes of snow plummeted from the sky, obscuring the woods so that we were trapped in a swirling vortex of frigid white. I could barely make out the wildly dancing flames only a few feet away. I could hear them snapping and crackling as they ate through any nearby brush, but their light was muted by the sudden snowstorm.

Lightning crashed to the ground just a few feet behind me, followed by the ominous sound of cracking wood. A tree had been struck and was breaking apart. I fought the urge to look over my shoulder to see if the tree was about to crash about my shoulders, reconciling myself to the thought that a falling tree would hit Rowe too.

A second roll of thunder was accompanied by a pair of sharp fangs embedding in my left calf muscle. A werewolf had jumped easily over the flames and was now gnawing on my leg like a chew toy. I screamed but didn't release the naturi. My hands were trapped and there was no way I could easily rid myself of the lycanthrope that wouldn't take my full concentration.

"Danaus!" I screamed, not caring who thought me suddenly weak. I needed help. I was surrounded and vastly outnumbered.

Coming! He was close, maybe only a few dozen yards away, but now I could also hear the growling of other lycanthropes. They were blocking his path, keeping him from saving me as I was trapped between a shifter and a naturi with a serious attitude problem.

"Doesn't look good for you," Rowe taunted as he twisted his wrist. I was weakening under the pain of the lycan that was tearing through vital muscles.

"Kill them, Mira," called a familiar voice in musical tones. "Use the bori and kill them all."

Rowe stilled suddenly at the mention of the bori. He jerked his head around so he could look over his shoulder for his mortal enemy. Nightwalkers were always good fun to destroy, but bori were a totally different matter.

I didn't hesitate. I couldn't lose this opening. I reached out for the powers that swarmed around Danaus. With only the barest of nudges, I activated the energy that seemed to lie sleeping around his soul. Something inside of me screamed in pain, blocking out the strain from Rowe and the pain in my leg caused by the lycanthrope. The flames that surrounded us were immediately extinguished and my hold on Danaus's powers grew stronger. I didn't question it.

I opened my senses as I tightened my hold on Rowe's arm. The souls of the werewolves in the immediate area glowed like beacons in the darkness. With a loud growl, I directed the powers out from Danaus, enveloping the werewolves around us.

No! the hunter cried in my brain, but I didn't stop. We were trapped and Nick was watching me. He expected me to use Danaus's power. If I didn't, I feared he would make a bad situation significantly worse. I was locked in a battle of strength with Rowe, and I couldn't come to Danaus's rescue if the monster decided to strike. Danaus would hate me, but in the end I figured I was probably saving his life.

The werewolves howled in pain as they writhed on the ground. Rowe stopped fighting me, staring at the werewolf behind me. It thrashed wildly on the ground, whimpering in pain. The naturi released me and jerked his one arm free of my grasp as he backpedaled away. His wide eyes jumped between the wolves that surrounded us. As death grasped them, they shifted back into human form in time for their flesh to split open. Boiling blood came spewing forth, hissing as it touched the snow.

When the last werewolf took its final shuddering breath, I released Danaus from my power. The hunter fell to his knees, his breathing ragged and labored. Using that power was exhausting and a heavy strain on his body after all the fighting he had already done. My own limbs were trembling in pain and fatigue, but I still had to deal with Rowe. It had been tempting to try to boil his blood as well, but more of a struggle to focus on his energy as well as the lycanthropes.

And in truth, I didn't want to kill him that way. Rowe and I had a history. He had been there at Machu Picchu when I was first captured. He knew me when I had been human. If I was going to kill Rowe, I would do it with my bare hands. It was something we both deserved. Not a death by these seemingly godlike powers that left us detached and feeling somewhat irresponsible.

"You missed your chance," Rowe said as he struggled to catch his breath.

I shook my head as I shifted my stance to take more of my weight off my wounded left leg. Blood poured down into my boot and pain radiated throughout my leg. "Never."

Rowe smirked at me. He lurched toward me with his knife slashing at my chest. I raised my own blade as I awkwardly stumbled backward a step. I was unstable on my feet, favoring my left leg still. The blade missed my throat by inches as he turned and threw it through the air. The knife cut through the air with amazing speed until it finally buried itself in Danaus. I screamed as I watched Danaus collapse backward into the bloody snow just a dozen yards away.

At the same time, Rowe ran into a small clearing and threw out his black wings. They immediately caught the rising wind and carried him from the vicinity. With a pain-filled grunt, I limped across the small clearing to where Danaus was slowly pushing up onto his right elbow. The handle of the knife protruded from just below his collarbone. It hadn't dug deep, as the blade had been caught up in several layers of thick clothing and a heavy leather coat. Kneeling beside the hunter, I pressed one hand against the wound as I yanked the blade from his shoulder. Danaus grunted once but said nothing for several seconds.

"You could have asked," he said in a low voice after a lengthy silence.

I frowned, biting my lower lip. The scent of his blood filled the night air, awakening the monster than inhabited my own chest, leaving it demanding a fresh meal. I could feel his warm blood against the palm of my hand, and it was all I could do to resist the urge to lick my fingers clean. I wouldn't feed from Danaus, not even indirectly. I wanted him to remain untouched by my kind. He was above them. He was above it all.

"I couldn't take that chance," I replied when I could finally focus on our conversation. Pain started to rise above the need to feed. My body was slowly mending the jagged bite that had been taken out of my leg. "There were too many of them and I was trapped with Rowe. I needed the lycans dead."

"So you used me?"

"Directing you—"

"Controlling me!" Danaus corrected.

"You could already see all the lycans surrounding us. I wasn't sure where they all were, and I couldn't risk searching for them."

"And Rowe? Why did you spare him?"

"We need him alive." I lifted my hands from his shoulder and immediately rubbed them in the snow, washing off the blood so I wouldn't be tempted to take a taste. I had succumbed to enough temptations tonight. "He's going to help us get closer to the naturi that are in the region. And if it becomes necessary, he can get me closer to Aurora."

"As her prisoner!"

"Possibly, but it's better than nothing. The queen needs to be destroyed, but we don't know how to find her. Even exiled, I have little doubt that Rowe can find his wife-queen in his sleep."

"That's insane," Danaus said, slowly pushing to his feet. Instead of rising with him, I turned and sat down in the bloody snow and mud. My leg throbbed but was mostly healed. The only lycanthropes in the woods were a good distance off, but we weren't alone. I could feel his energy permeating the air, filling the night like a heavy, perfumed fog. Only Danaus was blissfully unaware of it, and I wanted to keep it that way.

"Head back to the main clearing where we first met," I said. "Stefan and Valerio should be dragging Ferko back there."

"What about you?"

"I'll be right behind you. I just need to rest and clean up this mess."

"Grab a bite?" Danaus said in a nasty voice.

"Not from the dead. Besides, we ruined their blood for anyone else. I'll burn the bodies and then be right behind you."

Danaus started to walk back in the direction he had come from and then paused after a few feet. "And Rowe?"

"He won't be back tonight. We'll track him down soon, I promise."

"He needs to be taken care of. He's too dangerous to leave alive," Danaus said as he resumed his walk through the woods, the darkness immediately swallowing him up so that he was little more than a disembodied voice.

"I know," I whispered. Rowe *was* too dangerous to leave alive. I might have once hoped to use him, but that wasn't going to work. His only goal was to buy his way back into Aurora's good graces, and his only way of achieving that was through me. I couldn't take the chance.

Unfortunately, I had bigger concerns waiting for me in the darkness. I was on a deadline to learn to control Danaus's powers, and I was getting better at it. I could still feel the hunter fighting me, but in each situation he decided not to pull away. We had been desperate, surrounded. There had been no choice if we had any hope of surviving to see the next night.

Bending my right knee in front of me, I rested my right elbow on it and threaded my fingers through my disheveled hair. "What the hell do you want now? I did as you asked. I used his powers instead of my own."

"And I am so proud of you," Nick crooned, suddenly appearing before me in the form of my father. The snow crunched beneath his feet as he approached me with a slow, steady gait. It was like he had all the time in the world. We were in a dark, snowy forest surrounded by nightwalkers and lycanthropes. Now wasn't the time for a little family reunion, but then my life didn't matter to him.

"What do you want?"

"Just to tell you that you're close. You just need to try a little harder," Nick said.

"Try harder?" With my right hand, I tried to push to my feet, but with a slight wave of his hand Nick knocked me back down on my butt. I sat, balling my fists in the snow, barely suppressing the urge to hurl a fireball at him. I was getting over the fact that he looked exactly like my father. There were small differences now that my brain was beginning to pick out. He didn't walk the same. His gait was too confident and relaxed, as if he were lord and master of all that he saw. There was a twist to his thin lips that made him look like he was just about to flash a smug smile in my direction. And his eyes. They weren't the soft, loving brown that I remembered. Nick's eyes were the same shade of purple as mine. Maybe we were father and daughter, but that wasn't going to stop me from trying to fry his ass the first chance I got.

"You're struggling to maintain your hold over the would-be bori," he said. "If he were to really fight you, you'd lose your grip on his powers. That's not going to do you any good. And what if he comes at you with an attempt to control you? Do you even know how to fight him off?"

"He hasn't tried to control me. We've come to an understanding, which I am continuously breaking just to keep you happy," I snapped.

"My dear, you aren't trying to keep me happy. You're trying to save your own skin."

"Whatever. At this point it's the same thing."

"True." Nick shrugged, shoving his hands into the pockets of his dark pants. "But I'm not happy yet. Get a firm control on the hunter and then you need to go after the nightwalker."

"Jabari?" I asked, my voice cracking.

"He's the only one left that can directly control you. That nonsense needs to be stopped now before one of them discovers what you are truly capable of," Nick commanded, his expression growing grim for the first time. "I will not have you running rampant through the streets when you should be at my beck and call."

"Like an obedient dog," I growled as I struggled back to my feet. Reaching out with my mind, I tapped into all the blood magic that I could sense swirling in the air from the nearby nightwalkers and lycanthropes. I reached farther for the souls of the humans that lay slumbering in the nearby villages. I stretched for any creature with a soul and tapped that energy.

Holding my hands out to my sides, I summoned up two balls of fire that snapped and crackled with all the raw energy I could handle. I hurled them at Nick, willing them to not only hit his body but stick like tree sap to a leaf. I encased the creature in flames that grew to the point where it licked at the tops of trees and sent down a rain of melted snow. Clenching my eyes closed, I focused the energy on burning through flesh and eating through bone. I aimed for what I could sense of the creature's soul, trying to use the soul energy of others to destroy his.

I held the energy focused on him until my body trembled from exhaustion and I grew light-headed. With great reluctance, I released him, hoping to find that I had reduced him to mere ash. I didn't want to sense him in the area. I wanted to wipe him from existence. But he was a god and I wasn't strong enough.

A white skeleton stood before me with its morbidly grim smile mocking me. It seemed to shiver once, and in a matter of seconds, muscles, organs, tissue, and skin all grew back over him. Clothes came next, so that in less than a minute he stood before me again exactly as he had been before my fit of temper. Behind him the earth was scorched with trees reduced to thin black timbers.

"Now it's my turn," Nick said, and my stomach jolted in fear. Like an orchestra conductor, my father raised both of his hands. At the same time, it felt as if my soul had been lifted out of my body. I tried to open my mouth to scream in terror, but I no longer had a mouth to scream out of as my body went limp and dead to the ground. The world swirled around me, becoming pure energy. If Nick released his hold on my soul, I knew I would float away, never finding my way back to my body. Would this be death? Or something worse? Trapped forever between this world and the next, a part of nothing.

"I am not the bori or the naturi that can so easily be destroyed with your meager skills," Nick snarled. "I am a god and you cannot harm me. You have been given the great gift of my limited patience. Do not waste it."

I felt more than saw Nick lower his hands again, placing my soul back into my body. I curled up on the ground in the fetal position as if I could tighten my hold on my soul. "Lucky me," I muttered, looking down at the snow.

Nick was on me in a flash. Kneeling before me, he tightly gripped my face in one hand so that his fingernails dug into my cheeks. I could feel the blood streaking down my face and dripping down on my stomach and legs. He lifted my face so I was staring him directly in the eyes. They were two massive voids swirling around, nearly enveloping all of my thoughts and emotions. I gasped and tried to pull away from him. His power surrounded me and consumed me until I felt I was losing my grip on my very soul. He was everything, everywhere.

"You have no idea how lucky you have been," he snarled. "My patience wears thin. Control Danaus and Jabari: this is your last warning."

I blinked once, trying to nod, but he was already gone. I slowly let my eyes travel over the dark forest. There were no sounds beyond the clack of dead branches stirred to life by the wind. Around me were the dead bodies of the lycanthropes I had killed using Danaus. Their blood had cooled and there was the faint scent of burned flesh hanging fetid in the crisp night air. I still had to dispose of the bodies and burn around the blood-soaked snow. But for now, I didn't feel like moving. Nick was watching my every move, and Danaus's life hung in the balance. If I was going to keep him alive, I would have to make him my puppet.

Eighteen

F erko looked like shit. He had been beaten, stabbed, and dragged through the forest by Valerio and Stefan. When I arrived at the clearing again, the two vampires were flanking the lycanthrope as he kneeled in the center with his hands hanging limp at his sides. A deep cut slashed across his brow, dripping blood into his right eye. Meanwhile, his left eye was swollen shut, keeping him blind to his surroundings. Not that it mattered. His other senses were still keen and he knew the second that I arrived when he deeply inhaled my scent.

"Any trouble?" Valerio asked.

"Nothing important." I shrugged, pushing thoughts of Rowe and Nick to the back of my mind. This was supposed to be a hunt for werewolves, and those two had decided to join in the fun uninvited. Standing with my legs spread before the lycanthrope, I placed my hands on my hips and fought the urge to kick him under the chin. I restrained myself, barely.

"How many are left?" I asked, looking up at Stefan.

"Three, maybe four. Do you want us to hunt them down?" He smiled at me with frightening eagerness. Stefan loved his bloodshed, but then so did most nightwalkers.

I waved my hand, brushing off the question. "Don't bother," I muttered, turning my attention back to Ferko. "Hear that? You started with sixteen shifters and now there are only a handful of you left in all of Budapest. This could have been settled quietly. Lives could have been spared, but you chose to go this route."

"You have no business in Budapest," Ferko said in a rough, gravel-filled voice.

"The naturi are here. That makes it my business. But we have a more pressing matter." I glanced over at Stefan, who tightened his grip on Ferko's neck. The werewolf flinched, twisting in the nightwalker's grasp. "It seems that Stefan's assistant has gone missing in Budapest."

"What the hell do I care if someone has gone missing?" the werewolf snarled. "What the hell does that have to do with me?"

"A lot. Veyron pointed us in your direction."

"Bastard," Ferko muttered under his breath.

Stefan gave his prisoner a hard shake, making sure he had his full attention. "Her name is Michelle. She is a nightwalker with brown hair and brown eyes. Her hair hangs down past her waist. She is delicate. You would remember if you saw her."

Ferko laughed. "You think I'm going to remember some random girl?"

Stefan slammed his fist into the back of Ferko's skull, knocking him flat on his face. The werewolf shook his head slowly as he struggled to push back into a seated position with a low groan.

"You would remember her!" Stefan shouted, losing the last of his grip on his temper. "She is exquisite, like a dream. Dark hair, dark eyes, and pure white skin. She's a nightwalker. You would remember her!"

"When did she come into town?" he asked, finally taking the inquiry seriously.

"Weeks ago!"

As I started to walk by Ferko, I slammed my knee into his jaw, knocking him back to the ground while walking around to stand next to Stefan. Valerio stepped away, wandering over toward Danaus, lingering close in case Ferko did something truly stupid like attack me. I laid my hand on Stefan's shoulder, but he jerked out from my touch while a low growl rumbled in the back of his throat. He wasn't in the mood for any comfort from me, which meant he wasn't going to like the other part of my so-called brilliant plan.

We'll find her, I tried to silently reassure him.

You mean, we'll find her dead body, he snapped back at me.

I bit back a sigh and didn't deny it. At this point we'd be lucky if we found her body at all. She had been missing for a while now, and Budapest wasn't the friendliest city I'd ever visited. My growing concern was that we wouldn't be able to find the actual culprit in this rotating fun house of horrors. First we met the sensual Odelia, and then the power-hungry Veyron. It didn't ease my mind that we had Macaire lurking about, eager to offer a helping hand. And now the unlucky Ferko, who was not only doing the grunt work for Veyron, but also taking on all of the blame. This couldn't be the arrangement that the lycanthrope originally signed on for, and we had to find a way to use that to our advantage.

We need to leave him alive, I said reluctantly to Stefan.

The nightwalker jerked a step away from me, pinning his dark gaze on my face. *Are you insane? He may have killed her. If not him, then one of his people.*

Probably so, but we need him in order to get closer to Veyron. It's the only way to catch everyone in this twisted

*power dynamic. There's a warlock out there that's working
with the lycans as well. I want them all.*

So be it, he snarled at me as he stalked off a few yards.
Just so long as I kill him before we leave Budapest.

Agreed.

I walked back around so I was standing in front of Ferko,
who growled at me like a wounded dog. "Is this the agreement that you had in mind when you went in with Veyron?
Sacrifice your people? Get yourself killed just so he could
be the big bad vampire in Budapest? He wanted you for his
enforcer so you could do all his dirty work?"

"You don't know anything," Ferko said stubbornly.

"Really? Then enlighten me." I slipped my hands into
the back pockets of my pants as I came to stand before the
shifter. "Seems like you're getting the raw end of this deal.
You're going to die while he gets away without a care."

"What do you want from me? Names? Dates? The total
betrayal of everything? I'm no snitch."

I sighed, my shoulders slumping under the weight of
too many long nights with no real answers. Glancing up at
Stefan, I found the nightwalker growing more impatient by
the second. I thought he was getting closer to the realization
that he wasn't going to get his Michelle back, but he at least
needed the culprit behind her disappearance and death.

"Hasn't he already betrayed you? He singled out the lycanthropes for the disappearance of Michelle. Lycanthropes
attacked Danaus today, trying to kill me. Did you actually
think you would escape unscathed from such acts?"

"One can hope," he said, looking up at me with a lopsided
smile.

"You're no help to me. Kill him," I said, weary. I turned
on my heel to look at Danaus, who was watching me with
dark eyes. The hunter made no move to stop either me or

Stefan. Valerio leaned against a nearby tree, picking dirt and dried blood out from under his fingernails.

"No! Wait!" Ferko shouted suddenly. "Odelia sent me after the woman."

I turned back to face him, raising one hand to halt Stefan, who was holding the man with both hands around his neck. If Ferko had hesitated any longer, the nightwalker would have snapped his neck before we could procure this interesting and surprising bit of information. Odelia had struck me as another of Veyron's flunkies. She didn't have any particularly special standing within the nightwalker community other than being somewhat old. The true power, in my mind, had always been linked to Veyron. He was the oldest, strongest, and most powerful in the region.

"Odelia? Not Veyron?" I asked.

"Odelia likes the fact that she's the most beautiful of all those in the city. She doesn't like having competition," Ferko said quickly. "The bitch had two of my own females killed because of their looks. When this brunette showed up unexpectedly in town, Odelia didn't care that she was only passing through. She wanted her dead."

"So she requested that your people take care of her," Stefan said.

"Requested?" Ferko snorted. "You make it sound like we had a choice. Between Veyron and Odelia, we didn't have much choice in the matter if we wanted to continue to run in the city."

"You tracked Michelle down and killed her," I finished, my throat tightening around the words. The nightwalker had done nothing more than come into town so she could pick up a package for Stefan. She had been eliminated because she was simply too beautiful to live where Odelia was concerned.

"Where is she?" Stefan demanded in a trembling voice.

"Dead."

Stefan kicked the lycanthrope in the back, knocking him to the ground again. "I understand that! Where is her body?"

"Burned," Ferko admitted, slowly pushing back into a sitting position. "It's the only way to be sure that one of your kind isn't going to rise again. Her ashes were spread around these woods."

Stefan looked up at me, shaking his head. I could see the pain in his eyes. He couldn't stay here and not kill Ferko. And I couldn't blame him. If I had been in his shoes, I would have already ripped the werewolf's heart from his chest. Of course, I didn't think the werewolf deserved such a quick death. He deserved to suffer for the death of Michelle, and if I had any say in the matter, he would before we left Budapest.

Just give me a little more time, I begged Stefan.

So long as he is mine before we leave Budapest.

You can have Odelia as well if you would like.

Throw in a seat on the coven and I might not have to kill you myself, Stefan said, causing one corner of my mouth to twitch with a morbid laugh.

Agreed.

Stefan's eyebrows jumped as he looked at me, surprised by my promise. The nightwalker said no more after that, not waiting to spoil his sudden good luck. He simply disappeared into the darkness, leaving us to handle Michelle's murderer.

"Tell me about the warlock who was with your kinsmen during the day and I'll consider sparing your life," I said.

Ferko turned his face up to me, frowning. I doubted whether he could actually see me through his blurred vision, but I could tell he was considering my offer. He had to know that his life was dangling by a thin thread. "Warlock?"

"Oh, don't start playing dumb with me again," I huffed. "We were making such progress."

Ferko shook his head, turning his face back to the ground again. His shoulders were slumped and his breathing was labored. His body was having trouble healing all the wounds we had inflicted on him despite the full moon. Of course, if it hadn't been a full moon, I seriously doubted that he would have been able to survive. Valerio and Stefan liked to play rough.

I paced away from Ferko, walking over toward Danaus. Valerio looked up from his fingernails and pushed off from the tree with a jerk of my head. He headed over to our captive and took up Stefan's position behind Ferko. While Valerio might not like to get his hands dirty, he was still very good at it. If I gave the slightest indication that I wanted Ferko dead, Valerio would not only happily carry out my wish, but also make sure it was a particularly slow and painful death.

"I've been around for quite a while, Ferko," I started again, trying a different approach. "I've known nightwalkers and lycanthropes to work together on the rare occasion. I've known nightwalkers to rarely work with warlocks and witches. But this is a first. Warlocks don't generally get along with shifters. They see you as just a bunch of filthy, uncivilized animals that can't control your basic urges. Why would a warlock possibly want to work with your kind?"

"Maybe this one sees you as being less desirable to have around than a pack of animals," Ferko sneered.

"Maybe," I admitted. "I've pissed off my fair share of warlocks, but I have to say that I haven't been in this part of the world in a long time. I don't know who would find my presence undesirable."

"No one wants you to be the keeper here," Ferko said. "You don't belong here."

"And trust me, I don't want to be keeper here, but some-one has to rein in the chaos in this area before it leaks across the rest of Europe. Not every nightwalker is going to prove to be as tolerant as me."

"Tolerant? You've destroyed my pack!" he snarled, baring his fangs at me. Power filled the air so that the scent of the woods grew even thicker. Valerio leaned forward and clipped the werewolf behind the ear. The lycanthrope collapsed in a limp heap at my feet, unconscious.

"Valerio!" I shouted, throwing my hands up in frustration. I wasn't even close to being done interrogating our prisoner. I needed to know more about the warlock that was apparently working with the lycans, and by extension, the nightwalkers. This kind of collaboration wasn't something that set me at ease. Sure, at one time in my own domain my own people had gotten along with the lycanthropes, and I had a scattering of associates that were witches and warlocks. But this arrangement in Budapest was distinctly different and completely unsettling. The warlocks and ly-canthropes were acting as muscle for the nightwalkers during the daylight hours, extending that species' power more than it should have.

"Sorry," he said sheepishly, flashing me a weak smile. "I don't know my own strength sometimes."

"Is he still alive?"

"Yes," Valerio said, sounding put off that I would think he had so little control. "He's just unconscious. I am assuming that you want him awake when I kill him. Or should I call Stefan back? I'm sure he'd be happy to finish off this fleabag."

"Leave him alive. I promised him to Stefan later. Right now, we need him conscious so we can get more information out of him. I need to know who this warlock is."

Valerio sighed as he stepped over Ferko's unconscious

form and started to walk over to where he had left his coat folded over a tree limb. "We don't need him for that."

"Of course we do," I snapped, trailing behind him. "The lycans that attacked Danaus during the day were accompanied by a warlock."

"The night that we met with Veyron, Mira and I were attacked by a magic user," Danaus interjected. "I'm willing to bet that it's the same one. A city generally doesn't have that many powerful magic users on hand."

Valerio turned and arched one eyebrow at us as he pulled on his coat. "Agreed. Warlocks aren't very good at sharing. However, in this town, I would be reluctant to make such an assumption. It seems like everyone is working together here."

"Too true. Nightwalkers directing lycanthropes. Warlocks protecting lycanthropes."

"I'm surprised that they haven't also struck a deal with the naturi," Danaus added, earning a dark look from me. We didn't need to discuss potential deals with the naturi. We had already been down that route and the outcome was never pretty. The last time such a thing was spoken of, I ended up on the coven.

"The naturi don't like to make deals," I said. "Besides, Rowe's running around the city with his own personal band of followers. Their only agenda is to get their hands on me so they can hand me over to Aurora. He's not going to be into making deals with anyone. At least, I hope not."

"Unlikely," Valerio agreed.

"Thanks," I grumbled, but then turned my attention back to our problem at hand. With the toe of my scuffed black boot, I turned Ferko over so he was lying awkwardly on his back with one arm trapped under his body. His mouth was slack as blood trickled out of the corner and dripped onto the melting snow. "What about the warlock?"

"It's likely that it's Clarion," Valerio stated.

"Clarion? I'm afraid I've never heard of him."

"He's given me a little trouble in Vienna. He's a power-ful warlock who is based in Budapest, but he's come around some of the other big cities surrounding Budapest, looking to expand the reach of his . . . domain," Valerio said, strug-gling for the right word.

Warlocks and witches were not known for having a domain. They tended to settle in a central location for a time, and operated exclusively in that region until they either died, grew bored, or were run off by someone more power-ful. They didn't have followers or minions like nightwalkers or lycanthropes. And they didn't try to expand the reach of their home territory. This didn't sound good at all, and it clearly explained why Valerio was interested in this little trip to Budapest. It was a chance to make a grab at his an-noying neighbor, possibly scaring him into a new location if he didn't simply kill him.

"So you think that Clarion is the one working with the nightwalkers and lycanthropes?" Danaus asked.

Valerio gave a noncommittal shrug. "Possibly. Did you get a good look at him?"

"No, not at all. Just say a vague outline in the darkness." Danaus shoved his hands into the pockets of his long leather coat as he frowned at the vampire. "In the hotel room, I was too worried about keeping the lycanthropes away from where I *thought* Mira was. I could only sense his power in the air, marking him as a warlock."

"On the way to Veyron's, I got only a glimpse of the figure on the rooftop. No details," I admitted with no small amount of frustration. "But what are the odds that there is more than one powerful warlock in the region?"

"Pretty good, unfortunately," Valerio stated, pulling a growl out of me. I felt like I had stepped in quicksand. With every movement, I was getting sucked further down into the thickening insanity that permeated every inch of the dark occult side of Budapest. I was seriously beginning to long for my home of Savannah—away from Veyron, his flunkies, and the schemes of Macaire, which I had yet to figure out.

"How is that possible?" Danaus demanded. "I didn't think warlocks and witches played well together. Too territorial. Even more so than nightwalkers and lycanthropes."

"It's true, but this one seems to have found someone that he does get along well with. I have encountered Clarion only a few times during the past several years, but I had heard that he doesn't work alone. There's another magic user that he associates with here in Budapest. Unfortunately, I don't know whether it's a warlock or a witch yet. I can't gauge the creature's strength, but can only guess that he or she is at least as powerful as Clarion or he wouldn't bother with this creature."

"You mean, he would have either killed the person or pressured him or her out of the region already," I said.

"True."

"So what's our next step? Do we go after Veyron?" Danaus asked. "It doesn't take a rocket scientist to deduct that he sent a hit squad after you," he added, bringing a frown to my lips. "You were expecting him to send some people after you."

"Yes, but the problem is that I was expecting him to send humans with big guns and wooden stakes, not a pack of werewolves with a warlock as backup. That makes this whole situation more complicated, Mr. Rocket Scientist," I said, not caring how bitchy I was starting to sound. We were all getting more than a little frustrated by Veyron and his minions, and that didn't get us any closer to taking care of the naturi infestation we were originally sent to take care of. I might have let Rowe slip through my fingers tonight, but

I wasn't through with the one-eyed naturi. I wasn't going before Aurora again unless I had an edge that would finally take the naturi queen down. In the meantime, I needed to take care of Rowe so he wasn't constantly at my back with a knife.

"We first need to understand the power structure in Budapest." Valerio artfully wrapped his dark red scarf around his neck, showing the same skill as when he tied a cravat a few centuries ago just prior to our attending the various balls and soirees that filled our evenings together in Europe. "If we aren't careful, we could kill a simple pawn, which would leave the bulk of the power structure intact and us vulnerable to retaliation."

"Agreed. We need to be sure we take them all out before we leave Budapest," I said, smirking at his close attention to his scarf. Valerio shrugged, unmoved by my teasing.

Danaus frowned at us both, determined not to be distracted. "Could that be what Macaire planned all along? Why he's here now? If we destroy the reigning power players in Budapest, it will leave it vulnerable enough for him to move in and take over."

"I doubt it was his plan since he prefers to stay close to Venice," I replied.

Valerio reached into his pockets and pulled out a pair of supple leather gloves, which he proceeded to pull on. "Besides, Mira has spoiled that plan by claiming Budapest as her own. She may not truly want it, but she is the keeper of this domain now. As keeper, it's her responsibility to clean out old management."

"Which you approve of," Danaus sneered. "Being as Budapest is so close to Vienna and you're sure that Mira won't encroach on your territory."

"You make it sound like it's awful that I approve of Mira's new acquisition. Of course I like having her close at hand once again." Valerio paused and narrowed his dark eyes on the hunter as a wicked grin spread across his full lips. "Mira and I have a long history. It would be nice to have her around again."

Danaus took a step forward, his hand dropping down to his waist where I knew he kept an assortment of knives. Valerio was taunting him, seeing how far he could push Danaus. I had no doubt that he was also testing how far my relationship with Danaus went. The Ancient nightwalker smiled at the hunter, his fangs peeking out from under his upper lip. I didn't have time for this chest beating and territorial pissing. We needed to find Clarion.

"Enough!" I shouted, placing a hand on both their chests. "I need to find Clarion. Do you have any useful suggestions?"

Valerio laid his hand over mine, stroking my fingers in an attempt to annoy Danaus just a little bit more. I was about to smash my fist into his jaw. Instead I shoved. Valerio simply stood there, smiling down at me. "A coffeehouse called Gerbeaud Cukrászda," he said. "It's been around for ages and is located in Central Pest between the Chain Bridge and the Elizabeth Bridge. Any taxi driver should be able to locate it with no problems. I can come along—"

"No," I said sharply, causing his smile to widen. I was beginning to think that he and Danaus had spent more than enough time together. I knew that I had already spent enough time with Valerio. This was a case of too much of a good thing. "There are naturi hanging out on one of the islands in the Danube. Last I saw, there were three islands in the region. I want you to go check them out."

"This is my punishment. Taking on the naturi alone?" he demanded incredulously.

"Would I be so cold?"

"Yes."

I smiled up at my friend for the first time, shaking my head. "I'm not asking you to hunt the naturi. I simply want you to locate them for me. Find which island they have claimed as their own. It will be easier for the four of us to hunt them down if we are sure of their ultimate location. Don't engage if you can help it. Meet us later tonight back at my hotel room."

"Aren't you planning to change hotel rooms? Or are you planning to stay with me in Vienna?"

"I'm staying at the Gellért," I said. "I'm not leaving Budapest again until this mess has been cleaned up."

"It's not safe."

"Danaus will be there. I'll be safe."

"As you wish," Valerio said with an easygoing shrug of his broad shoulders. He took a single step backward away from Danaus and me before disappearing from sight. I looked forward to the day when I attained that ability. It would be so much easier than trying to grab a car or a plane or any other vehicle to get from point A to point B.

My eyes strayed over to Danaus's face and I winced inwardly. The hunter was not happy with me, and it was most likely Valerio's fault. Of course, Danaus could also still be upset over my choice to control him than use my own powers. My excuse had been extraordinarily thin and weak. I didn't think he actually bought it, but then I had been desperate and we weren't exactly in the best spot to discuss it. To my glee, we still weren't. The night was fading away and we still had to locate Clarion.

"I know." I sighed. "He's a complete pain in the ass."

"Reminds me of someone else I know."

"Yeah, well, that could be a long list. You'll have to narrow it down for me." We glared at each other before finally turning in separate directions. I looked over at Ferko to find that he had yet to move from where he lay. I didn't expect him to be unconscious much longer. He'd eventually pick himself up and scurry back off to Veyron to complain about the slaughter of his people. If Ferko was lucky, our destruction of the local pack might succeed in drawing out a few of the nightwalkers. I had a sinking feeling that this entire town needed to be thinned out. Veyron and his gang had a negative influence on everyone there, like a sickness eating away at the brain tissue.

"How is Valerio going to track down the naturi if he can't sense them?" Danaus asked, surprising me with his concern.

I smiled up at my companion as we trudged back through the woods toward the car we had stolen shortly after sunset. "He's a smart guy. He'll figure it out. A place where the humans have been murdered at an alarming rate, a heavily wooded area, or just a place where humans are afraid to tread. That's enough to ferret out the naturi."

"You're using humans as a guide?"

"Sure, they've got a natural sixth sense about danger."

"Then why do they flock to vampires?"

"I never said they were very good about listening to it. Besides, we're not trying to kill them, just feed off them. The naturi are the ones that actually want them dead."

"Nice rationale," Danaus said as he walked around to the driver's side and opened the door.

"Yeah, I thought so."

Danaus paused, standing next to the car with the door open. He stared at me over the roof of the little car. "We're hunting a warlock?"

"We're just going to have a nice little chat over coffee," I corrected with a shaky smile. I was beginning to think that Valerio had the easier task. For a brief moment I thought about reaching out to Stefan and requesting that he come along. However, I pushed the idea away as I climbed into the stolen car. Stefan needed some time to cool off and get back in control of his temper. As surprising as it was to me, he had lost someone important to him simply because she was beautiful. Michelle deserved better than that, and Stefan was determined to give it to her. He would need to kill both Odelia and Ferko to have his revenge. Unfortunately, to help him succeed, I first needed to deal with a warlock that was determined to see me dead.

Nineteen

Gerbeaud Cukrászda was stunning. I'd grown accustomed to cramped, dark little coffeehouses with people hunched over laptops or hiding behind a newspaper. But Gerbeaud Cukrászda was an old traditional Hungarian coffeehouse with its enormous arched windows looking out onto the city. Gold gilt and crystal chandeliers hung from domed ceilings, casting the room in a warm glow. Along the walls were rich wood sideboards that held delicate pieces of ancient china with slightly faded patterns, worn by the massive passage of time.

The coffeehouse was crowded, with people relaxing at small round tables laden with their coffee and frothy pastries that left me briefly longing for my more humans days when I craved things like sugar, milk, and airy whipped cream. Where coffeehouses in the United States were little dens of caffeine sin, Gerbeaud Cukrászda was a palace dedicated to the ancient art of coffee and decadence.

Danaus and I arrived looking as if we had just survived a fight for our lives. Our clothes were torn, dirty, and splattered with blood. I shoved one hand through my hair, trying vainly to smooth it back and into some semblance of order.

Danaus smiled at me, catching my eye in a nearby mirror. "You look vibrant," he said in a low voice, causing me to smile as well. He was being far too kind. We both looked a mess and had no business walking into such a civilized setting, but there was nothing that could be done about it. The night was still young, and the longer we remained in Budapest without taking care of this nonsense, the more dangerous it became.

It was tempting to cover us in a light glamour so people wouldn't notice our disheveled appearances, but I decided that it just wasn't worth the energy. Instead I turned my attention to scanning the beautiful restaurant for the one that would most likely prove to be Clarion.

He wasn't hard to spot. At the far end of the room was a man sitting at a table alone with a leather-bound book in one hand. He wore a fashionable suit with a dark blue and gray tie. I had little doubt that this person was Clarion. However, what I did find disturbing was that he wasn't the only magic user in the room. In fact, a quick scan of the coffeehouse revealed at least seven other magic users of varying power strengths in the room, though none was anywhere near as strong. Apparently, Danaus and I had stumbled upon a favorite watering hole for warlocks and witches. Fabulous. Simply fabulous.

I had known that this very public gathering would be a mix of talking, coercion, and grandstanding, but I didn't expect that I would be the one outnumbered at this gathering. If I had learned anything in my six centuries, it was that one did not go picking fights with powerful warlocks and witches, and never in their own territory.

Keep your temper and your weapons to yourself, I warned Danaus as I started to weave my way through the tables toward Clarion.

I can manage it. Can you? he taunted.

I was going to try, but I had my doubts. Ferko, Rowe, and Nick had all managed to push my buttons that evening. I suspected that Clarion was going to be happy to do the same once we sat down with him. He had every reason to suspect that he had the upper hand in our little game of cat and mouse. Danaus and I were the outsiders, while he was part of something far larger, which was attempting to kill me and my companions.

When we got within a dozen feet of the table, Clarion closed his book and laid it on the table as he turned to face us. He rose smoothly from his chair, running his hands over his jacket as if to brush away any nonexistent wrinkles. He smiled benignly at us while his dark brown eyes twinkled with some ill-concealed laughter, as if he held some secret delight that we did not yet know about.

"Clarion?" I asked as we drew closer.

"You must be Mira and Danaus," he said in heavily accented English. "Forgive me, but I noticed your entrance. Or rather, your scan of Gerbeaud. I naturally assumed you were looking for me." He motioned for us to take the two empty seats at his table while he resumed his seat.

"Do you frequently receive visitors here that search for you in such a manner?" I inquired politely as I took a seat opposite him. It was a struggle to ignore the grass stains on my shirt and the tear in my pants near my thigh as I sat across from Clarion in his tidy suit and precise manners.

Picking up the spoon from its place on his saucer, Clarion stirred his coffee a couple times before taking a sip. "Frequently? No. But I am aware of my standing in the community, and I would be the one you were most likely seeking in this place in such a manner."

I swallowed my next question as a server came over and

took Danaus's coffee order while I waved him off. Rowe and Nick had already pressed me to my breaking point, and I was in no mood to pretend to be human tonight.

"And I also deduced that it would only be natural for you to seek me out following your recent claim on Budapest," Clarion continued. "Congratulations."

"So you've heard already," I said, sitting back in my chair.

"Budapest may be a large city, but the supernatural community remains relatively small. Word travels fast," he said with yet another smug smile.

"I find myself reluctant to agree that the supernatural community is really all that small. Though it's a bit smaller now," Danaus interjected in a low voice that brought a smirk to my own lips.

"Since coming to Budapest," I said, "I've noticed that there is a large gathering of nightwalkers here, the Budapest pack was relatively large, and besides yourself there are at least half a dozen magic users in this coffeehouse alone. Not a bad showing for a town of any size."

"Forgive me, but what do you mean the Budapest pack *was* relatively large?" Clarion inquired, his hand stilling on his coffee cup.

"My companions and I are in town for a variety of reasons," I said, brushing some dirt off the leg of my pants. "One of them was related to the disappearance of a nightwalker. After some inquiries, we discovered that members of the local pack killed her. Retribution was meted out tonight and the Budapest pack has been nearly exterminated."

"Exterminated?"

"The pack has been culled, reduced, eradiated, destroyed," Danaus supplied.

"And you felt that this action was necessary?" Clarion asked, his brow furrowing as he sat back in his chair.

I shook my head, forcing a frown onto my mouth. "Unfortunately, yes. Pack alpha Ferko refused to cooperate with us, so we had to hunt down anyone who might have been involved with the murder of a poor nightwalker. We had to be sure that her death was avenged. Surely you understand?"

"Naturally," Clarion replied. "And have you completed your investigation into the matters regarding Budapest?"

"Not quite. Danaus and I have come to Gerbeaud to speak with you regarding a few minor little things."

Danaus placed his cup of coffee back on its saucer and turned his full attention to the warlock. "Being as you are obviously tuned into the supernatural happenings of Budapest, you should be able to provide us with some valuable information, which will help to shorten our stay within the city. The sooner we can fix matters here, the sooner we can leave."

"Are you in a hurry to leave? It's a shame that you're not enjoying your stay in our beautiful city."

"My time in Budapest has been entertaining," I said, "but my presence is needed in Venice with the coven. Once my duties to the coven are completed, Danaus and I hope to return to Budapest for a lengthy stay."

At that pronouncement, Clarion's smile wilted slightly, but he caught it quickly as he nodded to me. "Excellent. I'm sure your presence here will have a positive influence on our little community. We tend to be a tight-knit group."

"So I've noticed," I murmured.

"What can I help you with?"

"The naturi," Danaus said.

For a moment Clarion looked genuinely confused, but I wasn't buying it. "I beg your pardon," he said, sitting up straighter in his chair.

"The naturi. Apparently they've infested the city. They're

hunting down nightwalkers and humans within the city," I clarified, but the warlock continued to shake his head at me.

"This is the first I have heard of it."

"That's a shame." I sighed. "They are dangerous group who are hoping to wipe out all of humanity and nightwalkers in an effort to protect the earth. In Budapest, it appears that the local naturi have rallied around a ruthless naturi by the name of Rowe. He has dark hair, scars, and wears an eye patch. You would definitely know him if you were to meet him."

"I know I would recall seeing someone by that description, but I have to admit that I have not," Clarion stated.

I don't believe him, Danaus said silently to me.

Nor I. Dead humans or nightwalkers wouldn't be a particularly bad thing for him.

"Really? Hmm . . . that is strange, because Veyron assured me that you would know where to find the naturi. They were the initial reason for our appearance within Budapest."

"Veyron directed you to me?" he said a bit stiffly as the last of the amusement was wiped clean from his face.

"You do know Veyron, correct?"

"Of course. He's a somewhat powerful figure among the nightwalkers. It is only natural that I am aware of him. However, our meetings have been extremely limited. I cannot imagine why he might think that I know where to find this naturi called Rowe."

"He probably believed that you would be aware of the naturi simply for your own safety," I said with a wave of my hand. I let my gaze drift away from the warlock to a trolley laden with chocolate confections that smelled heavenly. For a second I wondered if Nick was causing more problems for me. I hadn't craved food in centuries, but then I hadn't even been faced with such amazing delights before now. Besides, I was content to let Clarion dangle a little bit.

"What do the naturi have to do with my safety?" the warlock demanded, finally dragging my eyes back to his face.

I lowered my voice to a whisper and leaned in a little bit. "Well, even though you are a warlock, to the naturi you are first and foremost a human. And second, the naturi have a history of singling out blood warlocks for execution."

"How did you know?" he asked, surprised.

"That you're a blood warlock?" I finished with a smile. "I can taste it in your powers. It's quite easy to spot. You have to remember, I've been around the block for quite a long time. I've had plenty of time to learn a few tricks."

"And you think the naturi would single me out?" Clarion demanded, starting to sound concerned for the first time.

"Possibly." I shrugged and then turned my attention to Danaus. "How's your coffee?"

"Wonderful," he said, refilling his cup from the small ceramic pot that had been brought to the table. "We'll have to come back after everything has been settled."

"About the naturi," Clarion snapped, drawing my attention back to him.

"Yes, it's quite possible they might come after you. Judging the energy that is flowing about you, I wouldn't be surprised if they were drawn to you. You represent not only a power player within the city, but could also prove to be a protector of the humans. You're a speed bump on the way to their domination of Budapest. They would see you as someone they would need to get rid of."

"And what about you?" Clarion said gruffly, eager to refocus my attention.

I gave a little laugh as I relaxed in my chair. "Oh, Rowe has special plans regarding my extermination. He's been trying to kill me for years. I'm sure he'll get around to it eventually, but right now he's set his sights on Budapest."

Clarion drummed his fingers on the table, rattling his

spoon on his china cup and saucer. His brow was furrowed as he turned over the selection of information I had carefully dropped into his lap. Some of it was true, but for the most part it was pure fabrication. I was trying to push him into making a rash decision, or at the very least, into confronting Veyron. Either would benefit me.

"I'm afraid that I don't know anything about the naturi," Clarion announced after nearly a minute of silence. "However, considering they are nature-based creatures and they are trying to take over Budapest, I would say that your best place to look for them would be Margit Island, which can be reached using Margit Bridge. It's a beautiful garden park. Recently, there have been a rash of disappearances on the island, but I have not given it much thought. Every city has its occasional murder and floating body."

"Of course," I said a bit sarcastically. "Thank you for the suggestion. Danaus and I will look into it this evening. Hopefully, we will be able to rid the city of its naturi problem."

"That would be a great relief to everyone, I'm sure," Clarion said, gritting his teeth slightly. "Now, if you will excuse me. The hour grows late and there are a few small items that I need to see to."

"Actually there is one other matter that you should be able to help with," I said, laying my hand over his on the table in an effort to keep him from leaping to his feet. "It has to do with a warlock in Budapest that appears to be stirring up some trouble."

"That . . . that seems . . . unlikely." Clarion stammered a bit, as if struggling to find the right words.

"I know, but it is true. I thought I would contact you first since you are one of the more powerful warlocks in the region. I thought you might be able to point us in the right direction," I said.

A patronizing smile lifted the corners of Clarion's mouth as he sat back in his chair, sliding his hand out from my touch. "You're looking for me to hand over one of my own kind to you?" he asked, tilting his head.

"Are you going to suddenly act as if there is any true loyalty among warlocks and witches?" I mocked. "Come now. I've traveled the world, and everywhere I have visited, the warlocks and witches have adopted a type of to-each-his-own mentality. Are you going to risk your neck for someone else when you've done nothing wrong?"

"Maybe things are different in Budapest than the rest of the world," he suggested, but again I wasn't buying it. Things were extremely different in Budapest from the rest of the world, but I was willing to bet that the warlock/witch community wasn't.

"Well, I thought you might help me. If not, I am more than content to contact Ryan in London," I said. Dropping the name of the extremely powerful and dangerous warlock that was the head of Themis caused Danaus to softly rattle his cup and saucer together. "He's been more than happy to help me in the past, and I'm sure that he would be able to ferret out the culprit in short order."

Mira! Danaus said in a warning voice in my head.

There's no way he's heard about our falling out, I replied quickly. *Ryan's not going to advertise that he failed to lure me to his side, and for all he knows, I haven't turned on him yet. He's still the one with the extra special blood that I can't resist. I'm just trying to rattle Clarion into making a mistake.*

Just keep Ryan out of this. We don't need any more problems.

"Ryan? From Themis?" Clarion asked.

"Yes. He helped us in the past with the naturi and I have no doubt that he'd be happy to help me with my little problem with Budapest. He does tend to know most of the powerful warlocks in the region."

"What kind of a warlock problem do you seem to be having?"

"The murdering kind," I said, losing all lightness from my voice.

"Oh. That is a problem," Clarion said, his whole body seeming to go stiff.

"Yes," I hissed, leaning a little bit closer to him. "Recently when Danaus and I were traveling to visit with Veyron, a warlock attacked us on a busy street. He not only threatened our lives, but threatened to expose our secret world. Not exactly something that is acceptable in our little supernatural community."

"No, it's not."

"And then again today, my hotel room was attacked by three lycanthropes and a warlock. Danaus didn't get a clear look at the warlock, but he's confident he would be able to identify him under the right conditions. Naturally, an attempt on my life needs to be dealt with."

"That is a problem," Clarion stated again, rubbing his chin with his right hand. He didn't sound as concerned as he should have. I knew I was sitting across from my would-be assassin, and I was sure that Clarion knew that I suspected him. My goal was to get him to run back to Veyron for help. Or at the very least, draw his magic-using companion out of the shadows. I needed a clear picture of the power structure in Budapest before I attempted to dismantle it.

"So you see, if you can't help me, I have no choice but to draw Ryan into the matter. As a power player in the warlock community, I am sure that he will want to personally see to it that our supernatural nature is not exposed by a warlock."

"Very understandable. I cannot currently help you, but I ask that you give me a day to look into the matter. This is all news to me, and I would like to be of assistance," Clarion offered, taking my hand in both of his. Energy zipped around me and pummeled my flesh as if it were trying to enter my body. His growing anxiety was making it difficult for him to maintain his tight control over his powers. The air around us seemed to jump with a seeming electrical current. "I'm sure that Ryan would be eager to help, but with the naturi running loose, I have no doubt that he is very busy. Allow me to assist you."

"Of course," I said with a broad smile that exposed the points of my fangs. "We would greatly appreciate it. This city is becoming too dangerous between the naturi, the brutal lycans, and now a rogue warlock. It seems that I became keeper of the city just in time."

"Yes, it would seem so," Clarion agreed, releasing my hand. He glanced at the gold watch on his wrist, but I doubted that he actually saw the time. "If you would excuse me—"

"I understand," I said with a casual wave of my hand as if I were dismissing him. "You may go take care of your business. I think Danaus and I are going to linger here a few moments longer so he can partake of some more coffee and one of these amazing little desserts."

"Wonderful," Clarion said absently. "I will seek you out soon with some new information." He then stood, turned on his heel and walked briskly out of Gerbeaud Cukrászda without a backward glance. I sat back in my chair and stared across the large room at where I last saw him. He was rattled, and I wasn't sure which had him more disturbed: the threat of the naturi purposefully hunting him down or the idea of Ryan coming into the region to hunt him down for trying to kill me. Either way, the hangman's noose was dangling over his head.

With a soft sigh, I motioned for the server to bring Danaus

more coffee as I turned to look at my private defender. He was frowning at me, less than pleased with my handling of the conversation. Unfortunately, he couldn't voice his opinion here. There were more than a few warlocks and witches in the room who would be hanging on his every word. Of course, I had tried to use that arrangement to my advantage when I positioned Clarion so he would have to start naming names, betraying his fellow warlock. If he didn't take care of matters very quickly, he was going to become a pariah within the supernatural community.

He's going to come after you again, Danaus needlessly pointed out.

Undoubtedly.

Are you going back to Vienna during the day?

Only if you refuse to protect me.

I'm not sure I can effectively protect you against a warlock, he admitted.

I laid my hand on his and squeezed it. "Would you like to stay for something sweet?" I asked for the benefit of everyone listening in on our vocal conversation. If one of us didn't say something aloud soon, they would grow suspicious.

"No, I'm fine. I'd rather take care of Margit Island so we can get back to the hotel," Danaus said, fighting to keep from gritting his teeth as he glared at me. He wasn't happy. He was worried about my safety now that we had successfully backed a dangerous warlock into a corner.

"Finish your coffee and then we'll go. The night is still young," I said, forcing a smile on my lips.

I continued our original conversation. *He might not come after me tomorrow. He may want to have a few words with Veyron first.*

He'll want to take care of you before you have a chance to contact Ryan. No one wants Ryan involved, Danaus countered.

That was an accurate assessment if I ever heard one. I had pulled Ryan into my problems once, in the belief that he could actually help me and I could keep the situation under my control. I had been seriously wrong and it nearly cost me my life and Tristan's. Ryan was too dangerous, especially when he claimed to be helping. Danaus and I were far better off if the warlock remained permanently out of our lives, but I didn't think even that was possible. He was going to come back to haunt us eventually.

But for now, we had bigger problems to deal with in the form of Rowe and his fellow exiled compatriots. It was time to clean house.

Twenty

The winter wind swept across the Margit Bridge, causing the waters of the Danube to whitecap. Snow swirled through the air in a lurid dance through the shafts of light thrown down by the iron lampposts. Danaus and I caught a cab from Gerbeaud Cukrászda to the Margit Bridge that led from Pest to Buda, connecting the two parts of the city with the island in the middle of the river. Margit Island was sparsely illuminated, and bare trees rose up from it like skeletal hands clawing at the night sky. A full moon drifted in and out from behind thick clouds that threatened to bring down a fresh blanket of snow.

"We shouldn't have come directly here," Danaus murmured. The hunter stood beside me on the bridge entrance the led to the island. He held one gun in his fist while his other hand gripped the metal railing. "We need weapons."

"What do you have on you?" I asked, my gaze not wavering from the garden spread out before me. In the distance I could pick out the sidewalk walking trails around the edge of the island, while old monastic ruins rose up from the interior like cancerous growths.

"Two guns. A spare magazine for each. A few knives."

I jerked my head to the side so that I could look at him. "And that's not enough for us to handle this?"

"I'd prefer to have my sword, more ammo, and you armed with two guns as well," Danaus snapped at me. He was right. I had only a couple knives on me. When it came to facing the naturi, I would have preferred to have a gun in my hand regardless of how bad my aim was.

"We'll manage," I grumbled, but I still couldn't force myself to step forward onto the island. Upon reaching the bridge, Danaus had confirmed that Margit Island was where the bulk of the naturi horde was camping. We needed to clear them out of Budapest if we were to succeed in the mission that sent us to this city in the first place. More importantly, I needed to finally get rid of Rowe.

"How many are there?" I finally asked, when it was obvious I wasn't ready to move. Thanks to Nick, I could sense the distinct signature of naturi magic, but it was just a large cloud of energy centered on the island. I didn't have the skill Danaus did in being able to pick them out individually.

"You don't want to know."

I sighed, my head falling forward. I had heard those exact words before when we were faced with nearly insurmountable odds in England. Cornered at Themis, we were attacked by the naturi, who were intent on destroying both Jabari and me. Now I was walking willingly into the nest of naturi in hopes of finally destroying them. For some reason, I doubted they felt the same hesitance that I was feeling at that moment.

"What about Valerio? We could use the help," Danaus reminded me.

I nodded, relieved by the idea of having someone else there to help us. Closing my eyes, I wrapped both hands around the railing and focused on locating my old friend. But something was wrong. I had known Valerio for centuries. I could have located him across any distance at any time as long as it was night where we were both located. Now, however, the feel of him was so faint. It was as if . . . he were dying. I could feel him on the island, but his energy was so weak.

"Something is wrong," I gasped, starting to lurch forward. "The naturi have him."

Danaus grabbed my elbow, stopping me from running headlong into the darkness. "They're waiting for you to come to his rescue. Go running in there and they'll cut you down in seconds."

"They're killing him," I cried, jerking my arm out of his grasp.

"At least summon Stefan!" Danaus ordered before I could take another step closer to the island. "There are more than twenty naturi there, with that number potentially including Rowe. We've gone up against him a few times now and not had much luck killing him. With this many naturi, it's not going to be any easier to get to him."

Clenching my teeth, I forced myself to stop and focus on the Ancient nightwalker. Danaus was right. We would need Stefan's assistance if we were going to have any hope of retrieving Valerio. No words were needed. Just the lightest brush of my presence against the ragged remains of his soul brought Stefan to our side with a sour expression. He was still upset about the death of his assistant, and I would have preferred to leave him to brood alone, but I knew I wouldn't be able to free Valerio without his help.

"The naturi?" he asked.

"How did you know?" I said sarcastically, but needling Stefan still failed to bring a smile to my face.

"We slaughtered the lycans, I don't sense any nightwalkers or warlocks, and this barren garden would be a refuge for only the naturi if they were determined to stay close to the city and cause mischief," he said, ticking each item off on his long fingers.

"They have Valerio," Danaus announced, causing Stefan's expression to grow even darker. While I doubted that he felt any real concern for him, I suspected he was more upset about the fact that the naturi dare lay a hand on an old vampire such as Valerio. In his opinion, they were above such things as kidnapping and torture.

"I sent him to look into which island they were hiding on," I said, then shook my head. "He wasn't supposed to engage them. Just look around. I can only guess that they managed to sneak up on him."

Stefan stepped around me and walked down the bridge to Margit Island. "Then we should get in there and kill them."

Danaus and I followed close behind him, weapons drawn. As we came to stand at the southern tip of the island, I pulled one of my spare blades and offered it to Stefan. "Take it. I've got a little extra firepower."

"Lame, Mira. Lame," Stefan said, but he took the knife from me anyway. With his ability to appear and disappear, I thought about sending him for more weapons but decided against it. We couldn't waste more time.

"There are three paths. Danaus, take the one to the left. I'll take the center one up the middle of the island, while you take the one on the right," I said, with a nod toward Stefan. "Kill anything that isn't in our party."

"The one that reaches the other end of the island first, wins?" Stefan challenged with an evil grin.

"I was thinking the one with the highest body count," Danaus countered.

I growled, tightening my grip around the blade in my right hand. "How about the one that safely retrieves Valerio wins?"

Stefan rolled his eyes at me. "Not much of an objective."

"Kill the naturi and free Valerio. Winner gets Ferko," I sneered, finally putting the light back in Stefan's eyes. Now he was interested in playing this game. The Ancient nightwalker floated off the ground, his long coat fluttering around him like a pair of wings. He gave me a small salute and then darted off into the darkness to locate some naturi.

"See you at the finish line," Danaus said, then started down the path to my left, leaving me standing alone in the night with the naturi waiting for me.

I sucked in a deep breath and slowly expelled it, sending out a white fog in front of me. The air was bitter cold, tightening muscles and making my body resistant to movement, but it didn't matter. Soon, I wouldn't feel the cold or hear the splash of the waves as they crashed against the side of the island. I wouldn't even notice the golden glow coming from Buda and Pest on either side of me. There would only be the naturi and my fight for survival. There would only be Rowe.

With a knife in one hand, I started off down the path, not bothering to try to mask my steps. Stefan was moving silently through the wind, and Danaus was a ghost on the ground. Let the naturi hear me coming so my companions would have a better chance of sneaking up on their enemies.

The first naturi attacked from my left, slicing his blade downward in an attempt to remove my head like a guillotine. I pulled up short, sliding a bit on the frozen sidewalk in my boots. I didn't bother to raise my blade to slash at his exposed neck. Summoning up my powers, I encased the naturi in fire, almost instantly burning him to a crisp. He ran from me to a nearby snowbank, but it wasn't enough to put out the flames. The bright light cast long, lunging shadows throughout the wooded island, revealing my enemies hiding around me in the darkest corners. They lurched forward as they tried to swarm me all at once. I extinguished the fire on the naturi that had attacked and created a wall of fire around me. The naturi was still breathing, but he wouldn't be in any shape to attack me anytime soon if he did manage to survive the next few hours.

Overhead, the sky churned with black clouds and the wind poured around the tiny island in a torrent as if it were a raging river running through a narrow canyon. The flames danced and thinned in some parts, allowing the naturi to sneak through. It didn't matter. I waved my hand and my approaching attackers went up in flames.

In a matter of only minutes five naturi had been dispatched, but there was a price. Surrounded by the smoking dead bodies of the naturi, I knelt down on one knee and stared at my trembling hand. I was exhausted and half frozen from the use of so much of my energy. The manipulation of fire came naturally to me, but there was a cost every time I used it. Energy was drained from my body, leaving me starving for blood and rest. Unfortunately, neither could be found here on this horrible strip of land. There were only empty trees and the naturi waiting to remove my head.

With a tired grunt I pushed off the ground and continued my trek into the island. The storm that was brewing gained strength with each passing second, until lightning streaked across the sky, arcing from one massive cloud to the next. A knot tightened in my stomach and I fought to keep my eyes on the path before me. Rowe and his fellow wind clan members were stirring up a storm that would either fry us with lightning or drown the island in the waves now crawling up the sides. In a small break in the trees, I could see the waves closing on the far sidewalk, casting sprays of icy water into the air. The hunter would soon have to move inland if he didn't want to get washed into the Danube. That was fine with me. By the little I could sense of Valerio, he seemed to be in the center of the island near what appeared to be a giant ornate water tower. It was a strikingly odd construction in the middle of what appeared to be a giant garden, but I didn't question it. I needed to get to him.

Picking up a short sword dropped by one of the dead naturi, I started a slow jog toward the center of the island. I was tempted to contact Danaus and see if he could give me an estimate of how many naturi remained and a location of where they were clustered. However, I kept my powers to myself and continued blind. I didn't want to take a chance that Danaus was in the middle of a fight and my distraction could potentially result in an injury. The hunter would have my heart in his hand.

They're at the tower, Stefan announced, obviously not caring whether I was in the middle of a fight.

Do you see Valerio? I picked up my pace to a run, reluctant to go too fast out of fear that I might succeed in stepping directly into a trap. The water tower was close now and I began to see the outline of a low building through the empty branches.

Valerio is there. Tied up on the stage.

Stage?

I'm going to fall back until you arrive. I will attack from the east. Don't singe me.

A weak smile crossed my lips as I softened my footfalls so they couldn't be heard over the wind. Reluctantly, I reached out to Danaus and briefly relayed the information that Stefan had supplied me. Danaus didn't reply, but I could still sense him. He was preoccupied, but it seemed that he remained uninjured for the time being.

My footsteps faltered when I found the enormous water tower, directly next to an open air theater with the name

"Szabadteri Szinpad" written across the top. Six more armed naturi waited for me. I raised my hand to conjure up a fresh wave of flames to burn through my opponents when a naturi created a wall of fire before I could. A string of low curses escaped me as I tightened my grip on my blade and took a step forward. No easy way out this time. The light clan naturi was going to keep me from burning any of the other naturi. I would have to fight each one of them.

"Kill the light clan while I handle the others," Stefan said as he walked past me and engaged the first two naturi. I nodded and rushed forward. Stefan was strong and skilled enough to handle anything the wind or animal clan naturi threw at him for the time being. He had no defense against a light clan naturi throwing fireballs.

In a couple quick slashes and lunges I dispatched the two naturi guarding the light clan member. I was surprised to find her siding with Rowe, considering that Aurora was light clan as well. I guess there was no such thing as loyalty between the various clans. The light clan naturi backpedaled a couple of steps until her back was pressed against the stone wall. With a broad wave of her hand, brilliant orange and yellow flames sprung up between us.

A wolfish grin spread across my face as I stepped through the flames, turning them from orange to a silent and steady blue. "You're going to have to do better than that."

"Done," she sneered, lifting her chin to me.

My only warning was the hair on my arms standing on edge. I dove forward, plunging my sword into the stomach of the naturi until the tip was buried into the wall. She grunted in surprise, but I barely heard it over the slam of lighting into the ground where I had been standing only a second earlier. Either Rowe or another wind clan naturi was close by, ready to make my night a nightmarish hell.

Pushing off the wall, I slowly pulled the sword from the naturi, but thrust a second smaller knife through her heart, making sure she was dead before I turned my back on her. The naturi were resilient and extremely fast healers. However, they couldn't recover from a missing heart.

"Rowe!" I screamed, staring up at the sky for a glimpse of the naturi that seemed to haunt my every waking moment.

"Inside, my friend! Inside!"

"Bastard!" I growled, turning to look for Stefan. He was detaching himself from his final opponent. He walked close enough to a shaft of lamplight to reveal that he was completely covered in blood. The jeans and sweater he had worn into the woods earlier in the evening were soaked in the blood of both naturi and lycanthropes. It dripped from his chin, where it had splattered across his face and poured in thin streams from his bare hands. A part of me longed to run my tongue along his chin, lapping up such waste, but I knew better. I didn't think Stefan would be opposed to it, but the temptation was tainted by the fact that naturi blood was poisonous to nightwalkers. Otherwise I would have been happy to bury my fangs into the devious monsters.

The echo of footsteps stopped my first comment to Stefan. I jerked around with sword drawn, but instantly relaxed when I saw Danaus pop through the trees. He slowed down to look over the bodies scattered around the area. With a wave of my hand, they all exploded into flames, burning away the remains so there would be nothing left behind for the humans to find. I could only hope that my companions were taking the time to dispose of their prey in the Danube. Otherwise we would have an annoying mess to clean up before we could finally leave this island tonight.

"How many are left?" I asked when Danaus finally reached my side. I didn't even bother to scan the region.

Now was not the time to hone that skill. We needed to get to Valerio.

"Only five more," he said after a brief pause to catch his breath.

I glanced one last time at the sky, inwardly cringing as I waited for the heavens to strike at me once again. "And one of them is Rowe."

"Is he truly such a problem to kill?" Stefan asked, leaving me wishing I could bury my blade in his stomach. He had no idea what kind of a problem the one-eyed naturi was.

"You take to the sky. Danaus and I will go in through the front on the ground. We'll take care of the naturi. You get Valerio out of there. I don't know how they're holding him, but he might be too weak to disappear and reappear in Vienna. Get him somewhere safe," I directed.

"As you wish, Coven Mistress," he said snidely with an elaborate bow before taking to the air like Superman.

"Has he always been such an asshole?" Danaus inquired.

I was about to reply when another bolt of lightning streaked through the sky, sizzling directly toward Stefan. The nightwalker instantly disappeared from the open air, but reappeared lying on the ground just a few feet away. I darted over to him, sliding on my knees as I reached him. "Were you hit? Are you okay?" I demanded, helping him to slowly sit up.

"Fine. Wasn't hit," he said, but his voice sounded wobbly and broken. He may not have been hit, but it was a close thing.

"Looks like you're walking in with us," I said as he slowly regained his feet.

"Walking into a trap," he groused, but he walked beside me as I approached the entrance to the theater. There was no doubt this was a trap of Rowe's design, but our odds were pretty good. Of course, I was hoping to leave with all my companions alive and in one piece. Rowe didn't care if we slaughtered the four naturi that were still at his side.

"Get to Valerio," I told Stefan. "We'll provide cover and a distraction."

I led the way into the outdoor theater with its massive seating. There was no missing the four naturi that stood on the stage next to Valerio, who was strung up on a massive wooden cross with a stake protruding from his chest. They must not have driven it into his heart because I could still sense him, but it was close enough that he was gushing blood and he was close to death.

"No!" I screamed mindlessly. I ran up to the stage, leaving Danaus and Stefan struggling to keep up with me. Lightning rained down from the gathering clouds, slamming into the seats so that they exploded in a shower of sparks and debris.

"Mira!" Danaus cried after me, but I ignored him. I wouldn't allow these nature-loving bastards to destroy Valerio, the one creature that didn't make me doubt myself. Valerio might have intended to use me to his best advantage, but I also believed that he loved and trusted me in his own unique way. I would not allow the naturi to kill him.

More lightning fell between the stairs of the stage and me, causing me to halt. The naturi on the stage jumped down and instantly surrounded me, while Rowe finally appeared, placing one hand on the stake in Valerio's chest.

"Surrender!" he shouted in a laughing voice. "Surrender and I'll consider not plunging the stake deeper into his chest. Surrender and they won't kill you now."

"You're not going to win," I snarled, looking up at Rowe as one naturi pressed the tip of his short sword into my throat. The blade punctured my flesh, sending a trickle of blood down my neck. "We've destroyed your numbers tonight. You're not leaving here alive."

"I think it's the other way around. It's your friends who are not leaving here alive. You, on the other hand, are coming with me to Aurora."

Despite the swords now digging into my neck, stomach, and chest, I laughed. My head fell back and a deep, dark chuckle rose from my throat. "Do you still believe that?" I looked around at the naturi standing directly in front of me. "Did he promise you absolution if you helped him hand me over to your queen?" I asked them. "Do you seriously believe that Aurora will forgive you for just me?"

The confidence and determination on the faces of my captors wavered ever so slightly, their eyes darting from me to look at their nearest companion. They were all asking the same thing: was I worth such a high price to Aurora? Sure, I was the Fire Starter, but to them I was still just a useless, dirty vampire. They began to doubt Rowe's promises, and that gave me my opening.

Get Valerio! I directed Stefan. The nightwalker disappeared and instantly reappeared behind Valerio. Out of the corner of my eye I saw him lay one hand on Valerio's shoulder as Rowe raised his hand to pound the stake deeper into Valerio's chest. It all happened in a split second. Not even enough time for me to scream. Valerio and Stefan disappeared from sight just as Rowe's hand passed through empty space and slammed into the wooden cross.

"Witch!" Rowe snarled, turning narrowed eyes on my face. "Just kill her. Aurora will be just as happy with her dead body."

With Valerio safe, I didn't hesitate to tap into my powers. I managed to dodge one sword at my throat, but wasn't lucky enough to miss the one that plunged into my stomach. I groaned as I set the naturi surrounding me on fire. Unfortunately, Rowe remained at my back, so I couldn't bathe him in flickering flames as well. I couldn't sense the naturi, so I needed to physically see him in order to set him on fire.

"Boil him, Danaus!" I screamed, keeping my focus on the naturi fighting the flames and still slashing at me.

"I can't," he said softly.

"What?"

"He's right." Rowe laughed manically. I turned to find him standing on the edge of the stage with one hand reaching up toward the heavens. "He might be able to boil my blood and kill me, but I guarantee that I'll be able to get off a couple lightning bolts before I go, and they'll all be aimed at you."

"Kill him, Danaus!" I screamed. The last of the naturi surrounding me had finally died, and I twisted around with a sword still in my stomach, ready to hurl a fireball at Rowe when I discovered that he had already taken to the skies on a pair of massive black wings. I threw the fireball at him, but he managed to easily dodge it on the heavy winds whipping through the park. In response, a bolt of lighting sizzled through the air. I jerked backward, only to slam my back into the wall of the theater near the stairs. I was trapped. The world exploded in bright white light, and for a moment I understood what it felt like to be burned. The lightning missed me by a few feet, but it was enough to singe.

When my vision finally cleared enough so I could see again, Rowe was gone. Danaus stood before me, one hand pressed to my stomach while the other pulled the sword free of my body. I clenched my teeth against the searing pain as the blade cut through muscle and tissue. A lump formed in my throat and I swallowed back a frustrated sob. Rowe was still alive.

"You're a fucking idiot," Danaus grumbled. He kept his hand pressed to the wound in an effort to slow the bleeding.

I leaned my head back against the wall behind me and closed my eyes. "I just want him dead," I whispered.

"Soon," Danaus promised.

But not soon enough.

Twenty-One

Danaus stood close before me, his breathing heavy from the fight. His warm energy danced around us, beating back the cold wind, which seemed to be growing quieter now that Rowe had vacated the immediate area. I stood still, fighting the swell of emotions that threatened to swamp me. Doubt ate at me. I should never have sent Valerio alone to look into the naturi problem. I assumed that with his ability to disappear and reappear, he would be able to easily escape any situation. I hadn't considered that he would be more vulnerable to a sneak attack since he couldn't sense his enemy. Of course, I'd thought it was impossible to sneak up on Valerio. He was old and powerful. No one could surprise him.

"It's not your fault," Danaus said when I remained silent for too long.

I closed my eyes and shook my head. "I shouldn't have sent him alone. I should have ordered Stefan to go along with him."

"Possibly, but there's a chance that they both could have been taken," Danaus conceded. "It's not as if Stefan's mind would have been completely focused on the naturi. They would have both been vulnerable."

"It doesn't matter any longer," I muttered, shoving both my hands through my hair to push it out of my face. I grunted as the movement stretched and pulled the still mending wound in my stomach. I glanced up at the sky one last time, gauging the night. "We're leaving here first thing tomorrow night."

Danaus's hand slipped away from my stomach as he took a step back away from me. "What are you talking about?"

"We're going back to Venice tomorrow. If we're lucky, we can be headed back to Savannah in less than three nights. This matter here is settled. I'm not playing any of Macaire's games."

"We can't leave." Danaus stepped in front of me as I shifted to start walking up the path I had come down only a few minutes earlier. "What about Sofia?"

My face twisted in confusion and frustration. "We were sent here to take care of the naturi in Budapest. Unless you're sensing some that I'm not aware of, there should only be Rowe left. And that naturi has no tie to Budapest. Hell, I wouldn't be surprised if he followed us back to Venice. I'm his target, not world domination by the naturi."

"What about Sofia? You said—"

"To hell with Sofia!" I snapped, finally losing my hold on my temper. "She got herself into that mess. Let her get herself out. It's not my job to save every pathetic creature that crosses my path!"

"You said we would help her!"

"I honestly thought we would. I thought in the end that we would have to kill Veyron before we finally got to leave Budapest. I was wrong. We don't need to kill him. What do I care about how Budapest is being run? So long as the humans aren't being exposed to our world, it doesn't matter what Veyron does with the other nightwalkers and the warlocks and the lycans. That's his business."

"They tried to kill you! You're just going to walk away from that?" Danaus prodded, earning a dark smile from me. I took a step closer to him, laying my hand on his chest. Beneath my fingertips I could feel his heart pounding like a tribal drum, urging me on.

"Now you're just trying to goad me," I purred. "Isn't it enough that I risked my neck for the coven to get rid of the naturi in Budapest? You want me to go hunting nightwalkers, warlocks, and whatever other creature that crosses my path. Anything just so long as the by-product is a free Sofia."

"Yes," he admitted. I clenched my teeth and attempted to push past him, but the hunter grabbed my arm, holding me in place. "You're not walking away from me."

"This conversation is over."

"It's not. We have to do something about Sofia. She's trapped. She's a poor human that has gotten ensnared by an extremely powerful vampire. Doesn't that mean something to you?"

"Not really," I said with a shrug.

"Damn it, Mira! We can't leave her. She doesn't have any chance of escaping on her own. Why can't you help her? You went out of your way to save both Tristan and Nicolai."

"Think about it, Danaus!" I shouted back at him, wrenching my arm free of his grasp. "Was I really risking that much when I rode to their rescue? In both cases, the coven needed to keep me alive. I was in serious danger of getting my ass handed to me by Jabari or Macaire, but they weren't going to kill me. Veyron doesn't need me alive. He's already proven that. Lycans and warlocks have tried to kill me in the span of just a couple nights. I don't need to go looking for trouble. I've got enough."

"You're not going to help me?" he asked.

"Damn it!" I growled, balling both of my hands into fists

as I fought the urge to light a fire. "Let her go, Danaus. She doesn't deserve to be saved."

"How can you say that?"

"Because she asked for what she got! She wanted to be Veyron's plaything. Why should I risk my neck to save her because she suddenly doesn't like what she got? What if we free her and she hooks up with another nightwalker in six months? Do you go free her later when she grows bored?"

"She's a trapped human! She doesn't deserve to be held prisoner by . . . by . . ."

"By what? A monster?" I supplied.

"Yes," he hissed.

"So you've made your choice." I crossed my arms over my chest, protecting myself from the words I knew were going to come next. "You're choosing her because she's human, regardless of what we've got going."

"What? Why does this have to be about us?"

"Because if this was some guy trapped with Odelia, you wouldn't care. But Sofia is an attractive young, helpless woman that desperately needs your help and you can't wait to play the role of the white knight. It's because you can't stomach the idea of being attracted to a nightwalker and would rather be with a normal human."

"That's—That's ridiculous!"

"It isn't! Being with me terrifies you because you know that deep down you are more like me that you care to admit."

Danaus shook his head at me, taking a step backward. "I won't discuss this now. I want your help to free Sofia."

"You also want me to take her back to Savannah with us and serve as her personal protector," I cried. "I can't do it."

"Why? You had no problem taking responsibility for Tristan and Nicolai."

"Because I won't risk my life to protect another woman that you are attracted to when I'm the one who cares about you!" I screamed, shaking my hands at him. "I've had enough. If you want Sofia free, you fight Veyron for her. I'm leaving for Venice tomorrow night."

Turning on my heel, I briskly walked back toward the bridge, leaving Danaus behind. A lump grew in my throat and it felt as if a hole had been ripped in my chest bigger than the wound that was healing in my stomach. I wanted Danaus for myself, but I knew deep down that I wasn't what he wanted, and it was tearing me apart inside.

Roughly brushing aside tears that had gathered in the corners of my eyes, I crossed the bridge back to Buda, where I snagged the first two available young people that crossed my path and fed deeply. I wasn't much in the mood for hunting, but I needed to replace the blood I had lost, particularly before I returned to Venice. I didn't know what Macaire's grand scheme was, and at the moment I didn't care. I had been dispatched to Budapest to get rid of the naturi problem, and that was all. The naturi were gone, so it was time for me to go home again.

At the hotel, I put out the Do Not Disturb sign and shuffled across the room to the large window that looked down on the city. It was just a couple hours before dawn, and I was trapped in Budapest for the night. Valerio would need to feed and heal for the next few nights before he would be of any use to anyone again. Stefan would need to remain at his side for at least one night to serve as protection and to help him hunt. I had no quick escape to Vienna available to me this morning. And this time I had a dark suspicion that Danaus wouldn't be coming back to the hotel. I had given him his choice—Sofia or me—and he was going to choose the human.

Leaning my head against the glass, I closed my eyes and tried to organize my thoughts. Danaus was determined to free Sofia, most likely leaving me to deal with Veyron since the hunter would need to focus on getting the little pet to a safe location away from Budapest. After my last run-in with Rowe, I had been hoping to avoid another encounter with Veyron and his flunkies.

The whole thing left me scratching my head. The power structure here was unlike any I had seen in any other domain. Nightwalkers didn't play well with other powerful creatures. It just wasn't in our nature. To make matters worse, there wasn't just one powerful creature in Budapest, but four.

Like the coven. Cursing, I stumbled over to the desk against the far wall and brushed off some debris from the earlier fight. The room was still trashed, and I shuddered to think what Danaus had to do or say to keep things quiet with the hotel management. It wasn't the first time a hotel room had been destroyed because of my daytime presence, and the incident was usually smoothed over with copious amounts of money.

Grabbing up a piece of blank paper, I wrote down Veyron's name and circled it. Beside it, I wrote Ferko and Clarion's names and circled each one individually. Reluctantly, I put down Odelia's name as well. My experience with her had not been impressive, but according to Ferko, she was the one to actually order Michelle's death, making her a power player in her own right.

I chewed on my bottom lip as I stared at the four names, and a knot twisted in my gut. It seemed they had formed their own coven here in Budapest, creating a powerful force for anyone to contend with.

But the fact that there were four ruling members in Budapest meant there was always the potential for deadlock, unlike the coven, which had five members. It felt like someone had to be missing. There could be only one lycanthrope pack alpha, so the chance of another lycanthrope was unlikely. Particularly since we had slaughtered most of them and there hadn't been another half as strong as Ferko. Another warlock was a distinct possibility. Valerio had indicated that Clarion was known to work with someone else, and that other warlock could be serving in the background with the other members of Veyron's ruling party. If I had to take on Veyron to protect Danaus and his new friend, then I would have to destroy all the members of this group in order to survive. I did not relish the opportunity to go head-to-head against not just one but two warlocks.

"If you had just used the half-breed, you could have killed that irritating naturi with little problem."

My entire body cringed at the voice. I didn't need to look up. I could feel Nick's power slowly filling the room as if he were pushing out all the air and leaving it thick and stuffy. If I still breathed, I would have suffocated in that tiny enclosure. I hung my head down and clenched my eyes shut as if I could will him away, but I knew it didn't work that way. Nick wasn't going to leave until he had finally succeeded in pushing me in the direction he thought I should be headed. At the moment, I didn't care what he wanted.

"I'm done using Danaus," I said in a low, hard voice, daring him to argue with me.

He chuckled. "You're not done by a long shot, my dear."

I slammed my fist against the surface of the desk and twisted around to finally face him. "I'm done! Just leave me alone."

Nick leaned against the far wall, looking like my last memory of my father, with his simple outfit and floppy hat to protect him against the harsh summer sun. The smile was all wrong, though. There was no warmth or compassion, only evil and malicious glee.

"I can't, my sweet daughter. We need each other."

"I don't need you."

Nick walked over and placed a hand on my shoulder to

keep me from rising when I tried to get out of my chair. "Without me, you will never reach your full potential."

"I don't need any more power than I've already got," I snapped.

Nick squeezed my shoulder hard enough to make me cringe and try to shrink away from his touch, but he refused to release me. "And I need you to help me once again reach my full potential. I want to reach the stars again, escape this weakened state."

I finally jerked out of his touch, but he had me pinned so that I couldn't get out of my chair. "I don't care what you want."

"You will if it means your life," he said, a grin growing across his horribly beautiful face. "If you're not going to help me, I will either impregnate you so you will bear me a child that can help me, or I'll kill you and go to one of my other children for assistance."

"I will not control Danaus again," I said stubbornly, daring him to contradict me. When he continued to just stare at me, I finally added, "Besides, I've already lost him. He won't speak to me, won't look at me. We're going our separate ways."

"Yes," he hissed. "I saw that. Not a good move. You should have just given him what he wanted so you would have his power at your disposal." Nick paced away from me. Some of the tension drained out of my shoulders as I watched him deep in thought. After a moment he shrugged his shoulders and turned back to me. "No matter. You still have Jabari. Once you return to Venice, you are to concentrate your attention on him."

"Jabari? Are you insane? He'll squash me like a bug if he gets even the slightest whiff that he can't control me any longer, let alone discovers that I can control him."

"Are you saying you don't want to control him?" he

asked, arching one brow at me. I couldn't ever recall seeing that particular expression on my father's face before.

"Of course I would love to control him. He used me for a century. I would love to have the opportunity to force him to take his own medicine. I'm just not strong enough. Jabari will kill me for even trying."

"Then I suggest that you get it right the first time," Nick said, and then disappeared, clearly indicating that he would offer me no help whatsoever if I failed to bring Jabari under control when I attempted it.

"Nick!" I shouted, but I got no answer. But then, that's how things were going at this point. I was alone to clean up this mess I found myself in. Nick had helped me to alienate Danaus, and now I was to stick my head in the lion's mouth that was Jabari.

Exhausted, I pushed away from the desk and wandered into the bedroom, where I plopped down on the edge of the bed and pulled off my muddy boots. With my legs still hanging over the side, I lay back against the thick comforter and closed my eyes. I wished for the world to fade away, and that we had never come to Budapest.

Twenty-Two

Sofia sat at the small table in the far corner next to Danaus as they shared a tray of food brought up by room service. I watched her cutting dainty bites of her chicken, wishing I could shove the fork down her throat. Danaus had risked both of our lives for this woman, and unfortunately, I was beginning to see why. In the broken, dimly lit room, she seemed almost luminous. Her features were delicate and perfectly formed, from her large innocent eyes to her button nose to her little rosebud mouth. It was as if she were a fragile, blown-glass ornament resting in the wreckage of the hotel room.

It didn't take a genius to see why Danaus was drawn to her. It was more than the fact that she was a helpless human tied to a ruthless vampire. It was that she represented the epitome of the beautiful damsel in distress. Danaus had spent a lifetime searching for good deeds, in hopes of winning his soul back from the bori. He had searched his life for just this situation. Now all he needed to do was vanquish the evil vampire and the heroic act would be complete. Then he and Sofia could ride off together into the sunset.

If it had been possible for me at that exact moment, I would have vomited with the thought. Danaus had no business with a woman like that even if her laughter sounded like jubilant little bells and her eyes sparkled when she gazed up at him. Danaus and I were a better fit. Dark, violent, and sarcastic, we could face whatever the world threw at us and still come back for more. We belonged together. But right now all he could see was a pair of wide blue eyes watching him.

Balling my hands into fists at my sides, I searched for an even, reasonable tone. "Does Veyron know you have her?" I demanded as way of greeting.

"I slipped out just before sunrise," Sofia said. "Veyron didn't know where I was going." She wiped her hands on her napkin before setting it by her plate. She rose to her feet and curtsied deep to me.

Meanwhile, Danaus sat back in his chair and crossed his arms over his chest as he stared smugly at me. "There was no fight. No one was killed. Sofia has been safely hidden here all day and no one has come to retrieve her."

"She's not hidden," I snarled. "She's Veyron's pet. The moment he wishes to know her location, he will. And then he will either come to fetch her himself or he will send some of his flunkies for her. Just because getting her was easy doesn't mean that it will be just as easy to keep her."

A flood of tears erupted from Sofia as she collapsed back in her chair. "Oh, she's right. It is only a matter of time before Veyron comes after me. I've put your lives in horrible danger."

I shrugged one shoulder as I shoved my hands into the back pockets of my leather pants. "Then go back. If you don't want to selfishly risk our lives, then go back to him."

"I can't," she gasped, raising her face from where she had it buried in her hands. "He'll kill me. I know he will. Veyron will kill me."

"I doubt that."

"Mira, you don't know that," Danaus growled at me.

"No, but I truly doubt that Veyron will kill her. Her only fear is that he's going to punish her in some way and she doesn't want to face it."

Danaus shoved to his feet while placing one protective hand on Sofia's shoulder. "The only thing she's afraid of is a lifetime of being a slave to that monster. She wants her freedom."

"Then she shouldn't have chosen to become Veyron's pet in the first place."

"Please, Mira. I need your help," Sofia said. "I made a mistake. I didn't realize what I was getting into when I made the deal with Veyron. At the time, he was just so powerful and mesmerizing. I wasn't thinking clearly."

I rolled my eyes and paced away from the woman. "And now you're thinking clearly? You want out of your deal and you're expecting us to protect you when it comes time to pay the piper."

"Please, I have nowhere else to go. No one who will help me. I'm alone, and you and Danaus are the only ones strong enough to take on Veyron. Besides, he said that you're the keeper of the domain now. Can't you just order him to release me?"

"I can order him to release you, but if he wants to be able to show his face in this city again, he has to challenge me for you. And truth be told, I don't want you. I've got enough problems on my hands already. I don't need to add to them."

"But I won't be a burden to you. I will leave Budapest. I will go somewhere far from here, like Paris or London or maybe even New York. I will never come to this city again," she promised.

I turned on my heel and shook my head at her. "Do you honestly think that it's going to work that way? Once Veyron

hears that you're out of my direct care and supervision, he
will come after you again. And then he will kill you to prove
that I wasn't able to protect something that was supposed to
be mine."

"But I don't want to be your pet," Sofia said in a breathless whisper.

"And I don't want you either, but you turned to another
nightwalker for help. That means I have to steal you away
from Veyron to protect you."

"But I ran away. You didn't steal me."

"Keeping you alive, keeping you safe, means stealing
you from him."

"We could just kill Veyron and then you wouldn't have to
worry about protecting her," Danaus suggested.

Sofia twisted in her seat and placed a hand over Danaus's
hand. "Must you? He didn't treat me that poorly. I don't think
he deserves to die because I made a mistake."

"I see no reason to kill Veyron," I said. "With the naturi
dead, I'm prepared to leave Budapest and not look back. The
coven is a more pressing matter for us."

"Then send her to Savannah," Danaus suggested.

"No!"

"Mira—"

"Absolutely not. If she boards my plane, she's going to
Venice, and that's where she's going to stay."

"Oh, please no," she pleaded. At the suggestion, the
woman grew considerably paler as she clenched both of her
hands in her lap.

"She wouldn't survive in Venice with the others," Danaus
said, "particularly since I know that you have no intention of
remaining there."

"I won't take her to Savannah and she can't remain in
Budapest. That only leaves Venice," I argued, struggling
to keep the smile off my lips. There was something very

appealing about sending a helpless Sofia to Venice. Deep down, I knew that I couldn't and wouldn't drop her off in Venice. I had moments when I could be truly cold-hearted, but there were limitations to even my vicious nature. She wouldn't survive her first night in Venice and we all knew it.

Unfortunately, I was still stuck with trying to come up with someplace to send her where she would be out of my hair, and preferably away from Danaus. Furthermore, the place had to be secure from a potential attack from Veyron should I decide to leave the nightwalker alive. At the moment I didn't care one way or the other. I just wanted to get home again, and now that the naturi were dead, I had no reason to remain in Budapest beyond giving Macaire a chance to kill me.

"Why not send her to Themis?" I suggested.

Danaus pushed away from the table and rose to his feet, looking far from pleased with my idea. "You want to put her in Ryan's hands?"

"She's a human who knows about our world. I can wipe her memory and set her free, but that's not going to keep her safe from Veyron and anyone else who might know about her. Ryan can watch over her, while she gives the researchers some interesting little tidbits about my world. It's a brilliant idea."

"It's a terrible idea."

"You had no problem putting Lily in his hands," I accused, hating to even say the child's name out loud. She didn't need to be brought into this conversation, but it didn't make any sense to me that Danaus would be willing to send something dear and precious to us to Ryan, but not this creature.

"Lily was going there under the protection of your name. I know that you wouldn't do the same for Sofia. Ryan doesn't owe me any favors and he's not trying to cultivate my friendship. Sofia would not have the same security that Lily would have had."

"It doesn't matter anymore. If she doesn't want to stay in Budapest, then she goes to Themis and is out of my hair as far as I'm concerned," I said, throwing my arms up in the air. "In truth it doesn't matter to me since she's not going back to Savannah, which is where I am headed after this coven nonsense is finished."

I cocked my head to the side and stretched out my powers as I felt a shifting in the air. Danaus grew instantly quiet when I raised my hand. Someone was coming, and I preferred that they did not catch us in the middle of this particular conversation. Sofia looked from me to Danaus, her expression growing tense.

A couple of seconds later both Stefan and Macaire appeared in the hotel room. A part of me had secretly hoped that the coven Elder had returned to Venice where he belonged, but apparently he was lingering in Budapest to make sure that whatever trap he'd set was properly sprung on Danaus and me. A frown pulled at the corners of my lips at Valerio's painful absence. The nightwalker had been my personal pocket of mischievous joy when he was around, and now I was just stuck with two nightwalkers that wanted me dead and a hunter that was trying to get me killed.

"How is he?" I asked, content to ignore Macaire for the time being.

"He'll live," Stefan replied as he unbuttoned his winter coat to reveal a handsome dark suit. "He fed heavily last night and I saw to it that he fed again as soon as I rose. He just needs another night of rest and food before he travels again."

"That is a shame about Valerio," Macaire murmured, rubbing one gloved hand against his chin.

"Valerio will be fine," I said firmly, fighting to keep from clenching my teeth whenever I spoke to the Elder. "The important part is that we have rid the city of the naturi. I need to still make a few phone calls to get arrangements in place, but Danaus and I will be returning to Venice tonight. I'm sure you two gentlemen can manage on your own. In fact, there's nothing keeping you here now."

"We're leaving Budapest?" Stefan demanded first, his mouth falling open in shock.

I nodded at him, but turned my gaze directly on Macaire, who was looking less than pleased by my announcement. "As I recall, the only reason for our coming to Budapest in the first place was the naturi infestation, which has now been cleared out. There is no reason for me to linger in this city any longer. We were to reconvene in Venice, and then Danaus and I will be returning home to Savannah."

So, you're going to permit me back in Savannah, but not Sofia? Danaus whispered in my mind, making me wish I could throw something at his head. Yet in all honesty, I wasn't sure which of us was acting more childish at the moment. I had a sick feeling that it was me. Sofia wanted her freedom, and Danaus was determined to give it to her. As his friend and companion, I should be willing to support him despite the fact that it went against my ways as a nightwalker.

It wasn't that I was unwilling to take on the protection of yet another creature, because I felt confident that Veyron would not travel to my domain of Savannah for her. It was more the concern that I would be protecting a creature that seemed destined to become Danaus's lover one day. I didn't think I had it in me to be that strong and not allow jealousy to crush Sofia.

"What about Ferko and Odelia? What about my Michelle?" Stefan demanded, taking a couple of steps toward me.

I smiled broadly at him, placing both of my hands on his stiff shoulders. "As keeper of Budapest, you have my permission to track them both down and eliminate them in any manner that you see fit so long as it doesn't endanger our secret."

"You're too kind," he replied, pulling out of my touch.

"I can well understand your eagerness to return to the coven and home again, but you can't leave this domain in the chaotic order that it is now," Macaire interjected quickly before I could turn my back on the both of them. "You need to establish your position of power within the city."

"I have. There was the language lesson at the Széchenyi Baths," I said, but Stefan was quick to speak up.

"That was in the name of the coven and establishing yourself as an Elder to be respected."

I forced a broad smile at Stefan as I clenched my teeth together. I didn't need his help. "There was also the slaughter at Bahnhof just the other night. I do believe that was in the name of establishing my position as keeper, if I'm not mistaken."

"Yes, I heard about Bahnhof and that was a very nice start," Macaire conceded.

"Cleared the place out," Stefan said proudly, referring to the nightwalkers that quickly vacated the nightclub rather than stay in our presence any longer than absolutely necessary.

Macaire heaved a heavy sigh and placed his hands into the pockets of his large overcoat. "Unfortunately, I get the feeling that the whispers of that event are still making the rounds among our kind here in this large city before you can comfortably vacate it, even for a short period of time. You need to make a larger display of your power, Mira. Take the advice of one who has been around quite a bit longer than you. When you took over Savannah, there were few night-walkers present. Budapest is considerably larger and older. You will need a grander display to have an impact on your people here."

"Do you have something specific in mind?" I asked, knowing that he did.

"The Solstice Ball," Sofia said in breathless tones. I turned to look up at her, but she had turned her wide eyes on the other Elder. "Tonight is Odelia's Solstice Ball. Everyone will be there."

"Exactly," Macaire said with a smile, then turned his attention to me. "Collecting another one? She doesn't seem to be quite your type."

"Yes, well, I'm open to new experiences," I said with an ugly smile before turning my attention to Sofia. "What can you tell me about Odelia's party tonight? Have you ever been?"

"I've been a few times. As far as I know, every night-walker in the city makes an appearance at this ball with his or her pets. It's a very formal affair with elegant ball gowns and beautiful suits. Veyron always called it the only civilized affair of the year because there was no fighting and no werewolves present."

"What about warlocks or witches?" Danaus inquired, before I could.

"Not as far as I know. Just vampires and their pets, which are always humans," she said with a pretty smile for him.

"Then I guess we're going to a ball tonight, gentlemen. It's a shame that Valerio can't make it, because this is exactly the kind of thing that would have raised his spirits. Where is it held?"

"I'm not exactly sure," Sofia said, "but it's always been in a private castle in the Castle District."

"I'm sure we can find it with little problem," Stefan interrupted, arching one eyebrow at me. "We can just focus on the heavy concentration of nightwalkers in the middle of the city."

"Then we should get going," I said. "The sooner this mess is taken care of, the sooner we can get back to Venice. Danaus, stay behind and protect Sofia while I am out tonight. Macaire, Stefan, and I apparently have a formal ball to attend."

"Is that what you're wearing?" Stefan demanded, looking me up and down. I was back in my leather pants and leather halter top with its varied selection of knives spread across my body.

My smile widened for him, allowing my fangs to peek out. I wrapped one arm around his shoulders, forcing him to place an arm around my back so his hand rested on my hip. "My ball gown is at the cleaners. I'm sure they will understand. Besides, this makes the impression that I want to leave behind."

A reluctant smile tweaked one corner of his mouth. "Blood, fear, and ruthless violence," Stefan said.

"Like Macaire said, it's all about leaving the right impression, and I have no doubt this is the one I want to leave behind in Budapest if I am to be both her keeper and a coven Elder. Let's dance," I said, grinning at my companion in violence. Despite the fact that he still wanted me dead, Stefan and I were starting to get along very well. But then he always loved a bloodbath and terror in his victims. Something I was starting to be good at once again.

No matter. It was time to crash Odelia's party, and for once, I couldn't wait, even if I did have Macaire tagging along.

Twenty-Three

Odelia's Solstice Ball was an extravagant affair. But considering what little I did know of her, I had expected nothing less. She was a relatively young nightwalker who liked to pretend to be much older than she was, reveling in the so-called "good old days," when she never really lived through them in the first place. This Solstice Ball was just another excuse for her to preside over the younger nightwalkers and strut about as if she were something truly awesome to behold.

The only problem was, the three nightwalkers walking into her party were truly awesome to behold, and we didn't like to share the limelight.

Unfortunately, Sofia either lied about the guest list or Odelia made some last minute modifications due to my recent behavior in Budapest. I had expected a lavish party of roughly one hundred people—half nightwalkers and the other half their human pets. When we arrived at the gathering, we discovered that the body count was well over two hundred, and nightwalkers accounted for less than quarter of those people. To prevent any kind of scene, particularly a violent bloody scene, Odelia had surrounded herself with humans. We could wipe only so many memories and control only so many minds at one time. This crowd was too big, and Odelia knew she was safe as long as she remained within it. It was a disappointing development, but I was not going to let it spoil my evening.

Macaire and I strolled into a grand ballroom laced in silver and gold decorations. A giant Christmas tree rose up in the far corner, glowing with twinkling white lights that reflected off red globe ornaments. Along either wall, enormous tables had been set up and were laden with gourmet dishes and artfully crafted ice sculptures. On the balcony overlooking the second floor, a string ensemble was playing music for the dancers in the middle of the ballroom.

Standing in that ballroom, I watched the swish and flow of the elegant ball gowns as the women were twirled around the floor. There was laughter and soft conversation in the air. I longed to have Valerio at my side. The scene played before me was like a crisp memory of a time not so long ago. Centuries ago, he and I had attended balls similar to this one, where we waltzed and laughed before luring our prey off to a secluded dark corner to feed. It had been such a seemingly innocent and light time in my life, which was now so far from my reach.

Stefan leaned close, brushing his chest against my shoulder so he could whisper in my ear. "I think there may be a problem with your attire." I didn't need to look over to know that Macaire was smirking. Both nightwalkers were at least wearing nice suits under their heavy coats, while I was sheathed in leather and steel. Not exactly what I would have preferred for a winter ball, but then I hadn't thought I would need a fancy frock while destroying naturi in Budapest.

I shrugged and stepped into the ballroom with the rest of the guests. "The point, I believe, was to cause a scene," I replied in a low voice. "I think this will help."

My appearance certainly grabbed the attention of the partygoers, as they quickly put some space between themselves and me while softly whispering among each other. I was proud of the fact that I didn't blush, and even more impressed that Macaire remained standing beside me, while Stefan stood straight and tall behind us both like a proper servant. Considering my aggressive attire, I had expected both of them to distance themselves from me at their first opportunity. It made me worry. *What was Macaire's game now?*

It took Odelia and Veyron only a moment to notice the uneasiness of the crowd and head in our direction. They had been holding court at one of the three tables at the far end of the room on a slightly raised platform. Odelia wore an elaborate dress of shimmering silver and black, while Veyron appeared in a traditional tuxedo. When they reached us, they both gave a respectful bow of their heads. It was enough to show respect without drawing too much attention from the humans. Unfortunately, that wasn't a particularly easy task, since nearly every human and nightwalker in the ballroom was staring at me.

"Welcome, great coven Elders Macaire and Mira. Welcome, Stefan. Please enjoy our small holiday gathering," Odelia said, spreading her arms wide to invite us in.

"Thanks for allowing us to crash," I replied. "We just heard about the party and thought we would drop by for a little while." I resisted the urge to lay my hand on the handle of one of the knives attached to my hip.

"You're most welcome here," Veyron said, though he refused to look directly at me. I had to wonder if it might have something to do with his missing pet. Surely there had to be a few nightwalkers present who noticed her glaring absence.

"In truth, we had not expected you to linger in the city

so long. Otherwise, I would have told you about the ball. It would have given you more time to find a proper ball gown," Odelia added, as her hand caressed a luxurious strip of black velvet on her dress.

I waved my hand at her and forced out a light chuckle. "Yes, it does appear as if I am a bit underdressed for the affair."

"In truth, it looks as if you should be part of the entertainment rather than a guest, but it is no matter. You are all most welcome here!"

"Why that's a brilliant idea!"

"What idea?" Odelia demanded in a rough voice, obviously terrified by anything that I could conceive of as brilliant.

"Entertainment! It would give me a chance to repay you and all the other nightwalkers for your warm welcome into the city as both an Elder and now her keeper. I would like to provide some entertainment."

"Oh, please, Mira. You don't have to trouble yourself," Veyron said, finally starting to look a little nervous. "Tonight is for your enjoyment and relaxation. You've done enough. We've already heard of the removal of all the naturi from the city. You've taken over as keeper for our protection. We can ask no more of you."

"But I insist! It will be fun."

"Please let her," Macaire interjected, surprising me. "Mira has such a special gift for entertaining those around her. She has such flair."

"Thank you, Macaire. Now, please, return to your seats at the far end of the ballroom and allow me to entertain you."

With anxious smiles plastered on their faces, Veyron and Odelia led Macaire and Stefan across the center of the dance floor, with me lagging behind them. I stopped in the center and sent out a slight mental push to everyone, indicating that they should back off to the sidelines and leave the center of the dance floor completely open. At the same time, I mentally directed the orchestra on the balcony to switch to a selection of pieces from Tchaikovsky's Nutcracker ballet. I thought it would make the whole performance seem more festive, since I was limited in what I could do at that moment.

Once Odelia and the others were seated at the head tables, I bowed deeply to them and then to my left and right, offering myself up to the crowd. As I stood upright again, I palmed a pair of knives at my waist and quickly began to juggle them. I wasn't a particularly accomplished juggler, but I'd picked up a couple tricks over the long years out of plain curiosity and boredom. The silver blades flashed in the twinkling light as they rose higher and higher. When they were more than five feet in the air, I added a third blade and pushed them even higher. The audience around me exploded in applause, but I wasn't even half done.

When one knife reached more than ten feet in the air, it became wrapped in a ball of flames. In a matter of seconds I was juggling three flaming knives to an awe-filled crowd of humans and a slightly terrified group of nightwalkers. To the humans, this was a bit of fake magic for their entertainment that could easily be explained away with logic and science. To the nightwalkers, I was a walking threat.

As the music reached its ending crescendo, I dropped to my knees, caught a knife in my left hand and another in my right. Then I tilted my head back and caught the third flaming knife with my teeth. The second the blade entered my mouth, the flames were extinguished. Thrusting the two knives in my hands back into the sheaths at my side, I pulled the other blade out of my mouth. With a wide grin, I puffed out my cheeks and pretended to expel a massive breath of air that turned into a ball of fire as it left my lips. Over the round of exuberant clapping, I could hear screams of genuine terror from the nightwalkers in the crowd.

Confident that I had everyone's full attention, I moved on to some more stunning tricks. With my blades returned to their sheaths, I raised my hands above my head and with a snap of my fingers four orbs of fire miraculously appeared hovering in the air. I waved my hands and the little fireballs spun and danced over my head in time with the music.

Want to have some fun? I silently inquired of Stefan.

I'm quite enjoying watching you make a fool of yourself. I don't need anything else.

Give me a hand, please. Float Odelia out here to me.

Float her out?

Imagine lifting her out to the middle of the floor like a silver angel descending into Hell. Stefan didn't say anything, but I could feel his inward chuckle at my description.

As the music shifted, I lowered my right hand and directed it toward Odelia, who magically lifted from her chair and floated out to the center of the floor, thanks to a little assistance from Stefan. Shock initially filled her face, but she quickly covered it up with a look of serenity—just like an angel floating down from Heaven. As her feet touched the ground before me, I used my left hand to direct the fireballs to change direction so they circled around her. With a laugh and a clap, they picked up speed and the ring around her became smaller so that she felt forced to cross her arms over her chest. A fragile smile lifted her lips, but there was genuine fear in her eyes.

We were completely surrounded by humans, and I knew it would be impossible for me to completely wipe all their memories if I decided to burn her right then and there. Of course, the real question was whether I cared if this gathering of humans watched as I burned her alive. No one knew me. I could easily disappear from sight and return to my beloved Savannah with no one thinking to look for me there. The nightwalkers wouldn't murmur a word of my identity and would most likely not admit to seeing anything at all. I was a bigger threat to them than anything that the humans could dig up.

I shifted my gaze from Odelia to Macaire, who was lounging in his chair, watching the performance with what seemed like only partial attention. I arched one brow at him, and in return he shrugged one shoulder, as if to say that it was my decision. Stefan, on the other hand, was sitting on the edge of his chair, watching the flames edge closer and closer to Michelle's executioner. I tilted my head toward him, and he gave me only the slightest shake.

Smiling broadly, I walked toward Odelia. With a snap of my fingers, the fireballs stopped circling her and returned to me. They settled on my thin figure and rolled over me, like a cat rubbing against my legs in want of affection. "It seems you've been given a reprieve. You've been promised to someone else," I whispered, winking at her.

Tumbling backward in a series of springing backflips that put some distance between Odelia and me, I came to a halt in the center of the massive ballroom and was instantly engulfed in flames as if they were a second skin. I bowed deeply to the crowd, and when I rose again, the flames were completely gone. It was only when I threw up my hands in triumph that the room exploded in applause. For the time being, my odd outfit had been forgotten and the crowd was left pondering my amazing pyrotechnic skills. The nightwalkers were terrified, but given the fact that Odelia had survived the encounter, they were now willing to give me the benefit of the doubt. I was going to behave myself tonight. For now.

I followed Odelia up to the raised dais where the three tables sat and chose the empty seat next to Macaire so that we were in the center of the platform. Stefan was on my right, while Veyron and Odelia sat at a separate table, like a pair of good humble court attendants. Above us the orchestra struck up a fresh melody, and the partygoers returned to dancing and mingling among themselves without casting an eye in our direction.

"Congratulations, my dear," Macaire said as he surveyed the dance floor before him. "You've managed to entertain all the humans in here with your amazing feats while openly threatening every nightwalker."

"Thank you," I replied with a slight bow of my head toward him. I sat back in my chair and crossed my left leg over my right, vainly attempting to relax while sitting next to my enemy. I wasn't worried about an attack. We were under the scrutiny of too many humans, and Macaire wasn't one for the direct approach. There was always the chance of things going sour on him and it ending badly for him.

I, on the other hand, had no problem with a more direct approach.

"I must congratulate you," I said, venturing out onto a very thin limb. I was taking a wild stab in the dark and hoping to hit blood.

"For what?"

"For what you've accomplished here. It appears that you've managed to set up your own little coven using not just a pair of nightwalkers, but a warlock and a lycanthrope as well. As a people, we're not known for getting along with the others."

"I'm afraid that I don't know what you're talking about," Macaire said blandly.

A smirk lifted my lips as I looked over my shoulder at him. "Please. You're not dealing with an idiot, and you know it. You sent me here to show off what you've accomplished. The naturi weren't a problem until I arrived. I must admit that it is quite amazing. The cooperation of nightwalkers, shifters, and magic users is rare. I can only guess that you've set yourself up as the liege figure. While somewhat treasonous, it's definitely interesting in its strength. It's a shame that all the positions have been filled."

Macaire shifted slightly in his chair so he was leaning forward, allowing him to get a better view of my face as I stared out at the crowd. "Are you saying that you would be interested in such a structure?"

"The addition of Clarion makes this structure very powerful, but woefully weak when you consider Ferko. I know too many lycans that would tear him apart. However, I guess you need that weakness in an effort to find someone who would turn his back on his own people for the good of the power structure."

Macaire said nothing, neither admitting nor denying my accusation as he sat back in his chair again. He stared straight ahead, drumming his fingers on the tabletop before him in time to the music.

"I will admit that the only one that I can't figure out is Sofia," I said, as if talking out loud to myself.

"She is quite the lovely pet," Macaire murmured.

"Quite lovely."

"I noticed that she was with your hunter this evening and not at Veyron's side. Have you taken on yet another new pet? This is becoming quite the trend with you."

"Oh, she's not mine. She convinced Danaus that she wanted her freedom so he's helped her run away."

"Will you be taking her back to your domain?"

"Definitely not," I said with an absent wave of my hand. "I'm not interested in her. I'm thinking of wiping her memory and dropping her somewhere remote, in a naturi country perhaps, like South America."

Macaire fell silent again, but I noticed that he had stopped tapping on the table and his hand had balled into a fist. I pressed my lips firmly together to keep the smile from rising. I was beginning to wonder if Sofia actually belonged to Veyron, since he had shown little concern about her absence.

"I just can't understand why she would take such risks," I said in a low voice. "She must have a powerful ally or two in her corner."

Macaire remained silent, staring straight ahead. He was no longer willing to be drawn into a conversation where he knew I was determined to corner him. I didn't know whether Sofia directly belonged to him or if she was simply taking orders from him. All I knew was that I needed to get her away from Danaus as soon as possible.

I looked over at Stefan, who appeared to be more than a little bored. He was another question hovering in the air. When the time came, where did his loyalty lie? There was no doubt that he would do whatever was necessary to get a chair on the coven. Furthermore, I was confident that both Macaire and I had promised him an open chair once the other was disposed of. Unfortunately, I knew there was going to be a point where Stefan would have to make a choice between who he was going to support in the end. While we had a common hatred of the naturi, I also had the nightwalker hunter at my side as a minus.

Stefan caught me staring at him. He raised one eyebrow questioningly, but I simply smiled at him and gave a little shrug of my shoulders. I could only hope that my promise to personally hand over both Ferko and Odelia was also buying me brownie points with the nightwalker. I was anxious to get out of this city and home again, but I'd be willing to stay another night to aid him in hunting those two down if it meant getting him to aid me when I attempted to overthrow Macaire.

Beside me, Macaire pushed to his feet as the music shifted. He turned to me and offered his hand. "It's been years since I enjoyed a waltz. Will you join me?"

I hated the fact that I hesitated. I knew that I was safe here at the ball and would easily be protected by the crowd of humans, but I still didn't trust him. He had to know that he was close to finally being rid of me. With stomach churning, I placed my cold hand in his and rose gracefully to my feet. We wordlessly walked out to the center of the dance floor and twirled about the area in an elegant waltz that was a faint echo of days long past. Like Macaire, it had been centuries since I had last waltzed as well.

A faint smile lifted my lips against my will as the memory of my last waltz spun through my brain.

"What happy memory has gripped you?" Macaire inquired.

"My last waltz," I replied. "With Valerio, in the middle of a dirty, blood-splattered alley in Munich too many years ago. We had spent an enjoyable evening out and he started humming a waltz."

"It is a shame about what happened to Valerio. The naturi, particularly this Rowe, are becoming quite a nuisance," Macaire said, clucking his tongue.

The naturi were far more than a bloody nuisance, but then Macaire wasn't the one being hunted by a fanatic and their queen. The naturi were a danger to our entire race along with the human race. To make matters worse, they risked exposing our secret as the battles grew bigger and closer to major cities. It was too early for the Great Awakening. The humans just weren't ready to know about us yet without it exploding in our faces.

I shook my head, hating to get into this argument while on the dance floor. "We need to develop a plan to go after Aurora. Once she is finally destroyed, we may finally be able to properly handle them. The naturi may be content to slip back into the quiet oblivion of the woods. They lived for centuries that way when the worlds were closed. I'm sure they can do it again."

"You're suggesting coexistence."

"I wouldn't mind if we quietly whittled down their numbers over the years, but if we're not careful, we risk all-out war, which would eventually expose us to the humans."

"Yes, it is too soon for that," Macaire agreed, surprisingly. But then, his life was quite comfortable now without the humans knowing. Why rock the boat? He only needed to get rid of Jabari and me. Then, with any luck, his own coven could move in and take over after wiping out our constantly absent liege and the all too quiet Elizabeth.

"I would like to see the coven start making plans for the hunting and destruction of Aurora when we return," I said. "Her death should dishearten the rest of the naturi and cause them to return to the shadows."

"What about this Rowe? He seems quite powerful and determined to have your head at any cost," Macaire suggested.

"He will, naturally, be eliminated with Aurora. I don't think the naturi would rally around him, considering that he's been exiled, but I'd rather not take the chance."

"I think you should definitely bring up your thoughts before the coven when we return," Macaire said.

I wanted to snicker. If I survived my time in Budapest, I had now developed a new role for myself in his life. I had no doubt that in his mind I'd become the one that would hunt down Aurora and kill her. But then I had always known that would be my job in the end. I had come the closest so far, and in truth I wanted to be the one that killed her.

As the music ended, Macaire and I bowed to each other and then silently returned to the raised platform.

We remained at the ball until a couple hours before sunrise. As we stepped outside of the ballroom, Macaire disappeared from sight, heading off to whatever location he was using for his daytime rest. Stefan offered me his hand with a smirk before we disappeared and reappeared in my hotel room. The nightwalker gave me a quick nod and then disappeared again, heading to his own secret daytime lair.

I frowned. The hotel room was completely empty. Unfortunately, the room was still in such disarray that I couldn't tell if there had been a struggle. Closing my eyes, I reached out for Danaus.

Where are you? I demanded when I finally reached him.

Getting Sofia settled, he replied immediately, to my relief. *We're in a hotel near the airport outside of the city. She's getting on a plane for London just after sunrise.*

You're sending her to Themis?

Just to London. If she wishes to seek out the researchers of Themis, that is her decision. I don't want her to be linked to us if she falls in with Ryan.

I would have preferred to wipe her memory before she arrived in London, but there wasn't time for me to get across town and back before the sun rose. I'd be cutting it far too close, and there were too many in this town that already wanted me dead.

Did you have any problems with Veyron's men? I inquired.

None. I should be back to the hotel by sunrise to watch over you. I want to see her safely on the plane.

I cut off the connection between us before I said something snide. Shuffling into the bedroom, I pulled off my boots and removed all of my knives before plopping down on the bed. I closed my eyes, forcing myself to ignore the growing anxiety within my chest. Would Danaus return to my side before the sun rose? I knew that I could always contact Stefan and have him take me to Valerio, but I tapped down the urge. The hunter had promised to protect me. I would hold onto that promise as I let sleep finally take me.

Twenty-Four

My ribs throbbed as if some of them had been broken. I lay with my eyes closed, mentally searching out the pain. It didn't make any sense. My ribs hadn't been injured at the Solstice Ball and yet I could tell that at least two were in the process of mending.

"Get the hell up!" shouted an angry voice. "The sun set more than an hour ago. I want to get out of here."

I lurched into an upright position and instantly regretted it as pain shot through my frame from my fractured ribs. My head knocked against a cold concrete wall as I tried to inch back down, creating a new pain that succeeded in scattering my already broken thoughts. I blinked and looked around the small dark room. Instead of pastel walls and heavy curtains, there were plain concrete walls and a steel door with a small window at the top. I was in a dungeon of some sort.

Standing in the far corner with eyes narrowed on my prone body was Rowe. I dug my heels into the concrete floor and pushed so I nearly slid up the wall in my desperation to put some distance between myself and the lethal naturi. Panic spread through my frame as a cold sweat broke out down my back. I had been trapped with my enemy while asleep. I had been completely vulnerable, and yet Rowe hadn't killed me, for some bizarre reason.

"What are you doing here? Where am I?" I demanded when I finally found my voice. I couldn't understand it. The last thing I remembered was falling asleep on the bed in my hotel room. Had someone grabbed me when I was unconscious? Had someone touched me and brought me here to this concrete prison?

"You're here for me to kill," Rowe sneered.

"Where's here? Where are we? Who brought me here?" I fired back at him, my brain chunking along at a slow pace because I just couldn't accept the notion that someone had gotten to me when I was at my weakest. Why hadn't Danaus been there to protect me? Why hadn't . . .

Because he had been busy protecting Sofia, I thought dismally. Something inside of me broke. I slid back down the walls to sit on my heels, hanging my head down so Rowe couldn't see the tears in my eyes. Danaus had abandoned me for a human, and I'd been captured as a result. Or worse, Danaus had been killed while protecting Sofia. A part of me didn't want to try to reach out and discover whether he was still there. I couldn't decide which was worse: his death or his betrayal.

"Still with me, sparky?" Rowe mocked, snapping his fingers a couple of times.

I lifted my head and glared at the naturi, fighting the urge to set him on fire. He was stuck in here with me and had ample opportunity to kill me, yet he hadn't. He was also the only one who might know where we were or who had us, though I had a couple guesses. "Still here, you fucking pirate. But where is here?"

He leaned back against the wall, relaxing his stance somewhat, which was surprising. I had the upper hand. I could set him on fire in the blink of an eye. His gift allowed him to call down lightning at will, but there were no windows to the outside, no way he could call down the thunder, so to speak. I could only guess that he was relying on my sense of fair play, since he obviously didn't strike when he had ample opportunity. "I thought you would recognize it. The place belongs to one of your kind."

"You're going to have to be more precise than that. Unlike naturi, there are a few nightwalkers in the area, from what I've seen," I retorted, causing his features to twist.

"The nightwalker that commands this territory. The one they call Veyron, I believe. From what I have seen, we're at his place, locked in the dungeon," he explained through clenched teeth.

I sighed as I bent my knees before me. Sure, I could go at Rowe now and destroy him. It was more than a little tempting, but it also wouldn't help me. I needed to get out of there, and I had a feeling I would need his help.

"I can make a guess at how I got to be here," I said, running one hand through my hair to push it out of my eyes. I frowned when I ran across a clump of dried blood on my scalp, bringing a smile to Rowe's lips. "Did you have to knock me around while I slept?"

Rowe shrugged, still smiling. "I had to make it convincing."

"Sure."

"I only stopped because it was far too easy."

"And you need me alive so you can hand me over to Aurora," I reminded him.

"Yeah," he muttered, looking away from me. I think he was beginning to doubt that his plan to get back into Aurora's good graces through my hide would work.

"How did you get here?" I repeated.

Rowe sighed and shook his head at me. For a second I didn't think he was going to tell me, but he finally spoke in a low voice. "I knew which hotel you were staying in and planned to grab you myself when the sun finally set. Unfortunately, I wasn't the only one with that plan. A group of six showed up: humans, lycanthropes, and a witch. Grabbed you before I could. One of the lycans spotted me, and the witch grabbed me with a spell before I could get away. When I found myself locked up with you, I didn't exactly see this as a bad thing."

"What about Danaus?" I demanded, pushing the words past a lump in my throat.

"Shot him."

Pushing off the wall, I was across the room in a blur, grabbing the naturi by the collar of his shirt and slamming him against the opposite wall. "What do you mean 'shot him'? Is he dead? Did they kill him? Was he coming after me?"

The smile on Rowe's face grew as he saw me twisting at his mercy. I was trapped. The walls of the cell felt as if they were closing in on me and the floor was crumbling beneath my feet. I had to get out of there and find Danaus. Pulling Rowe off the wall a little, I slammed his back into it again with more force, causing his smile to slip slightly. "Tell me what you know."

"Or what? You'll kill me? Won't get any information that way," he mocked.

I narrowed my eyes at him and leaned in so the tip of my nose was nearly touching his. "I can torture you slowly. I've gotten very good at it over the long centuries. Trust me, you'll be screaming answers before I am done."

Rowe stared at me for a long time, his teeth clenched. "He never got into the hotel. They shot him as they were carrying you out. He may not even know they have you. Don't know if he's still alive."

I released Rowe and walked back over to the other side

of the cell. He took the opportunity to put his foot against my butt and shove me away from him. I stumbled into the far wall, catching myself before my face smashed into it. Twisting around, I growled at the naturi, fighting the urge to lunge at him.

"Don't touch me again!" he snarled.

I chuckled at him as I straightened into a standing position. "I thought you'd like it. You're the one that kissed me all those years ago."

The anger slipped from his features and he smiled as well. When I was kidnapped by the naturi centuries ago, Rowe had tried to get me to betray my kind by convincing me he was a poor human about to be executed by the naturi. He kissed me as a last ditch effort to break me. It nearly worked. Even now my lips burned with the ugly memory.

"That was a special circumstance," he said in a low, amused voice.

Leaning my shoulders against the opposite corner, I took a deep breath and slowly released it. "We need to figure a way out of here."

"Brilliant grasp of the obvious you have," Rowe said snidely.

I ignored his comment. If I didn't, I would be forced to smash his smug face in. "Any suggestions?"

"He was told he would be released unharmed if he would simply kill you for us," announced a sweet voice from the other side of the door. I crossed the tiny cell and peered through the window in the door to find Sofia standing on the other side in a gauzy pink dress that floated around her like a thin wisp of smoke.

"Get me out of here, Sofia," I commanded, wrapping my fists around the bars in the window.

"I don't think so," she said with a little shake of her head. "You're too dangerous to be left running around. You've already slaughtered the werewolf pack. Who's on your hit list next?"

"You are if you don't get the key and get me the hell out of here," I snarled, rattling the door a little in its frame. The metal groaned and squeaked, but otherwise didn't budge.

"No, Veyron and the others certainly wouldn't like that."

"Set me free and I'll protect you. I'll return you to Danaus. I can help you," I offered.

Peels of laughter fell from her like the tinkling of bells. She wrapped her arms around her stomach and took a step backward to regain her balance as she laughed at me. "Free me? Who do you think led Veyron's people to you?"

My hands loosened from where they gripped the bars and slid back down to my sides as my mouth fell open. "You tricked us. Convinced Danaus you were some helpless human desperate for his help. You knew he would come after you," I murmured.

"And you're an old nightwalker stuck in your old ways. You don't meddle in the affairs of other nightwalkers, particularly when it comes to their human pets."

"You tried to separate Danaus and me," I said, still stunned by their plan.

"Of course." Sofia took a step closer to the door. "We figured if we couldn't kill you, the hunter easily could since he was able to get so close to you. When he failed, we thought maybe the naturi could. Unfortunately, he's proving to be useless. I guess we'll have to figure something else."

"Bitch," I snarled through gritted teeth. Focusing on her, I sent my powers out from my body and wrapped her in flames. I wanted to see her writhing in pain as the fire ate away at every inch of her flesh. She had deceived Danaus, separated us, and now she was trying to kill me.

But the flames never touched her. Sofia spoke a single, inaudible word and the flames swirled around her like a liquid shawl of fire. The flames danced and crackled with energy, but they never touched her. She looked up at me with glowing eyes. Damn it, she was a witch. It had all been an act, an elaborate hoax.

"Sorry, Fire Starter. You can't kill me, but don't worry, I'll be sure that Danaus knows the truth the moment before he dies," she said, then sauntered back down the dark hallway, leaving me alone with Rowe.

"Get back here, Sofia!" I screamed, pressing my face against the bars. "Get back here so I can kill you!"

"Oh, yeah. That's going to win her over," Rowe said sarcastically beside me.

"Shut it, pirate!" I snapped, pushing away from the door to pace the cell. Unfortunately, it was only a few feet wide. "I need to concentrate. We need to make a plan."

"A plan for getting out of here?"

"And killing all those that put us in here."

"I would be game for that," Rowe said, surprising me.

I looked up at him, my brows furrowed over my nose. "A temporary truce?"

"Extremely temporary. Just until we get out of his house."

I nodded, and returned to my corner in the cell. I lowered my eyelids so I could still partially see Rowe but was able to concentrate on what was going on outside the cell. I could sense Sofia and a scattering of other humans, but she appeared to be the only magic user in the house. I couldn't sense Clarion. Ferko was also in the house, but there were no nightwalkers about. The hour was still relatively early. I could only guess that they were all out hunting, not expecting me to actually survive the day locked up with Rowe. And in truth, I couldn't blame them. The only reason I could guess that I was still alive was because Rowe thought he had more use for me as a living entity to barter with.

I took another calming breath and reached out nervously

with my powers. Rowe had said Danaus had been shot, and Sofia seemed to think that he was still alive, but I was afraid to find out for sure. My powers crept slowly across Budapest, fanning out in all directions. I could have reached out directly but was afraid he wouldn't be there.

Mira! Danaus's voice rang true and clear in my head.

I stifled a half sob at the touch of his powers. He was alive and he felt strong to me. *Danaus! You're alive. Rowe said you were shot.*

I was. Where are you? Is Rowe with you?

Ferko and some others grabbed me. I think I'm at Veyron's. They grabbed Rowe, too. Are you all right?

Fine. Rowe's there? He's with you? he demanded.

Yes, we're both locked together in what looks to be the basement. We're going to try to break out. Where are you?

Near the hotel. I'm going to grab a taxi and get to Veyron's. Wait and let me get there first before you strike.

No, stay where you are. I'll get Stefan to come get you. We're going to need the help. I paused and took a deep breath. *Sofia is a witch.*

Mira—

No, listen to me. It was all a plot to separate us. She's a witch.

Mira, you can't—

I can't explain now. Just trust me.

Send me Stefan, Danaus said. He didn't sound happy, but at least he was willing to come get me out of my prison.

I looked up at Rowe to find him watching me expectantly. "Almost got the troops rallied," I said, then turned my attention to Stefan. He was a bit more pliable than Danaus. He didn't care about Sofia, only where I was and how he was going to set me free. While he preferred to come get me directly, he at last agreed to fetch Danaus before appearing at Veyron's place.

"Help is on the way," I said, finally turning my full attention back to the naturi watching me.

"So I would hope. Are they going to break us out of here?"

I walked over to the massive steel door and frowned. "They are going to act as support. I was hoping we could get out of here on our own."

"And then what?" he asked, not moving from where he stood against the wall. "You've summoned up your little soldiers, but there are no other naturi in Budapest to assist me. How far does this truce extend? The cell door? The front door?"

I held onto the tiny bars in the windows and stared down at the rough concrete ground. "I should kill you now for what you did to Valerio," I muttered, but then shook my head. "But you could have killed me while I slept and you didn't. That earns you a free ticket out of this house. However, if you strike at me or mine even once while we're on the property of this house, I won't hesitate to kill you. The truce extends as long as you behave. That goes for me and mine."

"Agreed."

I turned my focus to the door in front of me and the string of problems I had yet to face. I wasn't ready to contemplate the fact that I had just struck a deal with the worst of my enemies. I'd face that nightmare some night when I was home safe, away from the naturi and the coven.

Twenty-Five

Rowe pressed his hand and cheek against the cold steel door, sensing for any kind of spell that might have been wrapped around the opening. Not only was the naturi well versed in nature-based magic, but in his years of struggling to come up with a way to free his people, he had also become an expert in blood magic—the very thing that got him exiled. His hand slid across the metal in a slow caress, while I stood back from the opening, waiting to see if anything went awry. My skills did not lay with magic spells and other bits of hocus-pocus.

The naturi pushed away from the door and brushed off his hands. "There's no spell barring our way," he announced. "In fact, as far as I can tell, there's no spell in all of this basement area. Apparently, no one thought we would survive to attempt an escape."

"At least, they didn't think you'd have the strength to escape alone after you killed me while I slept," I added. "We should get moving. My companions should be arriving shortly and they'll need our help."

I wrapped my hands around one corner of the window in the door, while bracing my left leg against the stone wall. Rowe did the same on the opposite side of the door and we pulled. Alone, we were both stronger than the normal human, but neither of us were capable of pulling loose the steel door that was firmly bolted into the stone wall. However, working together, the door folded like a piece of warm cheese. A loud metallic screeching echoed through the stone basement, announcing our escape attempt. We had to get moving before someone arrived to investigate.

Climbing through the opening, I reached down to my side for my knife, to discover it was missing. I had forgotten that I'd taken off all of my weapons as I collapsed into bed. I was completely unarmed. I glanced over at Rowe, who simply shook his head at me. Apparently, his captors had taken the time to disarm him.

No matter. I'd tear Sofia apart with my bare hands if it came to that. She had caused me enough problems to last a lifetime and now it was time to take her life.

We hurried down the hallway to the entrance of the basement, not making a sound except for the occasional rustling of our clothes. I climbed up the stairs first and poked my head through the trapdoor, to find that we were actually in a subbasement below the real basement. On stone slabs there were an array of wood and metal coffins where Veyron and his companions obviously slept during the daylight hours. A quick count revealed more than a dozen coffins. Apparently, they subscribed to some of the old ways despite their talk of escaping the old-fashioned precepts of our people. I hadn't seen a grouping of coffins like this except for the underground rooms at the coven meeting hall.

"Can we burn them?" Rowe asked as his eyes scanned them, searching for any that might still be occupied.

"Why bother? We're going to kill them all eventually," I said with a shrug. The naturi smiled unexpectedly at me. Of course, he would be pleased with any plan that worked toward the demise of my kind.

"I think you're starting to come around to my thinking," Rowe whispered as he led the way to the only door in the vast dark basement.

"Hardly. I just don't take kindly to creatures that try to kill me," I replied, following close on his heels.

"I'm still here."

"You don't want me dead. Otherwise, you would have completed the task centuries ago," I said smugly, earning a low growl in response. I ignored it, though as I sensed the distinct presence of Stefan and Danaus close by. They had arrived at Veyron's and were currently seeking entrance into the house. I fully expected Sofia to invite them in. She needed to see to it that the rest of my party was disposed of properly, which would meet with Macaire's ultimate plan. He wanted Danaus and me dead. Unfortunately, Stefan was simply in the wrong place at the wrong time, caught up in the cross fire.

"Let's go. They're here," I said, giving him a little shove in the middle of his back to keep him moving up the stairs and through the door, which opened into the main hall. I peered through a small crack that Rowe had opened. The light was nearly blinding after walking around in pitch-darkness since awakening that evening. I couldn't see anyone, but I could hear Sofia's soft, desperate voice as she pleaded with Danaus and Stefan to help her escape Veyron's clutches. She claimed that Veyron's men had grabbed her again during the day and were threatening to kill her. She was plotting something, ensuring that Danaus and Stefan would be entangled in such a way that their deaths would be imminent.

The sound of approaching footsteps caused Rowe to pull back and soundlessly close the basement door. I threw out my senses to find six nightwalkers and three lycanthropes approaching my companions. Sofia was simply the bait in this trap.

"We need to get in there," I whispered, trying to get around Rowe so I could escape the dark prison.

"Unarmed? We'll be slaughtered in minutes," he snapped. "Your friends are surely armed. Let them whittle down their numbers a bit before we go jumping into the fray."

"Coward! Surely you're not afraid of a handful of weak nightwalkers and a few pathetic werewolves?" I goaded.

"No! I'm more concerned with the nightwalker I made a deal with stabbing me in the back because it's convenient. I would prefer to get the numbers down to something more manageable before I go jumping in."

Laying my hand on the doorknob over his, I took a step up the stair, crowding him. "Remain, if you like. I'm going. But know this, you may be missing your only chance to strike at your kidnappers."

A low groan followed behind me as I snuck out of the basement and down the hall in my stocking feet. In the light, I could finally see that I was dirty and splattered with my own blood. I hadn't had the chance to clean up from the new wounds Rowe inflicted on me while I slept. My palm itched to hit him, but it would do no good now. We had to take care of Ferko and Sofia before we left the house. Veyron and the others would have to be taken care of at another time—I was feeling too weak and we needed time to plan.

Rowe and I came upon the same large room where we had met Veyron for the first time. The garden room was ablaze with light, as if trying to cast away the evil spirits that lurked in all the shadowy corners. The wall of windows was black, reflecting back the furniture and occupants of the room. Sofia clung to Danaus's arm, pleading with him. The hunter placed one hand over hers, comforting her. I nearly set the house on fire. Stefan stood off to the side, looking completely bored.

Nightwalkers and lycanthropes are surrounding you, I

warned Stefan. There was no talking to Danaus—his eyes were only on Sofia.

I sense them, he replied blandly.

Then do something useful. Find out where Veyron and Odelia are. She won't confess to Clarion's location.

"If we are to help you," Stefan said to Sofia, not even trying to sound interested, "we need to strike while Veyron is away. Do you know where he has gone?"

"Away. Hunting," she said in a rushed voice. "But he should be back within the hour. Please, we must hurry before he returns."

"You're right. We must hurry," I said as I walked sound-lessly into the room. Rowe stood behind me, capturing Danaus's dark stare.

"Oh God! She's escaped!" Sofia cried, tightening her grip on Danaus's arm. "She came here last night out of her mind. She was trying to kill me, spouting nonsense about evil plots to destroy her. Veyron locked her up in hopes that a good day's rest would heal her mind. Please, you must pro-tect me!"

Danaus simply stared at me, his face an unreadable mask. I couldn't tell what he was thinking, and I was too scared to touch his thoughts. I didn't want to know if he believed Sofia. In the end it didn't matter. Danaus and I were already over, and I was going to kill Sofia.

As I took a step toward Sofia, the nightwalkers and ly-canthropes that had been patiently waiting in the wings at her disposal entered the room. Ferko brought a low hiss out of Stefan as he eyed the lycanthrope.

"Leave that one to Stefan," I said as I laid one hand on Rowe's shoulder. He stared at Ferko for a couple of sec-onds, frowning, before he finally nodded his agreement that Stefan would get the alpha. Rowe would make do with the nightwalkers.

Angry and frustrated, I was in no mood for a prolonged armed battle. I waved my hand, intending to set the lot of them on fire, but the flames merely swirled through the air and settled in a ball above Sofia's head before finally winking from existence.

"Witch," I snarled.

"You'll not win this one, Fire Starter," she said as she took a couple steps away from Danaus. "You are outnumbered and outgunned. Veyron needs you dead and that is what I shall deliver."

The nightwalkers and lycanthropes charged as one. Rowe launched himself at one nightwalker with lightning-fast agility, while Stefan sought to corner Ferko, tearing apart one lycanthrope in the blink of an eye as he moved to protect his alpha. Three nightwalkers flew at me but suddenly dropped to their knees, clawing at their flesh. A familiar warmth filled the air, brushing against my bare cheek and down my neck. I turned to find Danaus standing with one hand extended toward the nightwalkers, killing them with his special gift.

"Here," he grunted, tossing me a knife from his belt with his free hand.

With a wide grin I launched myself at the remaining nightwalkers. Slicing through tendons and muscles, crushing bones and lacerating vital organs, I left the nightwalkers shrieking in pain as they lay writhing in a pool of their own blood. They had chosen their path, siding with Veyron, and by extension Macaire. I'd had enough of the Ancient's games. Washed in their blood, I vowed that I would end this struggle for power with Macaire once and for all. I was tired of dodging shadows and running from every perceived threat, whether real or not. I wanted my life back, and I knew it would start again when I finally took out Macaire.

Placing a hand on the chest of each nightwalker, I set

them on fire, ending their suffering as I burned them from the inside out. I was too close and too focused for Sofia to be able to stop me this time. They screamed but for a moment, and then were silent forever.

Sliding easily on the balls of my feet on the blood-covered hardwood floor, I turned to face Sofia, who was watching me through narrowed eyes. Her face was twisted with rage, but she suddenly wiped it clean and turned to Danaus.

"Please, Danaus! She's gone mad! You have to protect me. The nightwalkers want me dead. I'm just some pathetic human for them to play with," she cried, clutching his arm again.

"Release him," I hissed, pushing into a standing position. It took all my will not to set her on fire. "He doesn't believe you any longer. He knows you're a witch. He knows you tried to use and trick us."

"It's a lie! She's insane!" Sofia screamed, growing more frantic. She was a superb little actress, but my patience was growing short and I was in no mood for games.

"Who stopped my fire attack?"

"How am I supposed to know?"

"Tell me what Macaire's demands were. What did he require of Veyron and Odelia?" I demanded.

"Macaire? I don't know who this Macaire is," she continued. She took a step away from Danaus for every step I took toward her.

"I'm quite confident that you do. I have no doubt that Macaire directed this entire farce. You already confessed that your goal was to come between Danaus and me. Separate us and force us to fight each other, to kill each other. For who better to kill me than my greatest ally? Definitely a plan of Macaire's making."

"Please, Mira, I never meant you any harm." Sofia extended shaking hands toward me, but there was an evil glint in her eyes. She was plotting something. "Veyron is the one that locked you up. I went to Danaus because I thought he could free me from Veyron's grasp. I never meant to come between you."

"I don't believe you and neither does Danaus. You locked me up with Rowe in hopes that he would do your dirty work for you. Macaire could then go to the rest of the world stating that a naturi killed me."

Sofia looked over at Danaus, but I refused to drop my gaze from her face. The witch dropped her hands back to her sides and then frowned at me. "A lot of good that did us," she finally confessed. "The naturi is now fighting with you when he should have spent the day ripping your insides out with his bare hands."

My hold on my temper finally snapped. Flames whooshed up around Sofia, burning through the carpet, drapes, and furniture. She kept the fire from consuming her but remained trapped in a tight circle. I stepped through the flames with my blade in hand. Above the crackling of the flames I heard someone shout my name, but I didn't look up. I couldn't take the chance. Sofia was a witch and I was sure that she still had a trick or two up her sleeve.

As I stepped into the circle of fire with her, she disappeared from my sight. I immediately extinguished the flames and scanned the room. I had felt the brush of power when she disappeared. She didn't have enough power to go far. She wasn't as strong a witch as I had thought, which was more than a little surprising. But then, Macaire wouldn't have been able to control a powerful witch very easily. Regardless, she was mine for what she had done to Danaus and me.

"Where did she go?" I shouted, my eyes whipping from one end of the burned and bloody room to the other.

"I feel her outside," Stefan replied after a second.

I darted outside, my blood-soaked stockings slipping on the hardwood floors. Gravel and snow bit into my feet as I hit the yard. With a wave of my hand the tires of the car that Sofia was climbing into exploded as the rubber melted under the fires that suddenly burned around them.

A roll of thunder rumbled in the distance, but the sound was approaching us. Rowe was outside and finally in the clear to use his own powers. The wind swirled around us, throwing up flakes of snow and the occasional dead leaf. I didn't need to look overhead to see the black clouds beginning to pour across the sky. Rowe wanted Sofia dead as much as I did. She was one of those responsible for his imprisonment.

"She's mine!" I shouted, pointing at Rowe.

"Not if I get her first!"

"Macaire!" Sofia screamed in terror, but it was too late. I lunged across the yard in a blur of color and grabbed her by the neck. I threw her away from the car and followed after her, narrowly missing the lightning bolt that came streaking from the sky to smash into the car. She landed in a mound of snow with a heavy rush of air expelled from her lungs. I landed on top of her and sank my fangs into her neck before she could make a sound, before she could even raise a fist to push me away.

As I drained her of blood, I pushed deep inside her mind. She felt me in her thoughts and tried to scream, but it came out as only a low gurgle. Once there, I showed her the horrors I had witnessed over the years. I convinced her of the torture that still awaited her when I was finally through feeding off of her. Her heart pounded in her chest until I was sure that it would soon explode, pumping her warm blood that much faster into my cold frame.

When I had drunk all I could, I lifted my mouth from her throat but not my presence from her mind. She stared off into oblivion, not seeing the world around her, but the horrible world of bleak terror and pain that I painted for her. After only a couple seconds longer, her heart finally gave out and she uttered a shuddering gasp. She died in the tight grasp of fear, convinced that a long existence of pain awaited her.

Wiping my mouth with the back of my hand, I rose to my feet and backed away from her corpse. Her blood still leaked from her neck, staining the white snow red. I felt both rejuvenated and disgusted simultaneously. It had been a long time since I'd last killed someone in that manner. Locked in fear, I left their mind a shattered mess of chaos and pain in their final minutes. It always left me wondering if the soul ever escaped those grim horrors when death finally came or if those same fears followed them through the rest of eternity. I didn't like it. Killing someone was a matter of blood, violence, and hopefully a quick death. This was a slow torture that damaged both mind and soul.

I had killed Sofia like that out of hatred and pain. I hated what I'd done, but at the same time I couldn't salvage any feelings of regret. Despite my distaste for the act, I still hated her with every fiber of my being. She had stolen Danaus from me.

"Mira?" Stefan said, drawing my gaze over to where he stood with a blade pointed at Rowe. The naturi glared at me, his hands lowered but open, showing that he held no weapon. For now he was abiding by our agreement. He had only struck at Sofia, the nightwalkers, and the lycanthropes that had attacked us. Rowe had made no move against me and mine.

"Let him go," I said in a low, weary voice.

"Are you insane?"

"I'm beginning to think so," I muttered. I had already

heard that enough from Sofia. I was starting to question my sanity.

"Mira, he's the one you've been after all these months! He's been trying to capture you. He's going to kill you. We won't get another chance like this," Stefan argued, taking a step closer to the naturi. Rowe never moved. He just stared at me with his narrowed eyes flashing in the light coming from the house.

"I know that!" I shouted back at him. "Do you seriously think I don't know exactly who he is and what he means to do to me? I said, let him go!"

Stefan glared at the naturi for another second before he finally straightened his stance and put the knife he was holding back into a sheath up his sleeve along his wrist. He walked over toward me, partially standing between me and the naturi as if he were still determined to protect me.

Rowe arched one brow at me while the corner of his mouth tweaked in a smile. "I am . . . surprised."

"Just go now before I change my mind," I growled.

Rowe hunched over as a pair of massive black wings sprouted from his back. He extended them to their full length, catching the wind that was still snaking through the city. As he lifted off the ground, I took a step toward him.

"Find Cynnia!" I shouted up to him.

The naturi hovered in the air like a piñata waiting for me to take a whack at him. Rowe cocked his head to one side in thought. "You think killing her will win me back to Aurora's side?"

"No, but I think you will find a home with Cynnia that you will never find with Aurora. Live your life, Rowe, while you can, instead of chasing after death."

"Same to you, Mira," he murmured before rising into the night sky. I watched after him for several seconds until he completely disappeared from sight. I knew he would leave

Budapest. All the other naturi here were dead, and he knew that I wouldn't be remaining there for long. I wasn't sure he would actually seek out Aurora's renegade sister Cynnia, but for him it would be a step in the right direction. I had a feeling that Cynnia would accept him, scars and all, where Aurora never could, no matter what he accomplished for her.

Closing my eyes, I buried my face in Stefan's chest. The nightwalker wrapped his arms around me, blocking out some of the cold wind that beat against my exposed flesh. I had killed Sofia, and soon I would have to face Danaus, but I wasn't ready. Not yet. Not tonight.

"Take me back to the hotel," I whispered, barely getting the words past the lump in my throat. I needed to be away from this place. I had woken up to find myself locked with my mortal enemy, a pawn in an elaborate game to turn Danaus against me so he would be forced to kill me. I'd had all I could take for one evening. I needed somewhere safe where the world could touch me no longer.

Twenty-Six

I stood in the shower for nearly an hour. Blood and dirt washed off me, but the gritty feeling of death and torture still lingered in my mind. I couldn't escape it, couldn't rinse it away no matter how long I stood in the steaming hot water. I washed my hair twice and scrubbed every inch of my body so that my flesh was rubbed red, but the memories and the pain stayed.

As the water finally started to chill, I turned off the spigot and towel-dried as much as I could. Wrapping a robe around me, I walked back into the bedroom as I rubbed a fresh towel through my wet hair. I paused just over the threshold, my hands growing instantly still. Danaus was in the hotel room with me. The door had just slammed shut and I could now sense him moving through the room.

My first instinct was to summon Stefan back to my side. He could take me away so I wouldn't have to face Danaus and his scathing words regarding my murder of Sofia. But I couldn't keep running from Danaus. I just wished I'd had enough time to become numb on the inside so that his words wouldn't have the power to reach my heart.

Pulling the curtains closed, I lit a handful of candles around the room with a wave of my hand, casting the room in a soft glow. I started to walk over to the closet when the bedroom door swung open and slammed shut.

"Just give me a minute to get dressed," I said softly.

"You left me," he replied. His voice was rough and ragged, as if it had been dragged across the concrete.

A sigh escaped me before I could catch it. "I'm not ready to do this now, Danaus."

I didn't have a chance to argue. He roughly grabbed my upper arm and spun me around. His lips found mine in a violent kiss as the back of my head hit the wall. Both of his hands cupped my cheeks as he kissed me again and again until his ragged breathing danced across my face. My eyes fell shut and I kissed him back, not questioning whether this was an illusion or just a hallucination of my own fractured mind. I didn't care. I would welcome death of this sort so long as he didn't stop kissing me.

My hand drifted down to his chest and I could feel his beautiful heart pounding beneath my fingertips. I knew the beat as if it were my own heart. His smell swam around me, that distinct scent of some distant sea and the soft caress of the summer sun. I wanted to drown in the smell so that it washed away my own scent. I wanted to become a part of him for a little while, just enough so the world would slip by us both unnoticed.

Danaus deepened his kisses, tasting me. My hands slid up to his arms and I kissed him back with the same passion, getting swept up in everything I had dreamed about for too many lonely nights. But he suddenly pulled back. He had pricked his tongue on one of my fangs—we hadn't had enough practice kissing each other to escape a little bloodletting.

"I'm sorry," I said, hating to ruin the mood. I didn't want to shatter it, didn't want him pulling away from me already. "I'll be more careful."

A frail smile crossed his lips as his eyes danced over my face, as if trying to soak in the sight of me. "I think my eagerness was to blame," he murmured before leaning in to kiss me again. I tried to pick up exactly where we had left off, but he pulled away again. His large hands caressed my cheeks and swept down my neck. "I thought I had lost you," he whispered in a wavering voice. "I came back to the hotel as they were leaving. They shot me. It knocked me out and I lost a lot of blood. I wasn't conscious again until you reached out to me. I had nightmares. I thought you were gone. Thought you were dead forever. I thought I had lost you."

"I'm here," I replied in a shaking voice, leaning my forehead against his. "I thought I had lost you too. Sofia . . . I . . ." I stammered. I didn't want to say the words out loud.

"I knew you were telling the truth. She was careless tonight, not bothering to cloak her powers. She used me," Danaus said, and I knew that I had been forgiven. Everything had been forgiven for tonight. Tomorrow there would be more words, and more arguments waited on that distant horizon, but not tonight.

"Kiss me again. I want to forget," I murmured, brushing my lips against his. Danaus leaned into me again, pressing me harder against the wall. He exhaled and I inhaled, drawing just a little bit of his soul into my body as he kissed me. My hands roamed down along his hard chest until I finally found the edge of his shirt. A low groan escaped me as I finally touched bare flesh. How long had I dreamed of the satiny warm feel of his skin? I wanted to run my lips along every inch of his skin, tasting him, memorizing him, but for now my mouth was trapped by his.

"Mira," he growled at me as my hands slid under his

shirt, exploring the sides of his stomach as they slowly worked higher.

"I need you, Danaus," I said as his lips slid down my jaw to my neck. The edge of his teeth scraped across my flesh, sending a shiver down my spine and lighting a fire deep inside of me that I knew I would never be able to put out. "Please say yes. Say you need me too."

He grabbed both of my wrists and stretched them above my head, where he held them with one large hand. He reached between us with the other hand and untied my robe, spreading it open so he could see my pale skin against the black silk.

"You're enough to break any man," he said in a low voice.

I smiled as I lifted my right leg and wrapped it around his left leg, pulling him back against me. "I don't want you broken," I purred in return. "It's more fun when you've still got some fight left in you." I'd run the tip of my tongue along his jaw and down his neck when I felt him stiffen but not pull away. Pressing a kiss to his neck, I nuzzled him once, chuckling. "I promise, no matter what happens I will never bite you."

"Thank you," he murmured before capturing my mouth in yet another rough kiss. His free hand slid up from my waist to cup my breast, leaving me squirming beneath his touch as I struggled to get closer to him. His hand was strong and firm, caressing me and pulling at the nipple until he finally got a moan out of me as I arched my whole body against his.

"Release my hands," I commanded, but he only laughed at me as his lips drifted down from my mouth to my neck. His hot breath trailed along my collarbone, lighting little fires down my body before he finally took my breast in his mouth. I jerked and groaned, my head falling back against the wall. He touched my hip bone before slipping around to cup my bottom, keeping me pressed tightly against him. I could feel his body growing harder beneath me, and the thought wrung another moan out of me.

"Release me, Danaus! I need to touch you!" I choked out as he switched from my left breast to my right.

"Are you not enjoying this?" he asked, sending his hot breath against my wet nipple. "It certainly sounds like you are."

"Damn it, Danaus! You're killing me. I want to touch you," I said between clenched teeth as I struggled to hold onto a single thought amid the pleasure shooting through my frame. It was unfair. I was standing there completely naked and shivering in pleasure, while he was still fully clothed and completely in command. Closing my eyes, I arched against him again, pressing as close as I possibly could. "I've dreamed of touching you for so long," I said, lowering my voice so it ran like a hand over his cheek. "I need to touch you."

A groan escaped him as he released my hands. His lips crushed mine as one hand tightened on my ass and the other closed over my breast. I kissed him back while I brushed both hands away so I could push his coat off his shoulders and down his arms. My lips never wavered from his as I ripped his shirt down the front, giving me full access to his chest. My fingers slid down as if I were reading him. I could feel hard unyielding muscle and smooth skin. My fingers tripped over the occasional scar from a wound too deep for even the bori-bound Danaus to heal completely. While his skin was soft and ageless, I could feel the centuries of life flowing through him. His powers brushed over me and through me, binding us together so that our powers were a single force within the room.

I dropped my hands from his body with great reluctance

and pressed my fingertips into the wall so I could push off. We stumbled blindly over to the bed, where I pushed him down and continued to strip him naked. Burying his hand in my hair, he pulled me on top of him. His kisses were hotter now and his body felt like it was on fire next to mine. I stretched out, pressing my entire length along his so I could feel all of him.

My fangs ached to enter his neck. Something inside of me craved his blood like a human craved air. The feeling crawled inside of me, burning away at my soul. I clenched my teeth and focused on his hands as they slid over my body, learning every curve and hollow. The craving finally subsided but the need to have him grew stronger.

"Please, Danaus, I need you," I panted, pulling him on top of me. He rolled over, positioning himself between my thighs. I grabbed two fistfuls of his hair and pulled his mouth down to mine as he grabbed my hips and thrust into me. My back arched off the bed and I moaned.

Danaus swore softly once as he started to slowly move inside of me. I dropped my hands to the bedsheets and raked my long fingernails along the fabric, shredding it. I moved in time with him, following each wave of pleasure as it pulsed through me.

Smiling up at him as his long black hair crowded around his face, I wrapped my legs around his and pushed him over onto his back while he remained inside of me. Straddling him, I rode him slowly, running my fingers along his rib cage and over his flat nipples.

"I take it you want to be on top," he murmured in a deep husky voice that sent a shiver down my spine. I wanted to take this slowly. I had waited too long to finally be able to touch him, to look down on his face wreathed in peace and pleasure. I wanted to savor this moment when the world wasn't crashing in around us.

But the slow ride couldn't last. I felt the orgasm rising within me, building so that muscles tightened and I could no longer form a coherent thought beyond the feeling of him moving in and out of my body. The need was on Danaus as well. He roughly grabbed my hips, forcing me to go at a faster pace as he pushed harder within me. I braced my hands on either side of his head and arched my back as the first wave rippled through me, tearing a scream from my throat in the form of his name. I rode him into mindless oblivion, where he joined me only seconds later. I felt the warm rush inside me as his own orgasm claimed his body. His arms tightened around my waist and he let out a low groan that seemed to have been torn from his very soul.

I collapsed on top of him, no longer able to hold myself up. My body was covered in his sweat and I rose and fell with each heavy breath he took. I felt at peace. There were no naturi or coven Elders waiting for us just around the corner. The world wasn't going to Hell in a handbasket. We weren't enemies sworn to fight until one or both of us died. We were just two people enjoying each other.

After several minutes I leaned up on one elbow and looked down on Danaus. His eyes were closed and his breathing had evened out at last. I brushed some of his long hair out of his eyes and smoothed it away from his sweaty brow.

"Feeling better?" I asked, unable to keep the contented purr from my voice.

"It's a good start," he said with a smile.

But to my dismay the smile faded almost as quickly as it formed and slight furrows appeared on his smooth brow. His look of peace and contentment crumbled before my eyes and I couldn't understand why. Reluctantly, I dipped into his mind. I just wanted to see where his thoughts were going. Were worries of the naturi and Veyron seeping back in already?

How are we going to make this work?

Danaus's words echoed through my brain, assaulting my heart. I could feel the doubt hanging in those heavy words and I felt paralyzed. I was losing him before we had ever really had a chance.

Sucking in a deep breath, I forced a smile on my face before pressing a brief kiss to his temple. "Don't think about it too much. It was just sex," I forced myself to say as I rolled off him. I briskly scooped up my robe from where I had dropped it on the floor and pulled it on while walking into the living room of the hotel suite.

I carefully erected a wall of stone around my heart, but it felt as if it were crumbling before the mortar had a chance to dry. I wanted Danaus. Not just in my bed, but in my life. I wanted him as my companion, my lover, and my friend. But I could feel the doubt rising within him. I was a nightwalker and he was a nightwalker hunter. He had spent centuries hating my kind. That was not going to be overcome with one night in bed.

Maybe he was right. How were we going to make this work?

I walked over to the desk and leaned my hands against the top, staring down at the piece of paper on which I'd written the names of the leaders of Budapest. Picking up my pen, I drew an X through Ferko's name. One down, four to go.

Out of the corner of my eye, I saw Danaus walk into the room still completely naked and oblivious to the broken bit of furniture and glass that still littered the ground.

"Why did you leave?" he asked as he came to stand behind me. "I wasn't done with you yet."

"I thought I'd give you a chance to recover," I said, not moving from where I stood leaning over the desk.

Danaus reached down and pulled up the edge of the robe so my backside was exposed. I started to stand upright when he placed a firm hand on my lower back, keeping me bent over. His other hand swept over my thighs before he reached between my legs. He inserted two fingers inside me, drawing a groan from my throat as my eyes drifted shut. "Why did you run from me?" he demanded as he drew his fingers in and out.

"I didn't," I croaked. My throat would no longer work and I was choking on the words. "I thought you needed to rest."

"You're wrong and you're lying," he said. He removed his fingers and immediately pushed his rock hard penis back inside of me. He slowly drew it out and then pushed it back inside. "So wet," he murmured. "Just for me. So tight and so wet, just for me."

His words sent a shiver through my body as I could feel his pleasure. He grew harder and thicker as he moved within me. From this angle he was deeper than he had been before, driving me insane with his slow movement when I wanted him hard and fast.

"It's never just sex between us, Mira. It never could be," he whispered in a rough voice. He leaned down and pressed a gentle kiss to my shoulder that nearly brought tears to my eyes. "Does this feel like just sex to you? Do you think that's even possible between us?"

"No," I groaned as I tried to quicken the pace, but he held me still. He moved with a slow pace, driving me toward madness as he brought me to the edge of an orgasm, but I couldn't quite reach it.

"Then why say it?"

"Because you have doubts. You don't think we can work. I heard your thoughts," I admitted. I tried to reach between my legs to touch myself, to finally push my body over the edge I was teetering on, but Danaus grabbed my hands and held them down on the desk and leaned forward.

"I have doubts, but I'm willing to try. It's the best I can offer," he said, growing still as his voice became deeper and huskier. "Will you try? I need you, Mira. Try for me."

"I'll try," I whispered. I leaned over and pressed a kiss into his arm, loving the feel of him wrapped around me and pressed deep inside of me.

"Thank you," he said. He reached down between my legs, pressing his fingers into my clitoris. My body jerked and hummed with a newfound tension as he pulled me back toward the edge. He picked up the pace, pounding his body inside of mine, earning a whimper from me as I hovered just short of an orgasm.

And then my world shattered. My bowstring taut body snapped and everything exploded as wave after wave of pleasure hammered through my frame, leaving me weak-kneed and shaking. Danaus held tight to my hips as he continued to pound into me until his body went stiff with the orgasm that swept through him.

Panting and covered in a fresh sheen of sweat, he leaned over me and bit my shoulder. "You're mine, vampire, from here until the end. You are mine."

I laughed at him. I was feeling light-headed and more than a little giddy. It had been too long since I'd last been touched, since I had last felt these warm feelings of concern and passion. It had been too long since either of us were happy.

"Then take me back to bed, hunter," I commanded in a weary but contented voice. "Take me back to bed so you can be sure that I stay yours."

Twenty-Seven

U nfortunately, any additional quality time was cut short by the appearance of Stefan in the hotel suite. He was considerate enough to appear in the living room instead of the bedroom where Danaus and I were spread naked across the bed. Danaus brushed his lips across my temple and heaved a deep sigh.

"Can I stake him?" he asked, running his fingers up and down my back in a slow caress.

I snuggled closer as I smiled. "No, you can't."

"Can you at least get rid of him?"

Leaning up on my elbow, I looked down at him. "I'm afraid not. We need to make plans for how we're going to get rid of Veyron and his companions."

"Back to work," he groaned, sitting up in bed.

"Back to work."

After pulling on some clothes, I went out to keep Stefan occupied until Danaus could join us. The nightwalker was also considerate enough not to make any comment on my obviously disheveled appearance. There was no question as to what we were doing.

Setting an overturned chair back on its four legs, I sat down on the soft cushion. "How's Valerio?"

"Better. He should be arriving shortly."

As if summoned by our words, Valerio appeared near the entrance to the room. He gazed about, arching one eyebrow at the chaos. "I see the cleaning service hasn't been through yet. Of course, if you're comfortable with this arrangement, who am I to judge?" he said blandly.

I jumped out of my chair and rushed over to him. The nightwalker gave a slight grunt when I wrapped my arms around him, but he returned the hug. Seeing him strung up on the cross with a stake in his chest had terrified me. I knew I'd come to close to losing him.

"So glad to see you still alive, old man," I said, brushing a kiss across his chin.

"I am glad to still be alive," he said with smile. His cheeks were still a little paler than usual and he didn't look as strong on his feet as he should. He was not up to his full strength yet, but coming back to Budapest was a start. As I stepped away from him, I noticed the smile fade from his lips. "However, I am disappointed to hear that you had a chance to kill my captor and you let him go. I'm curious to know why." His words were deceptively calm and neutral, but I could sense frustration boiling away inside of him.

"I would like to know why you didn't kill Rowe either," Danaus spoke up. I spun around to find him standing in the bedroom doorway with his arms folded over his chest. At least he looked as he always did, with his dark clothes and sturdy boots. I, on the other hand, was skipping around the room barefoot, trying to avoid shards of broken glass, chunks of wood, and spent bullet casings. "He's hunted you for months, Mira. He's going to continue to do so. Why take such a risk as leaving him alive?"

"I couldn't in good conscience kill him."

"You couldn't in good conscience kill the creature that

was going to end my existence?" Valerio repeated, humor and sarcasm filling his voice.

"I'm sorry, but no. Rowe was trapped in a tiny cell with me all throughout the day. He had more than ample opportunity to kill me while I was unconscious and vulnerable, but he didn't. I don't know why he didn't kill me, and in truth, I don't want to know. The only thing that matters is that he didn't. In repayment for that act of clemency, I agreed that no one would attack him so long as he did not attack me or anyone within my party while we attempted to escape Veyron's house. He kept to his part of the agreement, so I kept to mine."

"So, you're not going to kill him now?"

A deep laugh escaped me as I wandered back over to my chair and plopped down. "Of course I'm going to kill him. If I see him on the battlefield again, I'm sure neither one of us will hesitate to attack, but I promised for that brief period of time at Veyron's that I would not attack him. It was the fair thing to do."

"Fair thing? He tried to kill me!" Valerio said.

"And he had ample opportunity to kill a sleeping vampire that was his enemy for centuries, but he didn't. There is still time, Valerio. We will kill him soon enough. Please say that you understand why I did it."

"I understand. What I do not understand is where you got this strange sense of justice and fair play. Your conscience is going to get you killed," he warned, frowning at me.

"Possibly, but not tonight."

"No, Veyron is going to kill you tonight. Or rather, this morning," Stefan said grimly.

"If it's okay with Valerio, I would prefer to retreat to Vienna during the daylight hours and regroup here in the evening for our final attack on Veyron."

"You think Veyron will send another daylight raiding party?" Danaus asked.

"Not really, but I cannot judge Macaire's potential attachment to Sofia," I said with a shrug. "If he was fond of her, he may force Veyron to send people after me."

Valerio finally entered the room completely and sat down on the sofa after brushing off some of the debris. "So, tell us you've got this whole mess figured out. I don't believe that Macaire sent us here simply to get rid of the naturi."

"What you have to keep in mind," I said, "is that he only sent me to Budapest. He knew I would bring Danaus with me. You and Valerio are just expendable."

Stefan grimaced. "Nicely put."

I ignored his comment and continued. "There's a power structure here unlike any of the other domains, and Macaire was counting on it being strong enough to kill both Danaus and me." Pushing out of my chair, I went over to the desk and picked up the piece of paper I had been scribbling on. As I returned to my chair, I handed it to Valerio, who looked down at it.

"I don't understand," he said, handing the paper over to Stefan.

"Macaire built a ruling system here similar to the coven, with five shared rulers," I explained. "My guess is that he drew Veyron and Odelia, but also struck a deal with Ferko and the warlock Clarion. They held the city in a firm hand, killing off any creature that might have been seen as a threat to their control."

I looked up at Stefan and frowned. "Odelia may have given the excuse of Michelle's beauty, but if they knew she belonged to you, they might have feared that she was a scout for you, looking for new territory. She may have been killed simply as a poorly thought out warning against coming into their domain."

Stefan clenched the paper in his fist and stared down at it. "So, Veyron, Odelia, Ferko, and Clarion all conspired together to be the keepers of Budapest, and Macaire knew."

"Macaire didn't just know, he arranged it," I said. "We're not talking keepers. He was setting up a replacement coven. He had the liege role here in Budapest and planned to extend his power once his little group destroyed Danaus and me."

"Th-That's treason," Stefan stuttered. "Our Liege would never allow it."

"I think the hope was that he would never be able to withstand an assault by all five of them, particularly with the warlock in hand. Macaire's first goal was to get rid of me."

Valerio leaned forward and rested his elbows on his knees. "The odd thing is that this should have worked. If they all had acted in concert, we never would have been able to adequately protect you, especially not with Clarion as backup. You should be dead and you're not."

"How kind of you," I said with a smirk. "You're right, though. In a perfect world it should have worked, except that nightwalkers don't play well with other creatures."

"The agreement between the various members was falling apart?" Danaus asked from the other side of the room.

"Or it never really worked in the first place because it never really had a good test," I replied.

"They set up Ferko to take the fall for Michelle from the very beginning, knowing we would strike back by wiping out his entire pack along with Ferko, freeing the others from their agreement. They could have come riding to his rescue at any time, particularly earlier tonight at Veyron's house, but they didn't. Someone wanted him out of the way. He was sacrificed."

"And Sofia?" Danaus asked.

I frowned, still hating to hear her name pass his lips. "Just one of Macaire's pawns." I turned to look at Stefan and Valerio, wiping my face clean of expression. "Her job was to separate Danaus and me using his weakness for humans. Their hope was that we would kill each other so they wouldn't have to do the job themselves. If Danaus didn't kill me first, it was a given that I was going to kill Sofia for her trouble, even if I never discovered that she was truly a witch in disguise."

"How sweet! A crime of passion," Stefan mocked.

I bit my tongue. Stefan had committed his own crime of passion when he ripped Ferko to shreds over Michelle's death, and I had no doubt that he planned to do the same to Odelia when she crossed his path again.

"So, we're left with an intimate trio of conspirators against you," Valerio said, sitting back against the sofa again with a heavy sigh.

"Oh, no. This is a quartet, and I fully intend to clean house. I won't tolerate being hunted. This conspiracy was not only for our death, but yours as well. I don't find myself quite so forgiving as you when it comes to the planned assassination of those I consider to be my friends."

Skepticism filled Stefan's expression, and in truth I couldn't blame him. We'd never seen eye-to-eye on anything, and I had no doubt that he would take the first opportunity that presented itself to kill me for my seat on the coven. But by the same token, he had protected and defended me on more than one occasion since Peru. He was proving to be more useful than I initially anticipated, though I still didn't trust him. Stefan needed a seat on the coven if he was ever going to be satisfied.

"Mira, you can't mean . . ." Valerio started, but his voice faded off. Even as we sat in Budapest, a long distance from Venice, it still didn't feel safe to say the words out loud.

"I do and I will. It's the only reason that Jabari allowed me to join the coven in the first place. It's time I fulfilled my purpose so I can move on with my life," I grumbled, staring at the sparkling glass-covered floor before me.

"If you fulfill your purpose, then what reason will Jabari have to keep you around?" Danaus asked softly from the far side of the room.

"None," I whispered, then shook my head. "I'll deal with that problem when the time comes." Though I had a feeling I would have to deal with it sooner if Nick had any say in the matter. My time was running out. Soon I would have to deal with two coven Elders, not just one.

"What about the naturi?" Stefan inquired, drawing my gaze back to his face. The nightwalker leaned against the wall with his hands shoved into his pockets, looking very content with my plans. If I took on Macaire directly, there was a very good chance that a seat was going to open up on the coven. He honestly didn't care if it was mine or Macaire's. It was a win-win situation for him.

"They were just a red herring," Valerio said, his lips twisting around the words. He had been nearly killed by something that wasn't important in the grander scheme of things.

"Yes, it was either just luck or coincidence that Rowe happened to be in Budapest at the same time." I shrugged. "I hadn't seen any sign of the bastard since Peru."

"Or there's a chance that Macaire is still in contact with the naturi," Danaus said, "plotting new plots that would mean your eventual death."

"Macaire is plotting with the naturi?" Valerio nearly came off the sofa.

I inwardly cringed, wishing I could throw something at Danaus. I really wasn't in the mood to get into this with Stefan and Valerio. Neither knew that members of the coven had conspired with the naturi at one time to bring about the end of Our Liege.

"He did at one time," I muttered. "We don't know if he still is. I thought I had killed his contact, and I find it hard to believe that Rowe would cooperate with any nightwalker."

"He might if it means getting his hands on you," Danaus countered, sending a shiver down my spine.

"It doesn't matter. I plan to clean up this mess."

"Tonight?" Valerio asked.

"No. I need you in peak fighting form. I will need everyone's help to take down not only Veyron but Odelia and Clarion as well. We're cleaning out Budapest before we return to Venice."

"Will you ever return?" Stefan inquired. "You are the keeper, after all."

"Keeper," I grumbled. "I never wanted to be keeper of this city."

"It's not that bad a city. Once you clean out the rabble, of course," Danaus added, surprising me.

I leaned my head into my hand with my elbow resting on the arm of the chair. "I just want to go home at this point. I'll come back to Budapest eventually. It's not like we're going to be leaving behind any power players. The shifters are dead, and there aren't any old nightwalkers here."

"That's just the problem, Mira," Stefan spoke up. "You're leaving behind a power vacuum. Anyone will be able to move into this domain and take over."

"What? You want it? Take it!" I dropped my hand and glared at Valerio. "Or you. It's closest to your domain. You take it."

"I don't have a domain," Valerio said smugly.

I slammed my fist against the arm of the chair, causing the wood to creak. "Then man up and claim one finally!"

Valerio just smiled at me, enjoying my evident frustration. I didn't want Budapest. It was a gorgeous city and I had no doubt that I might actually enjoy it once Veyron and the others were cleared out. However, my mind kept drifting back to my sweet Savannah. I had left Tristan and too many others unguarded. I needed to get back there before something horrible happened.

"If nothing is going to be done tonight," Valerio said, pushing slowly to his feet, "then we should pull back to Vienna, where it's safer."

"We need to be at our strongest if we're going to take them on," I added, rising as well.

"Veyron got you worried?" Danaus asked.

I shook my head as I carefully picked my way over to the bedroom. "Clarion. You never know what warlocks are capable of until they have already cast the spell."

Danaus and I quickly packed our bags. Then Stefan placed an arm across my shoulders, while Valerio put his hand on Danaus's arm. In a blink of an eye we were whisked across vast empty miles to Valerio's private apartments in downtown Vienna.

Stefan released me once he was sure I was steady on my feet. He walked into the living room and relaxed across a chaise lounge. Valerio and Danaus appeared beside me a second later. The hunter frowned and shook his head as if to clear it of the cobwebs, while Valerio came over and picked up my bag so he could personally escort me to a room that I would use for changing. I would be sleeping in a more secure and private chamber with him and Stefan when the sun finally started to rise in the sky.

"It seems that you and Danaus have reconciled your differences," Valerio murmured when we were alone in the other room. He placed my bag down on the bed and leaned against one of the four wooden posters with his arms crossed over his chest.

"We're trying to make this work," I admitted, though

I was reluctant to speak about it. Valerio and I had a past together that stretched across several centuries. I'd taken different lovers during the times when we were apart, and he had not batted an eye at it. Why had he taken a sudden interest now? "What's your concern?"

Valerio smiled at me and extended one hand. I took it, allowing him to raise it to his lips and brush a kiss across the knuckles. "You are my concern. You are always my concern."

"You're also full of shit. What's your sudden interest?" I snapped. I tugged at my hand, but he refused to release me.

"A powerful nightwalker hunter has obviously won the heart of one of the most powerful nightwalkers in the world. Certainly that should raise a concern or two among the masses."

"Shouldn't you also consider that one of the most powerful nightwalkers in the world has potentially won the heart of a powerful nightwalker hunter? Wouldn't that benefit us?" I countered.

"Have you, now?"

"If not now, then soon I think," I said with a small smile. "He has stopped hunting us at random. Directed execution is not out of the question for him. He would be protecting the humans, and protecting my interests as well."

Valerio chuckled at me as he leaned down and pressed a kiss to my cheek. "You make it sound as if you planned this."

"Hmmm . . . wouldn't that be marvelous," I purred, and then grew serious. "I have plans for Danaus, but they have nothing to do with the coven or the naturi or anything of this world."

"And what plans would those be?"

"Going home to Savannah and letting the world forget about us."

"Ahh . . . *mi amor*, I don't think that will ever be possible."

"You're probably right, but we have to try. Even if it's only for a little while."

A knock at the door pulled us apart. I turned to find Danaus standing in the hall with his bag slung over his shoulder and his coat folded over his other arm. "Is this a private party?"

"No, we were discussing plans after we are done with Budapest and Venice," I replied, forcing a smile upon my lips.

"Savannah," he said with a sigh. *Home,* I heard whispered through his brain. He then turned his full attention to Valerio. "Does Clarion know where you reside in Vienna?"

"No, I don't believe so," Valerio replied. "No one has seen me come or go from this particular residence. The few times I saw Clarion in Vienna it was in some very public locations. He should not bother us here."

"Can Veyron or Odelia track me like the naturi can?" he asked, turning his attention to me.

"No. They found us at the hotel because I made no secret of where we were staying. We did not try to hide our movements within the city. We were easily followed, I have no doubt. They may guess that we have left the city with Valerio and Stefan, but they are more likely to believe that we have pulled back to Venice rather than Vienna."

"It may not be safe for me to stay here with you during the day." Danaus frowned down at me, tightening one hand on the strap of his bag. "I could go stay in a nearby hotel so you don't have to worry about Clarion getting close during the day."

I walked over and laid my hand against his cheek. I could spend a lifetime touching him. "If I know Valerio, we will not exactly be here during the daylight hours. He has some secret den tucked away for us to sleep in, which will be safe. You will have the run of the house until sunset."

"You'll be safe?"

"Completely."

I could feel the tension ease from his shoulders. The naturi were able to get to me in the past because they had been able to track him, following him until he finally met up with me. It was trick I was sure Rowe found handy more than once during our association.

"Well, if that's all for the evening, I must go feed," Valerio said in a louder than necessary voice to remind us that we weren't alone. I rolled my eyes, but I was still smiling when I turned to look at my old friend. "Feed well, but be back well before sunrise. We have to plan tomorrow's attack."

"Mmmm . . . sounds like fun." Then he disappeared completely.

Yes, the time had come for us to finally be on the offensive. I was done running and chasing my tail. The naturi were out of the way. The lycanthropes were dead. It was time to clean out the rest of the house, and Veyron was on the top of my list for Budapest. I had little doubt that Macaire had pulled back to Venice following the death of Ferko and Odelia. I would deal with the Elder in Venice.

Twenty-Eight

The silence was suffocating. I stared up the lonely street interspersed with trees gnarled and twisted by time. Without the presence of the naturi, the wind had gone still, leaving the tree branches standing like silent sentinels in the thick darkness. A fresh powder of snow coated the ground, struggling to glisten in the thin light that poured from the moon as it peeked from behind massive clouds.

The earth was holding its breath, waiting for the outcome of yet another battle. But then so was I. Each time I walked into a fight, I weighed the strengths and weaknesses of my opponents. I weighed the strengths and weaknesses of my allies. I played the odds in my head, and too often I came up as the long shot. It was getting old.

Among my kind, being the Fire Starter meant something. With a thought and a casual wave of my hand, I could wipe out an army of nightwalkers. When I faced the naturi, they needed to bring forth only a light clan member to counter my unique ability. A bori merely needed to extend its powers and I was under its immediate control. And a warlock . . . a warlock could counter my powers with a quick spell, leaving me nothing more than another bloodsucker with an attitude problem. In this fight, Valerio and Stefan had the true advantage, with their ability to appear and disappear at will. Sure, the power took its toll on their strength, but the battle wouldn't last more than a few minutes before one side was decimated.

Despite my place on the coven, it only made sense that I go in as bait. I was the ultimate target of Veyron and the others, at Macaire's request. I was also the youngest and the weakest of our quartet. Danaus was not thrilled with the decision, but he said nothing when Stefan took me to the end of Veyron's street and left me. I could feel Danaus as a ghost in my thoughts, along with Valerio. Both men were waiting for the first sign from me that it was time for them to appear.

My footsteps echoed off the concrete, the sound bouncing off the flat front of the homes and flying off into the nothingness. I resisted the urge to nervously check all my weapons once again. I was well-armed with a short sword across my back and an assortment of knives around my body. To Danaus's dismay, I didn't bring a gun with me. Guns were ineffective against nightwalkers, and I didn't think Clarion would allow me to catch him off guard with a spray of bullets.

In truth, I wasn't sure how we were going to kill Clarion. We would try to stop him if he decided to flee, but I wasn't sure if Valerio and Stefan could follow him if he did. I wasn't sure what the warlock was capable of, but I had a feeling he could cast some of the most basic shield spells to block our weapons and attacks. My only hope was that he didn't know how to control fire, but I wasn't counting on it. If Clarion was going to survive this ordeal, he would have taken the time to learn how to manipulate fire.

I paused at the edge of Veyron's yard and sent my powers flowing out from my body so they swept over the ancient structure. A single candle burned in the front window, while the rest of the massive house was dark. Inside, I sensed close to a dozen nightwalkers and a handful of humans. These humans would be heavily armed with guns that could blow apart the brain. That was the only way to kill a nightwalker with a gun—destroy the brain or heart so completely that it couldn't grow back. I would need to take out these humans before Danaus and the others stepped foot in the building.

Within their midst was a single powerful magic user. It would be Clarion, who was waiting for us. I could sense him over the aged Veyron and his companion Odelia. Clarion was the true danger here, not the nightwalkers or the humans with their weapons. Unfortunately, I had no idea how to defeat him.

I raised both of my hands out to my sides. Summoning up my powers, I directed them at the house, attempting to set the building on fire. It would have been easy if I could just burn the entire structure and everyone inside all at once. It would all be done in one quick and easy move, and I wouldn't have to worry about putting my companions in danger. But nothing is ever easy.

Electric energy filled the air around the house, sizzling like a lightning bolt looking for a metal pole. The energy dampened my own powers, keeping me from burning the house to the ground. I wasn't particularly surprised. It was a simple spell, one I had known for centuries and used in Peru to protect us from the naturi while we slept at the foot of the Machu Picchu ruins. I knew Clarion wasn't going to make it easy for me, but I had to at least try.

Dropping my hands back to my side, I could feel Valerio chuckling in the back of my brain as I walked toward the house. He could read my thoughts, hear as I cursed the warlock for making this more difficult than it truly had to be. But those fragments of laughter quickly grew still as I stepped to the front door and pushed it open easily.

Darkness waited for me as I stepped across the threshold.

Leaves and snow had blown into the open doorway, as if the house had been abandoned for years instead of just a few hours. Standing in the hallway, I waved my right hand, sending my power out, seeking candles, but no lights sprang to life. With a low hiss, I summoned up my powers again, this time attempting a small fireball that would hover just in front of me. Again nothing happened. Not only had Clarion cast a protective spell on the house itself, but he had found a way to dampen all fire. My ability was useless as long as the warlock lived.

Dropping my hand back to my side, I clenched my teeth and continued to walk through the house, weaving through room after room. The furniture was overturned and valuable knickknacks and paintings were now missing. The house had been ransacked in anticipation of my arrival. My guess was that Veyron was expecting to live through this fight but didn't believe that his residence would survive. He was planning ahead, but he wasn't planning well. If he was truly smart, he would have run and never shown his face in Europe again.

As I turned a corner to go through what appeared to be the dining room, gunfire opened up. Running across the hardwood floor, I dropped to my knees as I turned, sliding across the floor as I pulled a pair of knives from my side. Despite the heavy darkness in the room, I picked out my two assailants and flung my knives at them. One screamed as the knife buried up to the hilt in his arm, while the other man simply gurgled as the blade found his throat. He fell back, choking on his own blood, while the other man stumbled backward. He pressed his wounded arm to his stomach as he tried to awkwardly fire the gun with his left hand. He squeezed off several shots with the automatic weapon, sending two bullets clean through me before I finally reached him and snapped his neck.

Are you all right? Danaus instantly demanded as pain flashed through my frame.

Fine, I growled in return. My shoulder and leg burned but I could feel the holes already closing. I wouldn't lose much blood, and the pain was only a minor distraction. Bending down, I pulled the knives out of my two victims and wiped them off on their clothes before returning them to their sheaths.

The house was as quiet as a mausoleum now that the gunfire had stopped. I went completely still, straining to hear something. Above me, I heard the ever so faint creak of floorboards under the weight of heavy boots. There was the occasional deep breath and the slight sound of rapid heartbeats pounding away in anticipation. I sent my powers out from my body again. The humans were on the top floors, while the nightwalkers were in the basement. Clarion was completely missing. I could only guess that he was cloaking himself, but I had no doubt he was waiting for me in the basement with Veyron.

If I went directly after my prey, I would have a horde of humans with automatic weapons at my back. I needed to clear out the upper floor first before I went after Veyron and the others. Of course, I didn't trust this setup at all. I knew that Veyron, Odelia, and Clarion cared nothing about sacrificing a few humans if it meant destroying me.

I relayed my plan to Valerio and Danaus, and neither of the two men liked it. They demanded that they be allowed to assist me, but I told them to hold back. If I could pick off each human without risking more lives than necessary, then I planned to proceed in that manner. They would be taking on enough risk when they went up against Clarion.

Save Odelia for me, Stefan demanded, surprising me. I had not felt his presence in my mind, but then I hadn't been looking for him. Stefan abhorred my touch, and I had no doubt that he thought he was lowering himself to contact me in such a way, but at the moment it was a necessary evil.

I'll see what I can do.

Take a gun, Mira, Danaus ordered as I started to pass by the bodies.

I swallowed my argument and picked up an ugly black weapon. I didn't know how to load this monster and I could only hope that it didn't have a safety that I needed to flick off. I just wanted to be able to pull the trigger and have the thing send out a spray of bullets at my enemies, but I wasn't going to rely on it. I didn't like guns. Too unreliable and too noisy. Knives were so much more personal.

Heading back to the front of the house, I paused at the foot of the stairs. The second floor was open and overlooked the main foyer. I felt too exposed standing there, and knew I would be pinned against the wall as I climbed to the second floor. Looking around, I spotted an ornate chandelier directly overhead. With a smile, I leapt straight up into the air and grabbed a bottom section of the light fixture. There was a slight groan but the chandelier held. I swung back and forth a couple times like a circus performer on the trapeze before releasing myself. My left foot slipped on the edge of the second floor but my right foot held, allowing me to catch the railing.

As I climbed over the railing, gunfire shattered the silence and lit the darkness. Crouched on one knee, I swiveled from left to right, firing back at the men trained on me. Bullets pockmarked the walls and the wood railing around me. I was hit a couple more times but not before I managed to kill the three men that surrounded me with the automatic weapon.

Sitting on the floor, I clutched the gun to my chest while waiting for my body to heal. I was tempted to feed off one of my still dying opponents but decided against it. There was nothing worse than being interrupted in the middle of a meal. I gazed down at the gun in my hand and frowned.

I told y—

Shut up, Danaus. I had no doubt that the hunter had been waiting months to utter those words, and this time he was right. In a firefight with humans, guns were effective against guns. Well, at least they were effective when I couldn't set them on fire.

Do you need us? Valerio inquired. I wasn't accustomed to having so many people running willy-nilly though my brain. I was tempted to throw up some barriers and block them all out so I could concentrate but decided against it. They might be needed in an instant, and it was easier to contact them if they were already waiting in the wings of my mind.

Not yet. I sense only two more humans in the house. Let me clean them out and then you can come, I said, forcing myself to calm down and relax. The first stage was nearly complete.

Rising off the floor with ease only a vampire could show, I silently walked down the hall to my right. I eased past one open doorway after another, peering into the vast darkness to see the vague outline of a large bed and what were probably ornate bureaus. Nothing moved.

At the end of the hall was a pair of double doors, with one of them cracked slightly open. I could feel the two humans huddled in the far corner of what seemed to be a large room. With the gun tucked into my shoulder, I eased the door open, its creak echoing through the entire house. Before I took my first step into the room, thirty guns clicked in unison. *Shit.*

Get here now! I screamed at my companions as I dove across the hall and into an empty room. Bullets ripped through the double doors and pounded through drywall and timber. A trio of bullets scraped across my flesh in various locations, leaving a burning sensation behind. I clenched my teeth and pulled myself into a sitting position as Stefan, Valerio, and Danaus appeared next to me. Danaus knelt beside me, inspecting the latest laceration on my arm. The bleeding was slowing, helped by his constant pressure.

"There's a few more of them than I could initially sense," I said between clenched teeth.

"How many is a few?" Valerio asked.

I pushed to my feet with Danaus's help. "About thirty. Must be a freaking ballroom to fit them all." After handing the automatic weapon over to Danaus, I withdrew a pair of blades. I felt more at ease with the silver knives in my hands, as if I had regained a part of me.

"Kill her!" screamed a female voice from the other room.

"Oh, and apparently they've sent Odelia on ahead to deal with me," I said with a smile as I gazed up at Stefan. "Please don't kill her right away. I would like to try to get a little information out of her."

"I can't make any promises," Stefan replied with a bow of his head to me.

I smiled sweetly at him, trying to get under his skin. "Please."

Neither he nor Valerio said anything as they disappeared again. They would attack the room from behind, but first we had to get their full attention.

"Shall we go serve as live bait?" I asked, turning to Danaus.

"You put a lot of faith in your friends," he said.

My smile crumpled, but I raised my chin and met his gaze. "Yes, I do." Valerio and Stefan had ample opportunity to easily kill both Danaus and me. We were going to walk in front of this firing squad, dependent on them to strike from behind and save our lives. A moment's hesitation and Macaire would get his wish. Danaus and I would be ripped to shreds by the barrage of bullets, making it easy for Odelia to walk up and claim our hearts. At that moment, I was putting a lot of faith and trust in Stefan. It was more than a little unnerving.

Taking a deep, cleansing breath, I shoved the air out of my lungs as I stepped back into the hallway and kicked the doors open. Danaus stood beside me and emptied the last of the bullets from the automatic weapon as the humans facing us took aim. Muscles clenched, I scanned the room for an easy target while counting the milliseconds until Valerio and Stefan reappeared. It felt like an eternity.

Screams echoed from the back of the room, followed by the crunching of broken bones and the heavy thud of a limp body hitting hardwood floor. They came. Bullets still flew in my direction, but the concentration was not as thick as they should have been. Danaus partially hid behind the door and picked off attackers with his handgun, while I launched myself into the room, killing whomever I came into contact with.

Silver blades streaked red flashed in the pale streams of moonlight that danced through the windows filling three walls of the large room. Men fell to their knees, throats cut, intestines spilling from their stomachs. Bullets punctured me from all sides, but the wounds were largely superficial. I was moving too fast for them to get a clear shot, and we had them trapped in the room. Surrounded on all sides, there was nowhere to go and no room for mercy.

The entire battle was over in less than three minutes, but the devastation was massive. Bodies were flung and piled around the large empty room, while blood pooled in the cracks of the hardwood floors and soaked into the few carpets. When silence filled the room again, I turned to find Stefan leaning over Odelia, his fangs exposed and dripping blood. He had not killed her yet, at my request, but he wouldn't be able to hold out much longer.

Odelia was a bloody mess. Her face had a series of three long scratches across the front, and the way her left arm hung at her side made me think that her shoulder had been dislocated. Her dark hair was a matted mess of blood and knots from her struggle with Stefan. Long tears marred her clothes, revealing more wounds. She sat with her back pressed into a corner, her fangs bared as she tried to ward Stefan off, but she wasn't winning that battle.

"My dear Odelia," I purred as I walked over to her side. I slowly placed a hand on Stefan's shoulder and squeezed. The nightwalker drew in a slow breath through his nose as he straightened and put his fangs away. He was back in control of his emotions again. "It seems that Veyron and Clarion have abandoned you to your fate. Sacrificed like poor Ferko and Sofia. Did you know you were so expendable?"

"I'm not! Veyron will come for me! Just wait!" she cried even as she pressed deeper into the corner.

I laughed, twirling one blade in my hand. "Oh, I'm afraid it is far too late for that. I'm just looking for a little information before we kill you."

"And why should I tell you anything?" Her voice cracked as she spoke. I think she was beginning to realize that Veyron wasn't going to come riding to her rescue. Otherwise, he would have done so already. He would not have set her up against the Fire Starter and two Ancients with only a group of humans and guns.

I shrugged my shoulders as I kicked away a severed limb sitting near my foot. "It determines your death. You cooperate and you die quickly and painlessly. You don't, and . . . well, we can be creative." Stefan glared at me but said nothing. This had not been a part of our agreement, and I wasn't counting on him abiding by my wishes at just this moment.

"Did Macaire approach Veyron?" I demanded.

"Macaire came to Budapest months ago," she said, her eyes darting away from me.

"What did he want?"

"How should I know? I'm not the keeper of Budapest," she replied sarcastically.

I sighed dramatically. "Stefan."

Stefan moved forward to grab her and she screamed, "He wanted you dead! He wanted you dead!"

"Anything else?"

"You and the human. He wanted you both dead, no matter what it took. We were to do whatever it took to kill you both. It didn't matter who got caught in the cross fire," she admitted between broken sobs. She covered her face with her right hand as tears streaked down her bloodstained face.

"And Michelle?"

"Wh-Who?" she asked.

"Michelle. Vamp you had killed," I supplied. The edge retuned to my voice and I was about to hand her over to Stefan when she finally spoke.

"She didn't belong here. She had no business being in Budapest."

"No business?"

"She wasn't welcome here—we have enough pretty female nightwalkers in Budapest. There was no room for more."

"So you had her killed? How many others have been killed for that reason?"

"Dozens," she said, looking up at me with a confused expression.

I shook my head as I turned away from her in disgust. I had heard of hunting and toying with fledglings, but even that practice seemed to be dying out. However, I had never heard of nightwalkers being killed because there was simply no room in a city for another attractive nightwalker.

Ferko was right. Odelia had been jealous and ordered Michelle's death because she was threatened by the potential competition.

I merely had to wave my hand and Stefan was on Odelia in a flash as I walked back toward the double doors. Her bloodcurdling screams echoed through the room until they vibrated through my brain and rattled my teeth. The tearing of flesh and the breaking of bones was sickening, but in truth I hardly noticed. Those sounds had been background noises from my nightwalker childhood. They couldn't move me now.

Danaus frowned as he looked at me, purposefully keeping his gaze from Stefan and his work. "Wouldn't it be more painful to stake her out in the sun?" he inquired.

"She's asleep as soon as the sun rises. She would never feel a thing. Your idea is a slow death, but it's also very merciful. Stefan is quick and messy, but she dies in pain, which is what he wants."

After a couple seconds Stefan walked over, dripping Odelia's blood, a rare smile on his face. He might have lost an assistant that was important to him, but he had personally destroyed both of her killers with his bare hands. He couldn't ask for better justice. And in both instances, Ferko and Odelia had been my gifts. Stefan would now be more willing to fight at my side for the rest of the evening. At least, I hoped it worked that way.

"Veyron and the warlock?" he asked, pleasing me. Apparently he had a taste for blood this evening and was ready to get his fill.

"They are waiting in the basement," I said with a frown. "The entrance is single file down a set of wooden stairs. If we head down in a line, they will be able to easily kill us all. Let me go down first and scout it out so you can appear in their midst."

"Like we did up here," Valerio said, and I nodded.

"You're doing quite well in your role as bait," Stefan teased.

I was doing quite well as bait, but I wasn't enjoying it. In fact, I was downright terrified by the idea of heading down into a basement full of nightwalkers and a warlock without my powers. If my companions hesitated, I was staked. Sensing my unease, Danaus placed a hand on my shoulder and squeezed. At least he would not let me die without a fight. I just hoped that the others felt the same way.

Twenty-Nine

Air from the basement wafted up the stairs, smelling of dirt and mold. A heavy energy snapped and crackled from both Clarion and Veyron as they prepared for me to enter the place where they had decided to make their final stand. I resisted the urge to look back over my shoulder at Danaus and the others as I descended the wooden stairs into the basement. The heels of my boots clomped on the stairs, sounding like the drumbeat to a funeral march.

I frowned as I turned the corner and found that the coffins that had filled the basement before were now leaning against the walls, leaving the floor open for the fight that awaited us. Roughly a dozen nightwalkers were arrayed before me holding all manner of weapons, ready to attack me at the first indication from Veyron, who stood at the back of the pack. I would have to push my way through all the nightwalkers in order to get to him. To make matters worse, he was standing with his back against the wall, making it impossible for my companions to pop in behind him for a quick slaughter. This was not going to be a quick and easy fight.

And that didn't even begin to take care of the problem that Clarion presented. I wracked my brain as I slowly descended the stairs on effective ways to take out a warlock without the use of my powers. The only ace I potentially had up my sleeve was Danaus, assuming the warlock wasn't aware of the hunter's unusual gift.

At the foot of the stairs I found Clarion standing at the back of the room near Veyron. He leaned one shoulder against the wall in his neat suit and tie, looking as if he had just come from a business meeting. In his right hand he held a gold pocket watch, which he glanced at before looking up at me with a questioning gaze. I could guess what he was wondering. How was I going to handle this situation and survive?

And then it hit me, bringing a broad grin to my face as my gaze shifted to Veyron, who squirmed slightly. I didn't need to handle both of them. Only one of them was truly my enemy. The other one could still be made into my ally . . . if I could deliver what he wanted.

Stepping onto the concrete floor of the basement, I dusted off my hands and stopped a few feet away from the nearest nightwalker, smiling. "Ferko and the lycanthropes are dead. Sofia is dead. The humans are dead. Odelia is dead," I listed as I dragged my gaze over each one of the nightwalkers that stood ready to attack me. "Do you really want to join them?"

"You can't stop them alone!" Veyron laughed from the supposed safety of the back of the room. "You don't have your ability to control fire now. You're nothing. We will crush you."

"In other words," I said sarcastically, turning my gaze to the nightwalkers before me, "he will allow you to die trying to kill me so he doesn't have to get his hands dirty or endanger his life. He will let you die for him."

"Who doesn't want the honor of being able to claim that he killed the infamous Fire Starter?" Veyron asked sweetly.

"If it's such an honor, why don't you come here and try yourself?" I countered, smiling at him so my fangs showed. Veyron went quiet and I chuckled in the silence. "I thought so." I walked to my left, leaving an opening to the stairs while placing my back to the wall. "This fight is between Veyron and me. Not you. Take what's left of your lives and leave here while you still can."

There was a soft rustling among the nightwalkers as they looked around at each other, surprised by this unexpected offer. This wasn't an opportunity they would receive under most circumstances. But then, I wasn't like most nightwalkers. I was worse.

"You can't do that!" Veyron shouted.

"Of course I can. I am keeper of this domain. I am an Elder on the coven. I can offer them their lives if I so wish it," I said with a laugh. "But if you're going to go, go now."

There was a soft shuffling among the nightwalkers as a handful of them edged toward the stairs, cautiously moving around me. They were obviously distrustful, and they had every right to be. They had attempted to stand against me, to betray their keeper. They couldn't be allowed to live so they could betray me again at a later date.

Kill the ones coming up the stairs silently, I told my companions waiting for me up on the first floor.

Meanwhile, the ones that remained attacked at once. Blades slashed through the air and fists came crashing down, aiming for tender parts. I came alive in a flurry of action. With fighting quarters so tight, I opted for my small knives, allowing me to get close and personal with each of my opponents. I delivered a round of slashes and stabs that left three of my attackers rolling on the ground, gripping gaping wounds that would take several minutes to close. Stabbing one opponent in the stomach, I released my blade and slammed my fist into his chest. I grabbed his heart and pulled it free before he could fall over. Seeing his black heart in my hand, the remaining two attackers that I had yet to reach backed off immediately.

"I have survived six centuries, battled both naturi and bori. I have slaughtered nightwalkers, shifters, and warlocks with my bare hands. Do you think in all that time I haven't learned to kill without my powers?" I growled.

"Kill her!" Veyron screamed, earning a deep laugh from me, which simply danced around the dark room, leaving them jumping at shadows.

"Leave here," I commanded. Those that had the power to scramble out on their own two legs scurried up the stairs, where they were met with a silent death by my dear companions.

Dropping the heart, I licked some of the blood that was dripping from my fingers as I turned my attention to Veyron and Clarion. I smiled and cocked my head to one side as I looked at them, trying to decide how I would continue. There was a good chance that Clarion could crush me with a single spell. Besides, I wasn't sure I could manipulate Danaus's gift without him standing in the room with me.

I might need to use your powers, I warned Danaus. *I'm hoping to avoid it but I might not be able to.*

Do you need me there?

Stay where you are. All of you. I wanted to at least present the image of taking care of Veyron alone.

"Clarion, I would appreciate it if you released my powers now," I announced patiently.

The warlock arched one eyebrow at me and straightened where he stood. "And why would I do that?"

"Because I can more effectively torture Veyron that way."

"What's to stop you from trying to use your powers on me?"

I dropped my sticky hands to my sides and narrowed my gaze on him. "My business is not with you, is it? You've just been maneuvering everything so this city would be cleaned out of all the rabble."

Clarion gave a slight shrug of one shoulder and I smiled. Lifting my right hand, I snapped my fingers and a small teardrop of fire appeared. I suppressed a sigh of relief. I was not accustomed to not having this gift at my fingertips. While Clarion's magic had not gotten rid of my ability to manipulate fire, he had successfully suppressed the creation of fire within the house or around it. But now I had it back.

"Clarion! We had a deal!" Veyron screeched. The nightwalker turned to lunge at the warlock, but with a wave of my hand a wall of fire formed a semicircle around him, keeping him pinned against the wall. Veyron pressed his back against the wall while standing on the tips of his toes in an effort to get as far as possible from the flames. "Mira!"

You can come down now. Just follow my lead. I'm still digging for some information, I directed the others. Their footsteps pounded down the stairs. I didn't look over my shoulder, but I could feel Danaus in the lead, his powers rushing ahead of him and down into the dark basement. With a thought, a ball of fire appeared near the foot of the stairs, offering up a globe of light against the pitch-blackness that had barely been penetrated by the dim pair of bare lightbulbs that hung overhead.

"Now that the gang's all here, let's have a little chat, Veyron," I said, making sure that Clarion understood I wasn't including him in this nasty business. I had other, better, plans for him. "I want to know why Macaire came to you."

"Wh-Why would Macaire come to me? He doesn't have any business here," the nightwalker stammered.

"Please, Veyron, I'm trying to make this easy for you. Don't make me make you scream."

"Just kill him, Mira," Stefan grumbled. "I'm ready to quit this place."

"Soon. We will leave soon," I promised. I raised my left hand in a slow arc, and as a result fire jumped from the wall surrounding Veyron to his right arm. The nightwalker screamed and crushed his right arm against the wall, trying to put out the fire. I counted to seven and then extinguished the flames on him. "I can do this all night, and then get up the next evening and start it all over again. I can burn you until there is nothing left but a quivering mass of raw tissue and pain. Tell me why Macaire came to you."

"He wanted us to kill you and that thing," he shouted, pointing at Danaus with his left hand. "He knew our numbers were strong here. Sofia told him about Clarion and was confident that we could use him. Macaire also thought Sofia could break you both, so he told us to separate and kill you."

I turned my gaze to Clarion and smiled. "The Ancient put his money on Sofia to break us," I mused, and the warlock smiled smugly at me in return. He had been keeping to the shadows, biding his time.

"It was an interesting bet," he admitted.

Looking back at Veyron, I caused the fire to move several inches closer to him, shrinking the semicircle. "Have you communicated with Macaire recently?"

"No!"

"When did you last speak with the Elder?" Valerio inquired.

"The night of the ball."

"Did he give you any instructions regarding anyone else who might accompany me?" I asked.

"Kill them. Kill anyone who was loyal to you," Veyron said.

I smiled. Macaire had sealed his own fate by alienating both Valerio and Stefan. The Elder could have contacted Veyron again after they announced they would be accompanying me. He could have changed the orders so they would be spared, but he hadn't. Macaire wanted anyone associated with me dead.

"P-P-Please, Mira!" Veyron begged. "I'll do anything you say. Whatever you want! Please, I was only following orders. Macaire would have destroyed us all if we had not agreed to his demands." Clarion sent him a look of disgust as he returned to leaning against the wall while shoving his hands deep in the pockets of his trousers.

"Enough." I sighed. With a thought, the flames closed in around him, completely engulfing him. Veyron pushed off the wall and came running blindly in my direction, his high-pitched screams bouncing off the walls of the small room. I pulled my short sword from over my shoulder and stabbed it directly into his chest, spearing his heart and stopping him in his tracks. He thrashed about for nearly a minute before finally going completely still. Death had finally claimed him. I felt the cold touch of his soul as it flew past me in the wintry embrace of night.

Extinguishing the flames, I lowered Veyron's crusty black body to the floor. With my foot braced against his chest, I withdrew my sword and placed it back into the sheath on my back. One down and one tricky one to go.

When I looked up, Clarion was regarding me with a calculating stare, which I met with a slight bow of my head. We had to come to an understanding if anyone was going to leave this basement alive.

"So, where does this little escapade leave us?" he inquired.

"On shaky footing, I would say," I ventured. "Do you think it is possible for us to find a reasonable agreement this evening that would make everyone happy?"

Clarion frowned for the first time and every muscle in my body seemed to tense in anticipation of his attack. "I find that hard to believe."

"I could just kill you now and have it all done," I threatened.

"You know you can't use fire against me."

"I have other tricks." Narrowing my eyes in concentration, I reached out and grabbed hold of Danaus's powers. With a slight tug, I directed them at Clarion. In the back of my mind I heard Danaus growling at me, but he didn't fight me, which was reassuring. The warlock's face crumpled as he raised both of his hands to see the skin undulating.

"Mira!" he snapped, and I released Danaus's powers. I could try to kill Clarion this way, but doubted I would survive the spell he'd sling at me just before his death. I wasn't willing to risk it when I still had a use for him. For now, I just wanted him to fear me.

"I'm not limited to fire."

"I see," Clarion replied in a low voice. "What is it that you would like to discuss?"

"Budapest and her future."

He rubbed his hands together, seeming to try to massage away the unexpected heat that rested just below this skin. "Interesting topic."

"Macaire didn't approach you. He approached and ordered the nightwalkers to hunt me and my people down," I pronounced, leaving a wide opening for him to easily excuse himself from the madness. "If anything, you saw my arrival as an opportunity. You never wanted all these nightwalkers or lycanthropes within your city. I wouldn't be surprised if you hated sharing the city with Sofia."

"Interesting thoughts. Why would you say such a thing?" he asked, scratching his chin.

"I've known more than my share of warlocks and witches in my day. Sure, you might have your little covens where you cast spells together, but the really powerful ones don't play well with others. You don't like sharing a territory with other powerful spellcasters. Hell, you don't like sharing your territory with other creatures at all if you can help it."

"Astute."

"Lessons learned the hard way," I admitted with a shake of my head.

"So I took advantage of the situation," Clarion said. "I made sure that you had an easy target in the lycanthropes and nightwalkers."

"Even Sofia. Undoubtedly she secretly called for your help when I killed her. You could have easily come riding to her rescue but you abandoned her."

Clarion shrugged his wide, narrow shoulders. "She chose to go along with Macaire's silly plan. Who am I to deny Sofia her fate? But where does that leave us?"

"At an interesting impasse, I'm afraid. We could try to kill each other now, and I'm sure at least one person is likely to crawl away from this battle, but that won't settle the question of Budapest's future."

Clarion pushed against the wall and took a step toward me. "What do you want with Budapest?"

"Only peace and quiet."

"Will you renounce your claim as keeper?" he demanded in a rush.

I took a step forward and rested one boot on Veyron's chest. "Can't do that. It leaves the city open to any power-hungry nightwalker to move in and cause chaos. I can't allow that to happen. However, I have noticed that my name alone has the power to keep order."

"Yes, I have heard such things."

"I am thinking of being more of an absentee landlord. I keep my main home in the New World, while maintaining a vacation home of sorts here in Budapest. All I ask is that you maintain order here among the spellcasters. Keep the peace and quiet."

"An alliance?"

"No!" I said sharply, and then laughed. "I've seen how you operate in alliances. I was thinking of mutual acquaintances with similar goals. You go your way, I go mine. We both just protect the secret of our world from the humans, and otherwise don't associate."

"Sounds too good to be true," Clarion said with a distrustful shake of his head.

"Only because I'm at an interesting crossroads. Normally, I would go after anyone that tried to kill me or plotted the death of my companions. However, you're not the biggest fish in the pond, and I'm after him."

"Macaire?" Clarion guessed.

"Macaire."

"And once you've killed the nightwalker, will you come after me?"

"No. We're wiping the slate clean. You were simply going to steal this territory, and I got in the way. I'm willing to let you have it on behalf of the spellcasters so long as you let me handle the nightwalkers."

"Friends?" One corner of his mouth quirked in an odd smile.

"Not quite. Just not enemies. Try to kill me again and I will make you suffer," I warned as I extended my hand to him. I was taking a chance, and I could hear both Valerio and Stefan cursing me in the back of my head. Clarion could kill me in the blink of an eye this way, but I was trusting he wouldn't. He simply wanted this territory to himself without the politics, demands, or interference of any of the other races.

"Not enemies," Clarion repeated as he slowly took my hand. We shook twice and then quickly released, as we both were unsure of this tentative truce.

"Now, as a little advice from one nonenemy to another, I would leave. I need to burn this place to destroy the evidence of tonight's fun," I said with a smile.

Clarion returned my smile. "Next time you're in town, stop by Gerbeaud Cukrászda and we will chat over coffee. You can tell me how you did your new little trick."

"Right," I said sarcastically just before he disappeared.

"Are you insane?" Stefan demanded the second he was gone.

"Most definitely."

"How do you know he won't come after you again?" Danaus asked.

"Because he never truly came after me before. He didn't attack you at the hotel with the lycans, did he?"

"No," Danaus said with a shake of his head.

"And he could have definitely killed us in the taxi, but he didn't. It was merely a warning. He could have easily killed us tonight, but that's not his goal. He simply wants Budapest to himself, and now he's got it."

"So, he's keeper of Budapest now," Valerio chuckled.

"In a manner of speaking." I turned and started to trudge up the stairs with Danaus and the others following close behind me. "I don't want Budapest, but I need to be sure it doesn't slip into chaos. Clarion will keep things quiet here and my somewhat bloody reputation will aid that."

I paused in the hallway to find the bodies of the nightwalkers that tried to escape strewn all over the place. Heads had been ripped off and hearts torn from chests. They had all died as quietly and quickly as possible. I was proud of the work my companions had done, even if it was gruesome to behold.

"Besides, what I told him was true. I didn't want to die uselessly trying to kill him, when my true target was just beyond my fingertips."

We filed silently out of the house and onto the front lawn, which was still coated in snow. I sucked in a deep, cleansing breath. I could smell the crisp snow and pine needles over the thick scent of death and blood. I raised both hands over my head and flames instantly engulfed the house from top to bottom. I poured all my energy into the flames, melting glass and incinerating wood. Bodies were reduced to ash and made unrecognizable. I wouldn't be able to get rid of the evidence of gunfire, but I was hoping that the police would attribute the mess to a mafia hit. Regardless, a fight between nightwalkers wasn't going to be their first theory.

When the sound of sirens finally rang through the silence of the night, I lowered my hands back to my sides, leaving the fire to burn on its own. I leaned backward into Danaus, who wrapped a supportive arm around my waist.

"Mira, you need to reconsider your plan to take on Macaire," Stefan said in a low voice, surprising me. "He's a powerful Elder. You haven't a chance. You can't even teleport."

"I'll find a way to kill him."

"Stefan is right," Valerio agreed. "You can't do this. He won't give you the opportunity to use your gift."

I gritted my teeth and stared at the ground. My boots were leaving red footprints in the snow from all the blood I had been wading through. "If I don't, he is going to keep coming up with schemes to kill me and anyone associated with me. This time we got lucky. But next time, maybe not. I won't allow someone to die because Macaire has it out for me."

"And if you do win, what about Jabari?" Danaus asked. "He won't have a use for you any longer."

"I know." But right now Macaire was at the top of my hit list.

Thirty

Venice had never looked so good to me. It represented the last stop on a tedious journey; the last thing keeping me from my beloved Savannah. I needed to go home. My sudden departure from the southern city had left many things hanging in the air. Tristan needed me. His battered psyche was being eaten away by guilt from having a hand in Lily's death. The chaos created by the presence of the bori left the nightwalkers unsettled, and Knox had been forced to manage things in my absence. I needed to return home so I could smooth everything over. I needed to be there for Tristan.

But for now I was stuck in Venice while I waited for the members of the coven to reconvene. I sent Valerio on ahead to check in on the court and see what the recent gossip was. Danaus and I wandered along Guidecca Island as we awaited his return. The sidewalks were slick from a recent rainstorm and the water in the canals was high, slopping over the sides and past the railing. Storm clouds churned overhead with the promise of yet another storm that would leave many of the low-lying plazas underwater by morning. The lights in lampposts seemed to have dimmed, barely beating back the night, and an oppressive feeling hung in the air.

"Something ill is waiting around the corner," I said, slipping unconsciously into Italian. This place, with its centuries of bloody memories and violent flashes, pulled me into the safety of old habits.

"It is only the weather," Danaus replied in Italian as well.

Stopping near the edge of the island, I stared out across the lagoon toward San Clemente Island, the resting place of the coven. My stomach twisted into knots and I anxiously shoved my hand through my hair, pushing it away from where it had blown across my face. I couldn't remain waiting here. I needed to get on that island to find out what was happening. I needed to wrap my hands around Macaire's neck so I could rip his head off.

Everything will be fine, Danaus whispered across my brain. He laid his hands on my shoulders and attempted to massage away the tension, but the stiffness wasn't going anywhere until I heard from Valerio.

To my relief, the Ancient appeared beside us a few minutes later, but by his expression, I knew I didn't want to hear what he had to say. "The coven has gathered at the hall. They know that you're in town and are waiting to hear your report," he said.

With a jerky nod, I expelled a deep breath, trying to force myself to calm. I still had to deal with Macaire, and that would be no easy battle. "Then let's get going," I said, starting to walk toward a boat I had already chosen to use to cross the lagoon.

"There's more, Mira," Valerio said, stopping me in my tracks. I flinched, waiting for the news, but nothing could have prepared me. "Tristan's here."

I whipped around and pinned his with a dark stare that could have pierced straight through him. "What are you talking about? He can't be here. I left him in Savannah."

"Macaire has him."

My stomach heaved as if I had been punched and I felt my knees go weak, threatening to send me to the ground. "How long?" I whispered in a broken voice.

"Mira, you can't blame yourself. He—"

"How long, damn it? How long?" I shouted, sending my voice echoing through the vast nothingness of the night. I didn't care who heard me or what they thought. Macaire had Tristan again, and I hadn't been there to stop him. I hadn't been there to save him again from the court.

"It sounds as if he was here since our first night in Budapest. He's been here several nights at Macaire's mercy."

Mercy. Macaire didn't know the meaning of the word. I had no doubt that Macaire had taken advantage of Tristan's weakened and fragile state following the death of Lily to torture the nightwalker. I was just afraid to see what I would find when I finally reached the coven. I clenched my teeth and tightly balled my fists as I fought back the scream of frustration and anger. Tristan had never reached out to me for help. I had never sensed that he was in any kind of danger. I should have known that Macaire would strike someone from my home while I was away. I should have known and done something.

Blinking back angry tears, I boarded the boat and turned the engine over. I was only vaguely aware of Valerio boarding the boat, while Danaus untied us and jumped in as well. I shot across the whitecapped waves in a flash, cutting across the water with single-minded determination. Macaire would pay. He would pay with his life for nearly killing me, Danaus, Stefan, and Valerio. He would pay for the hours of torture that he undoubtedly put Tristan through because of me.

We crossed the lagoon in a matter of minutes and I circled to the back side of the island to dock at the small stone landing closest to the Main Hall. I paused only long enough to kill the engine before I jumped off the boat. Walking down the path, the glass in a nearby lamppost exploded into flames. My energy snapped and flowed around me as I no longer attempted to rein in my temper. It poured into the other energies I could feel in the air from the nightwalkers nearby. I didn't need to access any of it. For the first time in my existence I felt as if I was fully in tune with my abilities.

Two narrow rows of flames lit the sides of the path, flickering suddenly into life as they led us toward the Main Hall. I walked between the fiery lanes, clenching and unclenching my fists. I was going to kill him. I didn't know how, but before this night was I out, I knew I would be holding his heart in my hand.

"Mira, you can't just attack him," Valerio said, following close behind me. "He'll rip your head off. He's stronger and older than you by centuries. You have to be careful about this."

"We're beyond careful."

"I'm here for you," Danaus volunteered, but I just laughed.

"You're not to do a thing. I will handle Macaire alone."

"Mira—" Danaus started, sounding unsure for the first time, and then his voice firmed again. "My abilities are at your disposal."

That was somewhat reassuring. I would have tapped his powers whether he wanted me to or not, but it was nice to know that at least now he was willing to aid me in this battle, even if it was only from a distance.

As I mounted the stone stairs to the Main Hall, Danaus and Valerio stepped ahead of me and pulled the massive wood and iron doors open. I marched through the long foyer, sending candles sputtering into life as I passed. The second set of doors swung open of their own accord as I reached them.

On the dais, Jabari, Elizabeth, and Macaire sat in their chairs, appearing calm and regal as always. Meanwhile, I was windblown and looking as if I had crawled from the pits of Hell to confront them in all my fury. They were the Old World, with their old traditions and old schemes. I felt as if I were purely a force of nature, ready to rain down my terror on all of them. But for now all my energies were going to be focused on one smug face. He didn't think I would dare to confront him head on because of his age and powers. I was more than happy to prove him wrong.

"Where is he?" I growled as I marched across the enormous hall. Overhead, the candles in the crystal and gold chandelier exploded into life. The bright light reflected in the black marble floor under my feet and sent shadows scurrying into the far corners of the room. Around me, I could sense more than two dozen nightwalkers gathered along the walls, watching my long march into the room, but I didn't see them. My narrowed gaze never wavered from Macaire.

"And who are you referring to, my dear?" he inquired.

I mounted the stairs and grabbed the front of his suit jacket. I started to fling him out of his chair, hoping to throw him onto the floor, but the bastard disappeared from my hands. He instantly reappeared behind me, straightening his jacket.

"You know who I want," I snarled, starting to come back down the stairs. "Where is Tristan?"

"Oh, that young one," Macaire replied, his smile returning. He waved his hand and a pair of nightwalkers slipped through a door at the side of the hall. I was sorely tempted to follow, but I forced myself to remain standing in the hall. I wasn't about to let Macaire out of my sight for a second if I could help it.

"You know, considering your struggles with the night-walkers, warlock, and naturi, I grew concerned that you weren't going to make it out alive, so I thought it would be best if I went to fetch the boy. Sadira had been so concerned about him. She was sure that he wouldn't be able to survive on his own."

As he spoke, the fire in the candles overhead increased. Wax rained down, creating a sickening sound as it hit the marble floor. Flags that hung from the ceiling erupted into flames and nightwalkers screamed in terror as they scrambled frantically away from the fire.

Close the doors! No one leaves, I directed Valerio, knowing he could use his powers to hold the doors shut. I didn't know who was responsible for Tristan's torture beyond Macaire, but I would be sure that everyone witnessed this fight. I wanted to be sure that everyone understood that I was a force that was not to be messed with.

The side door opened again and two nightwalkers dragged a limp Tristan between them. His brown hair was matted and knotted and his clothes were in disarray. I scanned over him as I ran to his side. I could find no physical injuries beyond a handful of scratches. Of course, it wasn't bodily harm that had me concerned. The two nightwalkers dropped him near the center of the room and retreated again to the side, putting as much distance between me and them as possible.

Sliding to my knees before Tristan, I helped him sit up, cupping his face in both of my shaking hands. "Tristan, look at me," I said, pushing the words past the lump in my throat. His gaze continued to dance around the room as if he were struggling to process his surroundings. "Please, Tristan, I need you to look at me."

After another couple of seconds I finally got him to look

at me, but his gaze was vacant and lost, as if he weren't truly seeing me. Lines of pain and horror were etched deeply into his face, scarring and aging him by nearly countless years. My handsome, young Tristan looked as if he were trapped in a perpetual nightmare from which there was no escape.

"Tristan, it's Mira," I said, forcing my voice to firm. "Please, look at me and tell me you recognize me. Talk to me, Tristan. I'm going to take you home."

"No!" he screamed, jerking out of my grasp. He crawled across the floor a few feet before curling up in the fetal position in the middle of the floor. I heard someone snicker, and she immediately erupted into flames. Her screams of pain faded into the background as I crawled over to Tristan and pulled him into my lap as best I could. My heart was breaking into a million jagged pieces as I held my wounded Tristan.

"Why don't you want to go home?"

"She's there. She's waiting for me. She's going to kill me," he said in a trembling voice.

"Who?"

"The Fire Starter," he whimpered. "She's going to kill me."

"I'm not going to kill you, Tristan. I want you to come home with me. I will keep you safe. Macaire will never touch you again."

Tristan violently shook his head from side to side. "No, Macaire will protect me. The Fire Starter is going to kill me."

"No, Tristan. I won't hurt you," I said, forcing back a swelling of tears. I wasn't reaching him. He didn't see me. He was lost in his fear of the Fire Starter, his mind locked in the horrible world that Macaire had created for him.

"Fire Starter is going to kill me. Fire Starter. Killed her daughter. Killed little Lily," he murmured as tears streaked down his pale face.

"No, Tristan. It wasn't your fault," I argued as tears started to slip down my own face. "Lily's death wasn't your fault. You know that. I would never harm you." I carefully maneuvered him so he was seated on the floor again with his face in my hands. I tried to get him to look me directly in the face, but it was as if I wasn't really there. But in truth, he was the one that wasn't there. He wasn't truly in the Main Hall. He was locked in a never-ending nightmare surrounding Lily's death.

Closing my eyes, I plunged into Tristan's mind. His thoughts were a swirling chaos of fragmented memories. Nothing flowed in a natural order. The only constant was the vision of Lily's death running over and over again in his mind like a broken record. I could find no sliver of Tristan's conscious mind left. His sense of identity had been completely shattered, and that all that was left was a shell of fear and pain.

I pulled out of his mind and wrapped my arms around him in a fierce hug. I had failed him. I had promised to protect him and keep him safe from nightwalkers like Macaire. "I'm so sorry," I cried, choking on the words as they crashed over the silence of the hall. "I am so sorry."

There was no way to save him. There was nothing left of Tristan to save. He was trapped for the rest of his existence in a world of pain and horror. He believed that the one person that would defend him was going to kill him. He believed that Macaire was going to protect him, when the Elder was only going to add to his terror at every turn. I couldn't save him.

Roughly wiping away the tears with the heel of my palm, I pulled Tristan away from where he was curled against me. I forced him to face me again and gave him a hard shake in frustration. "Tristan, look at me!" I ordered in a rough voice. "It's Mira. Look at me. It's Mira and I want to take you home."

Tristan just shook his head, looking anywhere but at me as he whimpered softly in pain. A flicker of recognition would have stopped me. Just a glimmer of the old Tristan that would have indicated I might have been able to draw him out again. But there was nothing left.

Shoving to my feet again, I stalked toward Macaire drawing knives from my sides. With amazing speed I flung them at him, hoping that at least one would hit its mark before the bastard disappeared. I just needed to score a minor hit. Something to slow him down a bit so I could get a tiny edge.

"No!" Tristan screamed to my surprise. I watched as the spinning knives came to a sharp halt a mere inches away from Macaire as he stood before his chair. The blades hovered in the air, reflecting the shifting candlelight.

I turned around to find Tristan kneeling on the ground with one hand extended out toward Macaire. He was holding the knives steady in the air, his face twisted with fear. "You cannot harm him. He is my only protection from the Fire Starter!"

"He's trying to destroy you," I screamed in frustration as I grabbed more knives. I threw them at Macaire as well, but they hit the same invisible barrier. I was stunned that Tristan could stop any of them, considering how weak and fragile he was, but I could feel the fear radiating off him in sickening waves. It was enough to give him the strength to push on.

"He is my savior," Tristan said. He waved his hand once and I turned toward Macaire in time to see the knives shooting back across the room at me. Running a few steps, I dove forward and rolled into a kneeling position. Three of the knives clattered against the floor while the fourth embedded itself in my back.

Macaire's laughter echoed through the hall, pushing me past any rational thought. Not only had he tortured Tristan, shattering the poor creature's mind, but he had turned him against me. Still kneeling on the ground, I twisted around and threw out my right arm, sending out three fireballs hurling toward the Elder.

Again Tristan's desperate, terrified scream tore at the air. Pushing off the ground, he ran across the room and threw his body in front of the fireballs in an effort to protect Macaire. I didn't have enough time to stop it. The flames pounded him square in the chest, engulfing him for a full second before I could extinguish them. He flopped to the ground, twitching and writhing in pain as all his exposed flesh was scorched by the flames.

I pulled the knife out of my back as I rose to my feet and walked over to where Tristan lay on the ground. His wide eyes stared up at the ceiling as tears ran down his burned cheeks. He didn't see me any longer. He didn't recognize the love I felt for him. There was only the pain and the horror that Macaire had manufactured in his mind. Tristan was locked in that world now.

The only thing I could give him was release from the pain. I could give him peace. Gritting my teeth, I placed my left hand on his right shoulder and plunged my right fist into his chest. I pulled his heart out as quickly as I possibly could so I wouldn't cause him any more pain than he was already suffering. He slumped against me as I cradled his heart against my chest. His cool blood ran down my arm and dripped from the edge of my elbow onto the hard marble floor. I bowed my head and rubbed my lips against his soft hair as fresh tears rained down my cheeks. I had lost my dear, sweet Tristan, and Macaire had forced me to kill him in an effort to spare him from any more pain. I had lost my sweet Tristan and it was my fault because I hadn't been there to protect him.

Danaus walked over and knelt beside us. He gently laid Tristan down on the floor, straightening out his legs and folding his arms over his chest. I slipped his heart under his folded hands. I wiped away my tears, smearing his blood across my cheeks. I was ready to kill Macaire now. I was ready to kill them all.

Thirty-One

Macaire smirked at me. I rose from the floor as if pushed up my some invisible force and stood between him and Tristan's body. The hall was completely silent except for the crackle of fire and the steady thud of Danaus's heartbeat. My temper had reached the boiling over point. I simply wanted him dead. I didn't care how.

The Elder took a single step toward me and I threw my right arm out. Flames erupted from the floor around him. But before I could catch him, the nightwalker disappeared from sight. I hissed, twisting around to find where he had reappeared. I tapped into the energies around me, feeling him out. He was hovering just on the outskirts of the hall, close so he could watch, but safely out of my reach.

My head snapped over to Jabari, who was relaxing back in his chair. He waved his left hand at me as if to say that it was beyond his ability to help me. Like hell it was. If the Elder wasn't going to aid me in the disposal of our common enemy, then I was going to use his powers to trap me an Ancient. I could feel Jabari's powers curling around the room, mixing with Danaus's and my own. I knew I could wrap my hand around them the same way I could use Danaus's. I had no doubt that the Ancient was going to balk at being controlled by a pathetic creature such as myself, but I wasn't going to give him any choice. Jabari had drawn me into this mess, he had made me Macaire's enemy.

Waving my hand through the air in a sharp slicing motion, I extinguished the flames and stood perfectly still, waiting. Macaire reappeared by the dais, standing with one foot on the lower stair, his body partially turned toward me as if he had paused in the middle of climbing back up to his chair. "Do you blame me for your killing Tristan?"

"You destroyed his mind," I snarled.

"I'll admit that there wasn't much there to destroy when I found him. It seems that he had a run-in with a bori," Macaire said as he resumed his seat. There was an audible gasp that coursed through the room when he made that statement. I didn't cringe away from the new censor that was coming from Jabari and Elizabeth.

"We had some problems. The bori has been recaged," I said shortly. "Did you take care of the naturi problem you were assigned to?"

Macaire's smile faded and his face twisted into an expression of extreme distaste. "The naturi were exterminated. How was your luck?"

"The naturi were killed, but it seems that something else was waiting for me. Did you have a conversation with Veyron before I arrived? Directed him to dispose of me and my companions?"

"Why would I do such a thing?" Macaire asked smoothly, but there was a warning glint in his eyes.

"Because you're a fucking bastard that thinks of no one but himself. But I have to thank you. I needed a European territory, and now I am keeper of Budapest and Savannah."

My only warning was a low snarl from the nightwalker as he launched himself from his chair and streaked across the vast distance that separated us. I didn't hesitate. I wrapped

Jabari's powers around me and instincts alone helped me to disappear from that spot a half second before Macaire arrived. I hovered for a heartbeat in the swirling darkness, watching Macaire twist about as he desperately searched the room for me.

I reappeared right beside him and slammed my fist into his jaw before he realized I was even standing there. The nightwalker was thrown across the room, sliding several feet over the marble floor before coming to a stop directly in front of a group of nightwalkers that stared at me in utter shock. It was well known that I didn't have the ability to appear and disappear at will, and yet I just had, making me ten times more dangerous than I already was.

Fear filled Macaire's face for only a moment before it was replaced with rage. He had underestimated me, and that was only the beginning. I needed him to fear me. With Jabari's powers firmly in my grasp, I telepathically grabbed Macaire by the legs and tossed him across the room, slamming him into the far wall with enough force to crack the stones. I casually crossed the distance between us before once again grabbing him with magic and tossing him around the room.

"You can't do this!" he shouted with a slight waver in his voice. He was right. I couldn't do this, not without Jabari on hand.

Watch yourself, desert blossom, Jabari warned as he pushed to his feet.

With his powers still in the palm of my hand, I slammed Jabari back down in his chair. I was being reckless, but I didn't care. Killing Macaire was the only thing that mattered now. I would face Jabari later. *Sit down and enjoy the show.*

Macaire pushed back to his feet and launched himself at me again. Unfortunately, when I attempted to use Jabari's powers to disappear, Jabari fought me. I got control of his powers again, but only it was too late. Macaire smashed both of his fists into my chest, breaking my chest plate and nearly crushing my heart. I was thrown backward several feet. As I hit the ground, a tight circle of flames sprang up around me, protecting me from a second attack as I regained my feet.

Standing in the middle of the circle, I looked around the room to find that Macaire was once again missing. But I could feel his energy close by. As I grabbed onto Jabari's powers again, the flames that encircled me immediately went out. I fought for both for nearly a second before I finally gave up on the flames. Apparently if I was using someone else's powers, I couldn't tap into my own ability to manipulate fire. It would have been appreciated if Nick could have warned me of such a thing earlier.

With Jabari's powers in hand, I grabbed hold of Macaire's energy and forced him to reappear in the room directly in front of me. He stumbled a step backward as if to regain his balance, a stunned and horrified expression on his face. No one had ever pulled a nightwalker back once he had disappeared.

While he was still stunned, I released Jabari's energy and tapped into Danaus's powers. The hunter gave a slight grunt as I forced him to slowly boil Macaire's blood within his skin. The nightwalker ran several feet away from me as if the distance would help as he scratched at the skin on the top of his left hand. Blood oozed out, popping and hissing as it melted anything that it touched.

"Afraid I was going to burn you?" I called across the room in a voice the echoed up to the rafters. "I've got more tricks up my sleeve than you will ever know. You never should have touched what belonged to me. You never should have threatened my friends."

"You're a monster!" Macaire snarled. "You have no business living among the nightwalkers. No right to be on the coven." He continued to back away from me as he raised his right hand to claw at the heat creeping up his neck. His skin was growing a dark shade of red as if was cooked from the inside out.

With a smile, I released Danaus's powers and freed Macaire from their grip. The Elder's shoulders slumped in relief. At that second I struck again. Grabbing the lapels of his coat, I slammed him on the ground and straddled him. As I did so, I claimed control over Jabari's powers again. Telepathically, I pinned Macaire to the ground, blocking his ability to disappear from my grasp.

Frustrated and fearful, the nightwalker hissed at me, flashing his fangs in warning. I didn't care. My whole body was trembling with the energy that flowed in and around me. I felt as if I was about to shatter into a hundred pieces, but I couldn't stop. Nothing would stop me.

A part of me longed to burn him. I wanted to wash him away in a river of flames that reached nearly to the ceiling of the hall, but I couldn't risk him escaping me when I let go of Jabari's powers. Instead I was content to kill him the old fashioned way.

"No!" Macaire screamed as I raised my right fist. He tried to catch it with his wounded left hand that was still leaking sizzling blood, but he was too weak from my earlier attack. My fist punctured his breast plate and went straight to his heart. His blood was just below the boiling point, burning my flesh.

I screamed in pain and triumph as I wrapped my fingers around his shriveled heart and slowly pulled it free of his chest. Macaire immediately went limp as his soul fled his body, released from a long lifetime locked in that frail frame. It wasn't enough. I dropped the heart at my side and grabbed his head underneath his chin and ripped it from his neck with a sickening cracking of bone and tearing of flesh.

Standing on wobbly legs, I hovered over Macaire's headless, lifeless corpse. All the energy I had felt slipped from my body and resumed its flow around me as if I were nothing more than a large rock in a stream. Smiling, I walked over to Macaire's chair on the dais. Hooking the heel of my boot under the edge of the chair, I tipped it over onto its back, sending a loud crash through the silent hall.

"It seems we have another opening," I announced. I turned around to face the crowd of nightwalkers that was closely watching me. "Do we have any takers?"

Silence followed for several tense seconds before Stefan finally stepped forward. A part of me relaxed—I had been concerned that Valerio might go for the open spot, when I had promised it to Stefan already. I didn't want Valerio on the coven. I had other, better, uses for him. Stefan and I would never see eye-to-eye on most matters, but we agreed on one thing that was important: the naturi. I knew that he would not be making secret alliances with the naturi, jeopardizing the future of our kind or the life of Our Liege.

"I claim the open seat on the coven," Stefan proclaimed in a loud, strong voice.

I nearly laughed in my delight. Macaire's blood had not even grown cold yet and he had already been replaced.

"I recognize your claim to the coven," I replied. "Does anyone want to counter his claim?" Silence once again reigned. Stefan's quick claim to the coven and my obvious support left everyone fearful to move, let alone question the nightwalker's claim to the open chair. After watching my brutal slaughter of Macaire, no one was willing to question Stefan, which pleased me because it put Stefan in my debt. I could use a favor for him on a rainy evening.

"Apparently not," I chuckled. With a sweeping bow, I backed away from the tipped over chair, directing Stefan to come forward. The Ancient's face was expressionless as he turned the chair right side up. He paused, looking over the gathered nightwalkers as if surveying his new kingdom before finally taking a seat.

I turned as well, but toward the coven, my gaze traveling from Elizabeth's look of horror, to Stefan's expression of reserved contentment, to Jabari's quiet rage. He and I would still have to have words, but for now he could wait. He'd gotten his wish, and his enemy had finally been vanquished by his little protégé.

As I took my first step toward my seat, a low chuckle filled the hall. I paused and looked around, trying to determine where it was coming from when it finally dawned on me that it was coming from Our Liege's chair. Everyone looked up and a chill went through the room when they saw that the chair was still empty.

But it wasn't really. I could feel Nick's energy filling that chair. I could easily imagine him lounging in that chair with one leg thrown over the arm, looking for all the world as if he owned the place. He wasn't Our Liege. I didn't know who Our Liege was, and I wasn't looking forward to that meeting, but I knew it wasn't Nick. He had been around for my battle with Macaire, whispering dark secrets into the back of my brain. Nick goaded me on, firing the anger that seemed to burn relentlessly inside of me beyond all reason.

I had not only succeeded in fulfilling Jabari's wishes that night, but I'd also achieved what Nick wanted. I had learned to control the powers of both Jabari and Danaus. The only problem was that I knew Jabari could still fight me, stop me if I tried to do it at a moment when he wasn't in accord with my wishes. I had a feeling that Danaus could do the same.

The laughter stopped as suddenly as it started, and everyone was left scratching their heads, naturally assuming that Our Liege had made a rare visit. Nick's energy faded from the room, which was now filled with the heavy scent of blood. He seemed content to leave me alone for a while. I had accomplished his great task, but I knew he would be back for more at a later date. I would have to find a way to escape him.

But not now.

My legs were trembling with fatigue as I shuffled down to my seat on the dais. My body was suddenly filled with a hundred aches and pains I had not noticed earlier, and my chest felt as if a heavy weight rested on my heart. As I resumed my seat, my eyes fell on Tristan's limp body and my heart broke for a second time. I had destroyed the man that had tortured him, but I had been unable to save him. And that's all I ever wanted for Tristan. I just wanted to save him from the world.

My right hand trembled where it hung over the arm of the chair, sending a fresh cascade of blood drops to the floor. I slumped low and rested my head against my left hand while placing my elbow on the arm of the chair. My eyes didn't drift from Tristan until I felt fingers twine themselves around my fingers. I looked down at my right hand in confusion to find Danaus's hand wrapped around mine. Gazing up at his face, I saw a pair of beautiful blue eyes caressing my face. He was there for me, standing between me and the rest of the nightwalker nation. He was there watching over me.

In that moment, I knew that Danaus was my last refuge, my only harbor of peace and security. He was my happiness. And the only thing standing between me and complete oblivion.